Also by Marie Harte

The McCauley Brothers
The Troublemaker Next Door
How to Handle a Heartbreaker
Ruining Mr. Perfect
What to Do with a Bad Boy

Body Shop Bad Boys
Test Drive
Roadside Assistance
Zero to Sixty
Collision Course

The Donnigans
A Sure Thing
Just the Thing
The Only Thing

Veteran Movers
The Whole Package
Smooth Moves
Handle with Care
Delivered with a Kiss

All I Want for Halloween
The Kissing Game

MAKE
ME
BURN

MARIE HARTE

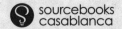

sourcebooks
casablanca

Published by Sourcebooks Casablanca, an imprint of Sourcebooks
P.O. Box 4410, Naperville, Illinois 60567-4410
(630) 961-3900
sourcebooks.com

Printed and bound in Canada.
MBP 10 9 8 7 6 5 4 3 2 1

Chapter One

"Oh, now that lady's looking fine. Yep. You could do worse than that redhead, son."

Firefighter Brad Battle ignored the Texan eyeballing the crowd and looked up, praying for rain. Spring in Seattle brought the wet weather, but not today. The temperature had warmed to a mild 54 degrees, the sky bright with the occasional fluffy cloud dancing across the sun when the wind deigned to blow. The Dog Days of Spring Festival, in Green Lake Park this year, had a decent turn-out. Such a turnout, in fact, that a man with a microphone flitted around, asking people questions.

Just what Brad didn't need. He *hated* reporters.

"We're here to work, not flirt, Tex," he said to his partner.

"You need to learn to multitask, Brad."

"I'm listening to you while not punching you in the face. How's that?"

Tex chuckled.

Brad glanced at his partner. They both wore Station 44 long-sleeved shirts tucked into dark-blue trousers accompanied by black boots. "Where's your hat?"

Tex typically wore a station ballcap when on duty and his Stetson on his off-hours.

With a sad sigh, Tex said, "LT wouldn't let me bring it today. Wants everyone to see my pretty face."

"Pretty face, right."

They both chuckled. With the lieutenant on them to be personable and *friendly*—directly aimed at Brad—there was no way Brad could duck out and avoid the press they'd been inundated with since opening up the new fire station.

Press like the man with a microphone striding toward him and smiling.

Tex saw the incoming reporter and drawled, "I got this. But you owe me drinks after."

"You're the man."

"Damn skippy." Tex intercepted the reporter and poured it on thick. "How do, friend. How about this amazin' weather, eh?"

Brad casually walked away from his buddy and lost himself in the crowd. He watched families cozying up to a few felines under one tent. To the right, a petting zoo had been set up, and the sight of small children smiling while riding ponies eased a bit of his stress.

He saw dogs everywhere, appropriate since it was called the *Dog* Days of Spring Festival, and wondered how the last stray he'd fostered was doing. His work for Pets Fur Life satisfied him, helping the helpless. His mood lifted even more.

Brad continued to meander, smiling and shaking hands with the locals. This he could do. But even so, after a while, he wanted to pare down on all the people.

He dragged a hand through his hair, counting down the hours until he could go home. At the beginning of his two-shift rotation, he worked twenty-four hours then earned two days off. He had plans to hang with the guys for a few beers tonight and a hike up Mt. Rainier on Sunday. Anything to stay outdoors and away from crowds.

A commotion just beyond a copse of bushes drew him, and he nodded at folks in greeting before moving closer to watch a short woman talking to a small group about adoption. She stood on a small stage under an arch of balloons in a shower of reds and blues, dressed in colors to match. Next to her stood a dark-haired woman in glasses holding a microphone—another reporter.

He stopped at the periphery and noticed a cameraman focusing on the group, but Brad's attention swayed toward the reporter. Beautiful, taller than the woman next to her, and smiling, she captivated with ease. He frowned. She looked familiar. But he couldn't see so well from his distance, so he drew closer.

"Mr. Fluffy Paws loves his catnip, long walks in the garden and mice, and is a raging Aquarius. So please, water signs need apply," the shorter woman quipped to much laughter. She had cropped blond hair that added to her all-around cuteness and wore slim-fitting jeans and suspenders over a long-sleeved red Deadpool T-shirt. She held the cat up like an offering.

The reporter sneezed. And sneezed again.

"Oh, sorry." The blond didn't sound sorry. Especially when she held the cat closer to the poor reporter. "But let this be a lesson, everyone. Do *not* adopt a cat or dog if you're allergic. You'll only end up giving the animal back, and everyone will be sad." She handed the cat to a nearby helper and brought out a large yellow Labrador retriever. "Meet Banana." Several children in the crowd perked up. "He's a three-year-old Lab needing a good home. He's friendly and sweet. And he loves to lick."

That wasn't all he loved.

Brad tried not to laugh as the dog sidled up to the reporter and rose on his hind legs.

"Look, he's dancing!" a little boy cried.

The dancing dog started humping the reporter's leg, much to the amused snickers of those around her.

"Dang it," she muttered as she tried to get some distance from the enthusiastic canine.

The laughing blond was no help. Nor were the amused onlookers. Brad couldn't help joining in. The "dancing" dog and helpless reporter were cracking him up.

She tried to make the best of it by taking the dog by the paws and dancing with him; not so easy to do with one hand still holding her mic.

Brad decided to help her out since no one else seemed inclined to do so.

The reporter laughed, keeping a good attitude, and addressed the crowd. "And this is why you need dog training."

Brad frowned as he drew closer to her. *Where do I know this woman from?*

"That would be my area of expertise." A tall, older woman next to the stage nodded. "Yep. We teach the little ones how to care for their dogs and take care of a dog's needs." She pointed to a large stuffed dog and a monster pile of fake dog poop on the stage right behind the reporter. "Come on over and I'll show you how we help our canine friends behave."

And that's when the situation went from bad to worse. Or, as Brad had the sudden thought, *it all went to crap.*

———

Oh no. Get off me! Please, not today.

Avery Dearborn's best friend was being no help whatsoever as the randy Lab kept trying to advance while Avery did her best to push the beast back and keep her microphone out of its mouth.

The colorfully dressed, short blond who should have been helping and wasn't finally choked back her laughter. In a low voice, Gerty said, "Uh-oh. Your dad's here. And he's looking at you."

"This is all your fault," Avery whispered back, wishing to be anywhere but in her particular circumstances just then.

The sun sparkled as a light wind whisked a few scattered clouds overhead. The weather was lovely. A little brisk, but the jacket she wore kept out the cold. A perfect day to film a short segment for the online e-news site *Searching the Needle Weekly*.

The opportunity to star in the piece that another reporter would normally be covering had been a gift from Avery's editor. And a chance to show her father she was more than just a glorified junk-piece reporter.

Unfortunately, the excitable dog kept trying to hump her leg.

The crowd seemed to grow as children and parents alike gathered to watch the spectacle she continued to make of herself. So *of course* her father had actually shown up to the festival in time to see her looking like a moron. His horrified expression spoke volumes.

Avery backed away and tripped over plastic poop.

Gerty burst into hysterical laughter along with the crowd. Banana woofed and licked Avery's face.

"I hate you," she muttered at the Lab and her best friend.

The dog cocked his head then turned to follow the trainer, who'd grabbed his leash. Behind him, Avery saw a mammoth Great Dane giving her legs a speculative glance.

She hurried to stand and pasted a smile on her face, aware her cameraman had been snickering and filming the entire time. She mentally added Alan to her revenge list.

Wiping the grass off her jeans, she pointed at the plastic poop and said to the amused audience, "And *that's* why we need to clean up after our best friends do their business. Because falling into that is something nobody wants, am I right?"

Several parents nodded, grinning. The children seemed enthralled with the animals up for adoption, letting Avery off the hook. She hoped.

"Dance with the doggie again," one of them pleaded.

"Yeah, dance with Banana. I think he likes you," Alan said.

Gerty looked over at Avery's dad and gave him a thumbs-up. "Keep going, Avery. You're doing great."

Avery's father took one look at Avery, grimaced, then turned and, dragging her mother with him, made way for the food trucks.

Avery swallowed her embarrassment and launched into an introduction of Gerty's newest furry friend. A gerbil, thank God. With any luck, this one wouldn't make her sneeze.

As Gerty talked about Jerry the Gerbil, Avery happened to glance at the crowd.

And spotted *him* next to the stage.

The man who had been the star on her journalistic walk of shame. She'd made him a household name, and he'd been so incredibly nasty about one lousy article that he'd managed to make her question everything about herself in the process. An emotional trial from which she was still recovering, even five years later.

Bradford T. Battle. Jackass Extraordinaire. No, *Sergeant* Jackass Extraordinaire.

He stared at her in bemusement before his eyes narrowed and his expression turned to one of loathing.

Ah, so he does remember me.

Too bad he hadn't gained a hundred pounds, lost some teeth or hair, and had his nose busted in the years since she'd last seen him. The jerk still had short, sandy-brown hair, light-green eyes that seemed to glow, a square jaw, and muscles on top of muscles. Oh, and even better. Not only was he a decorated war veteran, he wore a Seattle Fire Department uniform. Because apparently karma liked handsome dickheads.

He scowled.

Not one to miss an opportunity, Avery hustled to stand next to him before he could escape into the crowd. Gerty gaped, knowing exactly whom Avery stood next to. A good friend, she'd hated Brad Battle for years on Avery's behalf.

"Well, well. Folks, look who we have here. One of Seattle's finest. Let's give a round of applause for the Seattle Fire Department." She watched with glee as Brad's face turned red. Everyone cheered and clapped, and his hands clenched into fists. Ah, he still hated the limelight. Awesome.

He managed to glare at her without glaring. Some feat.

"Oh ho," Alan said under his breath. "More drama. What's this?" He zoomed in on Brad. Perfect.

"Please, sir, come on up and introduce yourself," Avery said in a super nice, super polite voice. "And tell us what the fire department is doing here today."

Despite not liking the spotlight, Brad joined her on stage and charmed the crowd in no time. "We couldn't pass up a chance to enjoy the fine weather while our furry friends find good homes. And of course, we're here to make sure everyone remains safe and sound while having a good time."

Such a Boy Scout.

"I'm Brad Battle, part of the new Station 44. We're happy to support Pets Fur Life, a charity that helps home strays. I just want to say on behalf of my station and myself, thank you all for being here."

"And thank you for your service," Avery said, sincere, even if she secretly consigned him to the same hell he'd put her through.

The Great Dane barked his approval, rushing past Gerty, and nudged Avery hard. She would have fallen over the plastic poop—again—if Brad hadn't stopped her from falling.

He pulled her close to whisper, "Still stepping in shit, eh, Dearborn?"

She muttered, "Oh, be still my heart, he remembers me," and smiled hard back, her jaw aching.

"Wow. You guys look so romantic under the balloons!" Gerty just had to add in a loud voice.

The crowd clapped, encouraging their hero for having helped a damsel in distress.

What-ever.

They quickly parted, both wearing fake smiles.

Avery stepped back from Brad and clapped as well. "My hero." She batted her eyelashes at him.

He gave a mock bow. "A firefighter's job is never done."

Everyone laughed while the children in the audience asked Brad fire station questions, giving Avery a chance to escape. Alan could film all he wanted. She needed a break.

She turned off her mic and quickly walked away, hoping to see her parents. But as usual, her father was nowhere to be found.

"Damn it." With a groan, knowing she'd hear about how embarrassing she'd been later, she got herself a lemonade and watched the festival. So much for a chance in front of the camera. The lemonade went down fast, and she sucked on the sour pulp, thinking bitterness fit with her current mood.

Of all the men she never wanted to see again, Brad Battle topped her list.

Alan wandered over to join her. The thirty-six-year-old cameraman had been working for *Searching the Needle Weekly* forever, first as a graphic designer, then as a video editor, and had become a good friend in the two years she'd been there. He had a warped sense of humor and the libido of a teenage boy still going through puberty. He often veered into goofy behavior—which she appreciated—did a decent job, and made her laugh. Usually.

Alan smirked. "We are *so* running all of that."

"Do it and die," she snarled.

"Oh, come on. This is video gold, and you know it!"

"Alan." She narrowed her eyes. "We're editing that piece before it airs."

He looked wounded. "Of course it'll be edited. What do you take me for?" He turned away, complaining about his empty stomach.

What do I take you for? A guy who thinks he's funnier than he is.

And speaking of not funny... She watched Brad Battle continue to charm every-freaking-one as he handled pets and answered questions about Seattle's newest fire station. She'd been bugging her boss to let her write a community piece on the hot topic, but he'd given it to a senior reporter instead. A bummer, but what could she do? The news stations and papers had all been covering Station 44 for months now, but firefighters never went out of favor, apparently.

Not if they looked like Brad Battle. Oddly enough, she hadn't seen him in any of the news segments played on the station.

She fumed, irked she had to run into him today of all days. She'd thought she'd finally found a safe enough topic for her father. He loved animals. Heck, he and her mother had adopted Salty the Rottie just last year at one of these adoption days. And with Pets Fur Life having financial issues, she knew the charity could use any help it could get.

Let's face it. If I managed to get an interview with Putin, Dad would find some way to criticize it. Because she'd prefer an interview with Putin's florist or hairstylist, not the man himself. Avery didn't do "hard news" anymore. She'd tried it; it didn't take.

Her gaze found Brad again. Dealing with him had been one of the hardest things she'd ever done. She'd been young and foolish, trying to impress her father, to live up to his name instead of doing what felt right. In the process, she'd burned more than a few bridges.

Brad met her gaze, quirked a brow, and deliberately turned away.

She glared. Well, that was one bridge she had no intention of rebuilding. Not since she'd discovered he was no hero but a troll sucking away the joy from any poor heroine determined to get close.

Hmm. Not bad. She'd have to use that line later while gaming with Gerty…*after* she made Gerty pay. Honestly, how tough was it to hold on to a dog's leash? And no warning that they'd be having cats for adoption either? It sure wasn't called the *Cats* Days of Spring Festival.

She turned to go and ran into another man wearing a Seattle FD Station 44 uniform.

"Oh, I'm sorry." He smiled, and she blinked. Did they send all the pretty people to Station 44?

"My fault." She fiddled with her glasses. "I seem to be tripping over my own feet today." *Today? Make that every day.* Her friends called her accident-prone for a reason.

He grinned and in a thick Southern accent said, "I caught your two-step with Marmaduke."

She laughed at that.

"I'm Tex McGovern." He held out a hand, clasping hers a bit longer than a perfunctory handshake would normally allow.

She gently tugged, and he immediate let go. "Avery Dearborn."

"Reporter?" he asked, glancing down at her microphone.

She tucked it into her jacket pocket. "I think so. That's if I still have a job after my idiot cameraman runs that clip of me dancing with Cujo."

Tex grinned. "I thought it was cute. You handled yourself well." He looked to be about the same height as Brad and close to her age. But unlike the angry fireman, Tex's smile felt warm, sincere. Shaggy, thick black hair framed a handsome face. His light-gray eyes stood out in contrast to his dark good looks.

She appreciated that this man didn't look at her as if Satan sat on her shoulder.

"Avery, I'm gonna grab something to eat. Would you like to join me?" He motioned to the food trucks.

She tossed her empty cup of lemonade in the garbage. "You know, I could eat something. Those tiny donuts are calling to me."

He studied the donut truck. "Hmm. That does look good. Maybe after I get something with meat in it."

She gave him a once-over and whistled. "I bet you need to eat a lot to fill those big shoes."

He wiggled his brows. "You know what they say about a man with big shoes."

Curious to see how far he'd go, she raised a brow. "No, what?"

"That he wears big socks." He winked.

"Nice save," she said drily.

He laughed. "Hey, we just met. I save all my unsavory comments for the second date."

"Don't we need a first date to get past?"

"If I buy you a mini donut, does that count?"

She scoffed. "A dozen, maybe. But one? Gimme a break."

He started to say something when a large hand settled on his shoulder. Tex looked at said hand and sighed. "Aw, man."

"Nice try, Tex. Time to mingle again."

It figured Brad would show up to ruin things. Avery sighed. "Don't you have some kittens to save? A pole to slide down? Trucks to clean?" *Another woman's self-esteem to ruin?*

Tex looked from Brad to Avery. "You two know each other?"

Brad huffed. Avery shrugged.

Tex seemed fascinated. "Avery, why don't you tell me over donuts?"

"She can't." Brad glowered at her. "We have work to do, slacker. Let's go."

"But—"

An angry Brad turned on Avery. "And before you try weaseling information out of my friend, don't bother." He tugged a protesting Tex with him away and disappeared into the crowd.

Totally annoyed and not sure how Brad had gotten the better of her, she stared after him. "Oh yeah. A total troll." As if she wanted to know anything more about him. Ever.

Gerty waved from across the way and threaded through the masses to Avery's side. "Did I just see—"

"Not a word. You owe me so big I can't even…" Avery blew out a breath. "Now break out your wallet. I need carbs."

"Yes, ma'am." Gerty bought them each a cup of sugary puffs of guilt. "Please tell me what the heck I just saw. Because it looked to me like your mortal enemy has returned with a vengeance." She rubbed her grubby little hands together. "This sounds like a job for Super Gert and her minion of stealth and subtlety. Or, you know, a gamer nerd and her clumsy, loud-mouthed friend."

Avery shoved a donut in her mouth and scowled, wishing she had something clever to say and coming up blank.

"Well, look on the bright side. At least your dad didn't stick around to see you and Super Hunk FD glaring at each other under my balloons of joy."

Avery ate another donut.

"Super Hunk FD. Balloons of joy." Gerty paused. "Nothing, eh?"

"I'm at a loss for words, I'm so mad." She explained her non-starting date with handsome Tex.

"That asshat! Messing with my sister from another mister. My pal from another gal. My wonder from another mother. My chick from another dick—"

"*And* we're done." Avery blushed when a passing mom frowned at them both. But Gerty had pulled her out of her funk. "Well, super geek, you put me in a better mood. Time to chalk Brad Battle back to the loser column and focus on work." She tried to put a positive spin on her day. "I guess that dance with Banana was kind of funny."

"Kind of?" Gerty chuckled. "Try hilarious. My money says the spot has you going viral."

"And won't my dad just love that." His loser daughter making social media waves by being silly. Just a hack journalist who'd fallen so far from the family tree she might as well be a weed.

Gerty held up a donut. "Cheers!"

Avery touched her donut to Gerty's and sighed. "Well, look-ing on the bright side, now that I know where the douche-nozzle works, I know how to avoid him. I'll never have to see that jerk again."

Chapter Two

Monday morning, Avery stared at her boss, unsure she'd heard him correctly. "I'm sorry. What did you say?"

"You were brilliant!" Emil Watts glowed with enthusiasm. He reminded her of an elf, with bushy white eyebrows and slightly pointed ears. His shock of white hair stood on end most of the time, as he had a habit of grabbing his hair when stressed, and he sported a white goatee that always appeared trimmed to within an inch of its life. Thin and neat, he liked to wear earthy colors and always did his best to take up environmental causes. She knew it was only a matter of time before they went completely paperless.

Searching the Needle Weekly had been around for more than a decade, starting out in print. The free paper had quickly become popular with the city, as much for its crazy stories about aliens and urban monsters as for its community pieces. But as times changed, so did the need to adapt to new technology. To compete with the many online news sources, Emil had enhanced their website with streaming video, increased the live broadcasts they'd been doing, and added a studio in the office to film the Friday news show as well as other series he was still developing.

Emil continued, "We're blazing on social media. The mayor called, thrilled with our coverage of Station 44 and Pets Fur Life. And after that mess with the health department last week, the city can use some positive energy. Heck, we're helping Seattle look good! Mayor Bentz is demanding follow-up interviews."

She blinked. "Demanding?"

"Encouraging with enthusiasm." He waved her question away. "You and that fireman have chemistry. Have you seen? We're getting national coverage out of your story. Even the AP picked it up."

Emil danced behind his desk, giddy and smiling so hard she worried his face might break in half. "Our website has gotten ten times the traffic it normally does in the past two days, and the views keep on coming." He gripped his hair. "Alan's a freakin' genius."

Alan was a traitor and so, so dead. "Hold on. Follow-up interviews? More stories about Station 44? That's Tara's beat, right?" Avery didn't want to mess with the frighteningly competent woman.

"No, she has more important things to cover."

Of course she did.

"Like what?"

Emil shrugged. "The city council, a few PTA sessions concerning diversity, tolerance, and some much-needed focus on math and science for young girls." He made the sign of the cross. Considering he was an atheist, she wondered what he thought might be protecting him with the gesture. "I can't tell you how many women seem to be unable to form quadratic equations."

"Sexist much?" *Math nerd.* "I can't name anyone—besides you—who likes spouting math for fun. Woman or man."

"Yes, my comment *was* sexist. Exactly. See what I'm saying? My nieces hate math because their teachers put them down. And Celia used to be so good at algebra. I'm so tired of—"

"Emil, focus. I'm not a newscaster. I'm a journalist." Barely. "Why do you want *me* to deal with Station 44? So what? I had one embarrassing scene with a fireman that hit the news. We have no chemistry, and frankly, I can't stand him."

"Him?"

She glared. "Brad Battle, the guy you want me to interview."

"You know, maybe we should have you do a more in-depth piece. That guy's a PR dream. He's a war hero, a Marine—"

"Former Marine." And she knew all about him. Her interview five years ago had put him in the path of media stardom. He should have been thanking her, but instead he'd buried his head in the proverbial sand and made her out to be a bad guy.

Guilt started its familiar churn. Anxiety flared, reminders of who she'd once tried to be filling her with shame. *No, I'm a good person. I will not fall into that mire again.* She had to work to get out of her own head.

"—women love him, and he's got pet lovers eating out of his hand. I wonder if he ever plans to enter politics."

"I wouldn't vote for him."

Emil frowned, in thinking mode. "Maybe you could do a continuing story on what it's like to be a firefighter in our city. But make it entertaining, not so dry. I haven't seen anything on that lately."

Shoot me now. "*The Seattle Times* just did a huge series of articles on that very topic last month."

"Yes, and it was boring." He ignored her sputtering and tapped his chin. "But that's taking you from what you do best. Warm and fuzzy." He nodded. "You're good at that. People love you, and they want to see more human-interest pieces. Let's scratch off the fire department's inner workings."

"But isn't the fire department human interest?" God, what was she *doing*? She didn't want to have anything to do with Station 44…unless she could somehow score a date with Tex that didn't ever involve being around Brad Battle again. And somehow, she didn't see that happening.

"You're right. It is. But it's too human. We want you fuzzy, remember? Think furry. The mayor is over the moon about Pets Fur Life. His wife's a huge supporter. I know your friend works with them, so you already have an in. But we want you and your fireman front and center." He snapped his fingers. "In fact, let's run a weekly streaming segment with you and the fireman featuring a pet of the week to adopt."

Her mouth went dry. *Weekly segment?*

"We'll run it before Tara's news piece in the early a.m. starting this Friday. Make sure you do follow-ups so we get the pet's picture and info into the paper as well as your fireman's billion-dollar grin."

"First of all, he's not *my* fireman. Secondly, the term is fire-fighter, not fire*man*. Third, am I getting a raise? Because that's a lot of work on top of getting my articles ready for the *Weekly* paper." Her salary barely paid her bills as it was, forcing her to freelance when needed. Maybe she could squeeze a few extra dollars out of her boss.

"You know what? You get me a fantastic piece with the fire-*fighter*, I'll see what I can do."

She blinked. "Really?"

"Really. You're due for a raise anyway. We both know you do the work of two people." *Try three, Emil.* "I just can't afford to bring anyone else on to help. Not without cutting all your salaries back."

"Yeah, I know." She sighed.

"But we've picked up two new sponsors thanks to your Dancing Dog and your comprehensive piece on the festival. That's in addition to the social media boosts, which are driving more traffic to our online presence. You've earned it." He looked so proud of her—something she wasn't used to seeing from a male authority figure.

"Thanks, Emil."

"Great. Now get out of here. I have to call Station 44 and get their cooperation. What's your firefighter's name again?"

If she didn't tell him, could she get out of this mess?

"Oh yes. Brad Battle. Love that name. Well? Scram. We have a lot to get done before this Friday." He grinned from ear to ear.

She left, feeling equal parts joy and dismay. Joy because she'd been acknowledged for doing a good job. Dismay because she'd have to deal with her mortal enemy, as Gerty had called him. Then again, Gerty had also referred to him as Super Hunk FD.

Meh. Avery would stick with Troll.

Deciding to spend the rest of her day prepping for the week's

articles, she got busy working. Though she didn't report on politics or world news, Avery told people about local events and
community spotlights. She did her best to bring joy and humor
to those who read her articles. Life shouldn't be so serious and sad
all the time.

While her father had labored for years to bring truth to the
masses, reporting on cruelties in other countries, on wars, fam-
ines, and brutal regimes, he'd been away from home, constantly
on the go, his work seeming more important than his family. Sure,
he'd received accolades and awards, both monetary and commen-
datory. Stuff Avery would never achieve in her current career tra-
jectory, to hear him tell it.

And maybe she was delusional. She'd had what he'd had for a
brief time, and though it hadn't exactly satisfied, she'd been young,
just starting her career… Until one day she'd woken up, tired of
dogging people for secrets they'd rather keep, like Brad and his
operations in the military. Tired of shoving herself in front of the
grieving and lost to get the emotional pull that made her news
pieces so gritty and engrossing. One day, Avery had just pulled the
plug. Then she'd gone a different way, one that included worry-
filled months to make rent and a lot of cheap meals.

Her parents lived in a lovely home in Ballard, traveled whenever they wanted, and worked semiretired hours. Her father occa-
sionally wrote for major news periodicals and did special interest
newscasts when asked. A success by age thirty, and over twenty
years later he was still going strong.

Avery still didn't know if she should regret her career choices
or not, and that bothered her. At twenty-eight, shouldn't she be
more confident about herself?

Lennox King—the pen name of her father, an investigative
journalist who'd gone all over the world, earned not one but three
National Journalism Awards and several global awards, and been
nominated for a Pulitzer.

Avery Dearborn—the real name of a washed-up city reporter now working for the *Searching the Needle Weekly* free newspaper and webcast, considered by Lennox to barely be a few rungs up from *The National Enquirer*, which Avery read cover to cover when she had the chance.

Was it so wrong to want to be entertained in a world too often saturated in tragedy and grief? Apparently, it was, to hear her father tell it.

She still hadn't heard from him after that fiasco on Saturday. Not even to tell her how she could have held herself better in front of the camera.

She hated that his distance bothered her. She should be used to it by now. *So why the hell does his opinion still matter so much? Mom loves me.*

Trying to put the great Lennox King out of her mind, Avery made calls and set up interviews with the Pets Fur Life people, arranging for photos of Banana. She'd let Emil handle Station 44. Once she'd finished her planning for this week's Pets Fur Life piece, she outlined her next series of articles in anticipation of spring planting. Then she tinkered with the quirky story about the "alien corpse" that had fallen in an older man's backyard. Great stuff. She buckled down and worked past quitting time.

Finally heading back to the apartment she shared with Gerty, Avery drove her peppy fifteen-year-old Volvo back to Fremont and let go of the tension giving her a headache.

Once inside, she embraced a positive attitude and laughed when she overheard Gerty swearing while zapping some barbarian on the large screen mounted to the living room wall.

"Die, rebel scum. The mage queen is done with you." Gerty continued to swear into her headphone mic as she decimated a barbarian army.

"Good to see some of my life is in chaos, but home, at least, remains the same."

Gerty glanced up with a frown. She pulled one headphone aside. "Huh? You say something?"

"Nope." Avery kicked off her shoes and hung up her jacket, tossing her purse to the counter. Then she grabbed a yogurt and settled on the arm of the couch to watch Gerty kick barbarian ass in their favorite streaming game, the popular *Arrow Sins & Siege*.

"So, how'd work go?" Gerty asked as she killed things on-screen.

Avery finished her yogurt and wondered what else she could gobble up that required little effort. She loved to cook, but not after working a ten-hour day. "Well, I got a ton done on the spring planting series and set up interviews with your Pets Fur Life friends all this week. Emil wants me to do more work with the charity. Apparently, I need to run a weekly Friday morning segment— that's streaming *live*—about adopting pets." She paused.

"That's great." Gerty beamed. "And neatly ties into the adorable puppy we're fostering."

"God. Gerty, you are seriously going to get us kicked out of here." In order to have pets, they needed to, one, be approved and, two, pay a monthly pet fee neither could afford.

"Please. If Landlord Larry finds out we have pets, I'll charm him into foregoing the monthly pet fee."

"Before long he's going to demand you actually go on one of the dates you keep promising him."

Gerty grinned. "Oh, I already have." She wiggled her brows then swore when she died.

"Already have?" Avery gaped. "No way."

Gerty nodded to the screen. "It was virtual, but it was really interesting. I wore red leather and—"

"I've heard enough, thanks." Their landlord, whom Gerty had for some reason nicknamed Landlord Larry, had to be a good twenty years older than them and gave off a weird vibe Gerty insisted was rooted in geekery. Frankly, Avery didn't like the way he never looked anywhere but at her boobs. He'd never said or done anything inappropriate otherwise, but geez, it would be nice if he made eye contact once in a while, not eye-to-nipple contact.

"Whatever. Landlord Larry loves us. Hell, he told me we could even foster a snake if we wanted and he won't care."

The hopeful look on Gerty's face disturbed Avery on every level. "No. No way."

"Aw, come on. Just that one? Patty is friendly."

"I watched Patty the Python swallow a mouse whole." Avery glared. "N. O."

Gerty sighed. "Fine. No snakes. But the puppy is in my room in his kennel, sleeping. We'll have him for another two or three weeks, I'm guessing."

"Fine." Avery knew better than to argue with Gerty over furry animals.

Her best friend since high school, Gerty had gone to a different university than Avery, had gotten a degree in computer science, and now worked from home more than she went to the office downtown. Gerty loved it and devoted her spare time to animals in need.

She proudly owned her geekiness, loved being different, and didn't seem to care what anyone thought of her. Avery wanted to be her when she grew up.

She sighed.

"What's that for? I said we wouldn't be getting a snake. Sadly."

"I didn't tell you the twisty part about my new pet spot on *Searching the Needle Weekly*."

"Uh-oh. That look on your face is scaring me." Gerty waited, wide-eyed.

"I have to partner with the troll—Super Hunk FD—for those weekly spots. Meaning I'm going to have to work very close to him for the next few weeks." She explained about the mayor's interest and all the publicity they'd gotten from Brad saving her from that dastardly Lab.

"Oh wow." Gerty blinked. "That's...um..."

"Exactly." Avery groaned. "I can only pray he refuses to go along with the spot." She perked up. "You know, maybe he'll hand off the pet segment to one of his firefighter buddies. Oh, maybe Tex will do it instead."

Gerty just looked at her. "You keep dreaming, kid. For what it's worth, my money says you and Super Hunk are going to be joined at the hip for the foreseeable future." She patted the spot next to her on the other side of the couch. "Now if you want to destress, why not join me killing monsters?"

"Trolls. I want to kill trolls tonight."

"You go, girl. Aim straight for the peanuts." She winked. "Because trolls have little dicks."

Avery grinned. "Sounds about right to me."

―――――――

Brad had tried. When he'd heard the news Tuesday morning, he'd argued, pleaded, and even cited his past history with the nosy reporter in question, but the lieutenant had refused to budge. By Tuesday afternoon, even his captain refused to hear him out, having orders directly from their battalion chief to go along with the publicity piece, declaring the effort "a win" to help the department look good. Unfortunately, the mayor loved the idea of Brad, Pets Fur Life, and *Searching the Needle Weekly* teaming up.

And when the fire department looked good, fiscal concerns might look even better when it came time to reevaluate the fire department's budget.

"Sorry, man," Tex said again, making sure to include the rest of their crew on Brad's misfortune. They all sat at the long metal table that served as a communal eating spot, large enough to fit a dozen. "I'd love to help you out with sexy Avery Dearborn, but it seems you've got all the luck."

"Bad luck," he muttered as he fixed the guys killer sub sandwiches. They'd had a brief pause in their busy day, and he hurried with lunch. He didn't do much cooking, but he wasn't bad with cold cuts.

"Hey, make sure to throw extra provolone on mine," Reggie ordered.

"Yes, *boss*." Brad shot him the finger.

Reggie grinned. Next to him, Tex rolled his head on his neck, making some terrible cracking sounds. "Damn, I gotta get a better pillow. My neck is killing me."

"It's killing me too," Mack said. "It's like watching *The Exorcist*, live. You start throwing up pea soup and levitating, and friend or no friend, I'm decapitating you. Just saying."

Tex grinned.

Reggie rolled his eyes. "Kill him later. Feed me now."

A big man, like the rest of their four-man crew, Reggie had a tall frame and dense muscle. While Brad and Tex had done time in the Marine Corps, Reggie had served in the Navy, Mack in the Air Force. A few others in the station had served in the military before joining the department, but Brad and his buddies had bonded years ago and formed a tight group that continued to work together.

Though he had to wonder why when Reggie and the guys didn't see fit to give him the sympathy he deserved.

"You have no idea what that woman is like," he warned Tex.

"Maybe because you haven't told us." Reggie motioned to the sandwich.

"Yeah, yeah, I'm cutting. Hold on, Reginald."

"Asshole."

Brad grinned and slid a plate Reggie's way. Six-one and two hundred twenty pounds of solid muscle, Reggie was the strongest of them, though Brad wouldn't admit it aloud. Dark-skinned, with a gruff kind of charm that somehow had kids and women all over the guy, Reggie'd had his share of issues with women, so Brad would think Reggie would be more compassionate.

"Well, it sounds to me like you're scared," Mack said, the moron thinking with his dick instead of his brains, as was often the case. With short, hickory-brown hair and laughing blue eyes, he never seemed to hurt for something to say. "Tex said she's fine, no doubt."

Tex tipped the brim of his ballcap up. The tallest of them, looking more like a poster boy for cowboys than a firefighter, Tex had bronze skin, always-mussed black hair, and gray eyes women seemed to fawn over. The guy had a new girl on his arm every week, or so it seemed. Apparently, solidarity with a fellow Marine meant nothing when a woman was involved.

Brad grimaced. "She's not bad looking, I guess. But she's a menace. She—"

"Is *super* fine." Tex smiled. "Really sweet, stacked, and kind of tall. Long, dark hair, big blue eyes, and those lips…" He sighed. "You just know she'd be able to kiss like a—"

"Reporter," Brad said and slid plates down to Tex and Mack. He took a sub for himself and sat to eat. "I wasn't even separated a year from the service when they unsealed those ops and the press jumped all over them." A series of classified operations that he'd been on had been cleared for use so some asshole politicians could justify their existence. "I was suddenly hot news, and I was having a bad time adjusting."

"That sucks." Reggie nodded.

"And there's Avery Dearborn, this fresh-faced reporter, invading my privacy. I asked her in the nicest way possible to leave me alone, to give me space, but she hounded me. And when I wouldn't talk, she went through my family." And had nearly opened up a huge mess that continued to haunt him. He did his best to forget a past that wouldn't stay forgotten, memories of Dana creeping in when he'd least expect them.

"Aw, come on, Brad. She was just doing her job," Tex protested. "Doesn't explain why she seems to hate your guts though."

"Oh, now there's a reason to like her," Mack teased.

Reggie grinned. "Yeah, there is that. Someone who hasn't fallen for Fashion Backward Ken."

"Barbie's—or should I say *Avery's*—future boy toy," Mack added. The dick.

The guys, minus Brad, laughed.

"Oh, and by the way," Brad growled, "the next naked Ken doll I find doing weird things with My Little Pony gets all three of you in the shit house. Yeah, you want to keep joking around? It's on." The gags around the station typically involved action figures doing things no child should ever witness.

"Oh, I'm so scared." Tex pretended to cringe in fright. "Lame-o. You ain't got nothing I haven't faced before." He paused. "Though for the record, I saw Hernandez coming out of your room last night."

"Ha. I knew it!" Then he noticed the sly look Mack shot Tex. "Oh, so it's gonna be like that, eh?" Baiting Brad with another member of C shift for something one of them had likely done.

"Not sure what you mean, son." Tex ignored him in favor of his sandwich.

"This is good," Mack acknowledged.

Reggie had yet to come up for air.

Brad picked at his food and tried not to feel amusement, doing his best to hold on to a grudge. But the guys were family, and even he had to admit the things that poor naked Ken doll had been doing all over the fire station had made the entire unit laugh.

And it wasn't just the guys pulling stunts. He'd seen Nat and Lori posing some action figures in questionable positions. He also wouldn't put it past his lieutenant to use his daughter's toys to screw with Brad. No way was the LT in the clear either.

Ken, sadly, had turned into a major pervert.

Tex drank down his iced tea and added, "Oh, and Avery wears glasses. These sexy black frames just make you think naughty librarian. Hmm. Or naughty boss, and I'd be her helpless secretary."

"Oh, I like that." Mack grinned.

"Her eyes are really blue. She's hot." Tex sighed. "Okay, it's settled. I'll talk to the LT about working with her while you take over my shift Friday, Brad."

Reggie frowned. "Fuck that. *I'll* work with her while you idiots clean Aid 44." Aid 44—one of the basic life support vehicles they were often assigned. "Good sandwich, Brad."

Brad stared at his mostly uneaten sub and sighed. "Trust me. I've tried asking for all of you to take my place. No go." He patted Reggie on the arm. "But thanks, bro."

"Oh, I wasn't doing it for you. I just don't want to be on cleaning detail with Frick and Frack here. They goof around too much."

Tex leaned forward. "That's crap. You're so busy flexing and staring at your reflection off the trucks you leave all the manual labor to me and Air Farce."

Mack was about to agree and paused. "Air Farce? Really? We're back to that?"

Brad started eating, thoroughly entertained by his buddies, his thoughts no longer on the pretty, annoying Avery. *And by "pretty annoying," I mean* very *annoying. Not that she's attractive.* Sad he had to keep lying to himself about that. Hell, he hadn't seen her in five years. Too bad her ugliness lay buried under that sexy exterior.

"Oh, come off it." Tex snickered. "Tell them, Brad. Once you go Corps, you always come back for more."

Reggie groaned. "That's both old and sad. And let's not forget, you Marines fall under the Department of the…what's that?"

"Uh, the Department of *the Navy*, is that what you mean, Reggie?" Mack asked, all smiles.

"Why, that's right, Mack. Sergeants Battle and McGovern are nothing without the help of the good old USN."

"Useless Second-Class Nerds?" Tex asked.

Brad chuckled. "Good one."

Reggie snorted. "Yeah, because I'm a nerd."

Tex sighed. "Sadly, yes. But it's a big step to embrace your truth, my man. Way to go."

"I hate you guys." Reggie grabbed the remains of Brad's uneaten sandwich and took a bite.

"Hey."

Reggie held up a finger. "USMC this."

Tex laughed and passed Brad some chips. "Here. Maybe barbecue will make you feel better. It ain't Texas barbecue, but you can make do."

Brad glared at Reggie while he munched, then pushed the chips away when a call came in for Aid 44, the unit he was currently working with Tex all day while Reggie rode with Mack in Aid 45. In Seattle, every firefighter had to also be an emergency medical technician, or EMT, since probably 80 percent of the calls they took turned out to be medical.

"Gotta go, losers. See you in a bit." He pushed his plate at the guys still sitting. "Yo, Reggie, grab me some tea to go, would you?"

"Sure thing."

Brad and Tex got their gear together, double-checked the truck, grabbed the tea from Reggie, then hurried to help an older man who'd fallen and couldn't get up—seriously—at the community gardens off Forty-Second.

Fortunately, they got in and on top of the patient right away.

Twenty minutes later, heading back to the station, Tex let out a breath. "Man, that was a good one. From a busted hip to a heart attack." Which would have needed paramedics, not two EMTs. "Thought for sure we were going to lose him 'til he farted."

Brad started laughing. "Yeah. Pressure in the chest due to gas buildup. Well, at least we're saved a ride to the hospital." The man's wife and son had insisted on taking him themselves.

"True." Tex shrugged. "Although there's one particular nurse I've been seeing that I wouldn't mind seeing again."

"Man, you need to relax on all the women."

"And you need to get a date instead of playing with Ken and Barbie in private." Tex grimaced. "It's kind of pervy having them in your bed like that. And in the station! Come on, man. Keep that stuff at home in private."

"Dick."

Tex laughed before turning to him with a more serious expression. "So, this reporter, you okay to deal with her? Seriously?"

Brad sighed. "It's no big deal, I guess." *It's a huge, hairy deal.* "More like a headache I'll have to handle." He thought back to the way Avery had glared at him. No love lost there. "On the bright side, I can't imagine she's all that happy to be working with me on this."

"Why not?"

Brad paused, looking back on the incident with Avery. "Well, you know, after I raised a stink about her unprofessionalism to the paper, she apologized. She cried, come to think of it. She was really upset." He didn't like remembering that.

"Oh, man. That's rough."

"But they still ran the story."

"I read it, you know, and you came across like Superman. She wrote nothing but good shit about your time overseas."

"So what? She invaded my privacy after I asked her not to." And had cornered his grieving brother one night when Oscar had indulged in one too many, telling her things Brad would have rather kept private.

"Huh. That's not cool."

"No, it wasn't." He'd been so focused on his own drama at the time he'd been unable to view any publicity as a good thing, wanting only to lick his wounds in private. But when she'd ignored him and talked to his family behind his back, he'd lost it. "And now she's working with *Searching the Needle Weekly*." A funny cross of local news and events mixed with outlandish stories that never failed to entertain.

Tex's eyes widened. "The free newspaper? Buddy, did you get her canned?"

"No idea. If anything, though, she got herself fired." Huh, how about that? In all his recollections of that disaster with Avery, he'd never thought about what had happened to her afterward, too lost in his own upheaval. "But Tex, she had it coming. I was having a tough time." He forced a smile. "I wasn't the same charmer I am today."

"Charmer, my ass." Tex snorted. "Yeah, right. You think if you turn on that five-hundred-watt smile, she'll be begging to drop her panties and forgive you for everything? Man, you are deluded."

"Why do I want *her* forgiveness? And who said anything about her dropping her panties?" Though the thought of Avery and panties interested him in a way he'd never before have considered. Hmm.

"And there you go. My work here is done."

"What?"

Tex looked smug until they got the call to head to a minor fender bender near an elementary school. Unfortunately, this one didn't look to be as easy to fix as recommending a roll of antacids.

Chapter Three

WEDNESDAY AFTERNOON, AFTER A DECENT RUN THAT brought about a good, cleansing sweat, Brad was lifting with the guys at the station, as they often did. Though he liked getting away from work to decompress, he also loved spending time with his friends. And since the station had a kickass new gym, why not make the most of it?

Unfortunately, Lieutenant Sue Arthur, currently on watch, had tracked him down.

"Yo, Battle. I have my own problem children to worry about. Quit ducking Ed's calls." The crews on D shift gave her hurtful looks she ignored. "Your lieutenant keeps calling me wanting to talk to *you*." She poked him in the chest, and he did his best not to look amused. Sue stood a good head shorter than he was and always looked so darn perky and cute. She hated it. He might be Ken, but she'd gotten her fair share of teasing for looking like Dora the Explorer. And yes, the teasing at the station seemed to favor kid cartoons. Between half of them acting like children and the others invested in their own kids, they had no shortage of toys to play with.

"I'm not ducking them." He totally was. "It's only Wednesday. I don't meet with the reporter until Friday. I was going to call the LT back after working out." Maybe tomorrow.

"Well, you're here, and it's official. I passed on the message. Meet the woman today. Now would be good."

Brad paused. "She's here?"

His buddies suddenly stopped working out, zeroing in on his conversation like sharks scenting blood in the water.

"She called the station. I told her you had time to talk, since you're here and all. In fact, she should be here in ten minutes."

Great. Now D shift looked all intrigued, neither the gang work-ing out nor the others standing around in the hallway leaning in making any attempt to appear disinterested.

Brad forced himself to sound casual. "Hey, Lew"—lieutenant—"can you do me a solid and tell her I'll meet her at Swirlie's instead?" Swirlie's was the station's go-to place for smoothies and snacks a few blocks away.

"Smoothies on Brad," Mack promised the guys.

"Yeah, yeah, sure," Brad agreed. "If you promise to leave me alone so I can be done with her fast."

"Sure we will." Tex didn't sound sincere.

Sue sighed. "I'll call her back. Just get out. You're not on shift, and you shouldn't be my problem." She opened her mouth to say something and frowned at the notebook in her hand. "And if I find the motherfucker who keeps leaving Dora the Explorer stickers on my crap, I'm going to fry your ass!"

The others around didn't bother to muffle laughter, though the smart ones cleared out while Sue muttered under her breath and stomped back into the main living area.

"Damn. That's got to smart." Mack shook his head. "I mean, Ken gets all the toys and the babes. Dora is always in the jungle with a monkey and a backpack. Not cool."

"You seem to know an awful lot about Dora." Reggie smirked. "Something you want to tell us?"

"You mean, that he's about as mature as my four-year-old nephew?" Tex chuckled. "We already knew that."

The four of them walked out of the station and headed for their cars. Since Brad had ridden with Reggie, he was forced to wait for Reggie's slow ass to get behind the wheel. A great guy to have in a crisis or to have at one's back, Reggie also believed in deliberating nonemergency situations to the nth degree. That included him taking his sweet-ass time getting anywhere.

"No," Reggie said. "I meant Mack's the one screwing with Lew."

Brad blinked. "Oh, really?" He grinned. "Nice."

Mack flushed. "Aw, it's nothing."

Tex slapped him on the back. "Way to go, hoss."

Mack grimaced. "Could I ride with you guys?" he asked Reggie. "Sometimes with Tex, it's like I'm stuck in a *Bonanza* episode."

Shoving a cowboy hat on his head as he sat in his truck, Tex glared. "What's wrong with *Bonanza*?"

"See?"

Reggie sighed. "Go ride with the cowboy. I have crap in my backseat I don't feel like moving."

"So much for being a band of brothers." Mack shook his head, his expression pitiful.

"For fuck's sake." Tex opened his truck and beeped the horn. "Get in or I'll sing along with Garth on the way."

Mack dragged his feet toward the truck.

Brad slapped the door of Reggie's car. "I have an appointment with someone I don't want to see. Can we get this over with?"

Reggie rounded the car to unlock the door, then stood back and waved Brad inside. "After you, Prince Pain in the Ass."

"Better." Brad buckled in. They reached the smoothie shop in no time, and he met the others at the door. "Now, before we go in, the rules."

Reggie sighed. "Here we go."

"No talking. No making faces at me." He moved aside to let a mother with her kids enter the place. "No getting little kids to embarrass me either."

"Can I call you Ken?" Mack asked.

"No."

Tex pushed back his Stetson, which should have looked ridiculous coupled with his workout gear but somehow looked normal instead. "Can I reintroduce myself to your pretty reporter?"

"No."

"But that's rude," Reggie said. "I mean, if we're all sitting with you and—"

"You're not sitting with me." Brad knew the idiots were loving this. "I'm going to sit with her and—"

"With Avery. Her name is Avery," Mack added.

Brad ignored him. "And we'll make sense of Friday, I'm guessing. You all will sit very far away. Like, on the opposite side of the shop."

"What if we need to go to the bathroom and you're sitting near it? Can we go near you then?" Mack blinked. "Just asking for clarification."

"You guys suck so much." Brad huffed and left them laughing at his sorry self.

He scouted the room, saw no sign of the troublemaking woman, and ordered himself—and the guys—smoothies. After dropping their drinks at a table far away from the one he'd selected with a view of the front door, he waited, annoyed to find himself nervous.

What the hell did he have to be nervous about? She'd made the mistake five years ago. It had been a spot of bad luck to run into her at the festival, but truthfully, he was surprised not to have run into her before now.

Though the Seattle metro area boasted nearly four million people, Brad always saw people he knew. Now working at Station 44, situated between the Beacon Hill, NewHolly, and Rainier Valley neighborhoods, he'd become familiar with several store owners, concerned citizens, and friendly neighbors. Being a firefighter put him in the public eye, obviously, and a lot of people seemed to still remember that interview the paper did years ago. But Brad had been working harder to be more outgoing and accessible.

He supposed he should look on this outing with Avery as a character-builder.

She arrived, walking through the door and almost colliding with an older man waiting to exit. She apologized profusely; the older man smiled and said something that made her laugh.

To Brad's bemusement, her pleasure made her prettier. Which was weird. He didn't like her, but he found himself attracted to her.

Not wanting to go down that particular road, he stood when she approached the table, reminding himself to be polite and professional and leave his baggage with the woman behind. He had a job to do. Plain and simple.

"I'm surprised you're here," she said brightly and sat down. "I thought for sure you'd have weaseled your way out of this." She glanced around and waved. "Oh, maybe Tex could sit in for you."

He sat as well. "Why? So you can dig for information without me around to protect the others?"

She lifted a brow behind those sexy—*no, functional*—glasses. "Protect them from what? Questions about what animals they like best?" She huffed. "Tone it down, Brad. I have absolutely no interest in your life. At. All. That article was published years ago, and I apologized for making you uncomfortable."

"You went behind my back."

"And printed nothing but the truth. You came out looking like a superstar." She glanced away and frowned, looking surprisingly ashamed.

"But you—"

"That was another life." She met his gaze. "I no longer work for that paper. And isn't it pretty arrogant to think I want to know anything more about you than whether or not you like corgis?"

He flushed, aggravated that he'd lost any hope of appearing calm and collected. What was it about this woman that got under his skin? She hadn't done anything but ask for another guy to talk to her. Something he actually wanted.

"Sorry," he said stiffly then forced himself to unclench his hands and sit back, loosening his muscles one at a time. "It's just, I don't want to be here."

She shrugged. "To be honest, I don't either. I tried to get out of this."

"That makes me feel better." He smiled. She smiled back. Bemused, he had to search for what he'd been wanting to say. "So, ah, so you know, I did ask the guys—my friends sitting across the room—to fill in for me. But the higher-ups want me with you. That news coverage at the festival nailed it."

"I know." She looked glum and kind of adorable in her misery. "It was bad enough that cute but quirky dog started humping my leg. Oh, go ahead, laugh. It was funny."

He couldn't help chuckling over the memory.

"But then *you* had to be there. Gerty and her stupid comment about you saving me." She huffed.

"Gerty?"

"The short blond with the overinflated sense of humor and bad fashion sense?"

"Oh, right. The suspenders." He nodded. "I liked her."

"Everyone likes her. She's Gerty." Avery fiddled with her glasses. "Let's be honest. You happened to stop me from falling. That's not that big a deal."

"Yeah?" He was starting to enjoy himself, loving the pique in her eyes. Tex was right. They were big and blue. "Because I saved you, on camera, from tripping over fake dog poop."

She covered her eyes. "That story is still getting hits, did you know that?"

He'd personally shared it with everyone he knew because he'd found Banana both endearing and hilarious. And yes, he was petty enough to admit he'd loved Avery falling over crap, fake or not.

"Fine. I guess you did prevent me from falling. Thank you." She looked him in the eye. "Now it seems we're both stuck doing this story together. I don't want to be here."

"I don't want to be here."

She nodded. "But we have to, so can we try to make the best of it?"

"I'm game. Provided you don't ask a ton of personal questions and start digging up the past." Before she could say anything, he leaned closer and lowered his voice. "That is nonnegotiable."

She leaned in as well, her gaze direct, her brows drawn in irritation. "Fine. I'd rather not revisit the past either. I never did understand what I did that made you so mad. Nothing the paper printed was untrue, and you came out smelling like a freakin' rose. But that's all done. Let it go, Battle, or this will sure as shit blow up in your face."

He leaned back, surprised. "Are you threatening me?"

"Yes." She frowned. "I'm tired of you acting like you're just so important I have to be interested in nothing but the great, glorious Brad Battle. Please. So what? You served in the Marine Corps. You serve now in Seattle's Fire Department. Thanks for your service. Yes, I appreciate that. Truly. But let's move on. The world does not revolve around you."

"But—"

"You don't want to talk about the past, right? Neither. Do. I." She poked the tabletop with a finger between each word. Then she relaxed and sat back. "Look, I know it's got to be tough being handsome and charming, with gobs of women fawning all over you. But sweetcakes, I'm not and never will be charmed. To me, you're just the pet guy I'm forced to deal with. We can be amicable, or I can show you what a grudge really looks like. It's up to you."

———————

Avery was so proud of herself for coming across as stern and unaffected. Because being this close to Brad again was doing strange things to her insides. He radiated masculinity, especially sitting so close in nothing but shorts and a T-shirt showcasing all those muscles. Man, his thick biceps would take both her hands to encircle. He'd been a jerk and still acted as if the world revolved around him, yet she could see why he'd act that way.

Since she'd sat down, she'd noticed the many gazes glued to their table. And not to her but to him. Women especially seemed to give him second and third glances.

If she was into hot guys with massive egos, she might be interested in dating him. But she'd been scorched when dealing with him long ago, and the man didn't seem to have gotten any nicer. So no, she'd much rather deal with his friends now standing just behind him than with Brad.

"Damn, son," said the tall, built man wearing exercise clothes and a cowboy hat she'd much rather have dealt with. Tex, the hottie from the festival. He had a deep, smooth tone that put her at immediate ease. "I guess that's that. Personally, I'd go with the grudge, but I'm ornery like that." He pulled up a chair, sat down, and held out a hand to her. "Howdy, ma'am. Don't know if you remember me, but we met at the festival. I'm Tex."

"As if I could forget you. Avery." She shook his hand, hers dwarfed in his.

Brad gave a loud, put-upon sigh. "Why are you here, Tex? Go back to your table."

"Avery, it's lovely to meet you in person. I'm Mack." Mack winked, sat on the other side of the table, and sipped his smoothie. He was leaner than the others but just as toned, and he seemed a lot more easygoing than Brad.

"Hi, Mack."

Brad groaned.

The other good-looking buff guy, the one she didn't yet know, said by way of introduction, "I'm Reggie. Nice to meet you." He leaned across Brad, who swore, and held out a hand.

Avery shook it and grinned, liking this guy. "Avery Dearborn. It's lovely to meet you."

Reggie pulled up a seat next to Brad, scooting the scowling man over. "So, you and Brad are working this pet adoption thing, huh? You know, it could have been me, but I was stuck cleaning at the station while Hollywood here and Tex got to attend the festival."

Mack sighed. "Yeah. I wanted to go too, but I got stuck doing Brad's work."

"Oh, please." Brad ran a hand through his hair, and Avery forced herself not to watch his muscles flex.

"Do you all work with Brad at the station?"

Mack nodded. "We're all firefighters and part of the same crew. We work C shift, so we're on and off at the same time. Been friends for years."

"Family." Tex corrected with a bright white smile her way. "So, when we saw our sad brother striking out with a pretty reporter, we had to come over and see what's what."

Avery had at first thought they'd come over to give Brad a hard time, which they continued to do, but she also saw the concern for their friend. She respected that, even if she didn't like being considered the enemy.

"For what it's worth, you guys probably know Brad and I have a weird history. Neither of us wants to do this story, but I'd rather just work together to get it done." She looked at Brad. "We can be nice to each other on-screen and not deal with each other unless we have to. I have no intention of causing any trouble."

Brad studied her, and she wondered if he saw the nerves jumping under her skin. All his friends could have posed for a man-candy calendar, and she'd have a tough time picking a favorite. Well, not counting Brad, in a purely superficial appreciation for his looks.

"You just want to do the piece on the pets and that's it?" Brad asked.

"Yes, for the *bazillionth* time."

His friends looked from her to Brad.

"Okay then. We should figure out how this is going to play out."

Before he could take charge of *her* news piece, she opened her mouth to speak.

Reggie beat her to it. "Whoa. Hold on. How come she's got nothing to drink?" He raised a brow. "You want something to drink? Or maybe to eat? They have snacks here too."

She shrugged. "What are you guys drinking?"

"A strawberry energy smoothie," Mack said and offered her some. "Want to try it?"

"Nah. She don't want your germs." Tex shoved Mack's drink back. "I'll grab you something. I had a whey protein banana thing that's pretty good."

Brad stood up in huff. "Oh relax, Romeo. I'll get her something." He looked down at her, his green eyes piercing. "What do you like?"

Sexy men with green eyes. The thought scared her straight. She did *not* like Brad Battle. Especially since he'd had to be shamed into buying her a drink. Not that he should have had to get her anything in the first place. But still.

"It's not a problem. I'll get myself something. You don't have to buy me anything."

Brad blew out a breath. "I'd like to make peace."

"Then why are clenching your teeth so hard?" slipped out of her mouth.

The others guffawed. Brad flushed then surprised her by smiling. "I have no idea. But hey, let me try to do my part to get along. We do have to work together, right?"

She hated that his smile gave her tingles. "I like mango. And thank you."

He grunted and left to grab her a drink.

"Get her some *passion* fruit too," Tex suggested in a loud voice. Then he laughed at the scowl Brad shot him. "Sorry, Avery," he said to her. "I had to. Anyone who gets under Brad's skin is A-okay with me."

"Be nice, Texas," Reggie ordered. "What is this pet thing about anyway, Avery? Brad's been a little vague about the details."

As she explained the segment, Brad returned and handed her a drink, and she included him on the particulars for Friday morning. "It shouldn't take more than an hour, max. Once you're in makeup and ready to—"

"Wait, wait. Makeup?" Mack's grin grew wide. "Like, eyeliner and blush? How about lipstick?"

Avery could see the humor in it. "Well, some foundation and blush, sure. Maybe some liner for his lashes."

"Oh, hell no." Brad glared at Mack then at her. "I'm not wearing makeup."

"I think you have to," Tex said before she could. "My momma used to be on TV, and without makeup, you look all washed out. Seriously, even dudes use it."

"Yep. Won't that go over well at the station." Reggie's eyes sparkled. "Just think of all the fun we can have with this."

Mack rubbed his hands together. "Oh, yes. Thank you so much, Avery."

Brad dropped his head to the table and groaned. "My life sucks right now."

Avery grinned. "Yes, it does."

Reggie winked at her.

She glanced around at the guys, ideas taking shape. "You know, if this works, we should definitely stream more of you on our site, helping out."

"Right, but first we need to see Brad do it, you know, so he can show us how to be all Hollywood and bright and shiny." Tex laughed. "Our own internet star. So excitin.'"

Avery liked his friends. They chatted while Brad remained quiet, watching but not saying much. A short time later, the guys rose to leave.

"Guess that's my cue to go." She grabbed her smoothie.

"No, you should stay." Reggie glanced at his phone. "You too, Brad. Make sure you're all set for Friday." He started to walk away.

"Hold on, you're my ride," Brad said to Reggie and stood.

Reggie grimaced. "Oh, man, I'm so sorry. I have to head back. My sister needs my help."

"With what?" Brad asked with a lot of suspicion, watching the other two wave and leave with a sudden quickness even Avery found suspicious.

She frowned at Reggie. "Yeah, what?" None of her business, yet she didn't like them leaving her alone with Brad. Not when she'd been having a great time with the others being friendly.

"Sorry," Reggie apologized. "I really do have to go." He gave Avery a friendly smile. "Say, would you be able to give Brad a ride home?"

"I'll get a ride," Brad said. "No need to put her out."

She didn't appreciate him talking for her. *I'm right here, Super Hunk FD.* "I don't mind taking you home." She added in a sweet voice, "Unless you're afraid I might find out where you live and start stalking you?"

He narrowed his eyes.

Reggie smirked. "Um, Brad. She's a reporter. If she wanted to know where you lived, she could find out pretty easily, right?"

She nodded. "I have no intention of doing anything but getting through these Friday mornings until we're done with them. I swear."

"Well, you two figure it out. I gotta go. Great meeting you, Avery. Later, Brad." Reggie left.

Brad watched her, looking for what, she had no idea.

She thought they'd made some headway, but apparently not. "Honestly, I think we covered everything we need to." She pushed back her chair and stood. "Thanks for meeting with me today. I'll see you on Friday at six forty-five a.m. You should get an email with the details from Emil, since it's his pet project. Basically, we'll talk a little about the animal we're spotlighting. Then we'll just spitball it. No script needed."

He nodded. "Sounds good."

She started to leave, her smoothie in hand, and felt him at her heels. She didn't make much of it until he stopped by the passenger side of her car.

"What are you doing?"

"Getting a ride. Or did you just say you'd give me one to look good in front of Reggie?"

She blew out a breath. "You have to be the most annoying man on the planet. Fine. Get in."

She clicked her fob to open the doors and slid inside. Unfortunately, her small car felt microscopic with Brad Battle sitting next to her, sucking up all the oxygen.

"Um, where to?" she asked.

He took his time answering, and she snapped, "Look, hero, I'm not interested in you. Period. So get the freak over yourself."

His smile was slow in coming and so darn enthralling her heart had palpitations. "'The freak over myself'?" He laughed.

"I try not to curse too much. It's an addictive habit." She scowled. "But you're pushing it."

"Sorry. I do appreciate the ride." He buckled up and gave her directions to an apartment complex in Greenwood.

"That's a nice area."

"Don't sound so surprised," he said, amusement in his voice.

"I am. I figured you'd live in my neck of the woods."

"Why?"

"I'm in Fremont, and I thought you'd hang out with your own kind."

"My kind?"

"You know, under a bridge…with the other Fremont troll."

He laughed. "Okay, that's a good one."

"So glad you approve."

She could feel him looking at her as she drove, her gaze on traffic. "What?"

"Were you serious about wanting to work together, and that's it?"

She sighed. "Brad, I don't know how many ways I can say that I'm not interested in you in any way, shape, or form." She paused. "No offense."

"None taken."

She spared a glance to see him looking her over. "Now what?"

"Nothing."

Yet he kept looking at her.

"Just tell me," she said.

"I hadn't thought about you in a long time."

"Join the club."

He nodded. "But then at the festival, there you were, and the past came rushing back."

"Yeah, that can happen." Although her past failures never seemed so far from her mind.

"Back then, you ran the interview. And I never thought about what happened after."

"You want another apology, is that it?"

"No." He frowned. "Maybe."

He deserved one, but she didn't like recalling what she'd done, who she'd tried to be back then. "I thought we were keeping the past in the past."

"We are, it's just… Did you lose your job because of me?"

She flashed him a surprised glance before turning back to the road. "Seriously?"

"I want to know."

"No. I did not lose my job. Hell, my editor loved it so much I got to interview all kinds of important people." Did he hear the sarcasm she couldn't hide? Brad's interview had made her a star, and she'd been miserable until she'd finally quit. And hadn't *that* made her father happy… "I worked at the paper for another year and a half before I left. Happy now?"

He didn't say anything more, and she turned on the radio to fill the awkward silence.

"Turn here," he said after a short while, and she turned off 85th onto a residential road featuring several apartment buildings. "Emerald Estates. That's me."

"This is nice." Not a super high-end place, but a quaint-looking brown-brick building that housed several units. "How many people live here?"

He shrugged. "About twenty units in the building, maybe. I'm not sure." He opened the door, got out, then turned to close it.

"Huh. I still think you belong under that bridge in Fremont."

He smiled. "Probably." He paused. "I'm sorry I gave you such a hard time back then."

She hadn't expected that, though his delivery seemed a little short of sincere. The fierce expression on his face alarmed her. "Oh, um, thanks." Then she gave him the apology he deserved, not the one she'd been forced to deliver all those years ago, mired in shame.

Though her editor had been pressured from some political bigwigs to leave the city hero alone, he'd been secretly pleased at her tenacity, insisting a printed apology would be enough to satisfy Brad's influential friends. "I'm truly sorry I pestered you. My editor at the time forced me to apologize, but I was sincerely sorry for going around you through your brother." She could still remember his brother's tears, his pleas to leave the sad, heroic Brad alone. She also felt the remorse that had followed, mixed with an unwelcome pleasure and guilt, since her father had never been prouder of her.

She continued, "I wasn't trying to hurt you. Just the opposite. I…never mind." She sighed. "I'm in a better place now. Life is good."

He lifted a brow but didn't comment.

Many people might not understand that her shift from a

critically acclaimed newspaper to writing for a weekly free news rag had been a great move for her peace of mind.

He nodded. "Thanks again for the ride."

"You're welcome."

They stared at each other, and Avery felt her lingering animosity for Brad shift. Not like she was burying the hatchet entirely, more like shoving it down deeper, away from her muddled emotions.

"See you Friday." That said, he shut the door and left.

She didn't wait to see him leave, not needing the imprint of his spectacular backside to ingrain into her brain any further. Instead, she drove away, praying she could get through the next few weeks alongside a man she didn't dislike the way she should.

Chapter Four

FOLLOWING HIS SECOND TWENTY-FOUR-HOUR SHIFT, BRAD spent the first of his ninety-six hours off defending himself from his idiot friends. Mack kept offering himself like a sacrificial lamb, to take that nasty Avery off Brad's hands, as if Brad had any say in the matter. Reggie teased him unmercifully about having to ride home with the sexy reporter, and Tex just smirked and said annoying things in that slow, Southern drawl of his.

By Thursday, Brad had needed a break, so he went to visit his mom and brother in Tacoma. His family should have cured him of any desire to enter into a relationship, yet confusing thoughts about Avery Dearborn continued to plague him.

He knocked on the door to his mom's house.

"Come in," his brother called.

Brad shook his head, wondering just when his mom would cut the freaking cord.

Freaking.

He grinned, remembering how prim Avery had sounding trying not to cuss him out.

Gah. Stop thinking about her.

Brad instead focused on the state of the house, pleased to see it looking worlds better than it had the last time he'd been by, with smaller piles of stuff stacked and pushed to the side. The house smelled clean, not stale and thick with the odor of decay.

A new couch had replaced the old one, and on a blanket sat his mom's ancient Maltese. "Hey, Tinker." Brad went over to scratch the dog behind the ears, pleased when the little guy's tail wagged. Each time he visited, he wondered if he'd find Tinker, praying he would. Not only did he love the furry beast, but his mother didn't do well with change.

Death was not a word she could handle at all.

Oscar had his back to Brad, the twenty-four-year-old dressed and working on the fireplace. Even better, he appeared to be clean, with a decent haircut.

"Hey, Oscar. What's up?"

Oscar turned with the vacuum in hand, the glass plate of the fireplace set aside, the inner workings of the blower in pieces by his feet. "Brad. Nice you finally showed up."

Like looking into a mirror, Brad and Oscar were the spitting image of their father. Sadly, yet more reminders of a life lost to constantly nag at their mother.

Brad had been just seven when his father had died during a tour overseas in service to his country, Oscar a baby. Vivienne Battle had been forced to raise her boys with little help. At the time, she hadn't been talking to her family. His dad's parents had passed long ago, and his mother's only sibling, a younger sister, had been dealing with demons of her own.

Fortunately, Rochelle had arrived eight years later, moving in next door. She'd become his mother's best friend and a part of the family, bringing joy and clarity with her deep laughter and thoughtfulness. Without her, Brad thought the family might have continued down a dark path—one his brother and mother continued to trip down when not careful.

"I thought you had a place across town from me." Brad kept his voice even, nonjudgmental.

"I did." Oscar shrugged and turned to vacuum up dust from the blower and fireplace.

So, that conversation had finished. Brad counted to ten in his head, deliberately not pointing out his brother's many issues, not when he had little room to talk. It appeared Oscar still had a job. Maybe. He waited for his brother to finish, wondering what next to say.

Oscar spoke. "Darcy and I broke up." He sighed. "Before you blame me for this, she was cheating on me."

"What?" Brad frowned. "That's not right."

"No, it's not." Oscar shook his head. "We were finally good. I mean, I have a steady job. She was working. We made enough to go out and hang with friends." Oscar shrugged. "But she was acting weird, and I kept getting overtime and working it because she told me to. Come to find out she was boning the neighbor when I was out."

Brad cringed. "I'm sorry. How did you find out?"

Oscar forced a smile. "The hard way. Found them naked in our bed when I got home early from a job. So, I fucked him up, shoved him out of the apartment just in time for his girlfriend to come home and wig out on him. Then I grabbed my shit and left." He gave Brad a sincere smile. "Darcy's name is on the lease, not mine. Let her find someone else to cover the rent."

"That's good at least."

"Yeah." Oscar sighed. "I still miss her."

"When did all this happen?"

"Two months ago."

"You never told me. I know I haven't been by in a while, but I have a phone." Brad scowled.

"Why? What would you have done? Nothing."

Nothing. Brad hated that word. Especially because it had a tendency to fit when it came to his actions concerning those he cared about. "You're better off without her."

"I know that, big brother." Oscar made a face. "But she was cool. We had fun." He frowned. "Never would have thought she'd cheat on me. I was better, you know? On track."

Brad didn't want to ask. He didn't want to know. He asked anyway. "You doing okay? Still working?" Still sober?

Oscar nodded. "Just got promoted, actually. All that overtime showed them I was serious about work. I'm also going back for some new certifications that will mean more pay."

"That's great." Brad smiled, feeling happy for his brother. But the sober part? Oscar didn't smell or look drunk, but Brad had been fooled before.

"Before you ask," Oscar said drily, "I'm still eighteen months and four days clean."

Brad tried not to let his relief show.

"You have the worst poker face." Oscar shook his head. "Loser."

"Please. You're"—*living at home with Mom* was not what his brother needed to hear right now—"still only the *second-best*-looking Battle in the house." Brad flexed. "See this muscle? I could break you if I squeezed that scrawny neck with just my biceps."

Oscar huffed. "And here we go. That ego has made your fat head so swollen it's cut off oxygen to your miniscule brain."

Brad grinned. "Yeah, I've missed you, little guy."

Oscar topped him by an inch but didn't have the muscle Brad did, so Brad figured the description fit.

"Little guy? Dream on." Oscar dropped the vacuum, toed his tools away, then crouched into a familiar stance. In seconds, Oscar caught Brad in a sumo hold, each of them gripping the other by the waistband as they tried to trip the other to the floor.

Oscar had almost managed to send Brad tumbling when Brad turned and body-slammed his brother over some couch pillows Tinker had shoved to the floor. Tinker leaned over the couch to watch them with approval. The dog was never so happy as he was when climbing all over pillows.

"Shit." Oscar did his best to get free, but Brad held him down then leaned closer, which had his brother in a panic. "No, don't. I swear, I'll start drinking again!"

Brad chuckled and breathed right into his brother's face. "You *loooose*."

Oscar pretended to retch. "Brush your teeth, dickface."

"Oscar. Brad." Rochelle had entered the living room and stood, her arms akimbo, glaring. "Clean this shit up. Your mom is five minutes behind me."

"I win," Brad said as he stood, offering a hand to his brother.

Who promptly yanked him down and turned to shove Brad's face into a pillow that smelled like dog.

"Whatever, civil *servant*." Oscar sneered and pushed off Brad to stand. "I'm the good son. I help Mom and Rochelle all the time. You're just driving an ambulance and fighting fires to get attention. Pathetic."

Rochelle laughed. "Both of you are morons. Now hurry up. You know we don't need more drama in this family." The level-headed one of the bunch, she'd eventually started spending more and more time with them, having no family of her own to speak of. She was more of an aunt to them than their mother's sister, whom they saw every few years at their mother's insistence.

With mahogany-brown hair and brown eyes, her skin tone a shade darker than their mother's, Rochelle dwarfed his mother in size, a woman with thick proportions, wise eyes, and a beautiful smile. Personally, he found her amazing and credited her with his ability to move on from disaster.

She'd been the one he'd gone to with his problems, the one who had talked him off the ledge of his own spiral into depression. A counselor by trade, Rochelle had done much for the Battle family, and they gave her the affection she clearly deserved but had never had.

His mother… He loved her, but half the time he didn't much like her. Weakness seemed to be her middle name. And just thinking that left a sour taste in his mouth, that he should be so lacking in character as to not love his mother without reservation.

"How is she?" he asked Rochelle.

"Better. She's been eating well and exercising, and that helps a lot. Seeing you will make her feel ten times as good though."

Great. Now he felt even more guilt for keeping his distance. Oscar's sardonic expression didn't help. His younger brother loved throwing Brad's savior complex in his face.

Brad knew he had issues. He didn't need his brother telling him that.

A few minutes later, they'd cleaned the chaos of the living room, and Vivienne Battle arrived. She entered through the back door, sweat clinging to her brow. Her blond hair now threaded with white had been pulled back into a ponytail. Her frailness, apparent in the birdlike bones of her body, contrasted with a healthy glow. She'd been getting plenty of sun, and it showed. Her blue eyes sparkled with vitality, and Brad was surprised to see her seeming so...healthy. She wore jogging pants and a sweatshirt and held up her wrist.

"Three thousand steps already, and it's barely noon."

Oscar looked at the clock on the wall. "It's actually after one, Mom."

"Details, details." She came forward to kiss Oscar on the cheek and gave Brad a huge smile. "Oh, a visitor. Do I know you?"

"Ha ha. Funny, Mom." He came forward to hug her, doing his best to focus on the now. He refused to look in her eyes and see blame for things he couldn't change, guilt for events beyond his control. Instead, he'd only look for the love she had for her sons, which had never been in question.

He let her go after she struggled to go free.

She patted his chest. "Bah, you keep getting bigger and stronger."

"Like a brainless ox," Oscar muttered.

Rochelle chuckled, then pretended to cough to cover the sound.

"I heard that." Brad gave his brother the finger when his mother looked away.

"And I saw that," Rochelle said. "Boys." She sighed. "Too bad you never had girls, Viv. Then instead of wrestling matches, we could have had tea parties and shopping days."

"Hey, I like tea. And I like clothes." Oscar tried to sound insulted. "Well, clean clothes. I don't suppose you could do my laundry, Rochelle."

She just looked at him.

He sighed. "I tried."

"I could wash—" Vivienne started.

"I was kidding," Oscar hurried to say, especially when Rochelle's eyes narrowed on him. "Actually, we should celebrate the prodigal son coming home. Got a fatted calf to kill?" A little bit of bitterness came through, but not as much as Oscar usually spouted when dealing with Brad's presence.

Progress, Brad supposed. "Actually, I was hoping to spend the day with you guys. I'm off until Monday."

"Your boyfriends on your nerves?" Oscar taunted.

Brad had never understood if his brother actually disliked his friends or felt jealous at Brad's closeness to them. Or if it was all an act to make their mother pay him more attention, something he could never seem to get enough of.

And there I go being petty again.

He cleared his throat and managed a grin. "Yeah, they are."

Oscar laughed. "I was kidding, man. The guys are cool. When you see them again, tell Tex I said hi."

"I will." *Tex? Why Tex?*

"If you're really here to help, there's some things you can—"

"Wait, wait," Vivienne interrupted. "Let's spend some time catching up first. Oscar, take a break, honey. You work too hard as it is."

"And you're on the early shift tomorrow," Rochelle reminded him. "You don't have to fix everything broken in the house." Under her breath but loud enough for Brad to hear, she added, "God knows how long that might take."

Brad bit back a grin. "Yeah, Oscar. Stop trying to make me look bad."

"Too easy. I'm gonna let that one go." Oscar grabbed a root beer from the fridge and offered Brad one.

He accepted it, as well as the food Rochelle prepared while

his mother sat with him and Oscar at the kitchen table. "Mom, the place looks great. You're doing an awesome job." No longer a hoarder's paradise, the house wasn't so crowded. His mother had made huge strides in getting rid of her many collections.

His mom beamed. "Thanks, sweetie. But it's really Rochelle and Oscar who've been doing all the work. I just sit back and let them clear it all away."

He frowned.

"I'm kidding. I've been doing most of the cleanup, so don't give me that look. I think the therapy you've all been hounding me for years to get is finally starting to take." She gripped the hand Rochelle put on her shoulder. "Oscar has gone with me a few times."

"More fun than AA and a King County holding cell all rolled into one." Oscar crossed his eyes.

Brad choked on laughter.

"That's not funny," Vivienne snapped. "Oscar, you were there. Tell your brother about our sessions."

"Um, how about we talk about the house instead?" Oscar suggested, shooting Brad a warning look that clearly stated, *You don't want to hear this.*

Rochelle grabbed more cheese and crackers, set them on the table, and took a seat. "Yeah, Viv. Tell Brad how your cleaning frenzy really started." Rochelle said to Brad, "She saw a show on Netflix and got super excited to be organized. It's actually catching. I've given away over half my shoe collection."

"Which leaves her with just five hundred more pairs," Oscar deadpanned, then laughed when she punched him in the arm. "Ow. You hit too hard. Go beat up on Mr. Biceps instead."

"I know you're not talking about me." Brad looked his brother over. "You seem like you've been lifting a little. Not bad." Oscar really did look better.

"Ech. Don't give me compliments. It gives me hives." Oscar had never liked Brad's praise, which didn't make much sense because Oscar continually angled for approval, then turned it away. Even now, he acted as if he wanted Brad to hang round, but when Brad did, he'd pretend Brad's presence didn't much matter.

Trying to figure out how Oscar's brain worked exhausted him...almost as much as trying to figure out how to handle their mother. He turned to Rochelle, who sat watching him with a smile.

"Rochelle, what have you been up to?"

"Same old, sweetie. I'm still working at the clinic, and your mom has been helping me at the community center. We're working with the seniors on a variety of programs."

"Seniors." His mother huffed. "I barely turned fifty-six and already I'm old."

To her credit, his mother appeared years younger. Instead of possessing a haunting, mournful beauty, she looked graceful and even elegant. A total contrast to her two bruiser sons and the tough chick-magnet that was Rochelle.

Vivienne cleared her throat. "Boys, there is something I need to tell you." Her voice shook when she announced, "I'm ready to start dating."

Brad and Oscar looked at each other, then turned to Rochelle, confused.

"Viv, I think they know that," Rochelle tried, as she did every so often, to air out the family secrets...that weren't very secret.

But Vivienne shook her head. "No, they still think I'm mourning their father."

"No, Mom," Oscar said. "He's been gone too long for us to think that." He reached across the table to grip her hand, and she squeezed it tightly.

"It's okay, Oscar. I know how much you still miss him."

"I never knew him. How could I miss him?"

Oscar's words fell on deaf ears as their mother tuned into her favorite topic—loss. She'd always been a glass-half-empty kind of person. Unfortunately, time and therapy had done little to change that. And Brad had been so hopeful about a drama-free visit home.

"Poor Bradford. Only seven years old when you lost your daddy. He'd be so proud of the man you've become. If only he could see you now..."

Brad sighed. He'd finished grieving his father years ago, the man a loving but distant memory. But God forbid his mother let it go. He didn't begrudge her feelings for her dead husband. He just wished she'd stop attributing that sadness to him. He had plenty of other reasons to fall down the rabbit hole.

Oscar squeezed her hand. "Mom? You were saying you want to start dating again?"

She blinked. "Why yes. I think it's time I found someone I can love with all my heart."

Finally. Brad and Oscar shared a hopeful glance.

Rochelle had been through so much for so long, only true love—and a sense of humor—could have kept her with Vivienne. Hell, Brad had moved out the first moment he could, enlisting in the Marine Corps at eighteen. Rochelle stayed close but not too close, willingly living in the proverbial closet as Vivienne's *neighbor* and *friend*.

"That's great, Mom." Brad smiled. "We only want you to be happy." *And how many times have I said that?*

Rochelle nodded. "The boys want you to be happy, Viv. I think you should feel free to tell them the truth." He hated the hopeful look in her eyes, having seen that hope dashed too many times to count.

But maybe, just maybe, this time...

Vivienne locked gazes with Rochelle and looked quickly away.

He saw Rochelle's disappointment and wanted to shake his mother. In what world could she possibly be living in that her sons wouldn't know about the significant other she'd been sharing a life with for the past thirteen years?

A glance at Rochelle showed her shaking her head, quietly asking him to say nothing.

It's not okay. He couldn't look at his mother, lest she see his sheer disgust for her cowardice.

Viv lifted her chin, her face red, hearing nothing she didn't want to hear. "I just want you boys to know I'm a woman with a woman's needs."

Oscar barked a laugh. "Okay, just don't. Date whoever you want." He smiled at Rochelle. "Love whoever you want. But by all that's holy, do not *ever* tell us about your needs."

"What he said," Brad agreed, determined to keep his visit amenable.

"Fine." Vivienne huffed. "Well, I'm glad that's out of the way."

Before his mother could add anything that would make him want to run for his car and not look back, Brad told them about his upcoming video spot with Pets Fur Life, being vague about Avery. His family was familiar with her name. They'd been by his side when his world had gone to hell five years ago, though his mother had been far from helpful.

"You're going to be on *Searching the Needle Weekly*? That's so exciting." Grounded once again, Vivienne sounded together, like a woman who cared. He wondered how Rochelle could stand it, living with a woman who only focused on what *she* wanted, what *she* could handle. Had his father lived, would he and Vivienne have stayed married?

He glanced at Rochelle and thought not. Hell, his mother couldn't even be honest with herself.

Words Rochelle had spoken years ago, when he'd realized just who she really was to his mother, came back to him. *"Don't judge her, Brad. You have no idea what your mother's upbringing was like. She's done the best she can for your family. I know you don't realize it, but she's a lot stronger than you give her credit for."*

"But how can you stand it? She acts like you don't exist!"

"*She loves me, and I love her.*" Rochelle had shrugged. "*None of us are perfect, Brad. Certainly not me. It's enough to know we love each other, and our lives are our business. Please don't make choices for me.*"

"*I love you, and I'm not afraid to tell anyone. I'll always love you, no matter what.*"

She'd kissed his forehead. "*I know, and that makes me feel so blessed. And you know what? I'll love you no matter what, too. You're my son in all but blood, sweetie. I'm so proud to be a part of your life.*"

Since he loved and respected her, he supposed he could understand her stance on leaving things be, wanting only for Rochelle to be happy. But he still thought she was the best of them, and that neither he, his brother, nor his mother deserved her.

Oscar frowned at him. "Hey, I asked a question. You're good with all this?"

"Oh, sorry. Yeah, I am. At first, I wasn't, but the reporter I'm working with is also being made to do this for the publicity. And you know, if it helps home strays, it's not a bad thing." From what he gathered, Pets Fur Life had been having funding issues.

"I guess not." Oscar glanced down at his drink then back up at Brad, a faint glimmer of need in his eyes. "Um, well, do you think I could come watch the taping?"

"Oh, me too?" Vivienne asked.

"I'm sorry. It's a closed set," he lied. "But maybe in the future?"

Oscar shrugged. "Sure."

"Okay." His mom smiled and launched into more questions about the festival, Station 44, the guys, and how he liked the new place.

He answered, feeling pleased about the turn of his visit. Afterward, helping Oscar repair a few broken shelves and tightening a few leaky pipes, he made a decision. In a low voice, he said, "I was lying to Mom. You can come Friday if you want to."

The look on Oscar's face unnerved him because his brother appeared overjoyed. "Oh cool. Thanks, man. I get you on Mom." He nodded. "You sure this reporter is okay?"

"Her name is Avery Dearborn."

Oscar blinked. "Seriously? The one who fucked with you all those years ago?" What went unsaid—the one Oscar had spilled his guts to in a drunken daze.

"Same one. She doesn't want to rehash things any more than I want to."

Oscar snorted. "She should have been fired after what she did. She was all over us, digging into shit she had no business looking at."

"I know." And it seemed Avery knew too. But what did that mean to him, exactly?

Chapter Five

THURSDAY EVENING, AVERY PICKED AT HER FOOD WHILE sitting on the couch, eating off a TV table that cost more than all of her secondhand living room furniture combined, while her father focused on his crossword puzzle and honey chicken. A rerun of *Jeopardy!* played on the television, but Avery had no enthusiasm for French poets or Yankee Hall of Famers.

Alex Trebek quizzed contestants while Avery pretended her father wasn't ignoring her and her father pretended she'd been born with a Pulitzer in hand. Ah, happy times.

Her mother entered the living room, glanced at them, and sighed. "Seriously, you two? Len, let it go. Avery, I, for one, loved the festival. You were the best part of it."

Avery smiled, wishing she could overlook her father's disapproval to bask in her mother's unwavering support. But she could never get past how much she disappointed her father. The fact he didn't respect her or the work she did was like an arrow to the heart.

"What's that?" Avery's father glanced up, confused. Or at least, *seeming* confused. With Len, Avery could never tell. He was a master manipulator, which was a great thing when dealing with stubborn informants. Not so great when trying to share real emotions.

He asked, "What's a five-letter word starting with *V* meaning mercenary?"

Her mother frowned. "Hmm. Good question."

"Venal." Avery nibbled at her chicken.

"Oh, thanks." Her father scribbled the word and continued to work down the crossword.

June Dearborn cleared her throat.

Len looked up. "What?"

"I was just saying how great Avery was on Saturday." She gave him *the look*.

He blinked, glanced at Avery, and smiled a little too wide. "Oh, yes. After you calmed down that dog, it went well. Good job."

Hmm. I've got a word for you, it's—she had to count on her fingers—*eleven letters and starts with P. How about* patronizing?

Her mother then gave Avery *the look*.

Avery sighed. "Thanks. It was pretty funny in retrospect. The paper is getting a lot of attention for it. The mayor's totally pleased with the support for Pets Fur Life as well as the positive reinforcement for the new fire station. Right now, the city is looking pretty."

Her father grunted. "Mayor Bentz isn't so bad. Would be good to get his attention. Imagine some meatier pieces. Maybe something on the new legislation he's been implementing." He sounded excited.

Legislation? Sadly, Avery had no idea what he was talking about. She didn't care for politics. At all. "Good point, Dad."

Her mother smiled, focused on the positive, ignoring everything else her father said. Like usual. "Yes, Avery was amazing, and of course people loved the segment." She winked at Avery. "It didn't hurt that you were saved from falling by a handsome fireman either. Is he single?"

"Mom." Avery flushed, wondering if she should mention Brad's identity as the man who'd been the start of her decision to torpedo her career all those years ago. Her father's attention had her rethinking that idea. He looked so pleased with her. "The fireman who's helping is really nice." Lie. "He's super excited to be working on the articles with me."

"Articles?" Her father's bright-blue eyes had always seemed more intense than hers.

"I'm doing a series on Pets Fur Life and Station 44, since a few guys at the fire station have kind of adopted their cause. *Searching the Needle Weekly* is covering pet adoptions for the next few weeks, and we'll help rehome—"

"That will help you get an interview with the mayor." Len nodded. "And that might segue into something a little more serious. You can use this fireman to step up the ladder to hit his battalion chief or, hell, maybe even so far up as the deputy chief if you do it right. I'd love to know what they think of the current funding they receive from the city. Our tax dollars could be better spent, you know."

She swallowed her desire to write about poppies and lavender, alien rocks, and the best cupcake recipes in the city. "That's true. Funding is always an issue, isn't it?"

He grinned at her, and his approval made her feel ten feet tall. "You're so smart. I just know you can push through this phase and get back on track, find your niche."

I have found it. "On another note, Gerty said to say hello."

"What's she up to lately?"

"She's been killing ogres and barbarians and making grown men cry."

Her parents laughed at that.

Her mother said, "You tell Gerty she's due for another Dearborn get-together."

"So, this Sunday then?" When they typically met for family togetherness. Tonight had been a one-off invitation for Chinese food. God bless her mom for not giving up. As if throwing her family together like last week's leftovers might salvage them into something palatable.

June shook her head. "Not this weekend. We're going over to Bainbridge Island."

Len stood with his plate and took it to the sink then stopped by June to give her a kiss. "I can't next weekend either. I'll be in New York." He watched Avery, looking for something she never seemed able to give him. "I told Erik I'd help him with something he's working on."

"For the *Times*?" her mother asked.

He nodded. "I'll only be a few days."

Avery swallowed the ball of disappointment, its weight heavy and sour in her stomach. Her ex-boyfriend, Erik, the son her father had always wanted, continued to call on his mentor. Len, eager to remain in the investigative game, was all too happy to help. He had a warm spot for Erik in particular, not that Avery could blame him. Her parting from Erik had been amicable, and she still considered him a friend. She just wished he wasn't always there to remind her father of her life that could have been.

Used to his comings and goings, her mother waved away his upcoming trip. "Well, then, we'll make it after that. Now, Avery, I want to hear all about your work." June tugged her by the crook of her elbow into the back sunroom. Salty, their dog, followed and sat next to Avery on the couch, her dark eyes full of compassion. And ever hopeful of a doggie treat.

Lost petting Salty, the cute Rottweiler just adorable with her head in Avery's lap, Avery wasn't prepared for her mother to join her on the couch with a commiserating hug, or for the tears that came with it. She sniffed, and her mom sighed and pulled back.

"Oh, Avery. Your father loves you, you know. He's stubborn and unable to see that what you're doing is just as important as what he does."

"Do you mean that?"

June smiled. "Of course. But we both know the truth of the matter."

"What?"

"You and your father are too alike, and you try to out-stubborn each other. You butt heads even when you're getting along. It's weird, but it's your dynamic."

"How can you say that?" Avery gave a harsh laugh. "He's successful. I'm not."

"You are too."

Avery hated that she needed someone to tell her that. Shouldn't she believe it of herself without outside validation? Money didn't equal success, she knew. She loved what she did, but she'd never be rich doing it. Having a job in her chosen field, which paid crap wages, would always be a risk. Something her artistic mother well knew.

"Mom, I'm more like you than him."

"Really? Because I'm content with my life, not always trying to go for bigger and better." June paused. "Or to talk a big game to please someone else."

"I'm not… I don't do that."

"Oh? Then why don't you tell your father that you're happy? Why are you always agreeing with his tips to get that next big interview? Honey, if you don't want the career your father had, just tell him."

"I quit my job. That should have told him."

"You said you didn't like the atmosphere there, not that you hated your job."

Because looking in her father's eyes and dashing his dreams had been an impossibility back then. And now. "Well, maybe I should want those things."

Her mother raised a brow. "I remember you years ago, twenty-three and on your way to an ulcer. Pushing people around to get at the truth isn't you, sweetie."

Brad Battle's face grew crystal clear in her mind's eye.

"Avery, if you're happy, your father will be happy for you."

"Now who's delusional?" she muttered.

Her mother popped her on the back of the head.

"Ow."

"This is my point. You're just like him. Sarcastic to the end. Always trying to prove yourself when you don't have to."

"Ugh. Now you're hitting me where it really hurts."

June smiled, a woman truly happy with her status in life. Avery had inherited her mother's need to create and to laugh. Whereas June Dearborn put her artistic efforts to paint and canvas, Avery used words to express herself. As a young girl, she'd written stories on note cards, making worlds where life felt light and happy. Her father had traveled the globe, doing important deeds, as he'd called them. He'd been larger than life and always with a smile for his little girl.

When Avery had started carrying around a tiny notepad and pencil, becoming a junior reporter to emulate her father, he'd been pleased, encouraging. And when she'd shown real aptitude for reporting the news in high school and then college, he'd been ecstatic.

But as she'd matured, she'd developed an aversion to prying, to lifting back the curtain on so much ugliness. Granted, news wasn't always bad. But so much of it turned her stomach. She liked butterflies, puppies, and fluff pieces. She'd loved covering the college Valentine's Day specials much more than she'd liked reporting on the assistant dean's scandalous affair with a few undergrads and his mishandling of personnel.

Her mother had a point, but every time Avery thought about coming clean with her dad and telling him, point-blank, that she had no intention of changing, she wondered if he'd just quit trying with her and lose interest forever. Unnerved at the thought, she wondered if perhaps he really did have the right of it. She'd made a hash of her career years ago, trying to find herself, and had changed track. Unfortunately, on the cusp of thirty, she still hadn't quite discovered who she should be.

"Okay, enough work talk." Her mother patted Salty, who groaned in pleasure. "Are you still dating that Jim guy, or are you two on a permanent break?"

"Jim?" Avery had to think hard. "Oh, Jim. No, we broke up a while ago."

"Why? I thought you liked him."

Bad sex and a need to talk about himself in the third person had not done Jim any favors. "He was nice but kind of boring."

"According to you, they're all boring."

Avery shrugged. "Dating isn't easy. Hmm. Maybe I should do a series of articles on that. We did one last year, but it wouldn't hurt for more advice on love."

"Love is never easy. Everyone thinks dating in my day was as simple as snapping your fingers to snag a man. Ha. I went on a lot of bad dates to find your father. And despite what you might think, he's a keeper." Her mom wiggled her eyebrows.

Avery didn't want to think about what those wiggling brows might be saying. "Great to hear. In my day, which is now, every-one's meeting up online. I've been striking out." Heck, she'd met Jim half a year ago, and after a month of texting back and forth, their schedules had lined up for a few dates. She'd gone out with him for two months before finally throwing in the towel. "Besides, I'm busy with work. My social life—"

"What social life?" June sighed. "If you're not at work, you're here hanging with your old lady mom."

"You're not old."

June snorted. "Or you're stuck at home. Avery, you're worse than Gerty. I love that goofy girl, but she's so wrapped up in her cyber world I'm amazed she was out under the sun this past weekend."

"She's got an animal charity she works with," Avery said, defen-sive. "She likes computer games, and she dates." Although cyber-sex with the forty-five-year-old landlord might not be considered a real outing.

"Gerty has a passion." June nodded. "You need that."

"Passion? I like guys well enough."

"No, no. Not physical passion." How cute. Her mom blushed. "I meant something outside of work that means something to you. A hobby, a passion for art, language, films, flowers. What do you like to do for fun, Avery?"

———————

An hour later, Avery lay on her living room floor, staring up at the ceiling, while Gerty drank hot chocolate and looked down on her from the couch.

"Gerty, I have no life."

"Could have told you that."

"Shut up. I'm serious. When my mom asked what I like to do for fun—not work-related—I came up blank."

Gerty sipped and sighed. "I love chocolate. So much." She wiped her upper lip with the back of her hand and burped. "Better. So, let's see. She asked you a question and put you on the spot. Come on, Avery. You have a life."

"No. I have work. I have you, my best friend."

"And me," Alan chimed in as he joined them in the living room. He'd just made a plate of s'mores in the microwave and handed one to Gerty. His penance for throwing Avery under the bus with that dog video. And yes, she was still making him pay. Though she loved Emil being happy with her, the added work was stressing her the hell out.

"First of all, Gerty, you're my roommate and best friend. You don't count."

Gerty scowled. "What? I count."

"Second, Alan, you're my work buddy. You don't count either."

"Fine by me." He shoved a whole wedge of graham cracker, marshmallow, and melted chocolate in his mouth. "I have so much life I'm full of it," she thought he said around the gooey treat.

"Full of it is right." Gerty shot him the finger, to which Alan said something unintelligible.

"Seriously." Avery glared at her friends before letting out a sad breath.

"Oh God. It's the Avery hour." Alan groaned.

"All drama, all the time." Gerty wiped an imaginary tear. "Pity me because I am."

"Suck it, you two." Yet Avery couldn't help grinning. "Okay, just hear me out. I know I'm being all whiny. I'm due. I had dinner with Dad tonight."

"Oh, well, go ahead." Alan nodded. "I like your dad, but he's like Babe Ruth and you're his kid who decided to follow him into baseball. Just…why? You have masochistic tendencies."

"I know. And can I ask why you always use baseball as a reference to life?"

Alan shrugged. "You get points for hitting things. There's a bat and balls—"

"Totally phallic." Gerty nodded.

"And guys who are always adjusting themselves. It's like if you don't touch your dick at some point in the game, the umpire will bounce you. It's a guy metaphor for life."

"You lost me there." Avery sat up and reached for a s'more. "But as to why writing? I can't help it. I like writing. It's fun and creative. And it's me. I'm not into art like Mom. I could give or take video games."

Gerty put a hand over her heart and cringed in mock horror. "Take it back, foul heathen."

"And let's face it. Photography is for those who wish they could write but can't," she added, gratified by Alan's scowl. "Kidding. But seriously, when Mom asked me what I like to do for fun, I came up with nothing. I mean, I'm not even into dating or sex anymore. And isn't that depressing."

"Early menopause?" Alan asked.

Both Avery and Gerty just looked at him.

"What? It's a thing."

Avery turned back to Gerty. "I have no passion. Not for art or sex or life, apparently." She groaned. "What do I like to do outside of work? That's such a simple question. So why is that so hard to answer?"

"I'll tell you why," Alan said. "Because you're overthinking it."

"This from the man who thinks dick pics are an icebreaker?" Gerty snorted.

"Hey, that was one time and an accident. I thought I was sending that to my girlfriend, Gillian. I got the G's mixed up." Alan looked as if he meant to say something, paused, then added, "But it was good, right? I looked huge from that angle."

"Huge," Gerty agreed.

"Anyway," Alan continued to Avery, "my point is you're a little neurotic when it comes to your dad and your career. Right now, you have nothing but work, so of course you're thinking you're some big loser with no life."

"I'm pretty sure I never said that." *Why did I invite him over again?*

"But you're hot and smart. Guys would love to get with you if you'd give them the chance. And no, Gerty," he said to stave off Gerty's pending interruption. "I don't mean me. Avery and I decided a long time ago that sexing coworkers don't work."

"I know that. Glad *you* remembered it," Gerty said.

"Don't get me wrong. I'd do her in a heartbeat, but I'm pretty sure she'd fall for me, and that would ruin my playboy image."

"Oh, thanks so much, Alan." Avery fluttered her eyelashes. "Great to know I'm good for a pity shag."

"You're not British, Avery. It's pity fuck." Gerty shook her head. "It's okay to say the f-word."

"Fuck. See? I said it." Alan smiled and continued, "And on top of all this anxiety you're suddenly feeling, let's not forget you have that video spot tomorrow with Super Hunk FD."

Avery turned to Gerty and glared. "You've got *him* calling Brad that now?"

"Hey, not my fault he has big ears." Gerty and Alan air high-fived. "But I'm more astonished that Alan actually sounds like he knows what he's talking about."

"Thank you." Alan nodded, taking a head bow. "I'm all about therapy. I'm actually dating a psychology professor at the moment."

"Oh boy." Avery groaned. "Great. Now you're going to be psychoanalyzing me all day every day."

Alan talked over her. "You're stressed about tomorrow. Considering this is the dude who was your first big story—and now your second big story—and he sees you working for the *Needle*, you're right to be a little freaked out."

"*Searching the Needle Weekly* is a great place to work." She glared at him. "Why are you acting like I should be embarrassed about writing for them? Like it's a step down or something?"

He just looked at her. "You write that alien baby piece yet?"

"Well, no…" She flushed, understanding but still annoyed. "Wait. How do you know Brad was my first big story?"

Gerty raised a hand. "I filled him in. What? He promised s'mores for the scoop."

"Traitor."

"You bet. I'm low on my chocolate stash." Gerty took another s'more. "But he's right. You're due to be a basket case over Super Hunk."

"I am?" Avery opened herself to listen, trying to come to grips with a mini early-life crisis.

"You are." They nodded, and Gerty added, "Your dad always makes you feel like you made a bad choice by not following in his footsteps. And the guy who pretty much made that blow up in your face is now back in your life. Plus, he's *really* good-looking. So even if you hate him, you can be attracted to him."

"I can?"

"You so are," Alan said around his s'more.

Avery bit into hers, losing herself in the mushy confection. After a few moments and a sugar rush, she asked, "I mean, I don't like the guy. But come on, you can't be attracted to men and not be attracted to him. Plus, he's all charming when he plays the heroic fireman." She'd always had a thing for a man in uniform, and Brad in his firefighter clothes unfortunately triggered a major attraction.

"Right." Gerty licked her fingers clean. "But to say you have no life isn't fair. You have to work extra hard lately because Emil has loaded so much work on you in addition to the stress of the Pets Fur Life thing. Cut yourself some slack. When this dies down, I'm sure you'll cook something up."

"Aha! I like cooking! I like it a lot."

Alan smiled. "See? There's your passion. Though I think you should return to the idea of sex."

Gerty rolled her eyes. "Of course you do."

"Dating is not a four-letter word, Gerty."

"Obviously."

"You know what I mean, smartass. We all know why Jim didn't last. He sucked in bed. Kiss of death for a guy."

Gerty gaped at Alan. "How do *you* know?"

Alan chuckled. "My last girlfriend, the one before the shrink, dated him and said he was terrible. Not into foreplay, as I recall."

Avery blushed. "You never mentioned that."

"I would have. But I thought it might make you uncomfortable that I knew the sexual history of your minuteman. Plus, he had that weird way of talking. 'Jim thinks Avery is fine. Jim loves tacos.' It took me a while before I realized he was talking about himself. It was like that *Seinfeld* episode."

"Everything can be equated to a *Seinfeld* episode," Gerty said and again air high-fived him. This time Avery joined in because she too was a fan of the old sitcom.

"I know he was a bit off," she admitted. "I just held on because I wanted to date someone for more than a week. Heck, I was turning into a girl-Alan before I went off guys." She pointed a finger at him. "Next time I date someone you know, tell me if he has a reputation. I can work with bad in bed if I know upfront, but he was also super-ficial and all about himself, which took a few dates to learn."

"Meh. At least you had a date for a while." Gerty sighed. "I'm in a dry spell. And no, Alan, I do not want your help."

"Your loss." He took the empty s'mores plate to the kitchen. Then he returned and looked down at Avery. "And you. Stop stressing so hard. Tomorrow will be fine. With any luck, Banana is busy. Because you get another dog humping your leg and I'm pretty sure you'll end up a bad meme. Something none of us want."

Gerty grinned. "Although, I could make it something fun and funny. Maybe—"

"No." Avery walked Alan out, giving him a hug as he left. She returned to the living room and shook her head. "I can't believe he knew about Jim and never said anything."

"I told you Jim was a dick the minute I met him."

"No, you told me our signs didn't align, and considering you didn't know anything about him at the time, that was pretty suspect."

"I just didn't like him." Gerty paused. "But I like Brad. He's a dick you know, yes, but watching him at the festival, I realized you don't know all of him." She grinned. "Did you hear that? *All of him*? Seems to me like there's a lot of Super Hunk to get to know. If you know what I mean."

"Gerty, you're about as subtle as a brick wall."

Gerty laughed. "Might not be a bad way to break your sad dating streak."

"You're the one in the dry spell. Why don't you date him?" Yet the thought of Gerty with Brad didn't sit right.

"Ha. Yeah, right. I'm not poaching Super Hunk FD from my best gal." Gerty left the living room and came back with her rescue dog, whom she'd named Klingon. The three-legged Lab puppy was wiggling his little heart out. Then he tinkled on the carpet.

"Crap. Quick, get the pet spray!" Gerty grabbed a leash and doggie bags and raced outside with Klingon. She returned ten minutes later to find the room cleaned up.

You're welcome, Gerty. A good thing Avery had taken the puppy out an hour ago or they might have had quite a mess to deal with.

"All good." Avery looked at the now-cleaned carpet, at Gerty holding a smiling Klingon, and told herself tomorrow would be "all good" as well. She just had to keep Brad Battle in the corner of her brain marked professional and pray the Pets Fur Life rep didn't try to pawn a cat on her and instigate a sneezing fit.

Did Brad prefer dogs or cats? She should ask him that. Nothing too personal. Stuff relating to animals and the fire department. Yes, she could handle that. Fun banter, nothing deep.

What she couldn't handle were the dreams of him, shirtless, carrying her up a flight of stairs into a bed surrounded by clouds, then proceeding to give her mouth-to-mouth for a very long time...

Chapter Six

At six forty-five on Friday morning, Brad looked around *Searching the Needle Weekly*'s tiny video studio, intrigued by the low stage, the lighting, and the cameras. Behind the cameras was room for a small audience, though the room appeared empty save for the folding chairs stacked in a chair cart against the wall.

An older man stood on the set. When the man turned, Brad recognized him as a funny old guy named Rupert, the nephew to Brad's octogenarian landlady. Rupert and his eccentric girlfriend often took in strays, and they'd started taking them in for Pets Fur Life.

Brad didn't ask questions, just accepted that Rupert wanted to help and did what he was told. Brad and his crew had been helping with adoptions lately, and they had another one coming up on Sunday.

He just had to get through this stupid live video thing.

Glancing around, he spotted his brother watching from behind the cameras, offstage, next to the blond from the festival—Gerty, he remembered Avery calling her.

He returned the wave Oscar sent him. Gerty narrowed her eyes and asked his brother something. Oscar grinned before turning to her, and their conversation seemed to heat up. Content his brother had a new friend, Brad looked to Rupert for a sign to get this show on the road.

Rupert, dressed in a suit that would have fit right in during the '70s, with frizzy brown hair threaded with gray and smiling eyes, crossed to him walking a large dog on a leash, a smaller one cradled against his chest. "Nice to see you, Brad."

"I like your friends." He smiled at the dogs, who seemed a little nervous.

Then Avery walked into Brad's view, all glammed up, and spoke to the cameraman. He had trouble catching his breath. Had Avery's legs always been that long? And her hair, it seemed wavier today, a bit of a bounce to that dark, silky mane. In profile, her curves were just...*wow*.

"Son, you okay? Hey, Brad, which do you want to go with? Henri or Rockslide?"

"What?" Brad did his best not to look flushed. But hell, he hadn't gotten a cup of coffee yet, and Avery looked amazing in a flowy skirt, form-fitting blouse, and heels. Even worse, she wasn't wearing glasses, and her eyes seemed to dominate her face. Or maybe it was her slick, cherry-red lips. He cleared his throat. "Sorry. I need caffeine. I was in here a little after six to get 'made up.'"

Rupert sighed. "I hear ya." Sixty-plus years young, dating a ball-buster of a woman who had erotic figurines decorating a house time had forgotten, Rupert could always be counted on to be entertaining.

"You were asking what, exactly?"

"Avery wanted to know if you preferred to hold Henri or Rockslide first. Henri, short for Henrietta, is this little Yorkie. She's cute but snappy. Rockslide is the sad-looking pit bull."

"Gimme the pit."

Rupert grinned. "That's what I thought you'd say. Oh, wait, there's Emil. I need to talk to him. Be right back." He left the pit bull with Brad and carried Henri with him.

Rockslide wagged his tail and grinned, and Brad couldn't help smiling. He had a thing for the much-maligned breed. Dogs were inherently good, in his opinion. People had made the mistake of turning them into killers. At heart, most canines just wanted love and affection.

Avery had joined Rupert and an older man. She was petting the little Yorkie, and he found himself wanting to trade places with the dog.

Which got his guard up. He had no intention of doing anything more than acting professional. Friendly but not too friendly.
Heck, maybe he needed to start dating again if the sight of Avery's
fashion sense had him so hot and bothered.

"I need a drink," he muttered as he bent down to let Rockslide
sniff his hand. The dog took a step back at the closeness and needed
a few seconds to warm up to him, but once he did, Rockslide stared
up at him with love. Brad kept reminding himself he couldn't keep
the guy. One, he worked bad hours for a pet, especially when at
the station where he couldn't take care of the dog. Two, he spent
enough time handling his family and his inability to let things go.
And three... Avery was walking over. He needed to get his head
on right.

"Hi, Brad." She looked him over, not sexually but critically.

His dander went right on up. "Avery." He smiled and gave her
the same once-over. Except deep down, he catalogued the lovely
shape of her breasts, her hips and waist, and the slender calves
shown off by those blue pumps. "No glasses today?" That seemed
safe enough.

She blushed. "No. I usually wear contacts for indoor filming stuff.
I've only done a few segments before this one, but today will be
quick and easy. I've already talked to Rupert. He said he knows you."

Brad nodded and stuffed his hands in his uniform pockets. He'd
worn his Class B uniform, usually referred to as his nomex—for
the material from which it had been made. The same official blue
working uniform he'd worn at the festival, but this time pressed to
within an inch of its life. "His aunt is my landlady. He's a good guy,
helps take in animals until we can find them a good home."

"We?"

"Pets Fur Life. The guys and I have been helping with the
animals for the past year, and even when we moved stations, we
decided to continue. It's good press for the station, and we love
animals."

She seemed to soften. Then she shocked him by reaching out and rubbing his collar—very close to his racing pulse. "Sorry. You had a little smudge on your uniform. Makeup, I think." She didn't seem to be making fun of him, so he thanked her and took a subtle step back.

"So, how are we doing this?" he asked.

Her rundown seemed simple. He would stand by while Rupert talked about Pets Fur Life. Then she would introduce herself and Brad, and Brad would introduce Rockslide, who had yet to take his loving eyes off him. They'd talk about dogs and pet rescues. Maybe she'd ask him something about being a firefighter. Nothing too strenuous. She handed him a note card with details on each pet, easy enough to remember.

"I think he likes you." Avery smiled and bent down to pet the dog, who sighed with pleasure and leaned into her. Avery seemed to wobble on her heels.

Brad could just see disaster written on the set and grabbed her by the arm to steady her.

She straightened, her eyes bright, and smiled. "Thanks. I'm a little uneven today."

"Uneven?" An old girlfriend had always referred to herself as uneven before adjusting her bra, which had Brad automatically looking down at Avery's chest. A brief glimpse he'd had no intention of taking. Unfortunately, she caught him looking. "What's uneven?" he asked, trying to play it off.

They both stared at each other, faces red.

Awkward.

She forced a smile. "I'm not used to these shoes, but my favorite pair snapped a heel."

"Bummer. I wore my favorite pair today. Nice, huh? They make my legs look terrific." He showed off his black boots, easing the tension.

Great job, Battle. Keep it up and you'll go down for sexual harassment in no time.

She laughed, thankfully. "With that sense of humor, we'll have the segment up and running with tons of people calling in for the dogs."

"Right."

Before he knew it, he and Avery stood next to each other on the small set, which consisted of a bar table with a phone, a bouquet of fresh flowers, and a backdrop of the city overlaid by the *Searching the Needle Weekly* logo. The bright lights centered on the stage made it impossible to see their audience, though he knew his brother and Gerty watched.

And wonder of wonders, they were streaming live. No correcting any mistakes. They had to get it right the first time. He should have felt more nervous, but public speaking had never bothered him. Though Brad didn't care for being the focus of attention, he performed well under stress. And standing close enough that he could smell Avery's light perfume definitely counted as stress.

Rupert introduced himself, made small talk with Avery, then turned the show over to her. She introduced herself and Brad while Brad kept an eye on Rockslide to behave. The pit was a gentleman until Avery drew closer. She had to be wearing some kind of dog-attracting perfume. That or she'd smuggled bacon in her skirt because Rockslide couldn't get close enough to her.

"Damn it," he muttered as he struggled to get the dog to obey. "Sit," he said in a firm voice. Rockslide froze, looked up at him, and sat on command.

"Wow, he's trained." Avery beamed and petted the enthusiastic bruiser. "And such a sweetie. Folks, you should see how lovely Rockslide is. He's only two years old, still a puppy really. He was found abandoned in a condemned house, chained up in the basement, all alone. So sad, skinny, dehydrated, and scared. But with a little love and TLC, he's turned into a seventy-five-pound bone lover." She rushed *bone* and *lover*, making them sound as if one word.

Rupert blinked. The set seemed to freeze.

Brad heard seventy-five-pound *boner* and did his best not to laugh. Rupert and a few others around them coughed to mask their amusement, though he swore he heard Oscar's loud laugh.

"What?" Avery asked, her smile starting to fade.

"Ah, right. So, Rockslide really likes being petted." Brad leaned down to hug the guy, which got him uber happy. Rockslide started licking him wherever the dog could reach. He nearly toppled back but had steadied himself, crouched and on one knee.

Avery tried to lend a hand. "Hold on. Oomph." The dog nudged her for kisses. She would have fallen…except Brad had a hold of her legs, keeping her upright. An accidental grab that caused every cell in his body to freeze.

He couldn't help feeling the silky smoothness of her skin, his left hand perilously high up on her thigh *under* her skirt.

"Well, now, what a good dog." Avery's voice had risen.

Brad needed to stand up, but the dog was blocking him, and honestly, his hold on Avery did as much to steady him as it did to steady her.

Rupert did nothing to stem his laughter. "Hey there, Brad. Great job giving Avery a hand."

The person working the camera laughed, as did more from behind the camera. Apparently, others had come in to watch the show.

"For goodness' sake." Avery took a step to the side and reached up to fiddle with glasses that weren't there. She put a strand of hair behind her ear instead. Then she glared down at him and said through a forced smile, "Wow, you firefighters sure are handsy. I mean, handy."

Handsy? Brad rose easily to his feet and smiled back at her. "No worries, Avery. I was glad to be here to lend you that hand. But hey, it's a good thing I was here to save you *again*." He stared into her eyes so she couldn't miss the mean glint in his gaze.

"Again?" Rupert asked.

Avery studied Brad as if she'd forgotten they had cameras on them. The dog sat like a rock by her feet, and she stroked his head absently. "It's so great that we citizens of Seattle can count on the brave firefighters of our city to save us from ourselves," she teased, but he saw the flare of anger she couldn't hide.

Rockslide chose that moment to nudge under her skirt, sniffing her legs.

"Whoa," she gasped. "Geez, he's curious."

"Well, he's a guy. Can't blame him for trying," Brad muttered, annoyed enough to feel the same "curiosity" for the snarky reporter.

"So you're saying all guys are dogs?"

"Nope." Brad did his best to remain cheerful. "But Rockslide is, and he seems to like you. Hey, just like Banana did! Remember that cute Lab you were 'dancing' with at the festival? Dogs really like you."

She smiled through her teeth. "My, the compliments are going to my head. What a charmer you are. Say, Brad, are you single?"

"I—what?" That didn't seem like fun banter. That seemed a little personal. Unless she was asking for herself? On TV? His heart raced.

"We're here to get Rockslide adopted, but maybe we can find someone to adopt you too."

A few people watching laughed. Rockslide barked on cue, encouraging more laughter.

He gave a fake smile, pretending she wasn't jumping on his last nerve.

"Are you housebroken?" Avery seemed to enjoy his discomfort.

"No, but Rockslide is." He would be the better person here. He could do it. No, he couldn't. Two could play at this game. He'd out-humane her. "Rockslide is one terrific dog. As we've said, he's housebroken, loves to play fetch, and wants a family. But he's a one-dog family. Like most men, he doesn't want to share what he loves."

"Right. I... What?"

She looked confused.

Brad turned to the camera and smiled. "Look at this great guy. His tail is wagging. He's so happy for affection. Like so many of us, he's been burned before. Rockslide, by the family that deserted him. So many other men, by the women who broke their hearts."

"Oh, please."

Rupert was grinning. "That's true, Brad. Some women just don't care how hard you work to put food on the table or how many sacrifices you make to keep them safe and happy. They have a roving eye."

Avery blinked. "What does that have to do with Rockslide?" She paused. "What does that have to do with *me*?"

Ha. Call me *handsy when all I'm trying to do is save you from falling while streaming live.* "Why nothing...unless the shoe fits."

Avery looked ready to combust.

He grinned at her and crouched down to pet Rockslide.

Rupert watched them, looking from Avery to Brad and back again. "Um, we also have Henri here?"

Avery stalked to Rupert and gently took Henri in her arms. "You know, Brad you make a great point. Let's look at poor Henrietta. Henri for short. She's a lovely little Yorkshire terrier, given up because her owner wanted a new puppy and didn't want to take care of an older dog too."

"That's not right. Pets are family and should be with you for life," Brad said, meaning it.

"I agree." She nuzzled Henri under the dog's chin. "She's a sweetie." She held the dog to him. "Done wrong by a man wanting a younger woman."

He took the dog in hand and rolled his eyes. "That's such a common stereotype. Not all men want a younger woman, you know."

"Sadly," she said, ignoring him, and turned to the camera, "Henri feels hurt and abandoned and is having trouble trusting men again."

"Yeah? Because she seems to be trusting me just fine." Brad cuddled the little dog while Rockslide leaned into him, wanting attention.

"She also loves cats, kids, and other dogs. She's got so much love to give." Avery was pouring it on thick. "And yet a man did her wrong."

The phone on the desk rang, and Rupert picked it up. He murmured something, then paused to say in a louder voice, "Hey, Avery and Brad, the station manager said we have a lot of calls asking about Henri and Rockslide. But wait a minute." He went back to the caller and paused again. "One lady wants to know if she gets a date with Brad if she takes on Rockslide."

Avery grinned. "That's a great deal."

"Now hold on," Brad said, not liking the turn the show had taken. This wasn't *The Bachelorette*!

Rupert grinned like a loon. "Well, we also have a few gentlemen wondering if you're single, Avery. Gosh, this is like a dating show! Let's find homes for dogs, cats, Avery, and Brad!"

Avery chuckled, though to Brad it sounded forced. "Too funny, Rupert. But I'm sure Brad has no problem getting dates. He's so handsome and available." She pointed to his arms. "Ladies and gents, look at those muscles."

She was *not* trying to auction him off. "Let's not forget Avery," Brad said with pretend cheer. "So beautiful, smart, and single, guys! Oh, and ladies, too. We're all about inclusion here."

"*So* outside our scope for this show," Avery said, smiling through her teeth at him.

"Yep." He smiled back.

Rupert cut in. "Don't forget about our adoption this weekend, everyone." He listed the times and locations for the event. "In addition to our friends here today, we have a lot more furry fellas needing a good home." He shot a wink to Avery and Brad. "And maybe a firefighter and reporter needing a good home too!" He guffawed. The audience clapped and hooted.

"Oh no. We're out of time," Avery hurriedly cut in. "Next week we'll showcase some new animals. And remember, Pets Fur Life is happy to take donations if you can't find room in your home for a new furry friend." She paused and, in a voice he clearly heard, muttered, "Or a big doofus dressed in blue." In a louder voice, she added, "Don't miss the phone number and website at the bottom of the screen. Thank you, and have a great day."

And cut.

Brad opened his mouth to retort, but whistling and loud clapping surrounded them.

Avery blushed, then turned wide, startled eyes on an approaching thin man with a wealth of white hair.

The man clapped with enthusiasm. "Brilliant! I love the dynamic between you two." The man held out a hand to Brad, who handed Henri off to Rupert in order to shake it. "Emil Watts. I run *Searching the Needle Weekly*. Pleasure to meet you."

Avery recovered her wits, apparently. "Emil, this is Brad Battle, a firefighter with Station 44. Brad, Emil, my boss."

"Boss, huh?" Brad gave her an evil grin. Before he could say something that wouldn't get her in too much trouble but that would make her sweat, his brother joined him.

"Oh ho, a sibling." Emil rocked back on his heels. "You two look way too much alike not to be related."

Oscar introduced himself. "Ah, hi. I'm Oscar Battle. Brad said it would be all right to watch." He shook Emil's hand, then Avery's. But his gaze fastened to Rockslide, and a wistful expression crossed his face. "I always wanted a dog."

"You did?" Brad hadn't known that. As a kid, his brother had been partial to reptiles.

Oscar shrugged.

Gerty appeared and elbowed him in the side. "Well then, adopt him." She turned to Brad. "Hmm. So, you're the troll."

"Live and in color," he deadpanned.

She surprised him by grinning. "Hey, Oscar. What do you know? Your brother has a sense of humor."

"Not when it comes to his precious car. He's never let me drive it, you know."

Brad groaned. "Don't make me regret letting you come today."

Oscar ignored him in favor of petting Rockslide, encouraging Gerty to do the same. The pair walked a few steps away with the dog, like Brad wasn't standing there after having been made a fool.

And this is why I hate the spotlight.

Avery seemed to be sneaking off as well, so he said in a loud voice, "Oh, before you go, Avery, could I get a moment of your time?"

Her boss watched them without blinking.

She smiled at Emil and blew out a breath. "Sure, Brad."

Emil grinned. "Brad, thank you so much for helping out today. Your boss wanted me to tell you thanks as well."

"Which boss?" He had so many.

"Well, there was a Captain Reynolds, and I think your battalion chief called. He's pleased to give us access to Station 44 for as long as we need it. From what I saw, we'll definitely need you for the next few weeks at least. Friday mornings work for you? Terrific."

Brad didn't have a chance to answer before Emil took a call on his cell phone and walked away.

"You have one minute of my precious time, Battle. Speak," Avery muttered.

"Not here." He stalked away from everyone, confident she'd follow.

In a dim, unused hallway away from the cameras and people, he glared at her.

She glared back.

"What happened to making this professional and courteous? You called me 'handsy' on TV!"

"You had your hand on my thigh," she said, her voice low, furious.

"Yeah? Well, I was trying to stop you from tripping over your own two feet and flashing your panties at the world. You're welcome."

"At the world? You do realize our audience is maybe a few thousand people at most. And what about my panties?" She gaped at him. "What the hell are you talking about?"

"If that wasn't bad enough, what's with trying to set me up with half of Seattle?"

"Oh, did I hurt your pride?"

He studied her, seeing the sparkle in her eyes. She liked their little fight. Hell. So did he. He felt himself growing warm and aroused and turned to go before he did something stupid.

Except Avery tugged him back to face her. "I'm not done with you."

"Avery, it's clear what this is."

"Oh, do explain 'this' to me."

He couldn't see her too well, but at least they seemed out of the way of everyone else in the less trafficked hallway. She moved closer, and her perfume went straight to his head. And other places.

"The problem, lady, is you want me, and that bothers you." *Because I know exactly how that feels.* "You think making a joke of me being available will make it seem like you don't care." What the hell was coming out of his mouth?

"You make no sense," she hissed. "You're so used to women throwing themselves at you that you can't stand it when a woman doesn't want you. And nice job, running those hands up and down my legs. You perv."

Incensed, he stalked her until she'd backed up against the wall.

Despite the low light, he saw no sign of fear on her face, just anger. "*I'm* the perv? You're the one constantly falling over so I'll save you. Jesus, that's lame, even for you."

"You jackass." She fumed, and he imagined steam coming out her ears. "Honey, I could kiss the breath out of you and come out the other end cold as ice. And not because I'm frigid, but because you're all bark and no bite."

"Oh yeah?"

Her hands gripped his biceps, her breath a rush of mint over his lips as she leaned closer. "I've met your type before. Pretty and buff with nothing else to offer. No idea how to please a woman."

"Avery, if you'd manage to get over yourself and plant a wet one on me, you'd end up shivering and begging for more while I did my best to keep you steady on your feet. I think they call that needy nowadays."

"Needy? Pucker up, asshole, and we'll see who's needy."

He'd been egging her on, hoping she'd do it.

He wasn't disappointed.

Avery dragged his head down and kissed him.

And as he'd secretly dreaded, her taste went straight to his brain, then traveled directly south and stayed there.

———

Avery had lost her temper and her mind, and not necessarily in that order. In a sane moment, she'd never have given in to temptation to kiss Super Hunk FD. He was masculine and hot and had a body worth killing for. His arms felt like steel under her hands, his chest broad and crushing her breasts, making her nipples stand on end.

His mouth was both firm and soft, and he didn't take charge of the kiss or try to manhandle her in any way. Instead he responded to every move *she* made, his body heating her up and making her burn.

She gasped at the fire inside her, and he took the invitation to thrust his tongue into her mouth, sweeping through to send her arousal into the stratosphere.

His large hands gripped her waist, and he angled his head to deepen the kiss, making her knees weak.

Something crashed nearby, startling them both into springing apart.

"Fuck me," he swore and took two large steps back.

"Oh no." Bad, bad Avery. "That was… I mean, I didn't mean to…" She leaned back against the wall for support, glad at least she wore her contacts. After that kiss, her glasses for sure would have fogged over.

He blew out a breath and bent over, as if having finished running a race. When he straightened after a moment, he gave her that sardonic look she loathed. "Now who's handsy?"

"Hold on, Battle. You have some nerve—"

"*You* kissed *me*."

"You kissed me *back*."

"I'm only human."

"What does that mean?"

"It means when a chick who's ripe for it grabs me for a kiss, I'm not dumb enough to say no."

"Wait. *Ripe for it?*" She wanted to scream at him, and herself, for being so close to the truth. Instead she said, "Ha. I proved my point."

He crossed his arms over his chest, and she did her best not to stare at his fine body like a love-starved "ripe chick." Brad snorted. "And what point might that be? That you can't control yourself around me?"

"That you're the needy one. I merely kissed you. A tame, simple kiss. You're the one who shoved your tongue in my mouth and got all grabby."

He narrowed his eyes. "You know what I'd like to shove in that mouth?"

"Oh, do tell." She took two steps closer and poked him in his rock-hard chest. "Because I have something I'd love to shove up your—"

"There you are." Oscar and Gerty paused at the mouth of the hallway. "Hey, Brad, what are you doing?"

Gerty grinned. "Yeah, Super Hunk. What are you doing?"

Oscar turned to her. "Super Hunk?"

She winked at him. "Well, you two do look alike."

Oscar flushed, then gave Gerty a huge grin. "True. He takes after me."

"Oh, then you must be a dickhead too," Avery snapped, came back to herself, and blushed. "Hell. I'm sorry." She glared back at Brad. "I have work to do. Great doing business with you, *Bradford*." She made sure to sneer his name. Immature, but right now it was the best she could do.

"You too, Ms. Ripe," he said, uber polite.

"I'll see you next Friday and not a second sooner," she sniped and tore past him, grabbing Gerty on the way.

Gerty yelped and waved. "Bye, Oscar. Text me!"

———————

"See you next Friday?" Brad repeated, watching Avery leave. "Not if I see you first." A lame comeback, but he had to have the last word. Either that or prove how needy *he* truly was with another bone-melting kiss.

He became aware of his brother watching him.

"What?" he barked.

"If I tell you how incredibly funny that pet skit was to watch, will you hit me?"

"Yes, but I won't leave a mark that will show."

"It was so fucking funny I almost peed myself laughing. And I wasn't the only one. Everyone watching loved it."

Brad groaned. No doubt about it, he'd be stuck doing this stupid bit with Avery until he quit the department or stopped helping at Pets Fur Life, neither of which was an option he wanted to consider anytime soon.

Then he made good on his promise and punched his brother in the arm.

"Ouch. She was right. You are a dickhead." Oscar frowned before grinning once more. "A dickhead in love…"

"Shut up."

Oscar hooted. "Oh man. I just realized how much crap you're gonna get when the guys at the station see this."

Brad mourned his life before Avery, back when he'd been respected. Because sure as shit, the station was merciless.

And every time he remembered how incredibly hot that kiss had been, he was reminded that things could only grow worse.

Chapter Seven

AVERY WAS SO SICK OF ALL THE CONGRATULATIONS everyone at work offered, especially because she had to pretend she and Brad had agreed to do that "bit" before being filmed. Emil thought her a genius and gave her the raise he'd been promising on the spot.

Sadly for her, the show was becoming a hit on YouTube, racking views right up there alongside her dance with Banana.

"You're becoming a minor celebrity!" Gerty said hours later on a lunch break phone call. "I am so glad I took the time off work to see you guys. That was so incredibly awesome. And say what you want, but that was *not* planned."

Avery groaned at her desk, conscious to keep her voice low. Most of those in the office had taken a lunch, but their star reporter, Tara, had been hovering, shooting Avery some curious looks from across the room.

To Gerty, she whispered, "I swear, I didn't mean to try to auction him off. But he was being so annoying."

"I showed my buddies at work, and they loved it. I'm telling you, they watched the entire segment. Twice. By the way, I have a few guys asking for your number. Should I give it to them?"

"*No.*"

Tara glanced over.

Avery lowered her voice. "No, please don't. I'm trying to put today behind me." *Oh my God. I kissed Brad Battle.* She'd been doing her best not to think about it, but she could still feel those sexy lips against hers, could feel the press of his chest brushing her breasts, all that strength while he'd had her pressed against the wall.

She started overheating and took a long drink of water. "Look, I have to go. I'll talk to you later, okay?"

"Sure thing. And hey, warning, if I saw what I think I saw between you and Super Hunk, you'd better give me details. Or else. Got it?"

"Yes," Avery said, miserable.

"Hot damn. I knew it!" Gerty disconnected on a laugh.

Avery wanted to bury herself in her desk and not come out for years. Not only had she screwed up the ten-minute streaming segment, but she'd kissed the hunky troll. If he hadn't grabbed her bare thigh, she never would have called him handsy for all of *Searching the Needle Weekly*'s viewers. She did have a few brain cells. But she'd been so riled by the feel of him she'd barely been able to string two sentences together. Then the thought struck that he might have been screwing with her on purpose.

She'd reacted.

Badly. Then badly *again* with that aggressive kiss. What had she been thinking to grab him like that?

She wanted to get that kiss off her mind, but as hard as she'd been working, she could still smell Super Hunk's aftershave. She shoved a hand in her hair and gripped it by the roots. *Son of a fuck—freak!* Who had taught the man to kiss like that? Squirming in her seat, she took deep breaths, trying her best to concentrate.

"So, you and Brad Battle, huh?" Tara stood by Avery's desk with a friendly smile.

Unlike how most of the world chose to look at professional women as being constantly competitive, Avery and Tara got along. Tara had the top spot, was damn good at it, and had a brain that never stopped working. She'd also been one of Avery's top cheer-leaders when Emil had brought her onto the paper. A few drinks and they'd bonded over years past dealing with toxic masculinity in the newsroom.

Avery smiled up at her, forcing away thoughts of Brad's lips.

"Yep. Emil liked the spot. We'll probably showcase cats next week." She sighed. "I'd better get more allergy pills."

"Are you guys dating?" Tara's eyes sparkled. "Because you had some serious chemistry. Go girl."

"Are you kidding?" Avery huffed a laugh. "That jerk? He's handsome, sure, but such an arrogant ass."

Tara seemed to deflate. "Oh, too bad. I thought you guys made a nice-looking couple. He seems like a nice guy."

"To you or his friends, maybe. But he doesn't like the fire department forcing him to do the pet adoption spot."

Tara frowned. "He shouldn't take his frustration out on you." Tara patted her on the shoulder. "Whatever. You still rocked it this morning. Kudos. Our numbers are really taking off. Maybe Emil will keep us in print a little longer."

He'd announced earlier that morning his plan to make their videos a bigger part of the network.

"I prefer print," Avery said. "Well, print or digital articles, not video."

"Why not? You're a natural."

Avery sighed. "Not like you. I just did it because Emil told me to. But I don't have your skill with people or your natural vitality on-screen. The camera loves you."

Tara preened.

"I am good, aren't I?" They both laughed, then Tara said, "Well, keep up the good work! Maybe they'll move you to morning news with me."

Avery looked Tara in the eye. "And maybe I'll quit. A short pitch I can handle. Five minutes, ten max. Actual city news? No thanks."

"I think you're selling yourself short, but it's your career. And speaking of which, I have an interview to get to. Later, Avery." Tara smiled and left, humming under her breath.

Too bad Tara can't do the pet segment. Friday mornings with animals—including you, Brad—are bad enough. No way I'd want to expand into other stuff online.

And she'd have to do it again next week. Stand next to Brad and pretend nothing had happened between them. She was disgusted at the amount of time she'd been spending mooning over her handsome troll. Guaranteed the man hadn't thought about her at all after leaving this morning. The jerk.

She dug into a candy bar left on her desk and furiously got back to work. Notes, two interviews, and a decent beginning into next week's feature took up the bulk of her day. But on the drive home, she dreaded talking to Gerty about Brad.

Work had pushed thoughts of their kiss aside, and she'd been more than productive. The fact of the matter remained she'd have to talk about that kiss sometime, and with Brad no less, because they had to work together. She didn't know why they couldn't get along. The past stayed in the past, didn't it? And with their current streaming segment getting so much attention, Brad was actually helping her, though he probably didn't realize it.

So why did she feel the need to antagonize him? To kiss him?

Her cheeks burned, as did the rest of her, recalling how good he'd felt. Yep, the return of her sex drive had arrived with no departure date in sight. So unfortunate that it took Brad Battle to rev her sad little engine.

She pulled into the apartment complex, parked, and steeled herself for Gerty's third degree. But when she entered, she found the apartment empty. A note left on table told her Gerty had gone out with a friend for dinner, giving Avery a brief reprieve.

Pleased to relax and kick back without worrying about anything, Avery allowed herself to just be.

———————

The next morning, she woke refreshed and ready to tackle her chores. "Yo, Gerty. You want to walk first or do chores first?"

Gerty didn't answer. Odd.

Avery knocked on her door and, hearing no answer, pushed it open. Gerty's unmade, unslept-in bed stared back at her. Worried, Avery shot to her phone, only to see a text from Gerty. *Drank 2 much. Had 2 spend nite. Back l8r* was followed by an alien and demon emojis.

Avery texted back, *B ready 4 your own INTERROGATION.* She signed it with a crowned girl and a zombie and received back a drunk face.

Grinning, because for once Gerty would have a story to tell that didn't involve digital wizards and barbarians, Avery decided to tackle some chores and set out for the grocery store. She picked up enough to last the next week. Frozen chicken, fresh fish, and tons of fruits and veggies for salads and smoothies. Totally healthy, she thought with satisfaction, determined not to add chips or chocolate for once. Back at home, she did her share of the cleaning and some laundry, exercised with a long walk by the river, made her bed, organized her closet, and stared at her shoes, not sure if she could part with any of them.

Resigned to keeping them all, she closed her small closet and went back into the living room. And stared at the clock on the wall.

The hour had just reached six in the evening. Gerty hadn't returned. Avery had done all her chores and had nothing but time on her hands.

She could get ahead on the next week's work. Edit her articles before she gave them to Emil.

But no, because she needed a life, and that meant not working all the dang time.

Hmm. With Gerty out, Alan no doubt enjoying his weekend with his girlfriend, and her parents living large in Bainbridge, Avery was at loose ends. She had other friends, though not as close. Many of them had significant others or even kids, and she hadn't been out with any of them in forever. No reason to call out of the blue now.

If she had a hobby, she could pursue that. She went back to the refrigerator and stared at all her healthy choices, craving chips.

The clock ticked.

She sat on the couch and laid her head back. She'd been up late the night before, and she'd gotten up extra early this morning for chore day. A nap would be great.

She stared wide-eyed at the ceiling. Not tired in the slightest.

"Hmm. Maybe I can give Gerty a break and clean the kitchen for her."

That done, she sat back on the couch, hoping for inspiration. A glance at the clock showed she'd wasted thirty minutes, and that had been dragging out the cleaning. Feeling beyond lame, she scrolled through her phone, found movie times, and decided to hit the AMC10.

Once there, she decided on the latest horror movie, hoping it would be terrible—her favorite kind—and needing something different to do to take her mind off how incredibly dull she'd become. Without Gerty, Alan, or her mom to give her companionship, Avery had...no one.

She groaned. "I am getting a life if it kills me."

After paying for a ticket to *Slice and Dice II*, she grudgingly parted with several bills to pay for the exorbitantly priced popcorn and small soda. Once inside the theater, she found a spot near the back, pleased to find the movie not all that crowded. Then again, she'd chosen *Slice and Dice II* because it had been out for two weeks and had terrible reviews.

The lights dimmed, and a sense of anticipation filled her. How long had it been since she'd seen a movie, anyway? She enjoyed the comfy seat, the darkness of the theater, and her favorite part—the previews—and kicked back to watch.

The movie progressed with plenty of gore, cheap effects, and a substandard plot. As she'd anticipated, not many people had opted to watch the movie, and she had room around her to stretch out.

Before she knew it, she'd gobbled up half her popcorn and a third of her drink. Toasty, comfortable, and slightly dulled by the plodding film, her eyelids started to drift closed.

Her prerogative, she thought with a smile, out on her own and enjoying herself, finally.

She blinked, yawned, and sank a little lower in her seat…

———————————

Tex elbowed Mack. Brad couldn't hear exactly what they said, seated at one end of their trio, but all the quiet murmuring annoyed him.

"Hey, shut up," he whispered. "Slice is on the move."

Tex chuckled and said no more.

Mack just had to say what Brad had been doing his best to ignore. He leaned across Tex in the middle and whispered, "It's weird the survivor looks like Avery. Right?"

Tex agreed, pretending to ignore Brad. "Yeah," he murmured. "I thought it was just me, but the too-stupid-to-live lady does look like Avery."

"Only not as fine." Mack nodded. "Still, I'd do her."

"Oh, me too."

Brad growled in a louder voice, "Would you two knock it off?"

Someone complained about the noise from a few rows down. Of maybe a dozen in attendance, they had to sit near a shusher.

"Sorry," Tex apologized in a low voice. He hunkered down in his seat between Brad and Mack and finally settled into the movie.

Considering Brad had been doing his best to forget all about Avery Dearborn since their unforgettable kiss yesterday morning, he thought it beyond ridiculous he was watching her twin avoid a maniacal killer on-screen.

If they'd stuck with the latest superhero movie, he might have been spared more memories of Avery. Instead, he could do nothing but reinvent that kiss. He clenched his fists, too easily recalling how it had felt to slide his hand up her thigh.

Overheating, he took a quick exit to refill his soda. On the way back in, he noticed a slumped individual a few seats above his and the guys'. She didn't seem to be moving, though he couldn't make out much of her face covered by hair and a pair of glasses. Out of concern for the woman, he bypassed his seat and went into her row that was all but empty.

A slight snore told him she seemed okay. But he sat beside her anyway, unable to process what he was seeing while someone on-screen shrieked.

Avery Dearborn, the bane of his existence, sat three rows above him in the same horror movie, in the same theater, in Seattle. What were the odds?

He looked down at his friends, who had yet to turn around. Had they set him up? Was Avery following him around for some reason?

The noise on-screen was deafening, yet Avery didn't move. The villain's laughter, in a deep bass, rumbled through him, and the heroine in the film kept yelling in a high-pitched tone that put him on edge.

He studied Avery, wondering how she could sleep through the screaming. Now worried something might be wrong with her, he prodded, "Avery?" He whispered her name again. No response. If she didn't soon wake up, he'd have to take more drastic measures. He nudged her shoulder. "Avery?" At the same time, Slice impaled the Avery lookalike on film, and the resulting cacophony of sound as the gates of hell opened up hurt his ears.

Avery bolted up and joined the screaming. She flailed and knocked her soda onto him, drenching his pants while her popcorn shot up and out over the seats in front of her. Fortunately, no one sat close enough to get doused.

No one but him.

From behind him, a guy grumbled about scared theatergoers. Down in front, fans clapped and cheered for Slice. Brad saw his friends clapping as well and couldn't help a snort of amusement. Sickos.

"Oh my God. What happened?" Avery breathed.

Her eyes wide behind her crooked frames, Avery stared at him, then at the screen and back again. She leaned forward and poked him in the chest. "Huh. Not dreaming."

"No." He sighed. "But thanks for spilling soda all over me."

"Oh man, I'm so sorry." She looked around her and sank lower. She whispered, "I cannot believe I fell asleep."

"I can't either. It's so loud in here."

"I'm a heavy sleeper. I must have been more tired than I thought." She handed him some napkins. "Here. Use these to blot the drink."

He cleaned up as best he could. "I saw someone up here not moving and wanted to make sure you were all right. I'll leave you alone."

Alone. Avery didn't seem to have anyone with her. Strange. He'd figure a woman who looked like she did would have a line of guys around the block wanting her time.

"Thanks." She gave him a hesitant smile. She had bits of popcorn on her shoulders, and her glasses remained askew. Yet she looked charming and innocent, and that put him on edge.

He seriously had something warped in his brain if he thought her innocent. Hell, she'd probably been spying on him and followed him to the theater looking for dirt.

So she fell asleep?

"Avery, come join us," Tex whispered loudly. "And bring Brad with you."

"Shh." An annoyed older couple sitting at the back glared at Brad.

What the hell did I do? I wasn't the one screaming. "Come on," he muttered before Tex started yelling his invitation and more people blamed *him* for it.

He seated Avery next to Tex, meaning to go on the other side of Mack, away from her. But Tex wouldn't let him pass.

"Move," Brad muttered, trying not to block those few behind him from seeing.

"No. Sit down."

"Sit down," yelled a teenager close by.

"Who let you into an R-rated movie, kid?" Brad yelled back.

"So much talking." "Shut up, man." A few more people protested the interruption, so he sat next to Avery, feeling foolish.

"This is the most exciting movie I've been to in a long time," she whispered to Tex, leaning closer to the big guy.

Annoyed, Brad said, "So exciting you fell asleep."

Then she had the nerve to shush him. "Shh. Look, there goes Slice. Nothing keeps him down."

Brad did his best to lose himself in the movie, but too aware of Avery next to him, he spent the next twenty-six minutes totally out of it. He only knew the movie ended when the audience clapped and the lights came back on.

"We're going out for a beer," Mack said to Avery, including her in a plan the guys hadn't exactly mentioned to Brad. "Wanna come?"

"I don't want to intrude." She looked directly at Brad.

Proving she didn't bother him, he shrugged. "Not a problem for me." He couldn't help himself. "Unless of course my being there bothers *you*."

She stiffened and stood, looking down at him. "Nothing about you bothers me, Bradford."

Tex snickered. "Bradford. Such a prissy name."

"Yeah, we should all be named Tex." Brad gave him a wide smile. "Or Roger."

Tex flushed. "Asshole."

Avery watched the byplay, a dimple appearing on her left cheek. "Roger's your name?"

"No."

Mack chuckled. "Yes, it is. Come on, *Roger.* Let's go grab that beer."

Tex sighed. "Fine. But just for that comment, I'm playing me some Blake Shelton on the way. Loud."

"Nooo." Mack walked away, bitching about country music. Tex continued to torment him with a compilation track of artists, and Avery chimed in with her knowledge of music, which was pretty extensive.

Brad followed, just listening, as they made their way to the parking lot.

"I'll follow you guys there," Avery offered once Tex had told her where they planned to go.

"It's dark. Let me walk you to your car," Mack offered.

Brad scowled at him, then noticed the others watching him. "What?"

"You jealous?" Mack asked, batting his eyes like a dumbass. "I mean, I'm sure Avery wouldn't mind if *you* walked her to safety. Or are you more worried that Avery's stealing me away? They all love me, you know," he said to Avery. "I'm the most popular guy in our crew."

"Mack, shut it." Brad would have said nothing more, but Avery's smirk got to him. "I'm not jealous, just worried for you."

Her eyes narrowed.

"Why's that?" Mack asked, playing along.

"Well, see, Friday morning, after the taping, Avery and I—"

"Come on, Mack," Avery snarled and yanked his friend away with her.

Mack followed like an obedient puppy.

"Avery and I what?" Tex asked. "I wanna know."

Brad felt weird about outing the actual details of his altercation with Avery. Baiting her was one thing, but he'd never been the kind of guy to kiss and tell, even if he didn't much like the girl he'd been kissing. Although, come to think of it, that had never happened before. Brad always had a connection with his dates. He didn't do casual sex and never had.

"She and I argued." Brad shrugged. "But Mack's a pain in the ass, so maybe he wants to argue?"

"With a pretty girl like Avery? Hell yeah. I wouldn't mind it myself." Tex grinned at him. "An argument, huh? If that's the way you want to play it, I'll back you. But it would help if you didn't keep staring at her ass."

Brad snorted. "Maybe I'm looking at Mack's."

"Nah. We've both seen him nekkid. Ain't nothing happenin' there." Tex laughed, and Brad laughed with him. "Now try to get your poker face back on because you need to prove to that gal you don't care. Am I right?"

"I don't care." He paused. "And why does everyone keep talking about my poker face?" First Oscar, now Tex. "I don't play poker."

"It's a good thing or you'd be flat broke all the time." Tex unlocked his truck and they both got in. Then he started fiddling with his radio.

"Hey, I thought the country music was a threat for Mack."

"Nah. It's my pleasure to play it for you losers with no taste. And I like it loud." Blake Shelton belted out a tune that wasn't too bad. Though Brad worried he'd suffer hearing loss as they trucked to a nearby bar. With any luck, they'd get pulled over by the cops for a noise violation.

No such luck.

They arrived at the bar, pulling in next to Avery and Mack, who seemed to be having a lively discussion they continued on their way inside the place. Avery greeted Tex—and ignored Brad—as she chatted.

Brad told himself he didn't care, that he didn't feel anything even close to resembling jealousy.

"Green as a mother," Tex muttered.

"I need a drink." He signaled down a waitress as they snagged a table in the back.

"A big one," Tex agreed, then slugged him with a friendly punch. "And because you were such a good sport on the way over, it's on me."

"What? I can't hear you." He tapped his ear. "Music. Was. Too. Loud."

Tex grinned back.

"Hey, *I* was a good sport." Mack grinned. "I took one for the team by driving with Avery."

Avery laughed. "There's nothing wrong with being a slow, responsible driver. And everything annoying with being a back-seat driver."

"Yeah, he does that." Tex groaned. "But Mr. Whiny over here can't handle his music too loud. I felt like I was driving with my ninety-year-old grandmother."

Brad pasted on a grin. "Oh, does she hate country music too?"

"Not as much as your mom. But she don't mind if I play it when we cuddle. You know, after...?" He wiggled his brows.

Brad couldn't help laughing. "You're an idiot."

"He really is," Mack agreed. Then Mack turned to him. "Did you know Avery loves bad horror movies? And the AMC10 is her favorite theater."

"The seats are the best," he and Avery said at the same time.

Flummoxed, Brad cleared his throat, ignored his buddies' cat-like grins, and asked Avery, "You had no better plans for a Saturday night?"

She turned red. "What? I can't like movies?"

"With all your friends?" he shot back, then felt that might have sounded more mean-spirited than he'd meant. "Where was the blond, Gerty?" She'd seemed pretty friendly with Oscar, though Oscar had shrugged off meeting her as if it had been no big deal.

Avery huffed. "I don't know. We're not joined at the hip, Bradford."

"She says your name like you're married," Tex said, laughter in his voice.

She pointed a finger Tex's way. "Keep it up, Roger."

Tex grimaced, making Avery smile.

Brad had no idea why his heart started racing.

Mack shook his head. "Don't look at me. I love my name. Mackenzie Revere. I go by anything. Nothing shames me."

"Sadly, that's true." Brad chuckled. "Even when he walked out of the bathroom at the station, wrapped in a tiny towel, while the battalion chief and his wife were getting the tour."

Tex leaned toward Avery. "They almost got the *whole* tour, if you get my drift."

"Hey, I made Mrs. Chief's day." Mack held up an impressive arm and flexed.

"He probably did." Avery grinned. "Man, and I didn't even get a tour of the truck at the festival."

"You know, that's a great idea." Tex shot Brad a sly look Brad pretended not to see and said, "You should come tour the station house, Avery. Maybe next Friday, after your pet thing with Brad. We're off that day, but I bet Brad would be happy to show you around."

Avery turned to Brad. "You have to do the segment even if you're not working?"

He shrugged. "It helps Pets Fur Life."

"That doesn't seem fair. I mean, not the part about you helping animals. But that you have to get up early on your day off."

"I bet our lieutenant will count it as overtime." Mack snorted. "And anyway, it's not like Brad's got anything better to do."

"Sad but true," Tex agreed.

Brad frowned. "Just what do you two have that I don't?"

"Lives?" Mack suggested. "Tex has a date next weekend." He smiled at Avery. "But I don't."

"I wonder why," Tex said drily. "Now let's talk about what's really been on all our minds."

Brad tensed, really hoping they wouldn't get on him about Avery the way they had all day yesterday. Avery didn't look all that much happier, probably anticipating the same.

Tex drew out the tension, talking even slower than normal. "Do we get a *Slice and Dice III*, or does the franchise end after this one?"

"They have to do another one." Avery insisted, sounding relieved. She looked way too cute and perky to be into bad horror and gore. "How will we know if Slice's dog comes back a hellhound?"

"That would be cool," Brad agreed, having thought that very same thing when Slice's dog fell through a dimensional portal in the movie.

Mack argued for the franchise to close. And Brad wondered if Avery recognized how often she agreed with Brad on things. Because he did, and it bothered him.

A lot.

Chapter Eight

Sunday afternoon, after Gerty had promised that Brad would be nowhere in sight at the Pets Fur Life adoption day, Avery had agreed to accompany her mouthy roommate, who toted Klingon with her.

"I still can't believe we got Henri and Rockslide adopted out already." Gerty beamed as they drove in her lime-green VW Bug. In the backseat in a tiny pet carrier, Klingon gave the cutest little bark. The fluffy golden/setter mix was freaking adorable. "You're next, boy."

"I'm just glad they found good homes. We do know that they're good homes, right?"

"We will just as soon as the adopters clear the screening process. But the homes are in nice parts of the city, and both families seemed super sweet." Gerty paused. "I kind of nosed through their application processes and ran their names through the computer."

"Hacker."

"Thank you very much." Gerty grinned.

Avery thought her friend seemed in too much of a good mood, even going to an animal adoption, which she loved supporting.

"Okay, tell me. Who was your mystery friend Friday night and nearly all of yesterday?" When Gerty blushed, Avery sat straighter in the passenger seat and gaped. "It was a guy!"

"Shh. Not so loud. You'll upset Klingon."

"I saw him eat a moth this morning before licking your dirty sock. Trust me, if he's fine with that, he's fine with the news that you had a date. Though *my* heart might not be able to take it." She pantomimed a heart attack.

"You're such a pain."

"You tell me about your Friday night, I'll tell you about my Saturday night." Since Gerty had been in bed by the time Avery had returned last night, she had no idea Avery had spent her evening with Brad and the guys.

"Wait. You mean there's more to tell than you and Brad shooting lusty hate looks at each other after the Friday morning show?"

"Lusty hate looks? What the heck are those?"

"The same thing I was throwing a guy's way Friday night at some party his friend threw."

"*What?*" She grabbed Gerty's knee and squeezed.

"Stop or I'll crash." Gerty strangled on laughter as she removed Avery's hand from her ticklish knee. "The party was fun, no booze though, so we went out to a club after. But I had way too many, so we stayed at my date's friend's in his guest room. Together." Gerty gave a sad sigh. "Not the way you'd hope."

"Wizard girl, that counts. You spent the night at a boy's house. I just shared a few lusty hate glares in public."

"You mean in private, in a dark hallway where you and Super Hunk FD were breathing hard."

"You spent the night at *a boy's house*," Avery repeated. "Heavy breathing or not, I can't compete with that. You win."

"Not really." Gerty groaned. "It's a long story."

"Yeah? Well, I have nothing but time because we are *not* here to adopt an animal. I mean it, Gerty. It's enough we're fostering."

"We? I'm pretty sure I'm the one doing all the pet stuff."

"I'm your emotional support friend."

Gerty gave her the side-eye as she parked down the street from the pet store holding the adoption. "Uh-huh."

They left the car with Klingon on his leash. The adorable fluffball strutted like he owned the street, and more than one person stopped to point him out or ask to pet him.

By the time they got to the crowded pet store, there wasn't a whole lot of room to work with.

Then Avery saw why. A guy dubbed the Viral Viking had been making the rounds on social media lately. He looked as if he could have stepped out of history—tall, muscular, and extremely attractive.

He stood by the adoption tables in the back, holding up a kitten at the moment, helping with Pets Fur Life.

Next to him Avery saw Reggie and Tex and tensed. "I thought you said Brad wouldn't be here," she growled at Gerty.

"He's not, genius. It's just those two and the Viking."

Avery relaxed while Gerty pulled away, Klingon in her arms, as she made her way to the adoption table.

Avery managed to find her minutes later, but before she could join Gerty, she bumped into Brad. Damn Gerty!

"Oh, sorry."

It wasn't Brad.

"My fault." His brother looked down at her with an apologetic expression. "It's so crowded in here."

"Hi. You were at the taping on Friday, weren't you?" She was doing her best to forget how she'd badgered him so many years ago, hoping he'd forgotten it.

He held out a hand. "Oscar Battle. We've met." To his credit, he didn't say more than that. "You're Avery, right?" His tone had cooled.

"Yes." She realized Brad had probably mentioned that she'd be working closely with him. "Look, the past is in the past. I was railroaded into the Friday show, same as your brother. I swear." She crossed her heart.

He shrugged. "Not my business."

"He's your brother. Of course it's your business."

Oscar seemed to lose a little steam. "Well, that's true."

Wanting for at least one Battle not to hate her, though last night had confused her for sure in regard to Brad, Avery put on an award-winning smile. "So, you're here to adopt an animal?"

"Kind of."

She frowned, then saw him glancing at Gerty with more than a little interest on his face. She recalled them both smiling a lot and talking after her taping.

"Wait a minute. Are you the reason my roommate never came home Friday night?"

"Roommate?" He glanced from Gerty to Avery. "Huh. She said you were friends, but I hadn't realized you were her roommate. The clumsy geek with the heart of gold."

"Gerty." She fumed.

Oscar laughed. "Hey, that's complimentary."

"*I'm* a geek?" She pointed at the dog Gerty held as she flirted with the Viral Viking. Next to the guy, Gerty looked about as big as a toddler. "She named that puppy Klingon."

"I know." Oscar smiled, and he looked so like Brad that Avery could only stare. "Klingon is such a great name. And man, that puppy is cute." Then he took another look at Gerty smiling up at the Viking and scowled.

"We're not keeping Klingon," Avery said, as if to remind herself. "You should see if you can adopt the little guy." She cautiously navigated forward, trying not to seem as if she were pumping the guy for information. "So, you and Gerty were hanging out, huh? She's pretty cool, my roommate."

"Yeah." He sighed. "And a little judgy."

"Gerty?"

"Apparently, she's not a fan of Brad." He frowned. "I could be just as judgmental, you know, but I'm not. I'm letting you prove yourself."

"Prove myself?" Gerty had fought with this handsome guy on Avery's behalf? Avery warmed at the thought. "Wait. Prove myself to you?"

Oscar shrugged. "Doesn't matter much what I think of you. It only matters that you don't screw my brother over. Again."

"Hey, I never screwed him over. I wrote an article chronicling his heroic achievements. And I never did dig for whatever he didn't want me to find." Which still bothered her, like an itch she couldn't scratch. But she'd done enough damage years ago despite her intent to help. "For the record, I never wanted to hurt your brother or use you to do it. I was so impressed by all he'd done overseas. I just wanted him recognized for it. People can be cruel, and he'd already been through a lot. I had no idea how adverse he was to being the center of attention." She frowned. "Why the heck is he a firefighter? No, don't answer that. I'm not asking, and I don't want to know."

Oscar studied her. "If you want to know about Brad, ask him."

"No. Nope, not gonna happen. I have to work with him ten minutes every Friday for the next few weeks. That's as far as I'm interacting with Brad Battle." Not counting that kiss or the movie last night.

"Don't you mean Super Hunk FD?" Oscar raised a brow.

She blushed, though it hadn't been her description. "Gerty's got a big mouth."

"But it's such a pretty big mouth."

Avery laughed. "You should go talk to her. Compliment Klingon. Donate to the charity or offer to help. She's a sucker for animals and computer games."

He brightened. "I know. She's really into *Arrow Sins & Siege*."

"If you can beat a level 49, you're in."

"Ah, a challenge. I love it." He left her when Gerty saw them standing together and headed over to talk to her.

Her BFF's eyes narrowed, and Avery wondered how Gerty would react to seeing Oscar. She still hadn't gotten the full story out of her roommate about the drunken sleepover.

Someone nudged her, and she fell backward into someone else. "Oh, sorry." She turned around to see her mother, of all people, staring at her in shock. "Mom?"

June recovered quickly, but Avery knew surprise when she saw it. "Oh, ah, hi, Avery. How are you, honey?"

"I thought you and Dad were heading to Bainbridge Island this weekend."

"Oh, we are. I mean, we did." Her mother's smile looked way too wide. "We got done early, so—"

"Hey, there, Avery. What are you doing here?" Her father asked from behind June.

Lennox Dearborn looked the way Avery felt. Baffled.

"Dad? Mom was just telling me that you guys were in Bainbridge."

"We were?"

Her mother laughed. A little nervously, to Avery's way of thinking. "Sorry, Avery. The line is getting really long. Come on, Len. Let's not waste time. Bye, honey."

"But—Bye." Avery watched them go, wondering what the heck she'd witnessed. Her mother and she spent much of their spare time together when Avery wasn't hanging with Gerty. Avery didn't mind. She loved her mom and was used to being an only child with demanding parents—parent, actually—because her father couldn't care less what she did when not at work. And sadly, she didn't have that much else going on with her life.

She stared at the back of her mother's head before the crowd swallowed her up.

"Hey, what's taking you so long?" Gerty grabbed her by the sleeve and tugged her forward. "You're helping too," Gerty insisted.

Avery frowned as she went around the table to stand with Gerty, Reggie, Tex, and the Viral Viking. She couldn't help looking way up at the guy, who had to be several inches over six feet.

"Axel, man, get a move on. That lady wants to see the kittens," Reggie dared order the giant. "Oh, hey, Avery." Reggie's welcoming smile invited her to move closer. "You know everyone except Rena in the back and Axel."

The big man nodded. She nodded back, praying he'd keep his

serial killer vibe to himself. He seemed much more approachable in pictures and from a distance. Still sexy, but now scary.

"I know, right? He's like an evil Thor," Gerty whispered, gazing adoringly up at the man. Oscar stood across the table, glaring at the guy, Avery noted.

"Well, your own evil barbarian is not happy with your fascination." She bumped Gerty to look over at Oscar. To Avery's astonishment, Gerty blushed. "Oh my God. You *have* to tell me what happened Friday night."

"Later," Gerty growled and fled to the back room.

Sensing a story, Avery started to move in for the kill when Reggie put a kitten in her hands.

She stood frozen, caught by cuteness overload and an automatic reaction to feline dander.

"Hey, Avery, can you deliver this little guy to the blond by the corner there?" His gentle shove against the small of her back didn't give her time to say no.

Avery sneezed. "Sure. I think." She sneezed again and again and barely made it to the lady before she sneezed her fool head off. Her eyes had started watering as well.

By the time she returned to Reggie, he was doing his best not to laugh. "Uh-oh. I'm sorry, Avery. I had no idea. Not good with cats, eh?" Reggie asked, his sympathy more than welcome.

"No." She sneezed and sniffed, not sure how accompanying Gerty had resulted in her holding a cat.

"Back here, come on." He led her back to Gerty, who was talking with a pretty woman about the same age. The conversation stopped as soon as Avery entered, and she started feeling paranoid. Why did everyone stop talking or look guilty when she arrived?

Reggie patted Avery on the shoulder. "Rena, do we have any antihistamines?"

Rena smiled. "Sure, Reggie. I'll get some."

Reggie turned and left.

Gerty shook her head. "You and cats. You're a menace, Avery."

Avery sneezed. "Me? I thought I was just being a good friend by coming with you to swing by, but you dragged me inside. Then Reggie put the furball into my hands and shot me toward someone like a guided missile." She wiped her eyes. "What was I supposed to do?" She turned to Rena. "Where do I know you from?" Avery would swear she'd recognized the woman's warm smile and sunny curls. She had medium-brown skin and wore a lovely sweater with strategically ripped jeans. Stylish and glowing with joy, she had Avery returning a watery smile.

Gerty pointed at Rena. "This is the other half of the Viral Viking. Rena's his girlfriend."

"And hairstylist," Rena added, holding out a hand in greeting.

"Ah. That's where I know you from. That shot of you and the Viking online."

"Great to meet you, Avery. Gerty's told me so much about you."

"Really?"

"Well, at our last event a few weeks ago. Axel—he's the Viral Viking—has been helping with the pet adoptions. And Reggie and the guys keep inviting us out, so I've been trying to help out more. Congratulations. I hear you're keeping Kl—"

"A close eye on those firemen out there," Gerty said loudly, narrowing her gaze at Rena.

Rena blinked. "Oh, ah, right. Yeah. I mean, those guys are just so handsome, aren't they? Station 44 has the best-looking firemen in the city. Or is it firefighters? Although I haven't seen the women there, so I really can't comment beyond Reggie and his crew."

"No idea." Avery's throat felt scratchy, and she hastened to accept the pill and water bottle Rena handed her. After she'd downed it, she used the sink in the nearest bathroom to splash her face with cold water. After a few minutes, she started to feel better.

She returned to find Gerty waiting for her. A thought struck. "Was that nondrowsy stuff, I hope?"

"Er..." Gerty looked at the box then back at Avery. "Nope."

"This is so not my day." Avery sighed, knowing she'd be asleep before long. She didn't do well with medications that could make her drowsy. No "could" about it. They knocked her right out. "Did I tell you I saw my mom out there? The same woman supposedly visiting Bainbridge Island right now. My dad too."

"Well, maybe they came back to shop or something."

"It was weird. My mom didn't seem happy to see me."

"She sees you all the time. Maybe she's tired of you." Trust Gerty to keep it real.

"Maybe."

"Or maybe it's all just an odd coincidence."

"Right. Tell me about Oscar."

"Here?" Gerty's voice rose. "Now?"

"Before I fall asleep." She yawned.

"Why don't you..." Gerty trailed off as Oscar entered the back room.

Rena took a look at all three of them and excused herself to help her boyfriend.

"Hi, Gerty." Oscar looked adorably awkward, kind of shy yet not as he devoured her best friend with his eyes.

"Oscar." Gerty sounded stiff and a bit...embarrassed?

Avery grinned. "I have got to know what happened Friday night."

"*Avery.*" Gerty looked mortified and turned back to Oscar. "We don't tell each other everything. I mean, we're friends, and we share. But it's not..."

Avery had never seen Gerty so off her game. Was it the drugs? Or was Elizabeth Gertrude Davis embarrassed about something for the first time in her life?

Avery glared at Oscar. "What the hell did you do to her?"

"Me? Nothing." Oscar blinked. "We talked and laughed a lot. And she slept off some drinks."

Gerty didn't contradict him.

"Huh." Avery bit back her questions, though Gerty's red face was killing her. "Hey, Oscar, can you watch Klingon for a minute while I talk to Gerty?"

"Sure." He accepted the puppy and lit up with so much happiness Avery could only stare. Did Brad ever look like that? She'd seen him laugh with his friends or smile on occasion at the animals, but never any real cheerfulness directed her way. *Well, is it any wonder? You aren't on good terms with the guy.*

Avery yawned and pulled Gerty with her into the bathroom. She locked the door behind them. "Okay, what happened?"

"Not here, Avery."

"I have no plans to move ever again."

Gerty sighed and said, in a low voice, "I'm an idiot."

"I know that," Avery whispered back. "What happened with Oscar?"

Gerty snickered. "I had that coming. Okay, in brief, *nothing* happened with Oscar. No-thing."

"And that's a problem?" Avery thought about it. "Okay, that's a problem. He didn't make a move, huh?"

"Not one. Not to hold my hand, hug, or kiss. He didn't even ruffle my hair and tell me I'm cute. We talked about everything, have a ton in common. I felt this immense connection, and I haven't felt that in a long, long time for anyone. Then he told me I was too drunk to know what I wanted, and I should put my clothes back on." Gerty's eyes shone. Avery didn't know what to say. Gerty never got super emotional, and especially not about guys.

"Wait. Back on? So you'd gotten naked?"

"Yep. But nothing I had impressed him that much, I guess." She clenched her fists. "Screw him."

"If he's not impressed, then why is he out there holding

Klingon? And why did he look as if he wanted to rip the Viral Viking's head off when you were talking to him?"

"He did?"

"He also said you have a pretty big mouth."

"That's rude."

Avery paused. "I mean, I called you a big mouth."

"Thanks a lot."

"And he said it's a pretty, big mouth. Like, that he's into you."

"Huh? Really?"

"I don't know. But I got a vibe he likes you."

Someone knocked on the door.

"Out in a minute," Gerty roared.

"Easy, girl." Tex yelled back. "I was just checking."

"We'll talk later," Avery warned her. "I have to get home now before I fall asleep in public again."

"What?"

"I went out to a movie last night, fell asleep in the theater, screamed my head off and knocked my soda all over Brad Battle's lap, then went for a beer with him and his friends. And if your eyes get any wider, they might fall out of your head."

Gerty punched her.

"Hey."

"Look, I told Rena I'd do some time here. You need to get home. I swear we'll talk when I get back."

"If I'm awake." Avery hated feeling so drowsy, but the sleepy antihistamines always affected her the same way.

"I have a plan…" Gerty shoved open the door and pushed Avery out ahead of her.

Tex blinked at them. "Ah, everything okay?"

Avery yawned. "Dandy."

"You tired again?" Tex looked concerned.

Avery laughed, trippy. "I don't have narcolepsy. I just took allergy medicine that made me drowsy."

"Hey, Oscar?" Gerty asked the guy playing tug-of-war with Klingon on the floor. "Can you do me a favor?"

He stood so fast Avery wondered that he didn't feel dizzy. His wide smile showed bright-white teeth. "Sure thing. What do you need?"

"Take Avery home for me, would you? Someone didn't show, so I promised two hours here before I can head home." She glanced at Klingon and sighed. "And would you mind taking the puppy back with you as well?"

"Sure thing." Oscar grabbed Klingon with one hand and steadied Avery with his other. "My car's out back."

Tex stood in the bathroom, just watching the three of them.

"Hey, Tex, you can use the facilities if you need to," Avery said. "You don't need our permission to pee."

He guffawed before slamming the door and yelled through it, "Later, guys."

Avery followed Oscar and Klingon and left through a back exit.

Feeling decidedly sleepy, she laid her head back in the passenger seat and closed her eyes.

And woke up as Oscar carefully helped her from the car.

"Wake up, Avery. Sorry, but you have to help me get you there."

"Where?"

"To your apartment. I'll come back for the dog."

"Sure, sure." She fumbled in her purse and found the keys. Then she steadied herself. "I'm good."

"You sure?"

"I seem to be constantly falling or sleeping around you Battles." She sighed. "Don't tell your brother I fell asleep, okay?"

"Um, okay." He gave her an odd look.

"He already hates me and thinks I have a mental condition."

"Condition?"

"Stupidity, craziness, his call." She blew out a breath as they traipsed to her floor upstairs. "I have to work with the guy, so I'd prefer it if he thought me professional and capable. And mostly awake."

Oscar smiled. "Okay." He walked with her, waited for her to enter, then promised to come back. He reappeared moments later while she did her best to get it together. Still sleepy but not as unfocused, she thanked him for driving her back.

"I appreciate it." She started to take Klingon from him, to put him into his crate in Gerty's room, when Oscar stopped her.

"I can do that."

"You just want to see Gerty's room."

"Well, yeah."

She waved him toward Gerty's door. He didn't linger, and Klingon for once didn't whine after being put in his crate.

Oscar took his keys from his pocket. "You good?"

"Yep. I'm planning on going to sleep just as soon as you leave."

He flushed. "Oh, sorry. I'm leaving, I swear. It's just… I tried to do the right thing the other night, and I think Gerty's mad at me. She's hot as hell, and I'd do… I mean, I'd like to get to know her better. But I think she has the impression I'm not attracted to her. And I am."

"Oscar, tell her all that. Later. Like, tomorrow."

"I can do that. Does she like flowers?"

"She's a sucker for roses. Red says love. Go for yellow or white."

"That I can do." He grinned, looking so much lighter than Brad. Despite the brothers' obvious age difference, Brad seemed constantly burdened with life. "Well, I'll let you go. Thanks."

"Thanks for the ride."

He smiled and left.

After Avery locked up behind him, she let herself fall into her bed and closed her eyes, her thoughts on dogs and Vikings and anything not related to Brad Battle.

So of course she dreamed about sexy firemen and what they wore under their overalls…

Chapter Nine

THE WEEK PASSED TOO SLOWLY. BRAD HAD NO IDEA WHY, BUT after seeing Avery Friday and Saturday, he'd expected to see her Sunday as well. Stupid since he'd intentionally not gone to the pet adoption, but he'd needed the break.

Reggie had mentioned she'd shown up Sunday with her friend...and that Oscar had given her a ride home.

Yet his brother hadn't mentioned her, and neither had Tex, who'd also been there.

Brad would have asked why not, but he didn't want to look like he cared, so he let it drop.

The days passed with the typical medical calls. A few burns, splints, bandages—basic medical help. One call had turned into the real deal, so they'd called out the paramedics to handle it.

Thursday, they caught a working residential fire. Finally. Firefighters respected life and death and did their best to help the injured and put out fires. But they couldn't resist that thrill when a big call came in and they could do what they'd trained for. Excitement surged through the team, and they rushed to help, Brad's crew on the aid vehicles and Hernandez's people on the engine.

Joined by Station 28 and a nearby Med unit, they had a total of two engines, two aid vehicles, and two medic units on a two-alarm fire. Their engine was first due. Since Engine 28 had been closer, they established a preconnect and laid a hose line for internal attack. Then Engine 44 arrived, and his lieutenant took command, Hernandez's crew onsite.

Bystander reports claimed three people still inside on the left side of the structure but no idea about the right. A mother and her oldest daughter insisted two cats and her younger children were inside, but she wasn't sure about her aunt. Neighbors got on the phone trying to reach the couple next door.

While the lieutenant managed assignments, Mack and Reggie helped two little girls dealing with smoke inhalation and a few cuts and bruises. Brad and Tex let the others work basic life support and rushed into their firefighting gear—their turnouts. All suited up, they waited to enter the home after Hernandez's team, rotating the two-in, two-out rule.

Brad met Tex's gaze through their masks. "Good to go." Meaning his breathing apparatus, with a radio attached, was working and he was ready. Tex returned a thumbs-up.

The heat was intense, the fire running up the walls and eating at the supports.

They didn't have a lot of time on this one.

Hernandez's crew had rushed by with a small girl, two cats, and a little boy. They hurried out of the building just as their LT reported one more person inside, an older woman, the family's visiting aunt.

"Gotcha. We're on it." Brad nodded at his partner.

Tex and Brad worked well together, and as Brad searched deeper into the first level, Tex kept his eye out for falling debris and structural damage, an ax at the ready.

"We need to hurry," Tex told him on the radio.

"I know."

The LT's voice came through again on the Ops channel. "The little girl says her aunt was in the main floor back bedroom."

Brad stepped over melting plastic toys and saw a woman lying in the hallway outside a room. "Got her."

He hurried and checked her for obvious injury, saw her cough into her hand once before hiding her head back under a wet towel. Smart. He tapped her on the shoulder. "Ma'am? We're here to get you out."

She nodded but didn't get up.

He lifted her carefully, her weight negligible, thank God, and followed Tex down the hall, only to have the rafters crash down.

"Back door," Tex insisted, pointing in the other direction.

"Lead the way."

Tex passed him, using his ax to break through the back door that refused to open. He made short work of it and kicked the rest away so Brad could hurry through with the woman.

Something inside exploded. *Shit.* They had a rippin' fire, for sure.

"Got her out back, LT," he informed his boss over the channel. "Bringing her around."

"She needs medical right away," Tex added to the lieutenant.

They hustled around the building, bypassing curious onlookers while the police did their best to keep people back. Fortunately, as they rushed the older woman toward Reggie, they saw a medic unit standing by as well and headed for the paramedics instead. Medic 28 was definitely a welcome sight.

Brad put her down on the stretcher the paramedic had prepared. "Saw a head wound. She took in a lot of smoke but was down low, her head covered by a wet rag."

"Smart," Station 28's medic said. "Good job. We got this." Her partner neared, and together they treated the older woman.

Brad left with Tex to help fight the fire. They helped on a hose to douse the delta side of the house, which burned hottest.

Two engines were needed to contain the blaze, so as to keep it from spreading to the duplexes on the adjoined block. The two stations worked like a well-oiled machine, providing coverage while the LT shouted orders. Hours later, they'd put out the fire that had to be chemical in nature, considering how fast it had spread.

An arson investigator had come onto the scene, and several reporters covered the blaze as well.

Exhausted and smelling like smoke, Brad finally left with Tex to return to the station. After cleaning all their equipment and finally himself, Brad fell into bed. Only to wake up four hours later on another call that luckily turned out to be an easy fix. A slight burn from a small backyard blaze taken care of before they'd even arrived.

After citing the unhappy homeowner, he and Tex returned to the station to find Mack and Reggie cleaning inside the common areas of the station.

"Man, this shift has been *biz-zee*." Mack grinned. "That fire was incredible."

"We did good," Tex said. "Everyone survived."

"Amen," Reggie added. "I like when that happens."

"Me too." Brad smiled. "But you know Wash is going to be impossible to live with."

They groaned. One of their fellow C shift firefighters, Wash was part of the Hernandez crew. Cocky, funny, and only slightly annoying, the other crew did their best to one-up Brad and the guys.

"Oh, and speaking of impossible, I got a brand-new stash of Dora stickers," Mack said. "You guys have to help me cover Sue's new notebook."

"No way." Tex frowned. "That woman's got spies all over the place. I think she turned a few of the crew in B shift. Don't trust 'em."

Mack shook his head. "No guts, no glory."

"At least my guts won't be splattered all over the wall when Lew finds out it's been you all along."

"Pussy."

"Oh, nice talk." Reggie scowled. "You kiss your mother with that mouth?"

"No, but I did kiss Tex's mother with it. Just last night, in fact." Mack smirked.

"Fuck off." Tex grinned. "My momma's a Southern lady. She doesn't have 'relations.' Claims the stork brought me."

"That's a lot of storks at your house." Brad shook his head. "Don't you have three brothers?"

Mack muttered, "The stork? More like the dodo."

"They're extinct, dumbass," Reggie told him. "So Brad, you going to give Avery the tour tomorrow after the show? Tex said you might."

Brad glared at Tex, who tried to look innocent and failed. "I don't know."

"You should." Mack nodded. "I think she likes you."

"No way." Brad huffed. "We're being forced to work this pet thing for *Searching the Needle Weekly*. That's all."

"I think you like her," Tex added with a grin. "You should have seen them at the bar, Reggie. All agreein' on shit and doing their best not to look at each other."

"Which is just a shame," Mack said. "Because Avery Dearborn is gorgeous."

"And klutzy in a cute way." Tex smiled. "I think she's adorable."

"Then you date her," Brad snarled, not sure why he felt so angry.

Reggie was staring at him. "Brad, you need to go out on a date. Not saying with Avery, but with someone. You've been alone for too long."

"Eight sad, pathetic months." Tex sighed.

"Oh blow me." Brad flipped them off as they worked, cleaning up the station house before they took another call. They had another two hours before they signed off. "I've been out since then." Losing his ex-girlfriend to a pediatrician who'd offered her a ring hadn't hurt the way he'd thought it might.

"You haven't been out with someone serious," Mack shot back.

"First of all, Mack, you haven't dated in a long time. Like, since high school, right?"

"Ass."

"Tex, your flavor-of-the-day dates are just pathetic."

"Keep it classy, dickhead. Flavor-of-the-day?" Tex snorted. "I respect women. I prefer flavor-of-the-week. You can't get to know nobody in a day. Oh, and note, wonder boy, I'm not lonely."

Brad ignored him. "And Reggie," Brad added, pleased to see his buddy not so cheerful anymore, "You're so closed off it's a wonder you even talk to us."

"Maybe I'll stop doing that," Reggie warned.

"Promises, promises."

"But I can't be silent until I get this off my chest," Reggie proclaimed.

Brad groaned and moved into the kitchen with a rag and bottle of cleanser.

"You're too tense, man. You need to relax."

"No shit," Tex agreed.

"Who asked you?" Brad growled.

"Nobody. But then no one ever asks me for my opinion. That hurts, guys, deeply."

Reggie chuckled.

"You have to have a heart to get it broken," Mack said, all sage-like as he dusted the living room.

"Wow, deep thoughts for a lightweight," Tex drawled. "Like Brad said, find yourself a girl. Then we'll talk."

Mack grinned. "Say what you want, but I am in love. Her name is Vella."

"Isn't that your dad's car?" Brad asked, impressed with Mack Senior's classic Chevelle.

"Nah. It's mine now. He gave her to me for being his favorite son."

Reggie laughed. "You mean the black sheep. Lone firefighter in a house full of cops. You're brave, I'll give you that."

"Or crazy," Brad added.

But Mack was lost in his own world. "Oh yeah. She's fast, sleek, and sexy. Tuxedo black with white super sport stripes and a mirror finish." He sighed. "Axel fixed the car up, and it's cherry. Seriously amazing."

"Sounds like Mack's in a relationship, all right." Reggie frowned. "A pathetic one, but he's got it all the same."

"I love her," Mac crooned and closed his eyes.

Tex frowned. "Isn't there some show about strange love or somethin'? I remember some guy getting it on with his car. Maybe you can tell them about you and Vella."

Mack stuck up a finger with several suggestions to Tex about what to do with it.

"But Brad, that leaves you," Reggie said.

"And you, to be technical about it," Brad retorted. "When's the last time *you* dated?"

The guys grew quiet, but Brad didn't care. They'd tiptoed around Reggie long enough.

"I think you know."

"I think we know Amy screwed you over."

"Yep, so I'm taking a break." Reggie showed a lot of teeth in that smile. "But you, you're obviously into Lois Lane."

Tex smirked. "I dunno, Reggie. Calling her that is gonna make Brad think he's Superman. I mean, I'd peg him a lame Robin to my Batman, but no way he's wearing a big S."

"*S* for *stupid*." Mack snickered.

Brad found himself grinning though Reggie was on his nerves, holier-than-thou about relationships when he had yet to come out of his shell after being dumped by his girlfriend. "Whatever. I'm amazing, and we all know that."

The lieutenant happened to pass by, overheard Brad, and laughed his way into the back.

Reggie chuckled. "Okay, Superman. So why is dating the reporter so bad?"

Tex cleared his throat.

Mack coughed.

"Oh, I know all about her being nosy way back when. But she never said anything bad about you. Not her fault you hate being the center of attention."

"Why are you a firefighter again?" Mack asked.

"But that was a lifetime ago," Reggie cut in before Brad could tear Mack a new one. "This is now."

Brad glared, but Reggie didn't budge. Not that Brad could completely blame him. No one knew why he'd been so upset about being interviewed five years ago. It had been about so much more than recovering from a bad op in Iraq. It had been about losing Dana, about the real mess that had been his life, a secret he held dear, keeping Dana close now as he hadn't back then. When he should have.

They could relate to a tough tour of duty, all of them having served, all of them having some skeletons rattling around in their closets. The reason they all got along so well—they knew about sacrifice and service. Brothers at heart.

Brad sighed, needing to be honest. If not with himself, at least with the guys who would never judge him. "Okay, Avery's hot. I like her, kind of. I mean, not really. She's annoying, but I can't stop thinking about her. And I don't date women I don't like."

In a low voice, Tex added, "You don't seem to be dating women, period."

Brad glared at him.

Tex leaned against the counter. "Sorry, but man, she's into you. I can tell. And you're into her. Why not see where it goes? Because I'm happy to offer her a shoulder to cry on when you strike out."

"Strike out? My money's on Brad." Mack grinned, joining them. "You in, Reggie?"

"No. I don't bet on my loser friends' love lives."

"Hey." Brad frowned.

"No offense."

"Offense taken, dickless."

Brad darted to Reggie and avoided a headlock but not the hold nearly taking him off-balance. He mock-wrestled with Reggie, not having an easy time of trying to take the mammoth down, but they did grapple a bit, much to the amusement of Hernandez's crew and the LT, who stood by the long, open counter, watching.

They broke up when another call came through, but this time Wash and Hernandez took it.

"Thanks, guys," Brad said.

"Anything's bettah than watching you two dance around each other," Wash said, the tall Irish guy sounding as if he'd been dipped in Boston and rolled around in Maine.

Hernandez held up his middle finger.

Reggie returned it and muttered, "You're such a dick."

To Brad, Hernandez winked. "Good luck with the hottie tomorrow. We'll be tuning in to see how many times you can feel her up or trip her before it's over."

Wash laughed. "Yeah, Hollywood. Go get her."

"Asshole." He watched them go and turned to Reggie. "You're wrong about me but so right about Hernandez. He is a dick."

"Amen." Reggie nodded.

They finished cleaning up the station house and settled down to wait until changeover. Brad hurried to clean himself up, needing to clock out early to go do his spot with Avery. Once back in the common area, Brad said to the guys, "I've got Pets Fur Life to do but plan on working out today. Anyone for a run later?" A nice beginning to their next four days off, even if he did have to see Avery first.

Tex and Reggie nodded.

"Sorry, I have to take Vella out for some action." Mack wiggled his brows.

Reggie shook his head. "It's a car, Mack. And your relationship with *it*—not *her*—isn't healthy."

Mack sighed. "Look at that thing you drive. It's no wonder you have no passion for a nice set of wheels."

Tex cringed. "You make me sad, Mack. A nice set of breasts, sure. Some kind of ass, you bet. Wheels?"

"That counts."

"If you're fourteen and waiting for your balls to drop, sure."

Mack and Tex started arguing.

Brad needed to unwind...and interrogate his brother about last weekend. "I'll talk to you later about the run."

Reggie winked. "Good luck with Avery. Ask her out, man. Don't be weak."

"Why? You going to take away my man card if I don't ask her out?"

"I should. You're just...sad."

"Stop pitying me. Pity them instead," He looked at Tex and Mack still arguing over breasts and cars.

"Good point. Later, Hollywood. And remember, we'll all be watching."

Brad groaned. "Thanks for that."

Reggie watched him leave, still laughing.

Brad drove to the *Searching the Needle Weekly* office, wondering if Reggie had a point. Thoughts of Avery continued to plague him. He wanted to think of her as that nosy reporter, but each time he encountered her, he found something new to like. The way she fiddled with her glasses. Her love of bad horror movies. How cute she was falling asleep. That his friends could see right through him told him to wake up. He had chemistry with the woman. That he definitely knew.

What would it hurt to maybe see if they had anything else? What if they became friends? Maybe even lovers? He could admit to wanting to be with her with an almost obsessive desire.

The plan had merit.

Except she got under his skin and on his last nerve half the time. He argued with her the way he argued with no one else. And he liked it. Brad didn't consider himself a contrary guy, so why did he continue to fight with Avery?

Tired and needing a break, he decided to save his questions for when he was more awake. Maybe after he and Avery nailed the morning segment. Brad would not look at her, touch her, or interact with her in any way that could be construed as rude or harassing.

That was the plan, anyway.

———————

They had managed to handle the morning spot professionally so far, though he hadn't been able to stop from laughing when the cat demanded Brad let go of him to twine around Avery's feet, which sent her into a sneezing fit.

"You aren't funny, Battle," she muttered and ordered him to collect the feline. "Mittens is very sociable," she said to the camera. "More than some firefighters I might mention."

Brad grinned as he picked Mittens back up. "It's been said some cats can sense evil. I think Mittens is attracted to it."

"Ha ha." Avery shifted away from the large dog behind her, a mix of Bernese mountain dog and Doberman. "Ahem. Folks, also note Hugo here. He and Mittens came from the same home and are friends. We're trying to adopt them together. Both friendly, great with kids and other pets, and totally housebroken."

Mittens purred and kneaded Brad's arm, digging his claws in. Brad smiled. "Mittens has his claws and can be both an in- and outdoor cat."

"Aw, Brad. He likes you. You're right. I guess cats *can* sense evil."

And the segment went downhill from there.

All Brad's intentions to play nice took a backseat to jibes and comments returned in a volley that didn't stop. The phone kept ringing, and without Rupert in attendance, Avery would stop to pick it up, only to continually try to pair him up with callers.

Another episode of matching pets and people ended to thunderous applause. It seemed even more people had stopped by to watch them, this time with Brad's captain laughing out loud with Avery's boss.

"Great job, Battle. Keep it up," his captain said after clapping him on the back. "Oh, and my wife wants a look at the cat and dog when you get a chance."

Brad forced a smile. "I'll have the Pets Fur Life people contact you, sir."

Avery looked no happier, wearing a fake smile as she talked to her boss. She finished and walked over to him. "We need to talk."

"Yep. But not there."

He left the building and stopped at his car.

"And not here," Avery said when he would have spoken. "We need to go somewhere private for this discussion."

He sighed. "I need to change out of my uniform. We can do breakfast if you like. Follow me." He took her to his home turf, intending to put this behind them and apologize. Why had he been such a dick today? What was it about Avery Dearborn that threw his sense of chivalry and common sense into the gutter?

Back at his apartment, as a show of good faith that he trusted her enough to enter his home—even if he didn't quite feel the sentiment deep down—Brad waited for her to enter before closing the door behind her.

"Can we talk here instead?" she asked. "Where no one can overhear us?"

"Probably makes more sense. Something to drink?"

She sighed. "I could go for some coffee."

"I can do that." He fixed them a pot then leaned back against the kitchen counter. He took pride in his home, an updated end unit he paid extra for that afforded two bedrooms, a large living space, and an upgraded kitchen on the second floor. He had one neighbor next to him and one below him, both friendly and quiet.

"I'm sorry," he said at the same time Avery did.

She blushed and rubbed her temple, no doubt reaching for glasses that weren't there. "I don't know what it is about you, but I can't stop from being sarcastic. I wanted today to be friendly and polite. And somehow I think I called you a horse's ass."

"Yes, you did." Brad shook his head. "I apologize for that crack about your two left feet."

She frowned. "Yeah. Thanks."

She took the cup he offered her, and their fingers brushed.

A bolt of heat shot its way through his hand and spiraled out to the rest of his body.

He should have been too tired to feel it and tried to ignore it.

"I appreciate you letting me come here. I realize this is your home, and I know how much it cost you to share it with me. You could have just met me at a diner or something."

"But you wanted privacy."

She nodded. "You and I have some issues to work through. I might as well get this out of the way."

He raised a brow, waiting.

"I'm sorry, okay? I know I said it before, but I really mean it. Because you and I can't seem to let the past stay in the past. Five years ago, I was pushy and invasive when you'd asked me to leave you alone. I sincerely regret it."

"Thanks for saying that."

"I'm not just saying it." She ran a hand through her hair, and he tried to ignore how that casual move looked sexy. "Look, you were a big story, and I was new with the paper. I'm not making excuses for hounding you. That was all me. I will say I was young and trying to push past the 'new girl reporter' stigma at the paper. I wanted to prove something." She paused and frowned. "I have issues, okay? There. I said it. Now you know something shaming about me."

"Shaming?"

"Because I know how bad it was for you coming back here." She swallowed hard, and he realized that though he'd been through a tough go, so had she. "I saw you break down with your mom. You didn't know that, but I did. And I felt horrible about it. But my dad and the paper kept pressuring me to get the true story. Once the Pentagon cleared the operation and made it public, I was ordered to make you tell me, in your own words, what happened during the conflict overseas and how it affected you afterward. I had to get to the truth no matter what. I couldn't let it go."

She took a sip of coffee, collecting herself, and added, "It made me uncomfortable and just miserable, to be honest. But I was the girl with game back then because no one could get near you to talk to you. And you were a hometown hero."

"I remember." His voice came out grittier than he liked, but not for the reason she believed. He clearly recalled the pain of that time, his crying fits not because of his work in the Marines but because he'd been dealing with Dana's death. The skirmishes in countries he'd done his best to forget had been terrible, but nothing nearly so personal as Dana passing.

"I'm sorry, Brad," Avery said softly, her gaze compassionate. "I had no business prying into your life, and I have no intention of doing that again. Ever. The joking between us on air, that's just fluff, you know?"

She stepped around the counter to face him. "I mean it. I was just messing with you about your dating life because you made me feel awkward."

"I did?" Could she not see how she affected him? How her sincerity and kindness right now were killing his ability to remain distant, nice but aloof? His entire body seemed to buzz when near her, as if magnetically charged to connect.

"Well, you're good-looking and charming and everyone seems to love you. I'm a klutz allergic to cats who fell over fake dog poop at an event I was covering." She huffed. "I'm no one's hero, and most of the city has never heard of me and never will…unless I'm humped by a large dog again."

He was trying not to smile.

She saw it and ended up grinning with him. "So yeah, I felt awkward and embarrassed because there I am trying to do my job and this handsome town hero arrives to see it all—the same guy I emotionally tortured years ago. The same guy who made me question what the heck I was doing with my life." She rubbed her temple. "Not sure why I'm telling you all this, but I wanted you to know I really am sorry. I know you hate the online stuff, and I wish you hadn't gotten roped into it." She held out a hand. "Friends?"

He stared at it, feeling full of…something. Attraction, hope, confusion. And over and above all, lust. He took her hand, and she must have felt some of the same desire because her cheeks turned a deeper pink.

"Avery, that was really sweet." And surprisingly healing. "I'm sorry I seem to act like an ass whenever we're together."

"It's okay. I deserved it." She tried to tug her hand back, but he wouldn't let her.

"No, it's not okay." He pulled her closer. Her eyes widened as their distance decreased. "For the record, I don't dislike you. You've been steadily growing on me from the festival."

"Really?" She sounded breathless, her sky-blue eyes growing darker.

"Really, and that's become a real problem for me."

"It has?"

He pulled her in tight, almost hugging her as he stared down into her upturned face. "Yes, because I don't kiss women I don't like. And I sure the hell don't want to sleep with them."

She gaped. "Sleep with them?"

"Or am I the only one feeling this attraction?" He cupped her cheek, stroking her petal-soft lips with his thumb.

She groaned. "No, it goes both ways. And not liking you and wanting you is really annoying."

"I know what you mean."

She licked her lips, and he couldn't help staring at her mouth. "So, ah, you want a kiss?"

"I want a lot more than that," he admitted, "but we can start with a kiss."

Before he could say any more, she dragged his head down and kissed him, sparking a fire that was bound to singe both of them at some point.

When he could come up for air, he stared down at her in shock, ready and willing to take her here and now. "*Fuck.*"

"Well, if you insist." And she yanked him back for more.

Chapter Ten

AVERY HAD NEVER BEEN SO IN LUST WITH A MAN BEFORE. Needing him more than anything, she clawed at his clothes as they kissed. Brad backed her against the counter. Pinned between it and Brad, she could feel *all* of him when he leaned against her. Jesus, she had no idea how she'd waited this long, but she had to have him. *Now.*

"Bedroom?" she managed as he ran kisses down her cheek to her throat. When he sucked, she moaned.

He pulled back and tugged her by the hand to follow him, moving so fast she nearly had to run to keep up. "This way." His voice was so deep. He wanted her, and that need only increased her own.

Inside his bedroom, he kissed her again. Her clothing fell away under his nimble fingers. She was naked and shivering when he pulled back.

His eyes widened. "Christ. I'm not going to last."

Not wanting distance between them, she kissed him as he unbuttoned his shirt and toed off his shoes and socks. But before she could reach for his pants, he stopped her.

"Hold on," he panted. "Let's keep these on so we're not done in two seconds."

She smirked. "Two seconds, huh? You're not impressing me yet, Battle." *I am such a liar. His body should belong in a museum, all sculpted muscle and strength.*

His grin was carnal. "Then I guess I have my work cut out for me, don't I, Dearborn?" He lowered her to the bed and followed her down, a fiery human blanket that incinerated on contact.

The feel of his chest brushing her sensitive breasts had her reaching for him with an embarrassing craving. Her body felt not her own, a trembling mass of desire on the verge of climaxing from some heavy petting and kissing.

He kept grinding against her, and the press of his large cock was destroying her ability to hold back her rise toward orgasm.

"I can't wait any longer," he confessed, his eyes bright as he stared down at her. "You're a beautiful pain in the ass, you know that?"

The bite of humor had her desperation easing a little, and she wanted to thank him for pulling back, letting her enjoy the moment before rushing headfirst into ecstasy.

He left her to remove the rest of his clothes and grabbed a condom from his nightstand. The sight of him in the nude stole her breath away.

He glanced up after sheathing himself and grinned at her. "Yeah, that's how I feel when I look at you."

She shook her head, amazed at the musculature of his thighs. And to be honest, by the size of his equipment. Handsome and hung, and he worried about slowing down for her. Man, she had to have this man.

"No words," he said for her, his gaze running down her body, centering on her breasts. "I'm really sorry for how fast this is going."

"Quit talking and get in me," she blurted. "We can slow down next time."

He nodded and joined her on the bed, crawling up between her legs. "Just one thing."

She groaned. "No talking."

"I'm about to go down on you."

She stopped groaning.

He gave a harsh laugh. "That shut you up. Look, Avery. Are we good to have sex? Both of us clean? I know I am."

She blushed, though being embarrassed about talking about sex while doing it seemed silly. "Yes. I haven't been with anyone in months, and we always used protection."

"Same." He didn't ask any more questions; instead, he kissed her inner thigh.

She arched up. "I thought this was going to be fast."

"I changed my mind."

She stared at him as he looked at her while kissing and caressing her, inching his way higher.

Then be bent his head, attuned to the task at hand, and put his mouth over her.

She cried out, the feeling incredible, as Brad made love to her body. He definitely knew what he was doing, driving her to orgasm as he massaged with his lips and tongue. Avery had never responded so readily to a man, especially through oral sex, and she lost herself in climax while he continued to stroke her to new heights.

When he finally moved back to give her a moment to breathe, she saw his satisfaction, the smile in his eyes. "I love the way you taste," he said as he licked his lips and covered her with his body. "I am so hard right now."

"Y-you're really good at that." What was she saying? She had no idea, drawing him down to her again while he spread her thighs wider and positioned himself between her legs.

Brad slowly entered her, kissing her while he did so. They shared a groan between breaths as he seated the whole of himself and paused.

He pulled his head back and watched her while he withdrew before thrusting once more.

"You're so big," she gasped, her body revved and ready to go again.

Brad was right there with her. "You're so hot. So wet," he moaned and moved faster, fucking her with a frantic need she felt as well.

But her rise to another climax was cut short when he groaned and stilled. He looked to be in agony, yet so incredibly erotic. He continued to pump, moaning her name, and finally ceased on shaky arms over her.

Before she could speak, not even sure what to say after her own earth-shattering orgasm, he lowered himself and rolled them over. Still joined, now she lay on top. She sat up to keep him inside her.

"Now that is a sight I've been missing." Brad sounded sleepy, his tension completely gone. And for the first time Avery saw the man behind all the bluster and responsibility. He looked boyish, soft yet not, and that sweet dichotomy had her feeling something more than desire.

"Yeah? You like me on top of you, hmm?" She'd like it more if he were hard again, but she couldn't complain about this new intimacy.

"I sure the hell do." Brad smiled up at her, focused on her breasts, and cupped them. "You feel good."

She warmed, the points of her nipples sensitive and aroused. "So do you," she said on a breath.

"Gimme a few minutes and then you need to ride me." He scooted her off him and removed the condom. A good thing he'd worn one because the man had a lot to give.

He saw her surprised reaction and grinned. "What can I say? I like you."

"Nice, Brad."

He grabbed a tissue and wrapped the spent condom in it before dropping it to the floor. "Do me a favor and grab another one from my drawer."

Did he have a special box for one-night stands? She wanted to care, to be thought of as someone more important than a mere sexual partner, but nothing much but the now existed for her while she was relaxing in a rush of endorphins.

"What did we just do?" she asked out loud.

"Put to rest some hostility, I'm thinking. That kiss we shared last week, that was angry sex. I could have done you there, against the wall, without missing a beat. You had me so hard and mad."

"I thought that was just me," she admitted and sat over him, staring down at him.

He sucked in a breath and let it out slowly. "You are so hot. You feel damn good on me, skin to skin."

With just a little movement, he could slide up into her.

"I know." She wiggled, feeling his cock growing thicker as he watched her.

"Oh, we're going again. I just need some time." He stroked her hips, then had her lean closer. "Put your breast in my mouth."

"The whole thing?"

He laughed. "Let's start with a nipple. Because yours are so pretty and tight and pink." He palmed her breast and glanced at her face. "Are you blushing?"

"No."

"You are." He blinked. "Seriously? You're sitting naked and wet on my cock."

"Would you stop already?"

"You really are adorable."

Adorable?

Before she could ask just what adorable meant on a scale of sexy to cute, he dragged her down for another kiss and teased her nipple. The friction over the tight bud had her squirming on top of him in no time, their slow build toward arousal stoked with little effort.

Avery was kissing him and rubbing all over him, surprised to find him hard again so suddenly.

But he wouldn't be rushed, and she was losing patience.

"Slow down," he ordered after they'd been kissing for an eternity.

"Speed up," she countered and wiggled her way down his body. She didn't give him a chance to comment before taking his erection between her lips.

"Avery, *fuck*." He palmed her head and started pumping into her mouth, his arousal back to where she needed it. "Gonna have to put it on me. Soon," he promised.

She learned what he liked, sucking him deeper, playing with the soft skin covering his firm balls. She loved his contrasts—the coarse hair over his legs, the smooth skin of his cock, the steel-hard muscle of his body yet the tender way he touched her. The man was driving her crazy.

She sucked harder.

He bucked and pushed her off him. "The condom. On me." His eyes looked wild.

She tore open the packet he handed her. "Watch." She rolled it over him, slowly, and loved how he squirmed.

Then it was his turn. With a strength she envied, he lifted her up and let her slide down him. She took him deep inside her and felt every move he made.

"Fuck, that's good." He groaned and palmed her breasts, kneading them while he pushed up.

She took the hint and put her hands on his shoulders, riding him up and down, letting him hit that spot inside her that made her see stars.

"Yeah, that's it. Harder, Avery." He watched her, so intent, and she felt vulnerable in a way that scared her.

Intense feels accompanied the physical pleasure, until she lost herself to it, doing whatever he said because she couldn't help teasing them both.

"Come, baby. All over me," he rasped, letting go of her breasts to put a hand between them, the other guiding her by the hip to move faster. He rubbed her clit, and she saw fireworks, coming with a cry.

"Oh yeah. That's it. *Yes*." He followed shortly after, holding her over him while he released.

The sound of their harsh breathing filled the room, a sexual catharsis relaxing every muscle in Avery's body. She slumped over him, and he stroked her back, whispering sweet words in her ear.

When she could function once more, she let him roll her to her side and closed her eyes, not ready to look at him. Not after feeling all that. She had no idea what to call it. Intense, sexual, yes. But the accompanying affection shouldn't fit with the carnal excesses between them.

"That was…" He sighed. "Let me think on it."

She gave a weak laugh. "Tell me when you can come up with words to describe it."

"Uh-huh."

They lay there, next to each other, just breathing. Until Avery started to feel the wordless silence.

She chanced a peek at him, saw him staring at her, and quickly looked up at the ceiling.

She heard his grin when he said, "Shy now?"

"Nope. Just wondering how the hell I got here."

"I spiked your coffee with 'Brad is great' pills."

She laughed. "No, it was the hand."

"The hand?"

"When you shook my hand. All that heat in your fireman body rushed up into me. Went straight between my legs."

He groaned. "Don't say that. You'll get me hard again."

"Not used to so much sex? I don't believe it."

"Not within the span of an hour. I like to stretch out my time. Not in a rush, not usually." He let out a breath. "Then again, I have another couple of hours before I need to get ready to meet the guys for a workout."

"Oh, I should go then." She couldn't get her body to work. She turned her head to see him still staring at her, propped on an elbow.

Brad's arm over her stomach stopped her from thinking too hard about leaving. "Now, now. No need to run out of here. I'm pretty sure we worked up an appetite, and I did promise you breakfast."

She narrowed her eyes, not sure if he was joking or not. "Is this where you try to get me to eat 'your sausage'?"

He blinked and started laughing, so hard he cried. "Oh, God. Please. Eat my sausage. That's classic."

She had never seen him so happy before and could only stare.

"I have bacon, actually. And that's not a reference for anything on my body, just to be clear."

"Well, I had to ask."

He kept laughing. "Of course you did." Then he surprised her by rolling over on top of her.

"Brad?"

"Avery?" he said, smiling. "You're actually pretty funny when you mean to be."

"As opposed to when I'm tripping over my own feet?"

"Well, yeah." He kissed her on the nose. Pulled back. Then kissed her lips.

The tender kiss deepened, until Brad was once again pressed up against her body, stealing her breath.

"Sorry." He didn't sound sorry, though he remained half-hard, not raring to go yet again.

She wanted to be thankful about that but wasn't. *I'm a nympho now? Relax, hormones!*

"So, you're really going to make me breakfast? I can go. It's okay." This was getting weird. No, she was getting weird.

Brad smirked. "Afraid you'll get too attached if you stay?"

And like that, their earlier sense of challenge reasserted itself, giving her an out from the strange emotions cascading through her. "I'm afraid you'll accuse me of taking advantage of you. Your fear is sexy though."

He sat up. "I'm sorry. My fear?"

"Of falling for me, so you're trying to rush me out of here."

"Um, Avery, I've been offering to feed you."

She arched up against his rising erection and raised a brow.

"Not my sausage, damn it."

She snickered.

Then he did too. "God, you make me want to spank you as much as kiss you."

"Back at ya, Bradford."

He kissed her, hard, and made her instantly horny again. Except he didn't follow through. The blasted man yanked her off the bed and over his shoulder.

"Brad!" So undignified.

He patted her ass, and it felt pretty damn good. "You're going to be nice to me if I have to force you to. We're eating breakfast, then I'm eating you out. We'll fuck. You'll leave. I'll go work out, and we'll never talk about this again. Ever."

An easy enough fix, and probably the best call they could make. Because dating Brad Battle would be a nightmare, especially with as much attention as they'd been getting. "Right. We had sex, scratched an itch, and we're done."

"Done and friends," he said as he gently stood her upright.

She nodded and held out a hand. He took it…and led it to his dick. She had to squeeze, instilling a groan or two.

He laughed when she refused to let go. "So, after all this, we're going to try to be friends. Right?"

"I think so, yes." She let go of him and did her best not to feel weird about being naked in front of him.

He stared at her. "You need clothes, don't you?"

"I do." She sighed. "But feel free to remain naked while you cook."

He left and returned in shorts with a large shirt for her to wear. One of his.

She put it on and rumpled her hair. "I look sexy, right?" More like messy.

He nodded, solemn. "You have the best 'just fucked' hair I've ever seen."

She groaned. "Good thing I have nothing but an interview at two. I'm going home to shower."

"Not yet." Brad fixed her breakfast, or tried to, but halfway through his attempt at fried eggs, she took over.

"You're not very good in the kitchen, are you?"

"No, but I want to be good. That should count, right?"

"Ah, not really." She made the bacon, eggs, and toast and let him pour the coffee.

When they'd finished eating, he stared at her with a strange look on his face.

"What?"

"Did this really happen?"

"The sex—yes. I was there."

"No, that food." He shook his head in wonderment. "You can cook your ass off. I mean, that was amazing."

She flushed. "It's just breakfast."

"You totally deserve a reward for that." He stared at her breasts as if she wasn't wearing his shirt.

"Um, isn't sex a reward for you?"

He stood and pushed down his shorts, revealing a long, thick erection, and just looked at her.

"Okay, it's a prize. I admit it."

He smiled. "Now let's take a walk back to the bedroom and investigate how flexible you are."

"With limits?" Did he want to get kinky with her? Like, bondage?

"With your body. You look pretty bendable to me, and I really want to try a new position."

"Oh." Her cheeks grew hot. "Um, well, okay, I guess."

"You guess?" He removed his shorts and started pumping his shaft.

"Well, fine. If you insist."

And insist he did, into two more orgasms for her. But they were just for today and nothing more than physical release.

She was halfway through her doorway at home when her phone rang.

"Yes?"

"It's me."

Huh. Brad must have found her number because she didn't recall giving it to him.

"I'm sorry. Who is this?" She had been trying the entire drive home not to feel bad that he only wanted sex between them. And not even continual sex, just that one morning. It made sense to keep things simple. And now that they'd fucked—*yes, just fucked, Ms. Sentimental*—they knew the answer to what it would have been like.

Spectacular.

"Very funny. It's Brad, smartass. The guy you were just playing bend over the dresser with."

"Oh. That Brad." She got a chuckle out of him and felt super proud for sounding casual about what had been a mind-melting sexual awakening.

"I, ah, I want to do this again. With you. This morning, I mean. Hang out, get together, you know."

I have no idea. "Okay, I guess."

He snorted. "You guess?"

"Well, yes. Fine."

"Took you long enough. I must not have been doing it right." His sarcasm she could handle. For some reason, it soothed her. This Brad she knew.

"Well, maybe if we tried it my way next time, you might last longer."

The pause had her thinking she might have pushed him a little too far. Although he couldn't have missed how she'd screamed his name as she'd come the last two times, pleading with him to finish her.

Then he laughed. "Longer? Okay, Lois. Next time we'll try it your way. I'm off 'til Tuesday. Text me when you want to get together again." He chortled. "Longer. Ha." He disconnected.

She took her phone away from her ear and frowned. *Lois? Who's Lois?* So she texted him. *Who the hell is Lois?*

And got a Superman GIF followed by *Lois Lane, doofus. Next time, wear glasses. You're hot in them.*

She just stared at her cell phone, shocked at the pleasure she derived from Brad wanting more of a relationship—whatever that might entail.

Avery smiled, so much her cheeks hurt. But she couldn't stop. Not even when Gerty arrived home later that night and demanded the full truth and nothing but the truth.

"Gerty, really?" Avery asked as her dorky roommate insisted she swear on top of Gerty's bible—a script she'd purchased at auction years ago, signed by Captain Mal from the science fiction television series *Firefly*.

Gerty glared. "Say it, Avery."

Avery rolled her eyes. "Do I have to?"

"Say. It."

"I promise to tell you the truth and nothing but the truth." *My edited version, at least.* She paused for effect. "So help me *Warcraft.*"

"Amen."

Chapter Eleven

BRAD DIDN'T KNOW HOW HE GOT THROUGH EXERCISING AT THE station with the guys that afternoon. Reggie and Tex had given him a few side-glances but didn't say anything. Mack, who had ditched Vella in favor of his friends, apparently, seemed oblivious...until the gym started to fill up. Then he approached Brad with a wrapped present.

"What's this?" Brad asked, taking it. Waiting for it to explode.

"Something from a bunch of us. To thank you for being you." Mack gave him a wide grin. "I'm just screwing with you. It's an early birthday present."

Brad would be celebrating his thirty-second next week, so the answer had some credibility. Yet the intense interest around him warned him to proceed with caution.

He eyed Mack warily. "Thanks. I think."

"Go on, Brad. Open it." Reggie nodded, smiling.

Knowing he might as well get it over with, Brad ripped through the paper and stared.

"See?" Mack helpfully pointed out. "It's got a neutral palette with some fun nighttime shades for your eyes."

"It's the sunset desire pack," Reggie added.

Everyone around them grinned, stifling laughter.

"Come on, Hollywood. Put it on." One of the D shift dicks said. "You're looking washed out."

"What? No lipstick? The guy needs to pucker for the camera." Freaking Hernandez.

Brad glared at the crowd. "Fuck all of you."

The laughter rang out, causing others in the station to swing by to see what the fuss was about. Tex made sure to explain in his slow drawl, instilling more laughter.

Lieutenant Sue happened by and stopped. "Hey, is that makeup?" Which generated more laughter.

Brad took it in stride, knowing he'd have piled it on had it been someone else getting all the attention.

One of the female firefighters sauntered up to him and asked to borrow his blush. Which had Tex in hysterics.

Brad handed her the kit. "Please, keep it."

"You sure you don't need it?" Nat asked with a smirk.

Brad snarled, "It's not that funny."

"No, it is. It so is." Tex grinned at her, and she walked away, the proud new owner of a sunset desire makeup collection.

"Thanks for your kind thoughts, dickheads," Brad said to the group. "It's not my fault I'm so pretty and manly."

"Yeah? Well, I'm happy to take that gorgeous reporter off your hands," one of the A shift guys said. Like Brad, a lot of the other firefighters spent their spare time in the station gym.

"I'm sure your girlfriend would love that." His buddy sighed. "Keep it in your pants, Joe."

"Oh? Well, let's talk about you and Marsha…and her mom."

"You really want to go there?"

"Oh, it's on," mock-whispered Mack.

"Sure thing." Joe grinned. "My girlfriend loves a real man."

"Then what's she doing with you?" Sue said, and not all that quietly.

Everyone started laughing.

"Lew, let me tell you about my girl…"

A collective groan went up, and Brad silently thanked Joe for taking the attention from him.

After Joe left, Brad took the ragging he was due, insisted he wasn't going soft for not making more of an ass of himself on the Friday morning spot with Avery, and pouted since no one would run with him, claiming they all had better things to do. Like sleep since many of them had just pulled a rough twenty-four hours.

"Even you, Reggie? Come on, man. You have no life."

Reggie said something less than complimentary and left behind Mack and Tex.

Feeling a spark he hadn't felt in a long time, Brad went home and used his excess energy to run five miles, clean his apartment from top to bottom, and do the laundry he'd been putting off. But since he'd started so damn early that morning, the hour had just reached seven in the evening, and he had nothing to do but think.

Thoughts of his upcoming birthday gave him hives, a celebration of life mingled with the death of his best friend. So no, not going there.

Avery Dearborn. A much more pleasant way to pass the time.

The woman was like a drug. She would no doubt be bad for him in the long run—a reporter, one who'd once pried into his life—but she'd addicted him from the first. Sure, he'd been thinking about what sex with her would be like. And he'd imagined some pretty spectacular fireworks. But his imagination hadn't come close to what being with her had actually *been* like.

He'd never have expected her to be so responsive, so damn open in bed. She hadn't masked anything. Just an honest chemistry between them that made every kiss and caress a magnified blast of pleasure.

He wished he could say he'd had better. Because then he could forget her. But she'd burned a place in his brain, and he couldn't stop seeing her in his mind's eye, naked and splayed out in his bed, waiting. Eager.

Damn. He was hard and hungry and wishing he hadn't been so stupid as to suggest they were done. He'd amended it, but too late. Now she'd be wondering why the hell she'd want to be with a guy who was satisfied by a few romps in bed.

Panicked by how much he hadn't wanted her to go, he'd made that stupid pronouncement. *"Done and friends."* How stupid could he be?

He wondered if he should just take care of his needs or hold out and hope to see Avery again. So soon? He sat on the couch and held his head in his hands, wondering where his legendary cool had gone. He groaned, recalling how he'd babbled on the phone with her. *"I, ah, I want to do this again. With you. This morning, I mean. Hang out, get together, you know."* Could he have been any more idiotic? Hang out, get together? Hell, he wasn't a kid and had no problem calling it what it was. Sex. Period.

But with Avery, it hadn't just been sex. And that worried him.

Unsure of what to do, he kept himself busy by adding another, shorter run to his routine, followed by some grocery shopping he didn't really need to do but would cut down on his chores for next week.

He somehow managed to finish the night by turning in by nine and was up early on Saturday with no clear agenda in mind. Until he realized he still hadn't talked to his brother about what Oscar had been doing with Avery last weekend.

After doing some arm curls, push-ups, and sit-ups, he skipped the run, feeling it in his legs after yesterday, and ate a quick breakfast before heading out to his mom's. Typically, he limited his visits to twice a month max, but this new development with Avery needed attention.

Oscar would no doubt still be asleep, though his mother and Rochelle woke by seven, even on Rochelle's days off. He was just leaving his brother's favorite donut shop with a box of sugar-filled goodness when he realized going home today might not be such a smart idea.

The anniversary of Dana's death was in a few days, the day after his birthday. Having lived a few doors down from Brad's mother's house while Dana had been alive, the Crawfords had since moved and sold the house to their nephew. But following their daughter's death, they made an annual pilgrimage back to remember her. They'd skipped last year, finally giving him a break from their yearly displeasure. But he couldn't count on that happening again.

He sat in his car and put the donuts on the seat, staring without seeing through the window. Hadn't he paid enough? Did he really have to consider avoiding his family, the home he'd grown up in, because the Crawfords *might* be there? Grieving, angry, and always wanting to point fingers, Dana's parents had made his life a living hell after her death, as if by placing the blame, they could come to grips with their loss.

Brad knew it didn't work that way. He'd lost friends fighting for an ideal not shared by many. He'd borne the brunt of scorn, hatred, and tears, condemned for all the ills of American values while trying to save innocent—and some not-so-innocent—lives. But that had been the job, and he'd done it well. He'd come home burdened but not scarred, healing in the care of his fellow Marines in Camp Pendleton. They knew, they understood, and they would never turn him away.

He hadn't been in the best place, mentally or emotionally, upon his separation from the military, so he'd been in no shape to deal with Dana, his best friend who constantly wrestled with her own monsters—namely, her parents. But he'd done his best to still be there for her, and they'd reconnected as if he'd never been gone.

But way too briefly.

Six months later, she'd died, and her parents had blamed him.

Truth be told, as much as he tried not to, as much as he'd heard what Rochelle and his brother had told him, he still blamed himself.

A horn beeped outside, taking Brad from his secret pain, and he buried it deep, trying to forget something he'd never wanted in the first place. Dana's face looked fuzzy in his memory, and he wondered if that was because he'd finally come to understand that he knew her so well she'd fractured in his thoughts—as she had in life—over time.

"Fuck this." He started the car, angry with himself for giving into the emotional cesspool he'd been doing his damnedest to ignore. *I guess I'm more like Mom than I wanted to think I am.*

He had only himself to blame. The time of year wasn't the best, and this thing—whatever it was—with Avery churned up emotions better left untouched. His last ex hadn't been wrong when she'd called him closed off and distant, but then, he'd never felt a need to go any deeper than fun and sex with Bella. Pretty, successful, and fun to be around, she'd been like the other girls he'd dated since Dana had died. Nothing too serious.

Just like Avery, he told himself as he drove to his mother's house. *She's just a woman I have to work with and amazing in bed. We have fun. It's not a thing.*

A thing? He had to stop talking to himself because even his subconscious told him he made little sense.

Fortunately, he closed a lid on thoughts of Avery as he pulled into his mother's driveway. He walked around to the back door, expecting to see his mother and Rochelle sharing coffee on the back porch. The porch remained empty, so he let himself inside and found them sitting and talking quietly at the kitchen table.

"I brought donuts," he announced as he joined them.

"Oh, good. I was hoping you'd swing by," his mother said, her eyes crinkled in a smile. She made no mention of Dana, and he let out the tension he'd been holding. A smarter man would avoid home at this time of year, coming back to the place where he and Dana had spent so much of their teen years, stirring more memories. But Brad visited on purpose, so as not to forget. And, as Rochelle had once told him, likely to punish himself for a death he hadn't prevented.

Uncomfortable at the sudden realization Rochelle was likely right, he forced a smile. "You're always happy in the morning, Mom. I wish you'd passed that trait onto me."

"Rochelle calls me cute and chipper but annoying." Vivienne laughed.

Rochelle nodded. "I do. And she is." Rochelle dragged him forward to kiss him on the cheek. "Go get your brother up, would you?"

"Why me?"

"Because we shouldn't have to," Vivienne said, a sparkle in her eye. "We've done our time getting cranky boys to wake up."

"You were the worst," Rochelle agreed and sipped her coffee. "Now let's see what you brought us. Oh, warm glazed. My favorite!"

Going with the flow, he bottled the past in the past—*and how often have I been saying that lately and not doing it?*—and woke up his brother.

"Yo, numbnuts, get up," he yelled.

Oscar lay half on, half off the bed, his head under his pillow. The sheets sat around his waist, exposing his broad back. He muttered something Brad couldn't make out.

Knowing how this worked, Brad left to grab a cup of cold water. "You have ten seconds. Then this water is all over you. Ten. Nine. Eight…"

When he got to three, his brother rolled over and tossed the pillow at him. "I'm up," he grumbled, his hair sticking up, and covered his eyes with his forearm.

"Jesus, I can smell your breath from here. Use a toothbrush once in a while."

"Go away."

"The countdown is still going. Three. Two…"

Oscar jackknifed to a sitting position. "I hate you."

"I brought donuts."

"Oh. Cool."

Brad turned away and drank the water while his brother stumbled out of bed. He didn't smell of alcohol, thank God. "Go shower and I'll save you a cream-filled."

"Two."

"Whatever. Hurry up."

Brad returned to see his mom and Rochelle laughing and planning their weekend as if it were any other weekend. He started to think maybe *he* was the one holding onto this tragedy. His mother

had a right to her grief over his father. But Dana had been his...
until she hadn't been.

He didn't like feeling so overemotional, especially after his
time yesterday with Avery. She'd been so full of life, so genuine.
Being with her made his time with Dana feel like it had happened
to someone else. So strange.

"Brad, help me in the garage for a minute, would you?" Rochelle
asked as she stood. "While you're here, there's a large box I've been
wanting to get down. It has some gardening supplies you were
looking for last week, Viv."

"Oh, right. My gloves."

Rochelle and Brad went into the garage, and Rochelle pointed
out a box she easily could have reached. He didn't question her
though. Rochelle was getting older, and it wouldn't sit well with
the capable woman to admit to growing weaker or more tired.

"Talk, Brad," she said.

He set the box at her feet. "Huh?"

"You always have that look on your face when you're troubled.
And we all know what time of year this is."

He shrugged. "I'm good."

She just stared at him.

He looked around the garage, noting a few things Oscar should
have taken care of, like the sagging shelving by the back corner.

"I'm waiting."

Brad returned his gaze to hers and blew out a breath. "I feel
weird. I don't know."

"Tell me."

"I met this girl. Avery. She's different than I thought. We hit
it off, kind of." *We had hot sex I can't get off my mind. And I like
her a lot more than I thought I would.* "But then I'm back here, and
the thing with Avery feels like it didn't happen. And I keep thinking about Dana even though I don't mean to. It's been five years. I
shouldn't be so weird, right?"

"Honey, give yourself a break. Suicide hits those who survive the hardest. Dana had real problems, problems her parents wanted to lay on you." She grimaced. "You do the blame game well enough as it is. Let it go. Dana was not your fault. She was a sweet girl who made a mistake. She loved you, Brad. Dana never would have ended her life if she'd been thinking straight."

He wasn't so sure. "She was...troubled." Her parents had been awful. Overly loving, smothering. Nothing they did could ever point to them as being abusive or neglectful because they'd love her. Too much.

"Yes, she was. Shit happens, and we have to deal with it." Rochelle sighed. "I work with plenty of people with mental health problems. Depression is a mental illness, and those who have it can't help it. Dana couldn't help her depression. Her turning to drugs didn't help either. She was your best friend, Brad. You know this."

"Yeah. But I should have been there for her."

"How? Brad, you were friends with that girl forever, even through that brief period where you dated, and Lord knows it's tough to hold on to friendships when you involve a romance. Still, you two were always tight. In all that time, did you ever see her parents let the poor girl just be?"

Only the fact that the Crawfords had known him since he and Dana had played together as children and grown up together under their supervision when at their house had made him an acceptable boyfriend for the brief time he and Dana had dated. But he remembered how pleased they'd been when he and Dana had gone back to just being friends.

He sighed, recalling the many times they'd controlled her. He'd be waiting for Dana to go out, standing by while her mother picked out her clothes. He'd often overhear her father lecture her about the fear she'd be throwing her life away if she continued to bring home an A– instead of an A. Seeing her sadness when she'd try her best only to come up short—but always loved—by her understanding parents.

They'd barely let her breathe on her own. And unfortunately, they'd grown more controlling after he'd left for the Marine Corps.

Rochelle was saying, "She could have left, could have gone anywhere for help. Hell, I was here for her, and she knew it. She had choices. She made her own decisions. And whether you were here or gone made no difference."

He felt tears building and willed them away, baffled at how he'd been fine one moment and super emotional the next. An image of Avery, smiling, appeared out of the blue and hit him hard. Grief and happiness made a mess of his mind, baffling and more than a little scary that he was losing control. Brad never lost control.

"I know all this. But sometimes I can't believe it. It doesn't feel right." *I should have done more. I should have known how sad she'd become. I don't deserve a life without her.*

Rochelle pulled him in for a hug, which made it worse. "You let yourself cry, baby. You earned it."

He had no idea why, but the tears made him feel better. After a while, he pulled back and wiped his eyes.

"Better?"

"I guess." Embarrassed, he didn't know where to look.

"I'll leave you in here to get the gloves for your mom. They're in the box." She touched his shoulder. "Brad, it's normal to grieve, even years later. What Dana did left an echo that's never going to go completely away. It's faded, but it's there. She was a part of you for so long. It's okay to feel sad that she's gone and angry that she left."

"I hate that she died close to my birthday." Hearing it aloud made him feel three inches tall. He snorted. "Selfish bastard that I am, it's all about me."

"Oh please. That's completely normal. Now tragedy is tied with something that should be celebrated." Rochelle paused. "Brad, I talked to her about her self-medicating while you were gone and about having someplace to go, about having options. Dana was tired, honey."

A lot like his mother had been. Was. *Still is?* But not at all like Avery.

"Yeah, but I—"

"But nothing. Dana never took me up on my information. She left in her own way. And all the finger-pointing in the world won't change the fact that nothing you did could have prevented her death. Unless you were willing to live your life shackled to that girl, you couldn't have stopped her."

"Okay." Rochelle was his rock. She'd told him that before, more than a few times, but hearing it helped him balance his responsibility with reality. "I know. I don't really even think about her that much anymore." Only in his dreams or in the dark when he was alone. Or he'd hear a song and think how much she'd like it. Fuck, he *did* still think about her. "I miss her, but I know she's gone. Lately, though, she'll pop into my head."

"Because it's the anniversary of her death." Rochelle nodded.

But it was more than that. He'd never come to grips with her loss, and maybe he never would. "Thanks, Rochelle."

"I'm good at what I do." She winked at him. "Brad, you can only save the ones you can save. Think about it." Something she'd said to him many times.

He felt the warmth of her affection and hugged her tight. "I love you."

"I love you too. Now hurry up before your brother eats all the donuts."

After getting a lid on his emotions, he rejoined the family and sat at the table with the others. Seeing the nearly empty box, he glared at Oscar. "You ate all the cream-filled ones."

"You said I could."

"I said I'd save you one."

"Two."

"There were four in there!"

"I'm a growing boy." Oscar smiled at him through chocolate and cream. "Be nice to me or I won't tell you how I met your new girlfriend."

"Girlfriend?" Vivienne perked up. "Oh, I have to hear this."

"Me too." Rochelle winked at him.

Brad felt himself turning red. His brother's laughter made it worse. He punched Oscar in the arm.

"Ow. Lighten up, Hollywood." He turned to his mom and Rochelle. "That's what the guys are calling him now. Hollywood, since he's doing those spots on Fridays."

Had to be Tex filling him in. The loudmouth.

Vivienne beamed. "I saw it yesterday on the computer, and it was fantastic. You're so funny, Brad."

Rochelle nodded. "And cute on camera."

"Stop, please." He hated that he was so quick to turn red.

"Ha! Big brother's embarrassed. Aw..."

"I'll hit you again if you don't shut up."

Oscar shoved his face full of another donut.

"The girlfriend, hmm? Has to be the reporter." Rochelle's eyes narrowed. "And you're okay with that?"

Great. So she knew who Avery was too.

"Okay with what?" Vivienne asked.

"Dating a woman he's working with. He's in the public eye now, and you know Brad hates that."

Thanks, Rochelle. His mother would freak out if she realized Avery was the Avery who'd gotten to Brad those many years ago. Right now, he could barely handle his own emotions. He didn't think he had it in him to help his mom deal with reactions to his worries.

"Well?" Rochelle raised a brow.

"She's nice. Avery is nice, I mean." Brad cleared his throat, hating that everyone was staring at him. "We're not really dating. Well, kind of. It's weird."

"You like her." Rochelle watched him.

"I guess."

"No, you *like* her. I can tell. She's different."

"Different?"

Oscar nodded. "They spark each other. You have to see it. It's like there's a connection you can almost feel between them. I saw it…" he trailed, realizing he wasn't supposed to tell their mother he'd been to the recording when she hadn't. "Ah, I mean, on-screen it looks so real."

Vivienne nodded. "That's how it was for me and your dad." Instead of going off on how much she missed him, their mother said, "When do we get to meet her?"

Brad blinked. "Meet her?"

"Yeah, Brad. Meet her." Oscar smirked.

"Well, um, maybe if we start dating seriously. I mean, we're just getting to know each other. It's new. Probably won't last." *Of course it won't last. It's just sex.*

So why had he been thinking about her and Dana? Why get so wrapped up that he cried?

He turned to Oscar. "I have some questions for you."

Oscar's eyes narrowed. "And I have some answers. But it'll cost you."

Brad sighed. "When has life with you people ever been cheap?"

"Well, I never." His mother tried to hide a smile.

Rochelle just laughed.

Oscar nodded. "Yep. We cost a lot. But we're worth it."

The question he kept asking himself as he drove Oscar back to his place—his family was worth it. But was Avery?

Chapter Twelve

AVERY STRADDLED GERTY'S CHEST AS THEY WRESTLED FOR the remote to the TV. "We are not watching *Zombie Parade* again. It's time for something different. I want to watch *The Christmas Cottage*."

"Oh man. That's a Hallmark movie!" Gerty slid out from under Avery. "Ha! Take that, sucker."

"Give it to me." She screeched when Gerty yanked on her hair, then rolled her friend under her and sat on her.

"Oomph."

"Yeah, that's right. I ate an entire large-sized burger meal an hour ago. I think I gained five pounds in five minutes. So that's gonna hurt when I let all my weight hit your gut. And didn't you just polish off a plate of pizza rolls?" Avery let her weight hit Gerty.

"Ugh." Gerty held up the remote in surrender. "You win. I think I'm going to barf."

Next to them, Klingon barked and ran around, his little yaps of excitement a perfect fit for the chaos that was their home.

Avery grinned as she got off her friend. "Quite an attack dog you have there."

"Don't mess with me. Klingon's a killer."

Hearing his name, the furry guy jumped onto Gerty's belly and hurried to lick every part of her face he could reach.

Avery couldn't help laughing and managed to take a few pictures before Gerty got a hold of the squirmy dog. For only having three legs, he moved like he had six.

After switching the television to something heartwarming to watch, Avery kicked back and sighed. She couldn't stop thinking about it.

"What's that for?"

"I slept with Super Hunk FD."

Gerty blinked, stared at her in shock, and screamed, "*What?*"

Avery covered her face with a couch pillow until Gerty ripped it away.

"Say. That. Again."

"I slept with Brad Battle." Keeping that nugget to herself had been sheer hell. She'd been dying to tell Gerty.

"When?"

"Yesterday, after the taping."

Gerty smacked her with the pillow. "And you waited this long to tell me? You swore on *Warcraft*."

"I didn't lie, I just didn't tell you the whole truth. Don't sound all hurt. I've been trying to wrap my mind around it."

"Well? Details, woman."

Avery breezed through the Friday morning banter to when she got to Brad's. "I apologized. And it felt like we really did put our differences aside."

"I'll say."

Avery flushed. "Then, well, I'm not sure how it happened. He was looking at me, and I was looking at him. And then we were kissing, and I couldn't think." She sighed and confessed. "Gerty, I have never been so well kissed in all my life."

"No kidding?" Gerty leaned forward, her eyes wide. "So, he was about more than getting to his happy place, huh?"

"Yep. I think his middle name is foreplay." She fanned herself. "And he's built proportionately. He's just… I mean, a lot of guys that good-looking don't rely on skills. They think because they're that hot, they don't have to work."

"No kidding." Gerty shook her head. "I remember Wasteful Will all too well." She grinned. "Say that five times fast."

They both tried it and ended up choking on laughter.

"Brad isn't wasteful." She paused in thought, her humor leaving her. "But he was pretty quick to get me to agree to it being a one-time deal we'd never mention again."

"Now that's a shame. I thought he was better than that."

"He talked a good game about us being friends." She didn't know why she still felt hurt about him trying to end them before they'd begun. "And honestly, it was the right call. We got off on the wrong foot from the beginning. We're forced to work together. Who knows how long that will last? Friday morning should have been a one-off."

"But…?"

"But before I even got home and through the door, he called me about wanting to 'hang out' again." She snorted.

"Well now. That's interesting."

"I thought so at the time. Now I'm not sure." Did she want to be with Brad just for hookups? She'd never had a strictly sexual relationship. She'd tried once but had felt so weird afterward she'd made herself go on a few dates with the guy to get her normal back.

"You're not sure? Why? Because you're crushing on your Pets Fur Life morning booty call?"

Avery glared at Gerty. "You really have a way with words, you know that?"

Gerty gave a shy smile. "I know."

"I just wish I could figure out what I want."

"Besides his body."

"Besides his body," Avery agreed. "I mean, I've seen the snarky, obnoxious side of him. And as much as that Brad annoys me, he's also pretty funny."

"I thought so."

"But then I talk to him, and I remember what I learned about him, how heroic and brave he is, and I get all tingly."

"You might need a shot for that. Did you guys have the safe sex talk? Because if you're tingling when he's not around, that's a sign you need to see a doctor."

"Elizabeth Gertrude Davis, that's disgusting."

Gerty cracked up laughing. "You look so mortified. It's like I'm talking to my Great Aunt Ethel."

"Ethel? Oh, Minerva's sister." Avery sneered. "Or was that Agnes Eudora?"

"Yeah, my family's just hell on antique lady names. But don't change the subject." Gerty didn't care, obviously, because at age seven, she'd decided to go by her cooler, unique middle name instead of boring "Elizabeth."

Avery cleared her throat. "Yes, we did talk about safe sex. We're both safe people."

"Boring people, more like."

"Really?"

"Look, I love you. But the truth is, you're pretty conservative. And I mean that in a good way. You date one guy at a time. You make him sign a waiver before agreeing to hold hands. Then there's that triplicate contract for a kiss."

"Stop." Avery couldn't help grinning. "I do not."

"And you have a minimum of three dates before you round any bases."

"Well, that's true."

"But with Super Hunk, you went for it."

"We're pretty attracted to each other."

"Hey, I get it." Gerty sighed. "His brother is so hot. And so damn slow."

"Yes, let's talk about you and Oscar."

"Don't worry. We'll get back to you."

"I can't wait." Avery felt for her friend. While Avery was still floating off what she and Brad had done yesterday, Gerty didn't seem to be as thrilled with Oscar.

"I told you about Oscar and me not doing anything, right?"

Avery nodded. "When you took your clothes off and he did the right thing and made sure you were sober before he kissed you."

"No kisses, no hugs. I got nothing."

"You got a guy who isn't into taking advantage."

"Yeah, yeah. He's a great guy. I know that. But I've been sober since the disastrous date that wasn't, and he hasn't made a move."

"Maybe he's shy."

"So what? I still want to ride him like a bucking bronco with a burr under his saddle."

No more going to the rodeo with Gerty. "And isn't that an image I'll take with me to the grave."

Gerty snickered. "Look, I want the guy. He acts like he likes me then pulls back. What did you do with Brad to get him to kiss you?"

"Well, the first time we were arguing. That happened at the news station."

"I knew it! Way to go." Gerty bumped fists with her. "And the second time you apologized, right?"

"Yeah. So maybe apologize for getting drunk and disorderly."

Gerty sighed. "I want disorderly so much I can taste it. But he's repressed or something. He doesn't drink, doesn't smoke, supports his big brother. He helps out his mom and aunt and has a great-paying job. He's an AC/heater repair guy. He has all his teeth, can talk without staring at my boobs, and did I mention he has a job?"

"I hear you."

"It's like he's a saint and I'm a disgusting little sinner." She groaned. "Because I have imagined him and me in about every dirty vice I can think of. Some twice."

"Okay, before you feel the need to describe those fantasies in detail, don't. And on another note, don't try to get the guy to have cybersex with you. If he won't kiss you when you're sober and putting out that desperation vibe you do so well"—she ignored the finger Gerty shot her—"then he's probably not into doing it with a svelte green orc."

"But she's got bigger boobs than I do."

"Gerty, no."

"Fine." Gerty sighed. "So what can I do to get his attention?"

"Why not invite him over for dinner next weekend? I'll make myself scarce, and you can have the place to yourself. I'll even take Klingon with me."

"Oh, really?" Gerty's big brown eyes shone. "You're better than Rokeg blood pie."

"*Star Wars* or *Star Trek*?"

"*Star Trek*. It was one of Worf's favorite desserts." Gerty stood and danced around. "What should I make? What if he hates my cooking? You have to cook it for me."

"Sure. But you have to promise to stop calling Brad Super Hunk FD in front of him."

"But behind his back, can I?"

"If you must."

Gerty clapped. "Hurray for Avery getting laid! She's so much happier now."

"Gerty, shut up."

Gerty laughed. "I'm so pleased with you, I'm willing to watch this mushy Christmas romance in April."

"Shh. I like this part."

"Wait. You've seen it before?" Gerty gagged.

"Twice. What can I say? I like this movie." And she'd bought the book too, but no need for Gerty to make fun of her even more. If it didn't have dragons and magic involved, Gerty was uninterested. What did that say for Oscar that Gerty still wanted him? Unless he had horns after all…

———————

By the middle of the workday Monday, Avery had no idea how to handle Brad. He'd texted her about grabbing coffee after work, and she'd stupidly said yes.

The entire weekend, she'd jumped if her phone so much as made a peep. She'd even turned off her email alerts so she'd be more attuned to her texts. That she was so nervous to hear from him again just annoyed her.

She did her best to pretend to forget Friday morning had happened. That he'd ever touched her, kissed her, held her. She couldn't help her oversexualized dreams, but when awake, she did her best to not think about Brad. Then out of the blue he texted her an invite to coffee after work.

She'd made herself wait a solid three minutes before answering.

And now she sat in Green Lake, at the best bakery in the city, and looked for him.

"So, when's a hunk of burning love showing up?" asked one of her favorite people.

"You're so not funny."

Elliot Liberato, owner of Sofa's Bakery, laughed. "I really am."

"In ten more minutes." Avery guzzled her coffee.

Elliot shook his head. "Man, you are frazzled. Let me grab you more caffeine."

"Which I probably don't need."

"But it will make you feel tougher. I'll be right back."

She'd done an interview on Sofa's owners two years ago, enthralled with their famous Halloween display. One of the owners, Elliot Liberato, had remained a friend ever since. Like Gerty, Elliot made friends without trying. He had a funny personality, was incredibly good-looking, and genuinely liked people.

He returned with her coffee and sat, waiting, his green eyes unblinking. She'd often likened him to a black cat she'd seen around the neighborhood. Both had sleek, shiny black fur (hair) and those same green eyes.

"You want to see him, I take it?" she asked as she sipped. "Oh, vanilla. I love you."

"They all do." Elliot grinned. "And yes, I want to see him.

Again. I've already been to three Pets Fur Life adoptions in the past two months. I saw the Viral Viking, who would be so much cuter without the beard—just saying. And your studly firemen are all anyone's talking about. Sofa's gets taken care of by a different firehouse." He glanced around and lowered his voice. "Great guys, but no one on Station 44's level of hotness." His voice returned to a normal volume. "I live in Queen Anne, so I'm not getting saved by your guys there either." He sighed. "With any luck, my car will catch fire south of Rainier. Wait, where's the station again? Maybe I'll need mouth-to-mouth in front of their building."

Avery laughed. "Please, if you do, let me film it."

"I'll do my best. But nothing beats you and Banana doing the tango."

She groaned.

Elliot laughed, then turned to the woman who'd slapped him in the back of the head. "Ow, hey. Cut it out."

"We have work to do. Quit flirting." His sister waved. "Hi, Avery."

"Hi, Sadie. Sorry for taking your brother from you."

"I'm used to it. I'm always picking up his slack."

Elliot stood and glared. "One, I'm not flirting. This is called being friendly to the customers. *Friendly*," he said slowly. Avery watched, loving the family dynamic. Elliot bounced around with a smile. Sadie glowered at everyone, had arms like a streamlined weightlifter, and wore nothing but Blackstone Bikes T-shirts no matter how much Elliot complained. Avery, like many of the other customers, enjoyed the sibling banter as much as she enjoyed the food. Plus, she had a feeling people hoped to see Sadie's fiancée, a former reality TV star who now crafted custom motorcycles for a living.

Sadie muttered something else under her breath and left to tend the counter.

Avery asked after his other sister, who had given birth to twins not long ago.

Elliot smiled. "She's coming back in a few more months, I think. She misses the bakery, but she's loving the kids." He leaned closer. "The boy looks just like me. It's awesome. He's going to be my very own mini-me. Just as soon as I can get his dad out of the way." Elliot stood. "Well, I'd better get back. But don't be surprised if I bring you guys some cookies on the house. You know, to show my appreciation for the city's selfless firefighters."

"Slick."

"I know. I've got moves. You could learn a thing or two from me."

"Yeah, like how to get out of work," Sadie called from the register, in front of which a line was forming.

"Man, you'd think finding a man would have made her nicer. No such luck." Elliot left on a sigh.

Avery had always wanted a family like Elliot's, with siblings and parents who doted on her. She knew from her interview that Elliot and his sisters ran the bakery, that his father couldn't be prouder, and that Sofa's was indeed a labor of love.

She hadn't talked to her parents in a while, but she didn't think they'd missed her much. Her mother loved her but for some reason had been too busy to pick up the phone lately. Her father, well, he was what he was. Avery would have been more bothered about her mother, except that Brad now occupied her every thought when not at work.

And even at work. Earlier, Emil had blathered about her amazing chemistry with Brad. Brad this, Brad that. She'd nearly told him she knew all there was to know about the man, including how he kissed. Then Emil had started badgering her about making Friday mornings a permanent spot. She'd finally told him she'd think about it just to get him off her back. Just like she did with her father...

She wondered how his visit with Erik the Ex had gone. Probably amazing. Erik knew people and had a way of getting information others couldn't. He was good-looking and sincere and radiated truth and dedication the way Avery radiated fluff and fun.

She sighed, wondering if she'd have to hear about how great Erik had been on her father's return trip, or if she'd be treated to his silence and disappointed sighs while he mentally compared her to the shining reporter that was Erik.

Either way, she'd be fending off her father's renewed zeal in trying to re-kick-start her career.

Brad walked through the door, taking her mind from her father, and had half the room staring at him. He wore regular clothes, not on duty until the following day, she gathered. He worked a set of hours, apparently. One day on, two off, then one on, four off, only to start the rotation again. It sounded like a pretty good deal, until she did the math and realized he worked a lot more hours than she did in a month.

He approached in jeans and a Seahawks T-shirt, his hair combed back, freshly shaven. She swallowed a sigh of appreciation.

"Hey, Avery." He smiled. "Want something? I'm going to grab a coffee before I sit."

Before he could, Elliot appeared with a plate of treats. Talk about Johnny-on-the-spot. She refrained from laughing at Brad's surprise.

"Well, hello." Elliot smiled. "You must be Avery's friend. I'm Elliot, owner of Sofa's."

Sadie passed by with a squirt bottle and rag in hand. "*Part* owner."

Elliot's smile didn't dim as he put the plate on their table. "Avery tells me you're a firefighter. Cookies on the house, drinks too."

"Brad Battle." Brad held out his hand, and Elliot shook it. "And please, I can pay for all that."

"Nope. My treat today. Besides, you're a friend of Avery's."

"I had to buy *my* coffee," she reminded Elliot, enjoying herself. Brad looked unsure, darting looks between Avery and Elliot.

"Only the first cup." Elliot smirked at her. "She's a caffeine addict. Watch yourself."

Brad sat. "Well, thanks. I appreciate it."

"Coffee, black? Or would you like a latte or something sweeter?"

"Black is fine."

"Black is boring, but whatever." Elliot walked away.

Brad watched him go before turning to her. "So, you and Elliot." He paused. "Have you guys gone out? Exes?"

She laughed. "I'm not his type."

"I find that hard to believe."

She took the compliment to heart and told herself to hold on to it. When they stopped doing whatever it is they were doing together, she'd try to remember the good stuff. "Well, if I told you that *you* were more of his type, would that make sense?"

Brad flushed. "Oh, ah, okay."

She laughed. "You're pretty red there, Battle."

"Screw off, Dearborn." He bit into a four-leaf-clover-shaped sugar cookie. "Holy crap. This is good."

"Don't sound so surprised." Elliot had returned with a cup of steaming coffee. "We are the best of the best. Tell all your friends." Elliot grinned. "Especially the pretty ones you do the pet adoptions with."

Brad smiled back. "Will do."

Elliot whistled as he left.

"He's so funny. A really great guy." Avery watched Elliot leave, aware several other patrons did as well. Elliot had style, she'd give him that. Even in jeans and a Sofa's tee, he looked like a runway model.

"So, is this you trying to set me up with someone again? The way you did last week on TV?"

She heard the teasing in Brad's voice and relaxed. "I thought you said I was more your type. But hey, I could have been mistaken."

Brad's gaze dipped to her chest. "Oh, you're totally my type. I love a woman with big…brains." He smirked and ate more cookies.

"Idiot." She took another treat as well, having a mouth-gasm as she devoured the creamy frosting of a spring cupcake. "I don't come here too much. I just gained ten pounds with that bite."

"Eat up. It's all going to the right places."

After a moment of silence while they ate and drank and stared at each other, Avery broke the obvious tension. "So. You texted. Is this us 'hanging out' or should we go back to your place for some 'getting together'?"

He flushed. "That was lame, I admit. But you fried my remaining brain cells. Besides, I didn't see you rushing to call me."

"I was giving you the space you asked for." She'd sounded snide. Damn.

One of his brows shot up, and she did her best to focus on his words and not his annoying good looks.

"Oh, so you were wanting more of me than that morning, huh?" His smug grin made her want to slap him silly. Then kiss his pouty mouth all better.

"You're good in the sack but totally annoying."

Her words seemed to brighten his day. "Thanks!"

She couldn't help laughing. "And weird. So, what have you been up to since I rocked your world?"

He'd been sipping his coffee when she asked and choked on his answer, which caused her to chuckle. "Cat got your tongue, Bradford?"

He managed to calm himself and took a fortifying sip of *her* water. "Thanks for offering," he said with no small amount of sarcasm. "And I'd rather *you* had my tongue, Avery." His heated expression dragged her thoughts past the gutter deep into carnal city. "Between your legs to start," he added in a soft voice.

Which caused her to choke on the water she'd taken back from him.

Brad left her and returned with a new glass. "Need help putting out the fire in your mouth?"

She bit back a grin. "Why? Got a hose I can swallow?"

He laughed, hard. When he'd finally caught his breath, he had to wipe his eyes. "Oh man, I've been needing that."

"Rough weekend?"

He nodded. "I've had better. You?"

"After getting the third degree from Gerty about you, I managed to cook a few new recipes. That's my new passion. Cooking."

At the word passion, Brad tensed.

"What?"

"So, you need a new passion? What am I?"

"Shh. Not so loud." Her cheeks felt hot. "I'm just saying that between work and having no life, I'm boring. I'm trying to find myself is all." Feeling foolish, she explained, "Not too long ago, my mom asked me what I like to do for fun. I had no answer."

He grinned. "Next time she asks what you do for fun, give her my name."

"What?"

"Your passion. It's me, right?" He chewed a bite of cookie. "I've been thinking about Friday, and I think we should see if last time was a fluke."

"Which last time?" She was fascinated by the looks he kept shooting her. Captivation mixing with confusion. She felt the same thing but had no idea what to make of it.

"The third time. The one right before you screamed my name," he said with satisfaction.

She leaned closer, not above showing out. "Oh, you mean before *you* begged me to move faster? That time?" She moved so that her breath fanned his lips. "Or when you asked, so very nicely, if I was a good girl?" She moved in to whisper, "You know. The kind who likes to swallow."

Chapter Thirteen

"You win." Brad had a tough time acting like he wasn't three strokes from coming in his pants. Seeing Avery in those sexy glasses, jeans, and a staid button-up blouse shouldn't have been so arousing. But it was. Then she laughed, and her joy with life made her that much prettier. He'd never in his life admit it to the guys, but what really turned him on with a woman was her laugh.

The face and body didn't hurt, obviously, but a woman's personality drew him in more than anything else did. A total blow to his claim about being a breast man. Although Avery had nothing to complain about in the curves department. They fit perfectly in his hands and even better in his mouth…

He shifted in his seat.

Avery winked and sat back, and he imagined her purring with satisfaction.

"So why didn't you text me before I texted you today?" he asked. He'd waited for her to call him and, when she hadn't, decided to take charge.

She lost her smugness. "You'd said you just wanted a one-time deal."

"But what did you want? Or did you just agree with me because I spoke first?" He genuinely wanted to know. He'd previously blurted a need to forget about their coupling out of fear. But why had she agreed so readily?

"I, ah, don't know." She fiddled with her glasses. "I had no intention of doing what we did. It happened fast."

"I said I was sorry about that."

She flushed. "No, no. I meant we kind of went from talking to kissing in a heartbeat. You—you were just fine."

"Oh." Now he felt awkward. "Wait. Just fine? More like incredible with a stamina that never quit once I got used to how hot you make me."

Her pink cheeks were adorable. "Yes, yes. You were amazing. Happy now?"

He'd be a lot happier if she'd sit on him and start moving up and down. Real slow.

"Yep." He nudged the last cookie at her, and she broke it in half. He took his piece and chewed, wondering what it was about Avery that made him both hard and happy. He'd had an emotional weekend, had even thought about canceling their coffee date today. Yet as soon as he'd seen her, everything settled, and he couldn't wait to get closer.

"Geez, Brad. Stop looking at me that way." She ate her half of the giant cookie in two bites and now resembled a chipmunk storing nuts for the winter.

"I can get more if you're still hungry," he managed without laughing.

She swallowed—oh yes, he looked forward to seeing if she was indeed still a good girl—and took a loud slurp of coffee. "You stress me out," she admitted.

"Me?"

"Yes, you." She lowered her voice. "After Friday happened, I had no idea what to make of it. I'm not a one-night—"

"One morning."

"—kind of person," she ended with a frown. "I don't do what we did."

"Me neither. I know people think most single firefighters are dogs, but we're not all like that. Well, Tex kind of is, but he's got a good heart."

She laughed. "I can see that."

"I date one woman at a time, and I don't always feel the need to be with someone. I broke up with my last girlfriend eight months ago, and she's happily engaged to a great guy. I have no regrets."

"Okay."

"I'm not hard up for sex. I can get that pretty easily." He looked her over. "As can you, I'd imagine. You're sexy, Avery."

"Um. Thanks."

"But Friday threw me. I think you and I fit on a level I'm not really comfortable with."

"Oh."

Oh? What did oh mean? "So, um, I was thinking we should explore it."

"Have more sex." She nodded, and he couldn't tell if that made her more or less comfortable with the idea.

"Yes, but not just sex." He felt like a moron. A lot of people had no problem with casual sex. If both parties wanted the same thing, they should go for it. Unfortunately, he couldn't separate the physical from the emotional. "I'd like us to get to know each other. You and me. And maybe we call it dating."

"Dating? Just you and me?"

"Well, I'm not asking Gerty to join us, if that's what you're asking."

She glared. "No, dumbass, I'm asking if you want us to be exclusive. Or will you be spreading the love on the days we're not together?"

"You're really cute when you get mad."

"Suck it, Battle."

He grinned, once again on an even keel with this Avery, the whip-wielding woman he wanted to cuddle until that sexy rage in her eyes fired up the rest of her. "I didn't mean to be confusing. Yeah, just you and me. I'm not into open relationships or having more than one girlfriend on the sly."

"Me either." Avery gave him a shy smile that made him feel funny. Not aroused or happy, but strangely content.

"So, um, I had an idea," he said.

"That squirrel is running really fast to keep the wheel turning in your brain, huh?"

He just looked at her, pleased when she laughed.

"Sorry. Go ahead, Hollywood."

"Okay, Lois." He enjoyed her frown. "My brother is trying to get with your roommate, but you're cockblocking him."

She blinked. "What?"

"Oscar. My brother. He likes Gerty, but he can't make a move because you're there."

"Why can't he make a move at his place?"

The tricky part. "He's been living with my mom to help out around the house. So, while he's looking for a place to stay"—*thank you, Gerty, for giving Oscar motivation to move out*—"he can't get her to himself. Alone."

"Huh."

He had no idea what that look meant, but she seemed to be thinking over what he'd said.

"Okay."

"Okay. Good?" At her nod, he continued. "I was thinking—"

"Be careful not to strain yourself."

He glared her into silence, secretly delighted at her muffled snort of amusement. "That if you do me a favor, I'll do you one back."

"Go on." She sipped her drink, which smelled amazing. He wondered if she'd give him a sip.

"My brother wants a date with Gerty. I was going to give him my place, but I'd need somewhere to crash. I could stay with you at your place this Saturday night, if that works."

She didn't ask why he didn't mention staying at any of his friends' pads. Oscar actually gave him the perfect excuse to be with her.

"How about if Oscar comes to my apartment and stays with Gerty, and I come to your place instead?"

"That would work."

"Gerty was thinking about asking him over, and I volunteered to get lost so she could seduce your brother."

He frowned. "What?"

"He's slow. Slower-than-a-turtle slow. Gerty's making her own moves. Don't tell him."

Brad grinned. "Didn't I say I liked Gerty? Woman knows her own mind."

"Yes, just like I know mine." She pointed at him. "A few rules, Battle."

He crossed his arms over his chest, enjoying this.

"We don't answer to anyone else. What goes on between you and me is private."

"Hey, I'm not the one telling my roommate everything."

"I'm not either." Yet that blush said otherwise. "Not everything."

He snorted.

"Also, if we're doing stuff with each other, I trust you to be honest with me. I take my health seriously."

"On that we agree. Just you. Just me. Anyone else in the middle, we're done."

She seemed relieved, and that emboldened him to add, "I don't want any of this advertised anywhere."

She frowned. "Advertised?"

He waved a hand. "You know. On the video stream, in the paper. Nowhere. You and me, we're private."

"Seriously?" She looked hurt.

"I'm not saying I don't trust you to keep this between us."

"That's exactly what you're saying."

He felt bad, but it had to be said. "Okay, so it is. Avery, you burned me once. I'm just asking you don't do it again."

She sighed. "I said I was sorry. And that was different. Brad, I've been trying to get out of the video spot. My boss won't budge."

"I believe you." And he did. "It's not that I'm embarrassed to be with you," he said quickly, in case she thought otherwise. "But I'm a private guy."

She huffed. "I remember. Look, this connection between us

freaks me out a little. I'm willing to see where it goes. Slowly, *without* an audience." She held out a hand.

He took it. "Me too." Instead of shaking her hand, he turned it over and planted a kiss in the center of her soft palm. He didn't know if she felt the heat, but he sure did.

"Now how about you tell me what Gerty really thinks of Oscar, and I'll tell you what Oscar thinks of Gerty."

"Oh, sharing details. I'm game." She paused. "But anything you tell me goes straight to Gerty."

"Go for it. My little brother needs all the help he can get."

And so do I. I have no idea what I'm doing with you. All I know is that I have to do it or go crazy wondering…

———————

Avery had a bad case of nerves Saturday night, which hadn't been helped by Alan popping over for a quick visit.

"Okay, I have to know. What's the deal with you and Super Hunk FD?" he asked, lounging against the kitchen doorframe while Gerty ran around like mad straightening their already spotless apartment.

"Alan, why are you here? Don't you have a date with Dr. Feel Good?"

"Ha. Good one." He sighed. "Sadly, we broke up. She said I shared too much, and I told her that wanting to date me just to spite her mother was both immature and showed she needed therapy."

Avery paused and stared at Alan, who seemed just fine with what he'd said. "What happened?"

He grinned. "We had angry sex after I apologized. On my knees." He wiggled his brows.

"TMI, Alan."

"Hey, I never said I was naked and on my knees."

"Oh." She imagined him groveling with flowers. Much better.

"I was, I just didn't say it."

"Stop talking."

He chuckled. "So why is Gerty flying around the house like the Death Star is about to blow?"

She stirred the pot, loving the scent of citrus and dill filling the air. "She has a date, and I'm finishing up her dinner."

"Oh, you cooked?"

She slapped his hand when he would have sampled her fish stew. "A tiny bowl for you. Hold on, Mr. Nosy." She fetched him a sample, pleased when he groaned his appreciation.

"I take it back. I'll date you, Avery. And we don't even have to have sex if you cook for me."

"Why? So I can be girlfriend number three hundred and six?"

"Well, I'm not exactly done with girlfriend number three hundred and five. We're on a short break while she decides if angry sex is as good as makeup sex. I'm hoping to have that tomorrow night."

"Your life is one big telenovela."

"I know." He gave her a smug grin. "It's awesome." He paused. "But not as awesome as you and Super Hunk FD."

"Stop calling him that." She fiddled with the stew then started on the salad.

"I know you hate to hear it, but you guys look really good together on camera. And I'm not the only one sensing all that delicious sexual tension between you." He tapped his heart. "So thick I can cut it with a knife."

"And that's not at all a cliché."

"Hey, I just take the pictures and shoot the video. You're the wordsmith. And speaking of pictures, I'm done shooting for your gardening series. If I never smell another flower or see another bee, it'll be too soon." He rubbed a spot on his arm.

"Bee sting?"

"Wasp, actually. But I was trying to make a point."

"Which was?"

He leaned closer to the soup. "I forget." He inhaled and sighed.

She warned him away with her spoon. "You already had a bite."

"More, please," he said in pitiful imitation of Oliver Twist.

Avery put a lid over the pot.

"You're so cruel." He settled for a homemade breadstick. "Oh man. Seriously. You can move in with me anytime. You just have to cook to pay off your rent. We'll still have an amazing work relationship."

"Where you dime me out whenever I make a mistake or have a dog humping my leg?"

"Exactly. We go together like Abbott and Costello."

"Who?"

He groaned. "Humor is wasted on you. I bet you've never seen *The Three Stooges* either."

She smothered a laugh. "Yeah, no. So, what other gossip have you heard at the paper? I've been so busy with the gardening series and Pets Fur Life I'm missing all the lunchroom noise."

"Well, Tara's a huge fan. I heard her talking to Emil on Friday."

"We've only had three shows. She's sweet, but I told her I wanted less, not more, screen time." Yet Avery had been having fun on air with Brad. And Emil's idea of a permanent Friday morning segment wouldn't leave her mind.

"You're still growing in popularity. Pets Fur Life has been pretty happy with the adoptions too. I heard they're having money problems, not just always needing donations but close to closing their shelter problems. So this helps."

"That's not good." She frowned. "Maybe next week we should do a more in-depth scoop on Pets Fur Life."

"You mean, instead of you and Super Hunk giving us ten minutes of flirty banter and furry love?" He paused. "And I don't mean that in a fetish kind of way, but in a cute, adopt-a-pet way."

"Yes, I know, Alan." She rolled her eyes.

"It wouldn't be a bad idea to do some interviews with the Pets Fur Life fosters. I know you were talking about that right after the festival."

"Yeah, I still like that idea. I'll talk to Emil."

He nodded. "So, about you and Brad."

Gerty popped in to taste the stew. "Oh, that's good. How did I make it again?"

Alan pretended to jot down notes while Avery went over details Gerty might need.

Gerty tapped her temple. "Got it. Thanks." Then she started shoving Alan toward the door.

"Hey. I was in the middle of interrogating Avery. And I want to try the salad."

"You need to leave. They'll be here any minute."

"They?"

"He, she, it. Look, Alan. I have a man to snag. I don't have time for proper pronouns," Gerty snapped.

Alan met Avery's gaze and worked on hiding a smile.

"I see your amusement. And I am not amused." Gerty gave him her lofty queen-to-peasant wave. "Get thee gone."

"Whatever. But I'm bored, so when you strike out with 'they,' text me and I'll hop on *Arrow Sins & Siege* with you."

"Oh, Gerty. You got him hooked on it, didn't you?" Avery turned to poor Alan. "Step away while you still can. I played straight through an entire weekend the first time I tried it. It's eee-vil."

"A lot like the tiny queen here." Alan sighed. "It's too late. I'm already a level nineteen paladin."

Avery scoffed, "Nineteen? Lightweight."

Gerty snorted. "Don't let her fool you. It took her two weekends and several late nights to hit level twenty-five."

"Twenty-five what? Because paladin is no joke, but the barbarian's not that hard."

Alan had just opened the door to leave with Gerty's constant shoving when Avery announced in a loud voice, "Level twenty-five barbarian *sorceress*, you whiny mortal! I, who am the wickedest of them all, who make men tremble in fear with my magical twin blades and merium-plated armor, will devour your intestines first, then—Oh, hey, Brad."

Alan, now in the hallway, looked behind him and grinned. "Well, well. It's the Battle boys looking all glammed up. Wish I had my camera. Oh wait, I do!" Before Alan could whip his phone out, Brad entered and pushed Oscar into the apartment, closing the door in Alan's face.

Through the door, Alan yelled, "I'll get you all for this! As the demigod Faelzeeboob declares it, so mote it be! I—"

They all heard him pause then apologize to the neighbors for the noise.

Avery laughed and saw Brad staring at her with a strange look on his face. "The wickedest of them all, hmm?"

She blushed. "I, ah, sometimes I play with Gerty." His eyes widened, as did Oscar's. *What's that look for?* She further explained, "In *Arrow Sins & Siege*, the *video game*."

Brad nodded. "Right. The video game."

Oscar chuckled. "That would be something to see, eh?"

When Avery realized what they meant, her face turned hotter. "Assholes."

Gerty shoved Avery aside and tugged Oscar into the living room with her. "Oh, hi, Oscar. Don't mind Avery. She's just on her way out." Gerty gave an obvious nod to the closet, where Avery's jacket and shoes sat.

"Right." Avery dusted her hands together. "Well, I'd love to stay, but I have things to do."

"You're a thing now, bro?" Oscar teased.

Brad glared. "I'd really hate to embarrass you in front of Gerty, but I can and will snap you in half if you keep talking."

"I…right." Oscar turned to Gerty and handed her a bunch of yellow roses.

She blinked. "Oh, these are so pretty. Thank you."

"Sure." He tucked his hands in his pockets as Avery dragged out her walk to the closet. She wanted to watch the pair and make sure Gerty would be okay before leaving. Brad too seemed in no rush to leave.

"Is Klingon here?" Oscar asked.

"Should I grab him?" Avery asked.

Gerty shook her head. "Nah. He's in his crate, sleeping."

"I'll check on him." Oscar darted to Gerty's room.

"I'm sure the barbarian sorceress's loud threat woke him," Brad said, grinning at her. "You're a nerd. Who knew?"

"I am not." Avery nearly toppled over trying to put on her shoes. "But I am a little clumsy. Don't even think of laughing at me." She gave him a warning glare.

He bit his lip and turned away.

"Something smells delicious," Oscar said as he returned, Klingon chewing on his fingers. The adorable dog had a Superman cape tied loosely around his neck. "Look, Brad. It's Super Dog."

Brad grinned. "Yeah, he's a keeper, all right. Does he shoot lasers out of his eyes?"

"He will if you don't get out," Gerty said, sounding super polite.

"I'm hurrying. Geesh." Avery grabbed her overstuffed, over-sized purse and jacket and preceded Brad out the door. "I'll see you guys later." She'd already worked out a plan with Gerty to stay away for the night if all went well and had a change of clothes and some toiletries in her bag. If not, she'd return to sleep in her own bed.

She glanced at Brad.

Alone.

No way she could sleep with him with Gerty in the next room. Unless they had a ball gag she or Brad could use. The thought made her laugh.

"What's so funny?" Brad asked as he walked her to his car.

"Oh, ah, nothing. Well, let's hope Gerty gets lucky."

"And Oscar gets a life. Amen."

They grinned and set out for an evening Avery hoped she'd remember…for all the right reasons.

Chapter Fourteen

BRAD WANTED TO TAKE AVERY BACK TO HIS PLACE AND NOT leave the bedroom for the next twenty-four hours. Instead, he did the smart thing and drove her to a bar he'd been meaning to visit, full of young professionals and regular people trying to have a good time. From what he'd read online, the place had music that wasn't too loud, decent food, and pool tables in the back. A great place to get to know someone.

The hostess led them to a table in the corner, and Brad waited until Avery sat to take his seat.

"I don't think I've ever been here before," she said, looking around. "It's pretty crowded."

"I've been meaning to come here. Yelp says the food is great and not too pricey. The drinks aren't bad either. There's music and pool tables. I think tonight's a live band."

"Nice." She smiled.

He had to say it. "So, *Arrow Sins & Siege*, huh?"

She flushed. "Gerty made me play with her."

A lot of guys at the station played the popular streaming game, though he never had. "You like video games?" A perfect segue into getting to know Avery better. Besides knowing the sensitive areas on her body, how she looked as she orgasmed, and how sweetly she could kiss, he wanted to fill in the blanks of what he knew of her character. Because everything he'd been learning pointed to her actions five years ago as being very unlike her.

"I do, kind of." Avery fiddled with her napkin and silverware. "I like reading. I like to cook." She glanced up at him, her bright-blue eyes stunning behind her trendy black frames. "What do you like?"

He paused as the waiter came to hand them menus. After a few moments, he and Avery ordered a plate of nachos and some beer.

"I'm not really into video games. Reading isn't bad. I don't mind a good thriller every now and then. When we get downtime at work, I like to break out a book."

"You're not super busy all the time?"

"It goes in waves. Sometimes, especially when I'm assigned Aid 44, it can get crazy."

"Aid 44?"

"Each fire station has different units. Like a ladder truck, an engine truck, medic units. The aid car is for when I'm playing EMT. Our station has an engine truck and two aid cars. We're Station 44, so we designate them E44 or Aid 44 and 45."

"They're cars?"

"I say cars, but they look like ambulances."

"Oh, right."

"But where a regular ambulance takes you to the hospital, we just zip around town patching people up. Minor care. We do BLS—basic life support. Burns, scrapes, splints. Stuff like that."

"You don't do open-heart surgery in the back of the ambulance on the way to the hospital like they do on TV?"

He grinned. "No. Even the paramedics don't go so far. To be a firefighter in the Seattle Fire Department, you need to be an EMT. I fight fires and I take care of basic medical needs. There aren't a whole lot of paramedics in town—they ride the medic units. We have seven to cover the entire city."

"That's not a lot."

"I know. But of all our medical calls, probably three-fourths of them are BLS that we EMTs can handle. The remaining fourth is advanced, for the paramedics. And we don't have any of those guys at our station."

"Wow. I had no idea it was so complicated."

"Yeah, well, Seattle likes complicated."

She grinned.

"On a regular day, I might pair with Tex and go out on five to fifteen calls—we have more when it's a full moon. I have no idea why, but we get all kinds of crazy then."

"Yeah, our stories are usually a lot weirder on full moons."

"Weirder than *Wolf Man Strikes Terror into Fremont Family*?"

She smiled. "I love that headline. It's fun. I mean, who takes that stuff seriously?"

"You'd be surprised."

"Not really. I have talked to a lot of people in this city."

"I guess you have." They smiled at each other.

The waiter brought their drinks and food, and they dug in.

"So, what about you?" he asked.

"No, we're not done with you. I find your job fascinating. First of all, you run *into* fire, not away from it."

"Not exactly." He tensed, wondering if this was where she would dig for the secrets she'd once tried to find.

"You get what I mean. It's a dangerous job. I've met you and your friends. You all work together and spend time together outside of work too. They seem like great guys, but don't you get sick of each other?"

He relaxed, realizing she really didn't want to pry into his history, not like that. And suddenly he liked that she wanted to know more about him. "Yeah, we do. But it's like family. You love 'em, but you don't always like them."

She nodded.

"I've been with Reggie, Mack, and Tex for years. We all bonded pretty fast because we fight fires, but also because we were all in the military. We know what it's like to go from the military to the civilian world to public service. Reggie's pretty chill. Tex is funny. We usually get paired together when we go out. Mack is a trip, but he can get on my last nerve."

"Why?" She munched on nachos, her attention like a laser beam, focused on him.

She made him nervous, which surprised him, and he had to work not to bounce his knee. "He just knows how to hit where it counts."

Avery laughed. "I like him and the other guys. I was kind of annoyed when you ruined my maybe-date with Tex at the festival."

"Is that right?" Jealousy struck hard and fast.

"But that was before. Now it would just be awkward. Tex would want to know how he stacked up to you, and I'd have to tell him that no one can compete with the mighty Brad Battle."

"Nice save."

"I don't want to hurt your ego more than I have to."

"Have to?"

"You're a handsome firefighter. A pussy magnet, I've heard said."

He nearly choked on his beer hearing that.

"Crass but true. Meanwhile, I'm just a lowly reporter who attracts horny animals. I can't compete with all that." She waved at his body.

"Aren't you funny?"

She grinned, and a dimple popped. "I really am."

"And clumsy." He chuckled. "I can't thank Banana enough for humping your leg."

"Brad."

"Him and fake dog poop. Man, do we have a great first-meet story or what?"

She sighed. "We met a long time before that."

"I know, but I like our second version better."

She softened. "Me too."

He leaned over and kissed her.

She stared, wide-eyed. "What was that for?"

"Because I can?"

"Okay, new subject, because if you keep looking at me like that, we'll end up back at your place playing hide the sausage and I won't have finished my beer."

He cracked up. "You have a way with words, Avery."

She smirked. "So I've been told. What do you like to do for fun, Brad? And don't say sex."

He opened and closed his mouth, earning more laughter. "Fine. Well, that's a tough one. I guess I like working out. And not just because I have to for the job, but because it makes me feel good. I've tried a lot of hobbies over the years, but not a lot sticks. Mack loves cars. Reggie is really into donating his time."

"His time?"

"Yeah, to Pets Fur Life, kids in need, that kind of thing."

"Wow."

"Yeah. I don't know how he does it. I tried a while ago, but I got so drained. I need more me-time, if that makes sense."

"It does."

Brad nodded. "Tex likes working out and fixing up his house. Crafty things. I'm pretty simple by comparison, I guess."

"You're like me, trying to find something that's just yours that's not work-related."

"Yeah." He finished his beer and drank water. "Fighting fires is a way of life, a lot like the military. There's a lot of sacrifice, some danger, but that feeling of making a difference. I love it. But sometimes it leaves little left for me at the end of the day."

She swirled her bottled, watching him. "What I do isn't making much of a difference, is it?"

"Wait. That's not what I meant at all."

"No, it's okay. I think about it all the time." She sighed. "I have always liked writing. My dad's a big-name journalist who's won a ton of awards for his dedication to the truth. He's been all over the world, in wartime, scouting major crime, threats to countries. You name it, he's done it."

He'd have to look the guy up.

"His name is Lennox King."

Brad blinked. "I've seen him on TV." Avery wasn't kidding. Her dad was famous when it came to serious news.

She wore a long face. "I grew up idolizing the man. Then when I showed some potential for reporting—and heck, I liked it back then—he was so proud of me. I wrote in high school and college, but I didn't like digging into people's lives. Sometimes I don't want the truth, you know? And that's anathema to my dad. He doesn't understand anything but going after a goal and achieving it." She paused. "That's why I was all over you for that interview back then. More to please my dad than the paper, if you want the truth. And I have to say I did a great job."

He gave her a sour look. "I know. I couldn't leave my house without someone telling me how great I was for months."

"You're welcome." She sighed. "But ever after that, my dad was always pushing me to find the next big story. Hell, he was mad I went so easy on you, wanting me to keep digging until I struck some real dirt." She must have seen the caution on his face because she hurried to say, "I kept on with the serious reporting for another year, but my heart wasn't in it. I hated it, started hating myself."

"Why?"

"Because I wasn't being me." She gave a self-deprecating smile. "I'm a puppies and festivals girl. I like sharing stories about the wolf man spotted in Fremont, about the haunted house in Green Lake, the alien sightings in Magnolia."

"In Magnolia, eh?"

They shared a smile.

"I like sharing positive news. Life can be so ugly sometimes. I want to share the good stuff, the stories that make people laugh." She looked so earnest, and he saw the real Avery under the film of her past. "Seeing how awful you felt after I kept bugging you for a story was one of the most miserable things I've ever done. And that made my dad proud." She huffed. "I told you I have issues—daddy issues. I'm never going to make that man happy, and it kills me. I'm an only child. I have one dad, one mom, and a small family on my mom's side that I never see. I still feel like a kid wondering what I'm going to be when I grow up." She paused, picked at the nachos, and shook her head. "I'm sorry I told you all that. I didn't mean to."

"I feel you," he said to make her feel better, believing her. Hell, believing *in* her. "Parents can be tough. My dad died when I was seven. A Marine who was on a mission and never came home. My brother never knew him, but my mom has spent the time since grieving him. I love her, but sometimes I don't like her. I can't rely on her for much because I don't want to burden her. She's so damn frail I feel like the wrong word will break her."

"That's rough."

"Yeah, and Oscar has had his own share of issues."

"No way. Gerty says he's a saint."

"Oscar?" Brad had to laugh. "Oh, hell no. He's a great guy, but he's far from perfect."

"Good. Perfect would be wasted on Gerty."

They paused to drink, and he ordered another beer. "Do you still want to make your dad proud?"

"Yes, and I hate that I do. My mom gives me unconditional love, and that should be enough."

"But it's not." He nodded. "I keep wanting my mom to be someone she's not. I want her to be more like her girlfriend. Her lover," he clarified, in case Avery didn't understand.

She just nodded.

He didn't mean to pour it out, but the anger had been festering for so long. "Rochelle moved next door to us back when I was a teenager. She and Mom became close friends, then more than that. Rochelle helped me when I needed it. She's a licensed therapist, and it's a natural fit. There's just something about her that calms you. She's an amazing woman. So strong and caring. And she's been in love with my mother for over a decade. But my mom won't acknowledge her. It's so fucking weird. We all know they're a couple. Rochelle practically lives at our house. But Mom won't come out and admit it. It drives me insane."

"That's got to be tough."

"Yeah. What makes it worse is that Rochelle is understanding and kind about it. She says not to force Mom to admit anything. But I love her. I'm not ashamed of her."

Avery sighed. "Shut up."

He was taken aback. "What?"

"Quit being so perfect."

It took a moment before he realized she meant it. "You think I'm perfect?"

"Not always, but right now, yes." Her eyes warmed. "You love your family, and by family, I mean your mom, brother, Rochelle, and the guys. You're real. I like that."

"Real. Yeah. That's you too." He caressed her cheek, feeling as if right now, he *knew* her. He dropped his hand to hold hers beneath the table. "You're kind of geeky, you're clumsy, you hogged the nachos—"

"Hey."

"—and you slurp when you drink coffee."

"Only early in the morning," she qualified.

"You make me laugh. I smile when I think about you. Especially because you're funny and sexy and don't seem to realize it."

She blushed. "Yeah, sure. I'm awesome."

He heard her disbelief and couldn't understand how he could see what she couldn't. "You're also a pain in the ass, and you don't let me get away with much."

She frowned. "Should I?"

"No." His smile widened, seeing her confusion. "Avery, it's easy to find people who'll tell you what you want to hear because they want something. A story, sex, attention. You've been nothing but difficult since I met you."

"Thanks a lot." She looked miffed.

"I see you, and I want you. I didn't want to like you, but I do. You confuse me, and I find myself intrigued instead of put off." Under the table, he brushed her hand over his crotch, so she could know he spoke the truth, and leaned closer to whisper, "Tonight, I wanted nothing more than to take you from your place back to mine and watch you come."

She cleared her throat. "Oh, um, right." Avery grabbed her beer and finished the rest. "Wow. You're good at the sex talk, Battle."

He loved her off-balance. "I'm even better at the sex act."

"Okay, I need another beer."

He chuckled. "Don't get too loopy. We have things to do later tonight."

"Only if your brother doesn't blow it with my roommate."

"Trust me, he won't." *Because if he does, I will personally serve his head to his ass and take pictures.*

―――――――――

"Is Klingon asleep?" Oscar asked.

Gerty nodded. "I just put him down. He's so cute." The little golden/setter mix had stolen her heart the first moment she'd looked into his big brown eyes. Born without a front leg, he'd been dumped by his breeder and rejected by the adoptive family when they'd found a "better" puppy for their son.

But Gerty had known. Klingon belonged to her. She'd fostered her share of pets, all of whom she'd loved. But not like Klingon.

She felt so warm when she looked at him.

A lot like the way she felt when she looked at Oscar Battle.

She wanted to keep them both.

Silly, since she had never fallen in insta-love with anyone. But talking to Oscar showed how much they both had in common. From loving science fiction and fantasy to eating pizza with ranch dip and reading books backward to know the ending before the beginning. He liked anime. He had a thing for animals, and he loved his mom.

All traits Gerty found highly encouraging.

"Gerty, dinner was amazing." Oscar smiled at her.

She smiled back, waiting. Should she make her move now? Later? Maybe snuggle closer and gradually cop a feel during a movie?

His smile faded. "I have to tell you something." He sounded serious.

"Okay." She sat on the floor, her legs crossed, her elbows on her knees.

He sat on the couch, leaning toward her. Close but not nearly close enough. "I really like you."

She waited for the bomb to drop. "Are you married?"

"*What?* No." He appeared genuinely taken aback.

Thank God. "I like you too."

He frowned. Oscar did look a good bit like his brother, which at first had weirded Gerty out. She and Avery had never gone after the same guy. And after what Brad had done to her roommate years ago, Gerty had not been inclined to like him or his family. But Oscar was different.

"I just thought, before this goes any further…" Oscar stood and paced, a towering hunk of nerves.

"Oscar, just say what's on your confusing man-brain."

He gave her searching look and grinned. "Watch who you're calling confusing, short stuff."

"Oh, snappy comeback."

He chuckled. "Damn it. I'm trying to tell you something." Pause. "I'm an alcoholic."

She needed to process that one. "Is that why you don't drink?"

"Yep. Been sober for eighteen months, two weeks, and six days. And yes, I keep count. I broke up with my girlfriend a few months ago. She was cheating on me, so I bailed. I live with my mom now, not because I have to but because I haven't done much to find a new place. She needs some help around the house, and I've been lazy about getting a new apartment because of it." He swallowed, his face seeming to pale. "I want you like crazy, but I'm done with lying and fucking around."

"Fucking around?"

He flushed. "Not literally. I mean, with saying what people want to hear. I'm all about honesty. I can't ever drink again."

"I drank around you."

"It's okay if you do." He wore a smile. "But never for me. And no drugs, ever. I'm not into that scene."

"Me either. I don't even drink much, honestly. Only socially." She studied him. "So, I have to know, when I stripped naked last week, did you want me?"

He groaned and crossed to sit next to her on the floor. "Like you can't believe."

"Do you want me now?"

He glanced down at himself. She followed his sight and blushed. "Oh."

"Yeah, oh," he said drily. "Does what I said bother you?"

"Should it?"

"I take life day by day. I'm far from perfect."

"Thank God. You being all nice and polite was driving me nuts."

He laughed, and Gerty felt the warmth all the way to her bones.

Time to go big or go home. And she was already home. *Big it is.* "Can I take you to bed now, or do you have any other dark skeletons rattling around?"

"If I tell you I'm just using you to get to Klingon, will that break the mood?"

"No, but will it kill you to know I'm adopting him? And I'm still fostering other animals when they need help."

He smiled. "Then I have to stick around."

"Hooked by my body, snagged by my puppy."

"Confession time. I can't look at you and not see you naked."

"Oh, good. Then it's my turn." Gerty urged them both to stand and waited until Oscar had completely undressed. She whistled softly. "Holy shit, I hit the mother lode."

He stepped forward, and she put a hand to his chest to stop him. "Wait. One question."

In a gritty voice, he said, "Make it fast."

"How do you feel about cybersex?"

"As a human or an otherworldly creature? Because I think orcs are sexy."

"Good answer."

———————

Much later, Gerty hugged Oscar under the covers of her bed. "Do you think we're the only ones getting lucky tonight?"

"If my brother has any game, then no. But we agreed—we never tell them this was a setup."

She linked her little finger with his. "Pinkie promise."

Oscar turned to her with a thoughtful look on his face. "So, about that cybersex. Can we do it in real life while also in the virtual world?"

Gerty leaped out of bed and returned with a set of virtual goggles. "Let's try it and see."

Turned out they could, and orcs really did do it better.

Chapter Fifteen

AVERY SAT WITH BRAD AT HIS PLACE, WONDERING WHAT HE meant with the mood music and wine. "Trying to get me sloppy drunk to take advantage of me?"

He snorted. "Please. All I have to do is whip off my shirt and you're drooling for it."

She grinned, liking their dynamic. After sharing so much she hadn't intended to at the bar, she'd been worried she'd gone too fast. But Brad seemed to soften toward her, no longer looking at her as if he wanted her one minute and distrusted her the next.

They were new, and this "relationship" would take time. What surprised Avery was her desire to try to make it work. Sex with Brad had been incredible. With any luck, it would be just as good tonight—that's if she could stop thinking about it every five seconds. Honestly, she'd been raring to go since she'd touched him at the bar. Being with him alone at his apartment made it worse.

"Tell you what, whip off your pants and I might give you a shot." She tilted her wineglass toward him, took a sip, then set it down. She didn't want to get drunk…unless it was on Brad Battle.

He laughed. "How about you take off your pants instead?"

"If I do, you won't last."

"Oh ho. More comments about my staying power, Lois?"

She frowned. "Quit calling me that."

"What? You look like a Lois."

"Well, you're no Superman."

"You sure? I have superpowers."

"Like what?"

He joined her by the couch and pulled her to her feet. "The ability to make you come in a single bound."

She flushed. "That was lame."

He grinned. "It was. But I still plan to make it happen."

"With my clothes on?"

He tsked. "Of course not. You stand still, and I'll do all the work."

"Yes, Sergeant."

He chuckled as he rid her of all her clothes, saving her glasses for last. "Seriously. These things are so damn sexy."

"Maybe you're just weird."

"Could be." He looked her over, staring hard at her breasts. "Here's what we're gonna do," he said, his voice husky. He walked her down the hall to his bedroom and positioned her with her back to the closed door. "You stand right here. If you can resist me, we'll stay right here and make out. If you want more, you just turn the handle, we'll go inside, and fuck."

She couldn't help the shiver that shook her, or the fact that Brad smiled with delight upon seeing it. A glance down his front showed him aroused. Then the bastard took off his shirt, and all those muscles seduced her as he'd promised.

"Drooling yet?" he asked and flexed, grinning.

"Is all that flexing for me or yourself? Because I think you're getting off on it."

"Honey, I'd rather be getting you off." He stared between her legs, where she'd left a trim strip of hair over her mound, shaved smoothly everywhere else.

Avery felt daring and lifted her arms over her head, bringing his attention to her breasts. "Well, let's get to it, Super Hunk."

He chuckled. "Fine by me." He kissed her, as she'd known he would. And even steeling herself for his touch, she couldn't stop herself from melting in his embrace. Especially when he drew her in for a hug and her breasts brushed his hard chest. He groaned and deepened the kiss, and she clutched his shoulders, needing to touch more of his hot skin.

Avery drew back against her will. "N-no touching. You can only use your mouth."

He slowly withdrew, his smile wicked, his breathing rough. "Even better."

Brad surprised her by turning her around to face the door and placed her hands on either side of the doorframe. "Keep them there." He pulled her hips toward him and spread her legs. If he looked closer, he wouldn't be able to miss how wet she'd become. But why turn her around? He couldn't kiss her with her back to him.

And then she felt his lips trailing her shoulder to her arm, kissing the side of her breast and down her ribs.

The soft touch sent electric shocks throughout her body and had her panting with need.

He continued to kiss her all over, running his mouth over her back and lower, along her spine. "I love your body," he whispered as he kissed down her ass to her thighs. "So soft over firm muscle. You work out?"

How can he think when I can barely stand? "Oh, um, sometimes. Not like you," ended in a gasp as he moved his kisses to the insides of her thighs.

"Mmm. You smell so good." He scooted around, between her legs, and knelt, his back to the door.

She glanced down at him and saw his face directly in front of her pussy. His kiss was a breath of air against her folds, and she trembled, so ready to feel him inside her.

"Only my mouth, huh?"

"Y-yes." She moaned when he nuzzled her folds to find her firm nub and sucked hard.

She ground against him and didn't complain when she felt his hands on her hips, holding her in place. He licked and sucked, making love to her with his mouth and bringing her to climax with little effort.

"God," she said when she'd caught her breath. "That was…"

He scooted away and suddenly stood behind her. "Fast?" He teethed her earlobe.

She gave a hoarse chuckle. "I deserved that."

"You deserve a lot more than that." His remaining clothing dropped at their feet, and he kicked it aside. "Guess it's okay to use my hands now?"

"Well, if you must."

He gave a mean laugh. She heard something rip. The condom wrapper. "I'm all about being handsy."

She groaned. "Never going to let that go, are you?"

"Nope." Those talented hands stroked her back, her shoulders, then rounded to her front to cup her breasts. She felt the heat of him behind her and sagged her head, leaning her forehead against the door.

"Tired, baby?" He ran those hands down her front and thrust a finger inside her. "You're so wet." He groaned, pumped his finger a few times, then withdrew. His hands returned to her breasts. "Spread wider for me."

She moved her feet apart, felt him along her back, and arched back into him.

"I'm a lot bigger than you are," he said, grinding his cock along her buttocks and lower back.

"Yes."

"Stronger," he said, his voice gritty. "Put your hands above your head on the door." When she did, he captured her wrists in one hand. "You like that?"

"*Yes,*" she hissed when he angled his cock between her legs.

"Ready for me?" He kissed her throat, sucked, and started to penetrate.

Was she ready? Was he dense? Could he not tell? "I—oh, *oh, yes.*"

He filled her with every inch, so thick and hard. So damn big.

"Christ. You feel so good." He turned her head to kiss her, one hand on her wrists, the other gripping her hair while he fucked her. He kissed her harder, his tongue thrusting in time with his cock. The passion overwhelmed, and she met him jolt for jolt while he manhandled her, taking her with brutal strokes.

"Too much?" he asked through gritted teeth and slowed down.

"Harder," she begged, and cried out when he hit a sensitive spot deep inside her. "More."

"Fuck. Yes." He took her with force, and she loved it, his dominance taking her to a new orgasm while he shuddered and jerked inside her, his climax joining hers.

He made the sexiest sounds, groaning and panting while he released.

They stood, joined, breathing hard, until Brad eased out of her and turned her around. He didn't speak, just stared at her before kissing her soundly. Then he drew her with him into his bedroom and left her, disposing the condom in the bathroom.

When he returned, he kissed her again, running his hands through her hair. The kisses turned playful, not as intense, and he pulled back. "I think you broke me."

She blinked. "What's that?"

He sighed. "I keep getting hard, and I can't stop until I come inside you."

She slowly smiled. "Is that right?"

"Sadly, yes." He hugged her to him, then hauled her up and into his arms.

"Brad!" *God, he's really holding me. I hope I don't break his back.*

He lifted her easily, pretending to toss her a few times until she gripped his neck. "Hmm. One forty?"

"You put me down right now." She fake-glared at him, taken with the teasing glint in his eyes.

"How about we have dessert?"

"I can't eat another thing."

"That's too bad."

It took her a moment to understand the naughty look on his face. "Seriously? You just came and you want a blow job?"

"Well, not right now." He laughed and sat them in the blanket-covered chair in the corner of his bedroom. He straddled her over his lap, and she liked being able to sit on her heels over him, to see his expression. He kissed her hand. "You ever have sex this good?"

"Did you really just ask me that?"

He rolled his eyes. "I did, yes. I'm a fucking moron. Don't answer."

She liked his lack of filter. "All those brain cells are taking a while to get back in line, eh?"

"Yeah." He blew out a breath. "Look, Avery. I don't just want you to hang out for sex. But I can't help myself with you. I thought tonight we'd slow it down. We'd have fun out, talk, come back here, learn more about each other, then maybe make love before bed. I swear I had no plans to fuck you against the door."

"Too bad. That was pretty intense."

"I know. I was inspired." He caressed her throat, her breasts. "You make me lose it."

"I'd say you were pretty controlled. I went crazy."

"Good." His satisfaction was impossible to miss. But she didn't care. Not after he'd made her come so hard. "You okay with this?"

"What? Us touching each other naked?" She didn't want to miss out and ran her hands over his chest, glorying in his strength as she felt his arms and shoulders, teased his chest, and stroked his nipples.

He sucked in a breath when she touched him there, so she leaned forward to kiss his nipples.

"Fuck. That's good." He groaned.

She pulled back. "I like knowing what you like."

He rubbed her hips. "I like you."

The simple statement packed a punch. She just knelt there,

looking at him, and realized he *saw* her. She smiled. "I like you too."

He brought her closer. This kiss felt warmer, deeper than the others. "Life can be so fucked up, you know? But here, now, with you, feels so good."

"Yes." It felt completely natural to tell him anything in this moment. "Brad, I like myself more when I'm around you."

"Yeah?" His hands kept moving, touching her, grounding her.

"You remind me of the mistakes I made and how I'm not making them now. And seeing what you do, how you make people feel better, it makes me think I can do that too. And that it's okay."

He paused, his hands leaving her hips to cup her cheeks. "Avery, what you do is just fine. It's your life," he said, his gaze intense. "Never let anyone make you feel bad for being who you are." He swallowed. "I had a good friend who made that mistake, and it cost her everything."

To Avery's shock, Brad's eyes turned shiny.

"She's gone now. Some days it's like she was never there. Others like she never left. I miss her."

She sensed his hurt and hated that he felt it, so she hugged him. "I'm sorry. I have no idea how much it hurts to lose someone close. You're so strong, Brad, but it's okay to give a little." She kissed his cheek and hugged him tighter, aware he let her.

Empathizing, she felt closer to him than she ever had to anyone else. Sharing felt so right. The void she'd always sensed but never acknowledged, a need for intimate closeness with a lover, a partner, had finally been filled.

Kissing and holding him, caressing with no other intent but to offer comfort, slowly turned into something else. Nothing existed for her but Brad, and she wanted to give him everything. They kissed and touched, her hands on his chest and down to his cock that thickened in her palms.

He moaned her name and pinched her nipples, rolling the buds with a firmness that triggered extreme desire. Her body lit up, totally in tune with his. She pulled back from a kiss and stared into his eyes as she held him, pumping his thick shaft, needy for more.

"I want you in me," she breathed, loving that he looked just as lost in his desire for her.

"In the drawer."

She knew what he meant and hurried to grab a condom. She returned and put it over him.

"God. Avery." He sat her over him, watched as she took him inside her so slowly while he stuffed her full. "I need you." His hands on her hips urged her to move. Then he pulled her closer to suck her nipple. Teasing. Demanding.

She moved faster. He reached between them, finding her clit and rubbing while she felt the rise to climax. He moved his mouth to torment her other breast then kissed her mouth, rising off the chair to deepen the contact between them while she slammed down, riding him with a furious desire.

Their coupling seemed to go on forever, a closeness weaving them together as one. And something in Avery gave, allowing Brad deeper inside the vault of her heart she kept locked.

"I'm coming. So hard." Brad swore as he jetted inside her, the pressure of his thumb between her legs pulling Avery with him as she moaned his name and joined him in bliss.

They sat together, locked in ecstasy, the knowledge of what they'd shared fading as time passed.

Avery couldn't believe how much she'd wanted to forego the condom. She was on birth control, and she trusted Brad when he'd said he was clean. Still, no condoms usually came after a long relationship. Her previous sexual partners had been around for months before she'd allowed skin-to-skin contact.

Brad? About three weeks and she was ready to throw caution to hell.

She groaned and, not wanting to dwell on what this meant

between them, kissed him again. Kissing Brad made everything right. Especially when he kissed her back and sighed her name.

"I came a lot," he whispered against her lips.

"I want to move, but I don't know if I can."

He grinned, and the sight of him happy, no longer with shadows in his eyes, took away any lingering doubt that tonight had been less than perfect. For both of them. What it meant tomorrow, she couldn't say. But she wouldn't bargain for trouble. Instead, Avery would enjoy his affection and not worry about the future.

That would come all too soon.

While Avery finished the shower they'd been taking, Brad got out and dried off. He needed time to process what the fuck had just happened, and to wonder if he'd been half-drunk or just stupid. "Take your time," he told her. "I'm going to get dressed. I'll be in the living room."

"Okay." She sounded happy, so he didn't rush to reassure her about his leaving her alone. *No, because she's a mature woman who just indulged in fantastic sex. I'm the basket case.*

Being with Avery, especially around the anniversary of Dana's death, had shaken something inside him. He'd been with women since losing Dana. Sex didn't often reduce him into a tearful lover. But fuck if he'd been able to hold it back when Avery had sat on his lap, seeing into the heart of him. Her blue eyes lasered into his soul, and he felt as if she knew his secrets yet still found him worthy.

It was nonsense, but he'd felt it all the same. He had no idea why this year seemed harder than all the others. Then again, he'd never known a woman like Avery. She owned up to her mistakes. She didn't cater to him, didn't treat him as if he could do no wrong. And she didn't seem to be asking anything from him.

Dana had been his best friend for years, starting in the second grade. Confidants, friends, and at one time innocently dating until they'd both realized they did better as friends. He'd been there for her while her parents' controlling grew heavier and heavier. His mother hadn't been the easiest woman to deal with, but erasing that part of his life while with Dana made the pain go away for a bit.

Then Rochelle had moved close and become another source of comfort. He only wished she could have been that same warmth for Dana. But Dana let few people into her world. Her parents wouldn't let her.

He sighed. All this feeling crap wasn't like him. He'd been through this a long time ago, had thought he'd conquered his demons. Then he'd cried with Rochelle and *again* with Avery. Hell. He hoped she hadn't seen how emotional he'd become.

Maybe it was the sex. Coming so hard had shaken his brain.

He let himself feel that pleasure all over again. No doubt about it, he connected with Avery on a whole other level. Jesus, he'd wanted to come inside her. Without a condom. When had he done that last? Three years ago with Jennifer, now that he thought about it. But like all the rest, Jennifer had found a lasting love with someone else because Brad "held too much of himself back and spent too much time with his buddies."

Well, sue him, but being with Brad meant being able to handle a firefighter's life. He worked a high-pressure job and needed to relax at home. Late nights, sometimes no nights, and understanding that his friends were family were part and parcel of being his girlfriend. Would Avery be able to handle that?

Did he want her to?

He fixed himself a bowl of ice cream and stood at the kitchen counter in his shorts, eating, nervous, and hating himself for it. Brad handled women just fine. With respect, mutual affection, and an eventual friendly parting. Avery would be the same. Just...their beginning seemed a lot different than his past relationships with lovers.

First, he hadn't been sure he even liked her before sucking face with her. Hell, he'd been pretty annoyed, to be honest. And he'd barely come to trust her before having sex the first time. Times? They'd gone at it like rabbits last week.

But tonight, he'd been closer to her than he'd been to anyone not family in years. Like the way he'd once been with Dana.

Was that it? The reason he felt so close to her, because some part of her reminded him of the girl who'd been his best friend? Avery and Dana didn't look alike, and they sure didn't act alike. Dana had been so unsure all the time, depending on him to make her happy, to be her wall when her parents kept knocking her down.

Avery told him to kiss her ass and challenged him to hold his own with her. Yet he'd seen her vulnerability. She wanted love from a father who had a hard time expressing it. He wanted a mother whom he could count on. He had it in Rochelle; he just wanted that support from the woman who'd given birth to him.

Was that unfair?

Brad swallowed more vanilla fudge and tried to bury his feelings. He normally had no problem. Other people's issues took priority. Saving lives, extinguishing fires, being there for his friends, his brother, his mom, Rochelle.

And maybe that way he didn't have to face the constant hurt buried so deep. He could almost hear Rochelle lecturing him to get that counseling he kept saying he'd get. They had a chaplain through the station, but he didn't want his private life to mingle with his work life. It was enough he knew he had an irrational need to save the world.

But he'd been doing better with that, accepting when his friends demanded to take on the more dangerous situations at work.

Mostly.

Avery came out wearing a nightshirt with a pink cartoon cat on it that hit her mid-thigh. And she wore her glasses. Brad's body stirred. He hoped she didn't notice. He wasn't a sex-starved teenager, but around her, his body reacted. All the time.

She smiled, seeing him with a bowl of ice cream. "Is there some for me?"

He held out his spoon.

"Ew. No way. I don't want any backwash vanilla fudge."

He blinked. "That's a thing? I thought backwash was only with drinks."

"It is to me." She just looked at him. "I'm trying to be polite by not rummaging through your kitchen, but I'm going to get my own bowl and spoon in a minute."

Snapped back to reality by a snotty Avery, he grinned. She didn't even try, and she had him feeling so much lighter, as if her snippiness eased the burdens constantly holding him down. "Snoop away. You are a reporter, after all."

"Sorry to break it to you, but unless you have an alien tomb buried in your bedroom or can tell me about your rose bushes, I'm not interested." She rummaged around and found a bowl and spoon, then dished herself some ice cream.

"Rose bushes?"

"Yeah, for my gardening series." She shared details of her new series of articles, and Brad kept asking questions, genuinely interested.

"My mom and Rochelle are big into flowers."

"Then they should love the series I'm doing. I'll save a paper for you to give to them." She ate her ice cream next to him at the counter.

She kept giving him side-glances until he blew out a breath. "What? Just say it already."

"Are you just pretending to be interested because we slept together? Or is your interest real?"

"Avery, everything with you has been real. That's one of the perks of this relationship." He grinned at her confusion. *Good. Glad I'm not the only one feeling it.* "I have no idea where this is going, but the sex is phenomenal, and I don't feel like I have to worry about hurting your feelings every time we talk."

"Oh. That's good then." She smiled.

"Yeah."

They watched each other.

She broke the silence. "Do you think Gerty and Oscar are getting along?"

"If he's not a complete moron, probably. He hasn't texted me, and I have no plans to text him." He looked her over, seeing those shapely legs when she shifted. Her nightshirt molded to her breasts, unfettered by a bra. He swallowed hard. "You cold?"

She glanced down at her nipples and winked. "Or am I excited because Super Hunk is standing so close? Tune in tomorrow to find out."

"So funny."

She smirked. "What's wrong? Am I distracting you?" She thrust her chest out and licked her spoon…suggestively.

He broke out in a light sweat. "Huh? Not at all. Your breasts are distracting me, not you. Because I will not objectify you as a subject of body parts. Your tits are fucking amazing. You, Avery, are lovely."

She blushed. "Well, I like being fucking amazing too." She licked that damn spoon again, looked him over, then took a big bite of ice cream as she watched him.

He should be too tired to go again.

But his dick had woken up and refused to go down.

She glanced at his cock and ate more ice cream before pointing the spoon at him. "Pull down your shorts."

His blood rushed between his legs and stayed there. "Why?"

"Just do it, Battle."

He pushed down his shorts and stood there, waiting. Excited by the gleam in her eyes.

She closed the distance between them, still nursing her vanilla fudge, and fiddled with her glasses. "Hmm. It seems to grow bigger when I get closer."

"Cause and effect," he growled. "Do the math."

She chuckled. "So easy."

He would have said something obnoxious back, but she removed her glasses.

"Ever had something really cold on your dick, Brad? Ever had it licked off?"

He just watched her lick her spoon for a long moment. "Oh my God. Stop talking and *do it.*"

She snickered, ate another spoonful of ice cream, then lowered to her knees.

Brad almost passed out when her mouth closed over him. And it didn't take him long to realize he'd found an expert in the fine art of fellatio, and that Avery was indeed a very, *very* good girl.

Chapter Sixteen

AVERY HOPED THE NEIGHBORS DIDN'T COMPLAIN ABOUT THE noise as she stood and put her glasses back on. A mouthful of ice cream followed the taste of Brad down her throat.

Ah, a weakness. Brad Battle loses his mind over blow jobs. Good to know.

She smiled at him while he stood gaping at her, so she helped him pull his shorts back up.

"I… You… I can't…"

She laughed. "Blew your mind, eh?"

He nodded, still trying to form words.

A loud knock at the door startled them both.

Crap. He'd been so loud he was getting noise complaints. She stayed behind the counter in the kitchen, visible if someone opened the door but far enough away they wouldn't be able to see she wore no bra.

Brad let out a loud breath and opened the door, likely to apologize, when Tex walked past him, agitated and in a rush. He wore jeans and a black T-shirt that clung to his amazing body. And his trademark cowboy hat.

"What the hell, man? I heard a yell. You okay?" He studied Brad, taking in the lack of shirt and shorts. "Dude, it's barely eleven. You going to bed this early on a Saturday night? You loser—" He caught sight of Avery and did a double take. Then he looked back at Brad. And grinned so wide it was a wonder he didn't break his jaw. "Hi, Avery."

"Be right back." She hurried down the hallway, hearing a low murmur of male voices, and put her bra back on along with a pair of shorts should her nightshirt ride up. Then she rejoined the guys in the living room.

"You're looking good," Tex told her, still smiling, sitting in a chair next to Brad on the couch.

"Yeah, yeah. Save all the innuendo for when I'm not around."

Brad sighed and patted the spot next to him. Avery sat, surprised when he curled his arm around her and dragged her closer.

Tex made a suspicious noise.

Avery frowned. "Did you just chortle? With glee? Like an evil villain when his plot comes together?"

He cleared his throat. "I might have."

"Okay, so why are you here?" Brad asked, sounding bored. "I thought you had a hot date?"

"It fell through. And it was nothing compared to what *this* probably is." Tex studied Avery, no doubt seeing her blush. "That was some yell, son."

"Tex…"

Tex's grin dropped. "I'm in trouble. No, *we're* in trouble."

Brad straightened in his seat, and Avery wriggled for some space. "What happened?"

"Pets Fur Life is worse off than we thought. They're close to losing the shelter they've been using. I guess their bookkeeper made some mistakes, and they need some big money fast. I just got the news."

"Oh man." Brad eased back.

Avery felt awful. Did Gerty know? "I can do a bigger spot in *Searching the Needle Weekly* for donations."

"Yeah, that will help." Tex frowned. "But I kind of pulled a few strings to come up with something bigger. Something faster."

"What?" Brad and Avery asked at the same time.

Tex grinned. "That is too cute. Makes me glad I came to you even though I interrupted your secret love nest." He pushed his hat back and lounged in the chair like he owned it. Tex sprawled and moseyed, as if the weight of Texas made it too difficult to move fast or sit in a confined space.

"Tex," Brad growled. "What are you talking about with bigger and faster?"

"Well, not you, hombre."

Avery snickered. "Sorry, that was funny. And you're blushing."

Brad glared, which started Tex laughing.

"Okay, sorry," Tex apologized when Brad threatened to throw him out. "A photographer I know is willing to take some pics of us looking all manly. She's gonna put pets with us and turn the pics into a calendar we can sell to make money for the shelter."

Avery smiled. "That's a terrific idea! But will your department go for it?"

Brad sighed. "If it's tastefully done and for Pets Fur Life, yes, because the mayor loves the charity as much as he loves Station 44. Who's this friend, Tex?"

Tex fiddled with his hat. "She's just a photographer I know."

Brad watched him a moment and swore. "Seriously? Didn't you learn your lesson last time?"

Avery looked from one man to the other. "Hey, inquiring minds want to know. Who are you talking about?"

Tex groaned. "My archnemesis."

"Wow, you have one too?"

Brad snorted. "You are such a nerd, Avery."

"And this is why *you're* my ex-nemesis."

"I am?"

"Not the point." She turned from Brad. "Tex, tell me."

Tex sounded so forlorn Avery had to fight the urge to pat his knee in sympathy. In a thick Texan accent, he explained, "She's this gorgeous, long-legged looker. Blond, stacked. Got eyes big and blue, eyelashes a calf would envy. We had one date, then she done broke my heart."

"Laying it on pretty thick, aren't you, *hoss*?" Brad rolled his eyes.

Tex looked at Avery with such sadness, she almost believed him.

She cleared her throat. "The truth?"

Brad shook his head. "Loverboy was on a date with her when an ex showed up and threw water in his face for two-timing her. He lost the 'long-legged looker' faster than he could spit." Brad chuckled. "To make it even worse, the woman is Brianna Gilchrist, professional photographer and…" He motioned for Tex to fill in the blank.

"Daughter of our battalion chief," Tex muttered.

Avery cringed. "That can't be good."

"It's not." Tex sighed. "For the record, the woman who claimed I was two-timing her wasn't my gal. We went on two dates and broke up way before I ever met Bree, but she wouldn't let go. Bree wouldn't believe me when I told her the truth, so I had to cut my losses and tend to my broken heart."

"Oh, Tex. That's rough." She could hear the frustration beneath his teasing. He didn't sound over the woman.

"So rough he found a new girlfriend a week later," Brad drawled.

"To mask the hurt, Brad. To mask the hurt." Tex sighed. "So anyhow, I begged and made a nuisance of myself. Bree said she'd do the calendar, but she gets to approve the models. I mentioned you, Mack, me, and Reggie."

"Oh."

Avery looked from one man to the other. "What's wrong?"

"Reggie will hate it. He always claims he's too real to be a beefcake."

She snorted. "Yeah, right. The sight of you four with no shirts holding puppies will sell through the roof." She considered Tex. "Wear the hat. Trust me."

Tex brightened. "I can do that."

Brad frowned at her. "You think Reggie's beefcake material?" He paused, his eyes narrowed. "Tex too?"

Tex watched, captivated.

Brad obviously remembered her comment about a date with

Tex he'd ruined. "You're *all* amazing," Avery said to reassure him. "But you're the best, Brad." She batted her eyelashes and laughed when he grunted.

"Just remember that."

Tex stared. "Wait. Brad Battle, jealous? Oh my God. I can't wait to tell—"

"No one." Brad stood and loomed over his friend. "Avery and I are taking this slow. We don't need an audience. I'm already in front of everyone with that stupid morning show." He stopped and turned to stare at her. "I didn't mean that the way it sounded."

She waved him away. "I get you." But that hurt. She'd started to warm to the show, enjoying her repartee with Brad. Even though she'd complained about it, she'd also started to seriously consider Emil's idea of a weekly spot on their web channel.

Brad hauled Tex out of his seat and shoved him toward the door. "Okay, we'll help. I'm in. Avery will do what she can to help promote it, right?" He looked back, saw her nod, and said to Tex, "And I'll get Reggie on board. But you have to do the rest."

"Thanks, man. And sorry for interrupting whatever it was that made you yell so loud."

Avery refused to look at Tex, pretending to focus on her toenails that needed a new color. Maybe yellow for spring?

Brad muttered something that had Tex laughing before throwing his friend out the door.

He returned to her and sat next to her once more, dragging her over him for a kiss. "I didn't mean to call the show stupid, Avery."

She buried her head in his chest so he wouldn't see her hurt. "I know."

"No, you don't. I can tell."

She raised her head. "You know me that well, huh?"

He gave her a slow, satisfied smile. "You know, I think I do."

She huffed. "Whatever."

"Now how about I show you exactly why I yelled when you put

that cold, cold mouth over my cock? I imagine you'll feel the same when my cold lips cover that clit."

She went from annoyed to aroused in a heartbeat. "You did that on purpose so I won't be mad at you. Which I'm not," she hurried to tack on. "The Friday morning spot is no big deal."

"Uh-huh." His fingers worked under her nightshirt to her shorts and dug between her legs. His slow smile made it worse. "Just the way I like you. Hot and wet."

"Brad."

"Go get the vanilla fudge. And hurry."

The next morning, an exhausted Avery took a healthy breath outside Brad's apartment building, needing the fresh air to clear her mind and body. She'd showered and dressed in shorts and a sweatshirt and waited for Brad to return with coffee—who the hell ran out of fresh coffee beans in Seattle?—so they could share before heading back to her place to check on his brother and Gerty. Why? Because they were nosy like that.

All Avery had received in reply from her texted question mark to Gerty had been a texted-back ogre emoji. Which could mean one of two things. Gerty was comparing Oscar to her much-loved ogres—which she found sexy—or the man was a figurative ogre, as in Brad *used* to be a troll.

She decided she'd had enough of the cool midmorning and returned inside to Brad's door, only to realize she'd locked herself out.

She glared down at her bare toes in flip-flops, now feeling the chill, and heard a door open and shut down the hallway. Great. Should she pretend to be waiting outside his door or dart down a nearby stairwell and hide? At least she looked somewhat presentable. What felt like an eternity later, an elderly woman walking with a cane, moving slower than dirt, stopped beside her.

"You casing the joint?" she asked.

"Ah, no. I got locked out."

The woman, who had to be in her eighties at least, had a gravelly voice and a pointed stare. She wore sweatpants, Nike hightops, and a *USMC Does It Best* sweatshirt.

"It's a new look. Like it?" The woman's watery blue eyes smiled though her firm lips didn't give.

"I do."

The woman cackled. "I'm Tilly, the landlady. So, you're Brad's girl, eh?"

"Um, well, we're kind of dating. Yes."

"Kind of?"

Avery felt all of five years old. Fighting her blush, she nodded. "Yes, we're dating."

"Well, come on, then. You can wait with me in my place or call him from my phone to verify you're really dating and not some girl with a vendetta."

Her eyes widened. "He has those?"

"Not that I know of. You could also be some animal lover." Tilly's eyes narrowed. "Are you?"

"I, uh, well, I like animals."

"You have any in there?"

"Animals? No."

Tilly eyed her up and down. "Why aren't you in church? God loves prostitutes too, you know."

Avery gaped. "What?"

"Not a working girl. Check." Tilly snorted. "I'm kidding. Come on."

"I'm not a prostitute." Avery wanted to make that quite clear… and decided to have a chat with her new boyfriend as soon as possible. *Tilly thinks I might be a* hooker?

"Obviously. Brad's fussy. Besides, you look like you're going out for a stroll, not out to roll a man. 'Course, that would be a refreshing change for the johns of Seattle, now, wouldn't it?"

Avery walked slowly, ready to catch the older woman should her cane not hold her. For all her bold words, Tilly seemed frail.

They walked even slower down the stairwell at the end of the hall before entering Tilly's apartment, a decent two-bedroom unit Tilly had one more of, should Avery be interested. "That's if you're not gonna shack up with Brad. I mean, I never see him with women around here."

"You see him a lot, then?"

"Not really. Now and then he'll give me a hand if I ask. Though we did have to check his place when his water heater got busted. Cost me an arm and a leg, I can tell you." Tilly handed Avery her cell phone. "Want to call him?"

Embarrassed not to know his number, she shook her head. "I'll just wait here with you for a few minutes."

"Suit yourself. I can call him if you want."

"Ah, okay. That would be good."

Tilly dialed, paused, then said, "I found a strange woman pacing in front of your place. Pretty, glasses, long legs, flip-flops. Says she's not a hooker."

Avery swore she heard Brad's laughter.

"Right, well, she's at my place when you get back. I didn't want her loitering and scaring the children."

Avery rolled her eyes. "I'm not a prostitute."

"Bye, Brad." Tilly disconnected and smiled up at Avery. "So, do you cook?"

———————————

Thirty minutes later, Brad found Avery and Tilly laughing over eggs and bacon in Tilly's home. He carried two pounds of coffee beans—who knew Avery was such a snot about coffee?—and a bunch of pastries.

Seeing the two bonding over breakfast made him smile. He had a warm spot for the older busybody. Though her handyman and his girlfriend watched over Tilly, Brad also kept an eye out for her. She'd once fallen in the basement, and he knew all too well how older people could break bones so easily, getting at least a call a day when working the aid unit.

"How about some coffee and pastries?" he offered, seeing them seated and eating.

Avery looked to Tilly, who nodded and said, "Saved you a plate."

He noticed an empty plate and silverware next to Avery. "Oh, so that's not for your boyfriend, Smith?" The handyman.

She grinned. "He's way too young for me. But how old are *you*, Brad? Thirty-two now, yes?" She turned to Avery. "He just had a birthday this past Tuesday, you know."

"Is that right?"

Brad felt like squirming. "I hate my birthday."

"But you're that much closer to my age." Tilly cooed. "I'm barely thirty-five, you know."

"And I have a bridge to sell you." Avery snorted. "You'd eat him alive, Tilly."

"Ha. She knows me already, and we just met."

Brad settled down to an enjoyable breakfast with Avery and Tilly, relieved Avery didn't make a big deal about him not mentioning his birthday. Time with Tilly amused him, and before he knew it, the older woman was shooing them out the door to go to church with her nephew.

"Get out, you heathens. Quit it with all your sexting and go visit God." Tilly whispered as she leaned closer, "I don't mean that. But I'm not getting any younger, so I have to put on a good front with the Big Guy." She pointed a thumb skyward.

"Right." Avery shook Tilly's hand. "Have a good one, Tilly. Great to meet you."

"Say hi to God for me," Brad said drily.

"There's the spirit, Brad." Tilly winked and slammed the door behind them.

Brad carried the coffee back down the hall, elated and trying not to be as he walked *hand in hand* with Avery. "Do I even want to know how that friendship came to be?"

"I got locked out. Tilly found me. Probably heard you yell last night and got worried."

His cheeks turned red, and she laughed.

"Funny girl."

"Funny *woman*."

"Sure thing, Ms. Politically Correct."

"Hey, I'm all for feminine power."

"Me too, which is why when you blew me last night, I blew you right back." He happened to say that as they passed an open door. A pretty woman with brown hair stood in front of a giant of a man. Both of them stood frozen.

"Brad," Avery growled.

The man grinned. "Hey, Battle. What's up?"

"Smith." He smiled at the woman. "Still with this lug, huh, Erin?"

Erin smiled back. "Life is good." She smiled wider at Avery. "Have a great Sunday."

"Ah, right." Obviously embarrassed, Avery hurried Brad to the stairwell and complained as they ascended to the second floor. "I can't believe you said that."

"What? It's true." All innocence, he shrugged and let them into his apartment.

"Yeah? Well, how would you feel if I said something like that in front of your mom? Not so hot." They both paused. "Not that I'll ever meet her, but still."

She looked even redder, and Brad wondered if it had been the mention of his mother that had done it. Did Avery want to meet his mom? Curiously, he wanted to meet hers. But exposing a partner to parents was a step in a serious direction. Did he want to take that yet? They didn't know each other that well… A lie, because he felt as if he did know her, and he'd told her things he never would have considered sharing with the Avery he'd once known.

Yet the past continued to fade, his hostility over her prying from years ago no longer important. He liked this Avery. Hell, he more than liked her, and that made little sense, yet there it was.

Perhaps meeting his family would show him more about her. And of course, she'd have to deal with the guys at the station, though he'd warned Tex to keep quiet.

"Okay, you've been staring at me with a really weird look on your face for a solid minute. What are you thinking?"

"That we should go check on my brother and your Gerty."

She chuckled, sounding relieved. "My Gerty?"

"She's not your sister."

"Not technically, but we've been friends since high school. I love her like a sister."

"Hence, your Gerty."

"Oh, you said 'hence.' Ten smarty points for you, Brad."

He didn't want to encourage her, so he bit back laughter. "Yeah? Well, twenty for you for using the word 'anathema' last night." He paused. "I had to look it up."

She snorted with amusement.

"That was gross."

"I'm sorry. Anathema? That's nothing. How about vapid? Contiguous? Ostentatious?"

"Facetious? Imperious? Bumptious?" At her glare, he returned a lofty look of his own. "Didn't I tell you I like to read?"

"Bumptious? That's a new one on me."

"Ha. Victory is mine!"

"Is it? What does 'bumptious' mean, genius?"

"Arrogant. Same as 'imperious.'" With a patronizing tone, just to annoy her, he added, "'Facetious' means—"

"I know what it means, *Bradford*." She sniffed. "See if I play any more word games with you."

"Oh, now we *have* to play Scrabble."

She grinned. "So long as you're not a crier. I like to win."

"Why am I not surprised?"

Her evil smile did more to break down the walls guarding his heart, and as they drove to her apartment, he wondered how soon he could get her to meet his mom and Rochelle and what they might think of Avery, whom he really, really liked.

Way more than he should.

Chapter Seventeen

BACK AT AVERY'S APARTMENT, THEY FOUND GERTY AND Oscar playing a video game on the big screen in the living room. Fortunately, the characters were dressed and seemed to be killing things, so Avery hadn't interrupted raunchy cybersex.

Gerty must have read her thoughts because she laughed at Avery and gave a sly glance to the screen. "Want to play?"

Oscar keeled over from the slap on the back Brad gave him and sprawled out on the floor. Talk about a melodramatic family. "Oh, the pain of brotherly love. Help! I need a health potion, stat!"

Brad and Avery shared an exasperated sigh.

"What did you do to him, you monster?" Gerty shrieked and cosseted Oscar. "Oh, you poor thing. Do you need medicinal sex to make you all better?"

Avery snickered. "Oh yeah. They hooked up."

Oscar rolled to his feet, rubbing his shoulder, and smirked at his brother. "I could say the same." He waved. "Hi, Avery. So sorry you had to participate in my brother's clumsy efforts at lovemaking. But Gerty and I made a tutorial if you need help, Brad."

Brad cringed. "Please tell me you're joking."

"Please." Avery agreed.

"Oh, relax, you prudes." Gerty huffed. "As if you should be so lucky to watch the very best cyber-porn has to offer. You could both learn a thing or two."

"Gerty. Ew." Avery leaned down to pick up Klingon, who danced at her feet. "You are so soft, little guy. Hi." She laughed as he licked her face with enthusiasm, wishing she could experience such joy, living in the moment like a dog.

Then she noticed the weird silence.

Brad was looking at her in a very strange way. Gerty and Oscar were staring at him, then exchanged knowing looks that made even less sense. Then Klingon peed on her and broke the tension.

"Oh, gross." She handed the puppy to Gerty, who couldn't stop laughing.

"You have some weird effect on animals, Avery. They either want to hump you or pee on you."

"Why me?" Avery raced to her room to grab a new shirt and bra—gross—and washed off in the bathroom before putting on her clean clothes. She returned to the living room to see Oscar and Brad chatting with…*her parents?* "Mom, Dad, what are you doing here?"

Her mother came over for a hug. "We passed Gerty on the way in. Sorry to hear Klingon still has bladder control issues." Her mom snickered. "Gerty looks great." In a lower voice she whispered, "I like her new boyfriend."

"I do too," Avery whispered back.

Her father looked intent as he spoke with Brad about Station 44. She would have rescued him, but her mother gripped her by the arm. "I like *your* new boyfriend too."

Avery blinked, trying to come up with something clever to say. "Ah, okay." Then she decided to ask what had been bugging her for a while. "Why have you been avoiding me?"

Her mom hushed her and pulled her into the kitchen. "I'm making coffee," she announced in a loud voice.

"Great, I'll have some," her father replied.

June sighed, hugged her daughter, then forced her to sit down while she rummaged for coffee and a paper filter.

"Third cabinet on your right," Avery pointed out.

"Oh, thanks. Honey, I'm sorry." June prepped the coffee pot before sitting with Avery, who still wanted to save Brad from her father. "I was avoiding you on purpose."

"Ouch. Why?"

222 MARIE HARTE

"Because I'm a crutch, and you need to get a life." Her mom smiled. "And it worked." She looked past the kitchen, where Avery could see the back of Brad with Oscar and her dad. Gerty returned, and everyone turned to her and the puppy.

Good. At least Klingon would take the heat from her hunky fireman.

"Mom, you are not the reason I'm with Brad. An unfortunate incident with Banana at the Dog Days of Spring festival a few weeks ago did that. We've been seeing each other Friday mornings on the show, and we recently kind of clicked."

"Which you wouldn't have if you were hanging out with me all the time. I love you, honey, but I think I monopolize too much of your time."

"Mom?" Where the hell was this coming from?

"Your father agreed."

Ah, right. Lennox once again doing his best to rearrange Avery's life as best suited *him*. "You know, Mom, I'm not afraid to say no to you. I could always say I'm busy if I didn't want to hang out." While part of her appreciated her mom giving her space, she also disliked her mother acting like Avery had no life.

"Yes, yes, I know. But I felt guilty for taking up your free time. I know you're super busy with the work you do for Emil and helping Gerty with Pets Fur Life on top of that." June smiled. "But now you're with your handsome fireman. He really is cute."

Avery flushed. "Mom."

"Introduce me." Her mother pulled her out of the kitchen like a ragdoll.

Avery assumed control and tugged her mother to meet Brad. "Brad, this is my mom, June. You already met my dad." She glanced at him, surprised to see Len looking happy to be there. "And Mom, this is Oscar. Brad's brother."

"I'm Gerty's boyfriend," Oscar said with a wide smile. "Pleased to meet you."

Gerty gave him a double thumbs-up. "How great is he? I trained him to say that to everyone new we meet."

"He's not a dog, Gerty." Her friend made her laugh, but honestly, Avery needed to give her pointers on how not to embarrass a guy.

Oscar, however, rolled with it. "Like Klingon, except I'm housebroken."

"Not if you could see his own bathroom," Brad had to add. "Seriously. He's a slob."

Oscar scowled. "Ignore my brother. His brain is fried from fighting too many fires."

"About that," Len said. "Brad, I was telling Avery she needs to talk to your battalion chief about the funding crisis. Do you think you could get her an interview?"

Avery wanted to sink through the floor.

Even her mother and Gerty cringed.

Brad handled the request like a pro. "If Avery asks me, I'm sure I can manage something."

"But I won't," she said firmly and stroked Klingon, keeping her hands from reaching for her father's throat. "Emil knows people in the fire department too, so if I needed anything for work, I'd go through him first." She smiled to take the sting out of the rebuke that went right over her father's head. He never had a qualm about using others to make the big story.

"Well, that's good then." Len smiled and shook Brad's hand. "Love the help you're giving our city. And maybe you wouldn't mind an interview for a friend of mine. He's doing a series of articles on fire departments across the country."

"Not Erik, Dad."

Her father beamed. "Yes, Erik. He's doing well, by the way. And he followed me home! He's actually coming Tuesday. Brad, how would you like to come to dinner next week? You could meet my protégé and talk to him. Or not. Just come to dinner. We'd love to have you."

Avery wasn't sure when events had spiraled out of her control. She met Brad's gaze with a helpless one of her own and started to answer for him when he smiled and said, "I'd love to, sir. My mom is a huge fan of yours."

Len preened. "Oh, that's nice."

"Sure. Just let Avery know and she can give me the details."

The coffee machine beeped. Gerty raced for the kitchen. "Coffee time! Who wants a cup?"

"Me." Oscar followed her, taking Klingon on his way. "But none for the pup. He's trying to quit."

Brad came up behind Avery and hugged her. "None for me. We had some earlier with a friend."

We, he said. She warmed. Her parents passed them, even her father smiling at them standing there like a couple.

"I'm so sorry for my dad," she apologized to Brad in a low voice.

"Don't worry about it. I said no to you once upon a time. I can handle my own with Lennox King." He faced her and grinned. "Besides, think of how excited my mom will be that I had dinner with him. He's right up there with her fascination for Dan Rather."

Relieved her father hadn't alienated Brad, she walked with him into their now packed kitchen. It took her by surprise, this sense of inclusion. No longer feeling like the oddball standing out when around her parents, she felt part of the family. With Brad by her side.

Strange yet welcome, she enjoyed their visit. It wasn't until after they'd left that she realized she'd overlooked one very important part of the conversation. "Holy crap, Gerty. Did my dad say Erik is coming to town?"

"Yep." Gerty nodded for Oscar to join her. "We're taking Klingon for a walk. Back soon." They left in a hurry, with Oscar giving his brother a shrug on the way out.

Brad leaned back against the kitchen counter, his arms crossed over that broad chest, a broody look on his handsome face. "Who the hell is Erik? And why did your father tell me I had some major competition if I wanted to hold on to you?"

———————————

Brad was still processing his meeting with the intimidating Lennox King. He conceded that the man had presence. A lot like Avery did, only hers was friendly, softer. Lennox seemed like a force of nature, breezing past everyone with probing questions and demands for answers Brad had felt duty-bound to deliver. Including the fact he and Avery were dating.

It wasn't that Lennox had a physically imposing presence. It was the way he held himself, radiating intelligence and focus. He dressed smartly, had a trimmed haircut and salt-and-pepper goatee, and wore glasses similar to Avery's. But while hers made her look sexier, her father's made him seem as if he could see the truth through those lenses.

Lennox hadn't said much about Brad dating his daughter except for dropping an innocuous comment about a visitor who might be major competition for Avery's attention.

So now Brad had to know who the hell this Erik was, why Lennox seemed so excited to help the guy, and why Avery seemed flustered.

And what he didn't like admitting to himself—why the fuck was he so jealous about a man he'd never met over a woman he'd just started dating?

He pretended to be a lot calmer than he felt, not used to handling such raw emotions. Brad was good at his job because he always kept his cool, especially under fire. And he'd just come under some major fire from Avery's imposing dad.

"Erik is my dad's dream of a son." Avery sighed. "He's the child my father should have had. Instead he got me." Seeing Brad's patience, she continued. "I met Erik at college. We shared the same interests, and we dated. Then he met my dad and fell in love." She teased, "With my dad."

Brad felt his tension slowly dissipate.

"They bonded while Erik and I drifted apart. I didn't want to move to New York or travel all the time for work. Not like he and my dad did. My dad used to leave us all for weeks on end when I was growing up, and I hated it. Erik wanted to make a splash in New York City, where all the action is." She huffed. "I was tired of journalism by then, and when he left, we broke up. We're still friends, but that's all there is between us."

"On your part," he said, feeling her out.

She nodded, and he didn't sense her hiding anything.

"What about Erik? How does he feel about you?"

"He's still tight with my dad, who flew out to help him last week. Me? We're buddies, that's it."

"Uh-huh." He watched her. "So why did your dad tell me Erik was my competition?"

"He really said that?"

"In so many words."

"Wow." She stared at him. "Seriously?"

He nodded.

"He's either pulling your chain to get a reaction, so good job not giving him one." She sounded proud of him. "Or Erik mentioned it when Dad was in New York, which I doubt. Erik has two loves. My father and his work. Period."

"Was that a problem for you when you were dating?"

"Yes. But it was more than that. He wanted to immerse himself in the job. I wanted…"

Brad prodded when she went silent. "You wanted what?"

"I wanted to get married and raise a family." She blushed. "I went through a mini-mom period. Then I realized I just wanted something different from what I had. No more digging through people's dirty laundry. I wanted a job that let me feel clean when I was done." She stood and crossed to him. "I'm sorry for that interview before."

He sighed. "If you apologize for it one more time, I'll get mean. And rough."

She pulled back and smiled up at him.

In that moment, nothing existed but Avery. Not work, his family, his past problems. Nothing.

He kissed her.

She kissed him back.

They stood there hugging and not speaking, and for a small bit of time, life was perfect.

Too bad perfection didn't last.

"Brad, move your gorgeous ass to the left. A little more. Let the puppy lick you."

"He smells like he just ate kitty litter," he muttered, but not quietly enough because Hernandez and Mack laughed.

"He probably did." Mack shrugged. "I saw him nosing around a litter box before you picked him up."

"Gross. Ken's smacking with cat poop." Hernandez made a face.

Like the others gathered in Brianna Gilchrist's small studio Thursday afternoon, he and six other members of C shift met with the photographer to get their moneymaking Pets Fur Life calendar started.

Hernandez, Wash, and Marcus had joined Brad and his crew, along with two guys from A shift and three from B. D shift had duty and had been pretty damn vocal about being excluded. As had the Station 44 ladies, but Bree had been insistent the calendar be for fire*men*, as opposed to the firefighters and later fire*women* calendars she intended to put together next year. Nat and Lori had been mollified, a little. Brad expected payback in due course.

But now they had twelve firemen to handle all the months of the year for Pets Fur Life.

"Yo, Mr. April, smile," Reggie called out, still annoyed he'd had to say yes or be party to dooming helpless animals to a life of vagrancy and despair. Brad had used Avery's nicely scripted guilt trip, then passed it on to Tex, who had done a hell of a job pouring on the guilts, so that every guy invited made sure to show up on his day off.

Wearing an unbuttoned shirt and jeans, his hair mussed by a cute stylist with neon-pink hair, Brad had been made up to look sexy and handsome and absolutely "dreamy"—according to Bree.

Tex, Brad had noticed with much amusement, didn't look happy about any of it. But Mr. December had to wait his turn. "Bree, we almost done?"

"Hell, no." The smart blond took a few shots, adjusted the lighting, then ordered him into more angles and poses while the cute but stink-breath of a hound kept squirming. "Okay, Brad, you're done. Hey, Rena, can you come collect Snoopy?"

The beagle puppy was adorable—and aptly named.

Rena, another hairdresser and a woman who often helped with the Pets Fur Life charity, hustled out, beaming. "Great job, Brad. Wow, you guys are so built." She stared at his chest.

"The Viral Viking let you come mingle with all the 'beefcake'?"

She grinned. "Hey, I'm on a job, supporting you with hair care." She nodded to the cute stylist. "Tommy too. This is about giving to charity and helping those who need help." She stroked Snoopy's head.

"Covering all your bases?" He grinned. He liked the pretty woman, and he liked her boyfriend. He was smart enough not to want to get on the guy's bad side though. Six-six and looking like a hit man on a good day despite the haircut that had made him famous, her boyfriend was not one to mess with.

"You know it." Rena winked. "Oh, there's Reggie. I think he needs a trim."

"He hardly has any hair."

"You are not the professional here, Brad. I am."

"Well, do your best. He's not happy about being here."

"Aye, aye, Captain."

"That's Sergeant, and...never mind."

Rena hustled over to Reggie and started *oohing* and *aahing* over him, which soothed Reggie's annoyance. A pretty woman would do that.

And speaking of which...

He looked for his own girl and found her hemmed in by Hernandez and Wash. He removed his shirt to wipe off the spritz of oil Bree had insisted he use and donned a T-shirt. Mack groaned as Bree's assistant dragged him toward the green screen and ordered him to lie down on a picnic blanket.

"Okay, this is going to be fast," Bree warned. "Look happy and get rid of the attitude, Revere. Pretty is as pretty does."

"Tex, she's being mean to me. Make her stop."

Others around them laughed until Bree shushed them. A bunch of Pets Fur Life people, Rupert included, centered around the shot, enclosing it with a moveable fence. Then three large pet carriers were opened and a swarm of puppies surged, covering Mack, who'd been spritzed with a bacon perfume—something Brad had never in his life thought might be a real thing.

Mack laughed uncontrollably as he was mauled by a dozen furballs.

Avery managed to duck the idiots surrounding her and made her way to Brad, who glared at the others before saying to hell with it. He leaned down and kissed her.

"I knew it!" Reggie crowed, "Washkowski, you owe me twenty bucks."

Brad knew he'd never hear the end of the teasing, but these asshats needed to understand Avery was with him...since she'd made no move to distance herself earlier.

"Very macho of you, Brad." Avery adjusted her glasses, not trying to hide her smile. "Way to keep us under the radar."

"Screw it. And screw them," he said in a louder voice, ignoring Reggie's thumbs-up.

She laughed. "You're cute, but not as cute as Mack and all those puppies! Oh my gosh, it makes me want to take one home."

"A dog, not the idiot in the middle, right?" he teased, not really meaning it.

"Relax. Not that I don't love the jealousy, but I'm not the kind who plays around." She gave him a hard look. "Just like you'd better not be. Go easy with the flirting."

"What?"

"I saw you with Rena. She's got a boyfriend, you know."

Feeling better about being possessive, he kissed her again. "I only have eyes for you… Watch out."

She stumbled over a cat, which hissed and took a swipe at her legs.

Then the feline ambled to Brad and wound around his ankles, meowing to be picked up.

Avery took a step back. "It's the cat or me. I took my allergy pill before coming today, but I really can't do cats."

"But Avery, I love pussy." Brad sighed. "What am I gonna do now?"

Mack bust out laughing. "Nice, Brad."

"Yeah, nice, Brad," Avery sneered.

"Perfect." Bree took more shots from different angles. Once the puppies started losing interest in Mack, she ordered the next victim to approach.

"She's like a drill instructor I had back in basic," Brad said as Tex joined them.

"No shit." He snorted then saw Avery. "I mean, no kidding." He tipped his hat at her.

He wore faded jeans, a black T-shirt plastered to his chest it was so tight, and that stupid hat.

"Wow. You look good, Tex." She stared, wide-eyed. "I want to look away, but I can't. All this eye candy is addicting." A glance at Reggie showed him flexing for Rena. Mack stood close to Bree, smiling. The other firefighters of Station 44 stood around, half-dressed and full of muscle. All there to help an animal shelter keep its doors open.

"Avery, close your mouth." Brad sighed, now amused instead of jealous. He and the guys were brothers. And, he had to admit, in damn good shape thanks to all the exercise they did. It was one thing for Avery to like the look of the guys, another for them to like her back. Though he'd ragged on her about Mack, he knew his buddy would never make a move on his girlfriend.

It took him a moment to realize thinking the word "girlfriend" no longer bothered him. Because it fit.

She fit.

Hell. Fluttery thoughts about Avery continued to plague him. Thoughts about tomorrow, the future, and a lot of possibilities he'd never even considered with anyone else dogged him when he thought about his sexy reporter.

"Bree is being so bitchy," Tex said to him in a low voice, breaking him out of his head. "That's a good sign, right?"

"Sure. I guess. Wait. Why is that good?"

Tex turned to him, looking serious. "Because if she hated me, she'd ignore me, right? But if she had conflicting feelin's, it's still there."

"What are you two talking about?" Avery asked and moved closer.

"He thinks Bree is still into him." Brad ignored the glare Tex shot him. "Hey, she asked."

"Breaking bro-code. Nice."

Avery smiled. "I'll feel her out for you."

Tex considered her. "Well, that's all right then." He glared at Brad. "You're still on my list, son."

"Whatever."

It took another hour before Bree took a break, and Avery hurried to talk to her.

"Seriously, Brad. Sharing guy secrets with the girl is a big step. Sure you're ready for it?" Tex asked him.

Reggie and Mack joined them. "So, you and Avery." Reggie nodded. "I like it."

"Me too," Mack agreed. "Even though she'll never know the wonder that is me, she got second best with Ken. Ah, well. Poor girl." He shifted a sly grin Brad's way. "But you know, now that the cat's out of the bag, so to speak, you are so in for it at the station." He waved to Hernandez and Wash, who were smiling widely at Brad. "They were asking Avery tons of questions about you and the pet show earlier. It's not looking good, Brad."

"What does that mean?"

Tex grinned. "I'm thinking dominating Ken gets some Paw Patrol buddies while he's doing black-haired Barbie in all kinds of ways."

Realizing he'd be the hot topic at the station, *again,* Brad groaned.

Reggie laughed. "I can't wait to see what they come up with."

"They? More like you," Mack said and winced when Reggie punched him in the arm and dragged him away.

"I knew Reggie was in on it," Brad said, planning a subtle revenge for his friend.

"She looks good," Tex said, sighing, and Brad agreed. He loved Avery in glasses, paired with jeans, a skirt, a T-shirt, he didn't care. But she had to wear those frames. "Man, how can I get her to go out with me?" Tex whined.

Brad froze before he realized Tex was talking about Bree.

I have got to stop thinking everyone wants Avery. And Jesus, but how possessive could a guy get, anyway? *Chill, man.* It felt as if someone had injected him with a shot of testosterone, but he knew the distance wasn't helping.

He hadn't seen Avery yesterday, as he'd been on duty. The two days prior to that they'd shared dinner but little else. By some mutual, unspoken consensus, they'd given each other space.

He didn't like it, though she seemed just fine with it. Yet she hadn't liked him being too friendly with Rena. That made him feel better.

Avery returned soon enough, a large smile making her blue eyes shine. "Bree agreed to an interview. I'm going to include it with some heavy coverage on Pets Fur Life this week on the show. And it'll be in the paper next week as well. Tomorrow morning, I want to focus on the Pets Fur Life people, so your part is going to be pretty minimal."

"Whatever you need."

She looked at him. "You're really okay with having to do the show with me now?"

"I wasn't at first, but we've been getting the animals adopted, fast. I like that." *I like you.* "Rupert told me he approves, which makes Tilly happy. I did tell you she's his aunt, right?"

"I love Tilly." She smiled. "Why was she so curious to know if I liked animals?"

He paused. "Well, ah, I'm not supposed to have any in my apartment, but a few times I've helped out with fostering in emergency situations."

"Oh, now I see. We're not supposed to have animals at our place either, but Gerty—"

"Gerty what?"

She coughed. "She, um, charmed our landlord. Man, I hope that doesn't backfire on us."

"What do you mean by 'charmed,' exactly?"

"She's nice. You've met her. Everyone loves Gerty."

"Oh, well, that's true." But he worried for his brother, who had been spending every spare moment with Gerty since Saturday. "Is Oscar being at your place bothering you?"

"Actually, no." She sounded surprised. "He takes out the trash, doesn't make a mess, and is really quiet. And he makes Gerty happy." She smiled. "Finally, a guy who gets my best friend."

"Yeah, but you and Gerty are tight. Is Oscar putting a kink in your girl time?"

"Speaking from experience?" She gave him a knowing look. "Is that a problem when one of your crew hooks up?"

"If it's the wrong woman, yeah." He watched her, wondering how she'd fit in.

She watched him right back. "I'm not going to ask."

He raised a brow.

"If I'm the right woman or not." She huffed. "I'm amazing. You'd be lucky to keep me."

"Is that right?" His lips twisted into a grin, hearing both her bluff and the shaky confidence underneath. "What about me? Would you be lucky to keep me?"

"That remains to be seen." She poked him the chest. "Just remember not to live up to the stereotype."

"Of?"

"Single firefighters who act like dogs." She nodded to the guys flirting with the pink-haired stylist and Rena.

He winced. "You have a point."

"I know." She kissed him quickly, blushed, and said, "I have to get back to work. I'll see you tomorrow morning?"

"Not tonight?" He didn't want to sound needy, but damn it, he missed her.

She sighed. "I wish. I have some last-minute work to get done for Emil. But we can spend tomorrow together after I get home. If you want."

He wanted. "Sounds good. I'll see you in the morning." He grabbed her hand and decided to tell her the truth. Glancing around and seeing no one close, he admitted, "I've been missing you."

Her smile blinded him. "Good."
Then she left.
Now what the hell did that mean?

Chapter Eighteen

AVERY SAT WITH EMIL IN HIS OFFICE FRIDAY MORNING, HAVING just finished the pet segment, and clasped her hands in her lap so as to stop with her nervous tells. Apparently, she fiddled with her glasses and nibbled at her thumbnail when nervous, as Gerty had oh so helpfully pointed out last night over dinner—otherwise known as the fiasco Oscar had attempted.

Bless him, but the man was all thumbs in the kitchen. Though with Gerty, he was all heart.

Avery really liked how he treated her best friend. She did reserve some judgment after Gerty had confided in her about his alcoholism. Yet he'd been upfront with Gerty about it, and Avery liked that. If Gerty could handle his issues, it wasn't Avery's business to intervene.

"So, have you thought about it?" Emil asked, apparently done babbling about his favorite perennials.

"About...?"

Emil sighed. "Are you hungry? I can almost see your brain floating away." He tossed her a peanut bar. "Go ahead. Take mine."

She loved the caramel holding it all together and gladly accepted, asking through a sticky mouth, "About what?"

"The video spot. Our new, highly successful streaming web channel. Alan's handling production of the thing. I want you on right after Tara hits the hard news. Live streaming spots Friday mornings at nine instead of seven."

"Um, well..."

"And you don't have to be joined at the hip with your fireman. You two are terrific, but at some point, his chief will be breathing down my neck to let him get back to work. Another few weeks and he's done. We can use his fellow firefighters at the station too, I've been told. But we don't need to focus on Pets Fur Life forever.

"Avery, you're really good on camera. You come alive. And you draw in a younger audience than Tara. Our demographics show the older set likes you as well. You come across as friendly and sincere. I want to turn the ten-minute spot into a twenty-minute Friday Feature. And if that does as well as I think it will, we'll do more."

"W-what?"

"We're going to keep the paper in both print—for now—and digital, and we'll take some of the onus of all our story ideas off you. You still get to write about features in *Searching the Needle Weekly*, but you get creative control of what we stream live. What do you say?"

"I say that's a lot of pressure."

"Did I also mention your work nailed the two dream backers I've been courting for months? They like a softer, more human-interest aspect to what we do. As well as the city myths. You know, alligators in the sewer, ghosts of the underground, that sort of thing." When she still said nothing, he swallowed hard. "And did I mention another raise on top of the one I just gave you?"

"Are you on drugs?"

He laughed. "Just desperate. A lot is riding on you, I won't lie. But this is a new direction for us, and I think you're up for it." He rubbed his hands together. "More advertising and a lean toward social media mean more opportunities for expansion."

His wheels were spinning, for sure.

Avery's gut told her to go for it, but her head told her to wait because this new direction seemed the exact opposite of the hard news her father wanted her to hit. What would Lennox say?

Then she remembered Brad telling her to be her own person, to not let anyone keep her down, the way his friend had. "Okay, I'm in."

Emil smiled, turned, and tapped a key on his computer. "Great. I just sent out a group email announcing it."

"Sure I'd say yes?"

"Hoping." He stared at her. "Well? Get out. Take the day to enjoy your upcoming success and be prepared to go longer in two more weeks. We start our new format in May."

"That's pretty quick."

"And you'll be pretty busy, so take your time off when you can. I expect you here bright and early on Monday for our first streaming meeting. I want you to meet our new backers."

No pressure. "I think I need a drink."

"It's five o'clock somewhere," Emil told her. "Now, unless you want to sit here with me while I explain to Mark that he has to take on some of Alan's duties, I suggest you go home."

"Oh, right." Avery zipped out of the office, grabbed her purse, then grabbed Alan on her way out for a coffee.

"Whoa. What's the rush?" he asked as they found a new local beanery and ordered lattes.

"I just agreed to a new twenty-minute Friday show. You'll be producing it."

Alan grinned. "Outstanding. I told Emil I'd be the right guy for the job." He studied her. "I don't think you realize how this is going to blow up. We're going to make you a YouTube star."

"Yeah, Banana and I will go far," she said wryly. "I'm still events lady for the paper, and I'm still the human-interest focus for the video spot. Period. Except now I have to fill twenty minutes instead of ten."

He scoffed. "Easy. Just bring on more firemen and start a hookup service. Ratings will go through the roof."

"Ha ha."

"She thinks I'm kidding." He swallowed his coffee loudly. "So, what's up with you and Brad? Rumor has it you two are getting serious."

"Rumor?" Had Gerty been talking to Alan behind her back?

"It didn't escape my notice that the Battle brothers, all two of them, came to your house for Gerty's date. Anyone with eyes can tell you and Brad are hooking up."

She blushed. "We are not."

"Ha. Right. You're such a bad liar."

She toyed with her cup. "Can I tell you something?"

"About Brad? Sure." He leaned closer.

"About the show, doofus."

"Oh." He sounded disappointed. "Okay."

"I'm nervous. I actually want this to work."

"It will. Emil and I have been talking about it. And I know a guy who knows a gamer who has over ten million followers, and he thinks you're hot. He's all set to share."

"Oy." She tugged on her hair, nerves aflutter. "My dad is going to hate it."

Alan patted her on the shoulder. "Ah, so that's what's got you nervous."

"And the idea of a million people seeing me. I'm not a celebrity. I do puff pieces."

"The kind of stuff people eat up. You were made for the spotlight, I'm telling you. You're funny and good on paper, but face-to-face, you have what a lot of people in this industry don't."

"What's that? Glasses?"

"It. You have *it*. Tara is good, but she's too polished. You come across as goofy."

"Thanks a lot, Alan." And there went her small step of confidence, that she might be able to pull off twenty minutes of fluff.

"Goofy and relatable. People like relatable. Trust me." He gave her a toothy grin. "I'm the guy who made you and Banana Seattle stars."

She groaned. Apparently, she and Banana had been spotlighted on *TMZ* last night. "Let's change the subject. How are you and the good doctor? Back together yet?"

His smirk said yes. "She realized she's been sublimating mommy issues with me. Now we're working through them." Alan leaned closer. "Sexually."

She groaned.

"Each day we try something new. Reverse cowboy to ride out her demons. Missionary to get her closer to God."

"Really? Now you're a religious experience?"

"What? Sex with me brings her closer to heaven every time. It's like being blessed for a good three, no, five minutes."

Avery refused to laugh.

"Then there's blowing the old johnson."

She coughed. "I hate myself for asking, but how is that helping her?"

"It's a hand-to-mouth stimulus kicking in. Plus, it's like sucking on a straw, which oddly stirs her creativity."

"A straw? Not a great comparison for *your* johnson, Alan."

He cringed. "Good point."

But he made her forget to be nervous, and they spent the next half hour teasing and laughing before Emil texted him—in all caps—to get the hell back to work.

Avery walked Alan back to the office, then drove herself to the library, giving herself a free day. She found a few books she thought she might like, got herself a massage last minute at her mom's favorite place in Queen Anne, bought a pound of chocolate from a pricey candy shop, then decided to surprise Brad.

Some mind-blowing sex would top off her Friday, and since Brad didn't have to go in until Saturday, she'd have him all to herself.

She gleefully contented herself with how she now held the upper hand. Not one for games in a relationship, she nevertheless knew she'd best be cautious when dealing with a man like Brad.

He missed her.

That warmed her in all the right places.

Because she missed the heck out of him. They hadn't said much about just spending dinner together—sans the sex—the past Monday and Tuesday. It was as if by unspoken mutual agreement they wanted to see how they felt apart.

She missed the crap out of him, which made her feel needy and pathetic. A guy as good-looking and friendly as Brad would never hurt for companionship. And when that calendar dropped, the wolves would be out, gunning for him.

Was she really the best sex he'd ever had, or had he just been saying that? For her part, no question, Brad rung her bell. And continued to ring it.

But it had been several days. She was due some heavy chiming.

She pulled into his apartment complex and took her chocolates with her to his door. She knocked, curious as to how he'd handle her pop-in. Then she decided to surprise him even more.

The door opened, and Brad smiled down at her, wearing lounge pants and a T-shirt. Lounge wear. Perfect. "Hey, Avery."

She launched herself at him and planted a doozy of a kiss. When they parted, both breathing hard, she declared, "Your barbarian sorceress is here for the sex. Get naked, Hollywood."

Loud laughter erupted from behind them in his apartment. Whoops.

———————

Brad blew out a breath, his body tingling all over. *Shit.* He had to clear his throat to speak and raised his voice to he heard over laughter. "Uh, the guys are over, hanging out. Why don't you join us?"

His gorgeous, red-faced barbarian sorceress looked from him to the guys inside and sighed. "Might as well."

He leaned closer. "We'll get to the sex after they leave."

She grinned up at him.

He was falling deeper for this woman with no sign of stopping. "Guys, Avery's here."

"No, that's a barbarian sorceress," Mack corrected him, smirking. "What level, Avery?"

"Twenty-six, so suck it."

Mack and the others just stared at her.

Brad frowned. "What's the problem?"

"That's amazing." Tex patted the spot next to him. "The nerds at the station can barely clear fifteen."

"Gerty—my roommate—is a forty-seven."

Even Reggie blinked. "No kidding?"

Brad snorted. "Video games are for kids."

They all gave him pitying looks.

"You sure you want to attach yourself to that?" Mack asked her. In a loud whisper, he added, "He has no idea what a level even is."

Reggie laughed. "I don't play *Arrow Sins & Siege*, but even I know it's massively popular. Hell, my sisters play."

"And how are your lovely sisters?" Mack asked, all innocence.

Reggie glared, and Mack turned to Tex. "He has absolutely no social grooming. He needs help."

"*He* is right here."

Avery turned to Brad, biting back a grin. "What did I interrupt?"

"We were trying to decide what to do. We're bored." Tex sighed. "And going for a run ain't gonna help, Ken."

"Dick." Brad gave Tex the eye.

"Ken?" Avery looked from Tex to Brad. "He called you Ken? Is that your middle name or something?"

"We call him Ken because he looks like a Ken doll," Mack announced. "All hard body, blondish, and with that understated male anatomy."

Avery snorted. "Ken. Classic." She saw his face and started laughing.

"It's not that funny," he said.

"It is," Reggie and Tex said together. Reggie explained, "Everyone at the station has this Ken doll they put with other dolls doing unspeakable things. It's hilarious."

"It's not, really."

Mack looked at Reggie. "Do they make brown Ken dolls?"

"No idea, but my sister used to play with my GI Joe action figure, Roadblock."

"Doll," Avery corrected.

Reggie repeated, "*Action figure*, and used to bury him in the backyard while she did spells, hoping to bury me for real. Nadia's a little scary."

Brad stared. "Nadia? But she's so sweet."

Reggie snorted. "To you. She didn't like me messing with her crayons and pretended she was a witch, treating poor Roadblock like a voodoo doll."

"Voodoo and witchery are two totally different things." Everyone turned to Avery, who flushed. "What? They are."

"Roadblock, huh?" Tex looked at Reggie with interest. "Hmm. I wonder where I can find one of those."

"Your turn to be Ken, I'm thinking," Brad said, fervently wanting everyone to start picking on someone else.

"So, Avery. You just here for the sex? Should we go?" Mack asked, super polite.

Tex snickered. Reggie cracked a smile.

Avery sighed. "It's like in another life I was a complete ass, so in this life, I'm constantly either tripping over my own two feet or embarrassing myself."

"You're saying Brad's your punishment." Mack nodded. "Makes sense."

Brad wiped a hand down his face. "You probably want to go now, don't you?" he asked her.

"Depends. I've earned a day off and a raise, so I'm treating myself to fun."

"A raise? Nice." Tex held up his glass of water in a toast.

"A raise? Congrats." Brad kissed her in front of everyone, aware the guys were staring and not caring. "That's awesome."

She flushed. "Yeah, well, I also got an offer for a twenty-minute regular Friday Feature. Streaming live on our new-and-improved streaming channel." She swallowed loudly. "And apparently I was on *TMZ* last night. That clip of me and Banana. I'm getting kind of popular. It's weird."

Brad didn't like the popular aspect so much, but he could see her doing amazing things with it. "Are you happy about it?"

"I think so. Yeah. I accepted the job." She shrugged. "I just hope my dad doesn't freak."

"Oh."

She sighed. "Yeah."

Brad realized they'd been ignoring the guys, so he turned to include them and had a better idea. "This calls for a celebration."

"We should go—" Mack started before Brad cut him off.

"Scrabble and ice cream. Who's for it?"

"I'm in." Tex nodded. "I don't normally go for games where we keep our clothes on, but I want to see how many words Brad knows."

Brad flipped him off.

Reggie grinned. "Count me in. Scrabble over a five-mile run? Hell, yeah." Reggie said.

"Just don't blame me when you lose," Mack said. "Warning for you, Avery, Reggie's a sore loser when he doesn't win."

"Bite me, Air Force."

"I'm sensing sobbers. My favorite kind of losers." Avery gave an evil laugh and cracked her knuckles. "Prepare to go down, gentlemen. I'm a sorceress, or didn't you hear me earlier? And with words, I'm a freakin' queen."

Two hours and much laughter later, Avery had proven herself victorious. "You miserable curs should bow to my righteous acuity in the face of such plaintive doltishness."

"Okay, now you're just being abhorrent." Mack sniffed. "And in case anyone cares, I came in second."

Reggie snorted. "I don't care."

"Me neither," Tex agreed.

"A rat's ass, I could not give," Brad had to add, which made Avery giggle.

"Sorry. I'm heady with my victory. And maybe a little light-headed. Some victory chocolate should do the trick." The sore winner took two and offered Mack, and only Mack, one. "He did come in second. Which is first place…for losers."

Reggie snickered. "True."

"Well, now that I mopped the floor with you big strong guys, I should probably go. Don't want to interrupt the bro time." She smiled as she said it, apparently having changed her mind about aftergame sex, and gave Brad a chocolatey kiss. She then danced toward the door singing queen's *We Are the Champions*. "Text me, my handsome loser. I mean, Brad." She grinned, a hint of chocolate on one tooth. "We can 'hang out' later if you're game."

Then she left.

They sat in silence before Reggie, Tex, and Mack all gave him a thumbs-up.

"Huh?"

"We like her. Keep her." Reggie nodded. "She's good for you."

"And she knows words like 'cazique.'" Mack sounded in awe. "I had to google it. It's a bird in the American tropics, by the way. Next time we play Scrabble, I get her as a partner."

Brad scoffed. "How's that? She's *my* girlfriend."

"Yet her intellect is more along my level," Mack explained slowly.

Tex grinned. "You gotta love when he does that snooty voice."

Reggie nodded. "Oh, I do."

Brad sighed. "Now I have to go convince the woman I'm not as stupid as I look."

"Which is pretty damn dumb," Tex murmured. "Really, Brad? Spellin' 'czar' without the 'c'?"

"Like you knew how it was spelled." Brad had brain-farted. It happened.

"I did indeed." Tex grabbed his hat and shoved it on his head. "And since I can't stand another insult without calling you out, I'm outta here." He winked. "See you at work tomorrow, Romeo."

Mack followed him, a last parting shot over his shoulder. "That ends in an 'o,' by the way."

"Asshole."

Reggie was the last to leave, and he studied Brad for a moment. "Don't treat her like you do the others."

"What does that mean?" Brad had never been cruel or ugly with his exes.

"It means let her get close and see where it goes. Don't break up with her because she likes peas. Or because she didn't put the salt back in the right cabinet. Or because she put on her right shoe before her left."

"What?" Brad suddenly remembered breaking off with women and using those as excuses when teasing with the guys. "Oh, come on. I broke up for better reasons than those. I was just joking."

"Yeah? Because you break up with *everyone* after a few months. Women I actually liked for you, if you want the truth."

"Like who?"

"Sal was cool. She let you be you, but you couldn't take her laughing all the time."

"She laughed at weird stuff." Funerals, death, balloons. Sally had been gorgeous but a little flighty.

"Bailey?"

"She wanted marriage. I didn't."

"Why not?"

"I don't know. She wasn't the right one." He'd known it but couldn't exactly explain it.

"Amelia?"

"I can't remember."

"She was the salt chick."

"Oh, right." She'd had a thing about rearranging his cabinets and toiletries. And her intrusive sense sent him packing.

"Look, man. I liked all of them, but they didn't fit you like Avery does. We can all see it. The question is, can you?" Reggie sighed. "And that's my lecture for today. Before you tell me to shut up and get out, I'm leaving." He paused. "And for the record, don't be flattered if some smartass poses a Roadblock *action figure* with a Ken *doll* next week. You're not my type."

Brad flushed. "Ken's not a doll."

"Whatever. Just remember, Avery's not a doll either. You can't throw her away like the others, Brad. She's special."

"Thanks, Dad."

"Fuck off." Reggie paused at the door. "See you tomorrow."

"Later."

Brad stared at the door and wondered about what Reggie had said. Did he really break up with women for no good reason? At the time, he'd felt stifled by them, not ready to commit. Not wanting to commit.

Scared to commit.

He paused, thinking about Avery. Thinking about Dana.

Tired of hearing himself think, he grabbed his phone and his wallet and keys and headed to Avery's, wanting to see the woman growing ever closer to his heart.

Chapter Nineteen

Avery answered the door on the first knock. With Gerty out with Oscar at his mother's house—meeting the parents!—Avery had the apartment to herself for once.

Talk about a heck of a day. A raise, a new—though intimidating—job, fun with Brad and his friends, and now free time. The only thing making her day complete would be an orgasm, but she hadn't wanted to overstay her welcome at Brad's.

A knock came at the door. She answered, hoping but not expecting Brad, and stared at her own Super Hunk FD. He walked toward her, so she backed up.

Once inside, he shut and locked the door behind him. "Can I come in?"

"Duh." She looked around her. "Already in."

He laughed. "I am, aren't I?" He studied her, looking her up and down. "Oscar's introducing Gerty to my mom and Rochelle."

"Yeah. Can you believe she's already meeting the parents?"

He nodded. "Oscar's pretty into her. He didn't take his ex to meet my mom until they'd been going out a few months."

"Gerty's got game."

"She must." He stepped closer. "But as much game as you?"

"I, uh, no. I'm the master." She flexed, her arm pitiful next to his.

He didn't smile.

"Brad?"

Instead, he swung her into his arms and marched down the hallway. He paused by Gerty's room, but before she could tell him hers was the next one, he was already moving. "Yeah, this is more you."

The plain room had an unmade bed, clothes on the floor she'd meant to put away yesterday, and her neatly stacked library books because one did not have disorderly reading content.

He set her on her feet, shut the door, then came back and removed her glasses. "Sorry, these have to go. I was ordered to give the barbarian sorceress a lot of sex."

"Well, that was an order." She nodded and opened her arms. "And you must obey. I beat your ass at Scrabble."

He nodded, solemn. "You also crushed and demoralized my friends."

She paused. "Demoralized?"

"Just Mack, who cares about winning word games. The rest of us were crushed."

He slid his pants down and pulled off his shirt, leaving him in nothing but tight boxer briefs doing nothing to mask his arousal. "But me, I was turned on. Still am."

She let him remove her clothes, slowly, his hands brushing her belly, her breasts, lingering over her hard nipples. Then they were sliding between her legs, her thighs, and back up and inside her. His finger caught in her damp heat.

"And maybe demoralizing everyone aroused you too," he said with a smirk. "You're such an ugly winner. I'm enchanted."

She couldn't help laughing, though he didn't remove his finger. "I'm both turned on and amused. Can we have sex first, then laugh about it?"

"Sure." He lowered himself to the floor, kneeling, and kissed her clit, but he didn't linger. "It's been days, Avery. I'm not gonna last the first time."

She sighed, brushing his hair back as she stared down at him. "I won't either."

"Did you miss me?"

Should she admit it?

Wasn't it obvious?

"I, ah…"

"I asked if you missed me." He drew her down to kneel in front of him, now both of them nearly at eye level. "The truth."

"Maybe." She smiled. "I—"

"Not good enough." He turned her around and pushed her to her hands and knees. Then he shoved her knees wider. She heard a packet rip and after a second felt him angle into her, sitting at the entrance to her sex.

Wet and wanting, she inched back, taking the tip of him inside her.

"I know we're being safe, but I want to get to the point where we don't use a condom," he said, his voice gruff.

"Me too." She had missed him, too much for such a new relationship. "Maybe after—"

He shoved hard and fast, filling her so tight. She gasped and groaned as he rode her, his taking thorough and rough.

His hand fisted in her hair, the small bite of pain making her body quicken. Her breasts swayed as he thrust, and she moaned his name.

"Say it. Tell me you missed me."

"I missed you," she said when he slammed particularly hard.

She clamped down on him, wanting to keep him there.

He inched back and thrust again. "Say it."

"I missed you."

"Again."

He rode her like a damn horse, and all she could say was "I missed you" as she came hard around him, dragging him with her into an explosive climax that left her shaking.

Brad was moving in and out of her with a slow thoroughness. "Fuck, you feel so good." He reached around her to cup her breast. "I can't get enough of you, Avery."

"God, I missed you," she said on a breath, squeezing him with her inner walls.

"Yeah, that's it." He ground up deeper into her. "You make me lose it. I can barely think when I'm inside you."

"I know." She paused, having thought about it a while. "I'm safe. On birth control, and I'm disease free. I just had a physical a few weeks ago and haven't been with anyone since. Well, besides you." *I want you in me, skin to skin.*

"Good." He sighed. "I'm clean too. Maybe we can do this again without the condom." Before she could respond, he added, "But if you need my last physical or something more before you trust me, I'm down. Or if you just want to use condoms, fine. Whatever you need." He shifted inside her. "I just want more of whatever this is between us."

"Yeah." She felt his hands on her shoulders as he withdrew so slowly, only to return with a cool washcloth between her legs.

"No, don't move." He cleaned her, then pulled her gently to her feet. "In the bed. Now."

She raised a brow, liking this aggressive side to her lover.

My lover. My boyfriend. Oh wow, I like him way too much for him to be a mere boyfriend.

Alarmed yet also sated from being taken so thoroughly, she lay down on the bed on her side, facing him. He drew her close for a kiss. Then another. "Reggie told me I should give us a chance."

"What?"

"Do you like peas?"

She had no idea where the conversation had gone, but he kissed her again, distracting her. "N-no."

"Does the salt have to sit next to the pepper?"

His hand found her breast and massaged.

"It should." She sighed. "But doesn't have to." She rubbed his chest, taken with this strength.

"Did you like being with the guys today?"

"I liked being with you." She kissed him this time. "And I'm sorry, but I love your friends."

He stared into her eyes, looking for what, she didn't know.

"But my favorite part of today?"

"Yeah?"

"It's not the raise, the chocolates, or whipping you losers at Scrabble."

His lips quirked.

"It's this. With you." She kissed him, tenderly, showing him how she felt because she couldn't fathom the truth to say it. She stroked his lips, petted his shoulders, his neck, his hair. The strands so soft and silky, like straw turned into molten gold. *Oh my god, I'm thinking poetic thoughts. I'm in so much trouble...*

He kissed her back, patient, loving. And when he pulled her closer, so that she felt all the hard contours of his body, she sighed into his mouth, lost in pleasure.

The kissing seemed to go on forever, Brad a part of her, giving and taking. She didn't mind him rolling them over so that he lay over her. He propped himself on his elbows, keeping his weight from crushing her. But his cock continued to brush against her front, over her mound and lower belly.

"You're so soft." He palmed her breast, slid his hand to her stomach, stroked her belly with care. "So fucking beautiful."

"Brad." She kissed him, the slow burn of desire building once more as he dragged his growing erection over her stomach, sucked her tongue, and kissed his way down her cheek to her neck, then to her breasts.

"I love tasting you here." He sucked one nipple into a tight peak and startled a pleasured cry from her when he nipped the bud with his teeth. Then he turned to her other side and did the same, causing her to writhe, needy and surprised at the depth of her desire.

"And here," he murmured as he played with her nipple. "And here." He kissed his way down her belly and settled between her legs. He parted her folds, staring at her, then licked her clit. "I came in you, so hard. And I'm ready to do it all over again."

"Yes. In me this time, no condom."

"You had me at yes." He moved up her body, kissing her inch by inch, and settled at her mouth as he slid inside her, pausing at the entrance to her sex. "Jesus. You feel so good." He closed his eyes for a second. "You make me lose control. I don't like that."

She arched up as he speared her with one big push. "You d-don't?"

"I like being in control." He held himself over her, their bodies joined. "Usually. But with you, everything goes away but this. Us." He watched her as he made love to her, the connection so intimate she felt more than vulnerable and closed her eyes.

"No, watch me."

She opened her eyes, staring into his. The connection between them snapped back into place.

He moved faster.

She lifted her legs to wrap her ankles behind his back.

"Yeah, that's it. Let me take you. Harder." He slowed his thrusts, making each one deeper. "Watch us." She looked down, seeing him leave only the tip of himself inside her, then shoving back in, until his body stopped and hers began. "I love this." He continued to move, his strokes growing choppy, rushed.

And then he brushed against her clit one more time and she came.

"I love—" His breath caught as he groaned and spilled inside her. So tense she feared he might break, he caged her beneath him as he spent, the jolts of pleasure so damn beautiful.

When he again opened his eyes, he stared down at her, making no move to leave. Instead he held himself on his elbows and swirled his hips.

"Oh." She sighed. "You feel so good." She ran her hands over his thick shoulders. "You're so big."

His intensity faded, and he smiled. "Why, thank you."

"I mean, all of you. Not just your..."

"Dick? Cock? Penis? Snake? Hose?" He grinned at her blush. "I could have won at Scrabble today. You're not the only one with a knack for words."

"Yeah? Well, you forgot tallywacker."

He frowned. "That's not real."

"I read historical romances. It is."

He laughed and started to slide out of her. "Oh. I think I should move."

"I guess." She groaned when he left her. But this time she made haste for the bathroom and returned to find him lying in her bed, still naked. Still drop-dead gorgeous.

And hers?

"In what universe does this happen?" She motioned between them and joined him in bed, squealing when he dragged her over him in a burst of speed.

"There. I needed a blanket."

"Funny."

"What's wrong with 'this'?"

"Nothing. But it's like I'm the smart girl in bed with the quarterback."

"I wrestled. Sorry."

"You know what I mean." She tugged at the light spatter of chest hair, pleased when he winced. "Well?"

"How the hell should I know? I'm a sucker for a sexy woman."

"We went from mortal enemies to boyfriend-girlfriend. How does that happen?"

"Magic? You are a sorceress, right?" He raised a brow.

She had to laugh. "You're not just all brawn, are you?" She remembered some of their conversation earlier. "What was the bit about me liking peas?"

He flushed. "Forget I said that. So, ah, something I want to know."

"Yes?"

"Are you okay with me going to dinner with your parents?"

"Sunday night, by the way. Mom texted me earlier. And yes. That's if you are."

"I'm fine with it." He looked at her hair spilling over his chest between them. "I'd like you to meet Rochelle, actually. She's pretty cool."

"Oh." *Now I'm meeting the parents!* "That would be nice." She smiled at him.

He smiled back.

God, I think I might love you.

She stiffened.

"What's wrong?"

No, not love. Just like. It's too soon. He's too soon. And too much. Too handsome, too hunky, too amazing. And I'm...

"Avery, baby, you okay?"

She forced herself to relax. She'd been overwhelmed by all the terrific sex. That had to be it. "No. I'm a klutz and a spaz. And I magicked you away from your friends."

"How's that?"

"I horned in on your downtime with your buddies." The more she thought about it, the more she wondered at her own audacity.

"And?"

"And then I unmanned them by beating them all—*you* all—at a board game."

Brad chuckled. "We like board games. I love Scrabble, and it was my turn to pick. And yeah, you're magical. So you seduced me into playing. I seduced you right back. We're even."

She studied his smile, his patient eyes. "Even."

He nodded. "Although I did make you come twice. And you only beat me once."

"Actually, I beat you dorks three times. So sad."

"So, what you're saying is I owe you another orgasm."

"What? No." She didn't know if her body could take it.

"Sure I do. You're a chick. You can go for days doing it."

"Oh, that's not sexist at all."

He chuckled. "It's true, right?"

"I mean, sometimes. If I'm in the mood."

Which she shouldn't have been now. Not after realizing she had real feelings for the super hunk, and that she'd gotten in deep without trying.

"And that's my cue. Challenge accepted."

Oh yeah. She was in *way* over her head…

———

Sunday night at dinner, Brad sat in an impressive home in Ballard with the Dearborns. June and Len were as nice as they'd been when he'd met them a week ago. June, an artist, had a creative, upbeat mind. He could see a lot of her in Avery, the uplifting attitude, the wide smile. But Len lived on in his daughter, even if neither father nor daughter could see it.

He witnessed the stiffness when she'd greeted her father, and even now, as he stood next to her while Len grabbed him a drink and the uber professional Erik took his measure, Avery continued to glance from Erik and her mother to her dad, who did his best to ignore her.

What a crappy dynamic.

"So, Brad, you're a firefighter." Erik, tall, slender, with dark hair and dark eyes, wore glasses that made him appear intelligent. Brad disliked him on sight. The guy acted polite, smiled, and hadn't stepped a foot wrong.

He also looked perfect next to Avery, the Woodward to her Bernstein. The jelly to her peanut butter. The… *God, I'm lame.* Reggie would be laughing his ass off if he could hear Brad's thoughts.

"Yeah, I'm with the new Station 44 here in Seattle." Brad

thanked Len for the drink, a disgusting Scotch that seemed more sophisticated than the beer he really wanted.

Avery eyed his drink with a question, but he only smiled before doing his best to listen to Erik blather on about something work-related. As if Brad never talked about anything but fires and emergency calls when he had time off.

Reggie, that bastard, would have loved to know how much he'd gotten in Brad's loop. Ever since his comment about Brad not committing to women for superficial reasons, Brad couldn't stop thinking about it.

He had a real hard-on for Avery. The good kind. And it wasn't all sexual. He thought about her when he wasn't with her. He didn't care if she moved the salt or liked peas. Nothing mattered but seeing her smile or watching her eyes light up when she found something interesting. He'd been learning her tells, and he knew she fidgeted with her glasses and nibbled her thumbnail when nervous. That when aroused, a subtle blush lingered on her cheeks and she had a habit of looking at his chest. Not his face or his crotch but his pecs.

She also loved his body. Couldn't get enough of it in bed and loved when he took charge sexually.

He inwardly sighed, nodded at Erik's banal remarks about needing more paramedics in town, and wondered why memories of Dana tended to crop up when he thought too hard about Avery.

He knew Dana would have liked her. Dana, who loved goofy cartoons and read books until the spines broke, had a lot in common with Avery. He'd been able to tell Dana everything, even emotional crap.

With Avery, he'd shared his feelings about his family. And last night, in bed with her before Gerty and Oscar had returned, Brad had told Avery how proud he was of his brother for dealing with his addiction and how he wished he could be a better man and love his mother without always noticing her flaws.

"But you're human, Brad. It's good to have problems you can fix with yourself. Because that keeps you humble," she'd said and smiled. "Or it should keep you humble. You're a nice person, and kindness is vastly underrated."

For once, being called a nice guy hadn't grated. The compliment had warmed him. Avery saw beyond his physique and his lifestyle. She wasn't a firefighter groupie and didn't want him to further any of her own goals. She seemed to like him for him.

"Right, Brad?"

He blinked at Erik, at a loss.

Avery clutched him by the arm. "You know, Erik, Brad and I were just talking about that, how I have no intention of returning to hard-nose journalism, right, Brad?"

Silence filled the room.

"What's that?" Len asked, frowning.

"Dinner!" June hurried everyone into the dining room.

"Way to drop the bomb," Brad whispered to her as they followed.

"I'm easing him into it," she whispered back.

She wore a shimmery green skirt that reached mid-calf over leather boots, paired with a cute pink blouse. She reminded him of a flower, and he promised himself to buy her pink tulips to show he'd been listening when she'd mentioned her favorite flower on the drive over. Back when he'd been taking a few glances at her full breasts, wondering if her nipples would be as pink as the tulips she so loved.

They sat with her family, Brad and Avery on one side of the long table, Erik facing them. Her father took one end, her mother the other. A retro '60s lampshade overhead accompanied the teak dining table and modern chairs. The whole home had an eclectic feel, as if some big money designer had whisked his or her way through and made everything expensive-looking and chic.

"This place is really nice," Brad said.

June blushed. "Thank you. I designed it myself."

"Really? I would have said you paid a lot of money for a top-notch decorator."

"Suck up," Avery said, not softly.

Erik grinned. "She's good. As amazing with design as Len is with words. You get your abilities honestly, Avery."

She smiled at the guy, and Brad nodded. "She's gifted, all right." He hadn't meant any innuendo by what he'd said, but he noted a side glare from Avery and a frown from her father. "I mean, have you seen her show on Friday mornings? The *Searching the Needle Weekly* pet segment is now super popular."

"Pets Fur Life?" Her father snorted. "Anyone can smile and play to the audience. Avery, you're so much smarter than that."

Brad didn't like the guy's tone.

Avery responded, calm, collected. No doubt used to her father's dismissive attitude. "It's not about being smart. It's about playing to my strengths."

June got up to grab something for the table, already set with fine china, cloth napkins, and real silver, was Brad's guess.

"Let me help you," he said to her mother.

June smiled her thanks. "You can carry the roast."

"You made a roast? You sure you want to stay married to that guy in there?" he asked as they entered the kitchen. The place looked like a cook's dream. Dark-gray cabinets, marble counter-tops, stainless-steel appliances. And a huge kitchen island and prep sink filled with food that smelled so good he felt himself drool. "So, this is where Avery gets her love of cooking."

"She's cooked for you, hmm?" She handed him the roast and grabbed two casseroles in large dishes.

"Breakfast, but she says if I'm good, I'll get a real dinner soon enough."

"Ask her to make her capellini salad. It's amazing."

"I have a feeling she could make cardboard taste amazing."

June laughed. "Do you cook?"

"I can make ramen and hot dogs. Does that count?"

Avery looked up when he entered the dining room once more, her expression one of relief. "No, noodles and hot dogs don't count."

Erik huffed. "Oh, come on, Avery. We had plenty of that in college, and you know you liked it."

Avery gave him a small scowl. "Back when I was a pauper, sure. But now I have a more refined palate." She winked at Brad, who set the large roast down and sat by her again. Right by her side across from dickface, who frowned.

"What's wrong with hot dogs?" Erik gave Brad a look Brad couldn't read.

"You're telling me you eat Oodles of Noodles and franks at your posh place in New York? Really? Is that how you're hobnobbing with the celebs and power players in the Big Apple?"

"Well, no." Erik grinned. "But I still like a fresh New York City hot dog."

"Oh yeah." Len agreed. "Gray's Papaya. The best, hands down."

Erik scoffed. "What? No way. Feltman's trumps Gray's. Hell, even Nathan's is better than Gray's Papaya."

"Well, if you gentlemen would rather eat hot dogs than my rib roast, feel free. But Brad, Avery, and I are sharing this fine food."

Len and Erik looked at the food then at June. "You know, hon, I think you're right. Erik, we should agree nothing beats my wife's cooking."

"First true words you've said all night," June piped back. "Let's eat."

Brad didn't have to be told twice. Fortunately, June took the helm and directed the conversation to upcoming Seattle events and some new plays she wanted to see. Avery and her father managed to have civil conversations about life in the city, and Brad saw them interact like a loving father and daughter for the first time that night.

He was enjoying himself when something licked the hand he

had on his leg. Startled, he immediately looked to Avery, as if she could have done it. Stupid.

Then he heard a little whine. Expecting a small dog, he leaned down to glance under the table and spotted a giant Rottweiler.

"I see you met Salty," Len said with a sigh. "She's in stealth mode, praying someone drops some meat. Erik, don't you dare."

"Both hands on the table, mister," June said, her lips twitching.

"Ha. I told you he was always the guilty one, not me." Avery chuckled and elbowed Brad. "Ignore her and she won't pester you. Give her one bite of any kind of people food and she'll be your shadow. *Forever.* Salty never forgets."

Erik nodded. "True enough. I haven't been here in a year and she's still waiting for me to drop something."

"Gotcha." Yet as Brad peeked at her again, seeing those big brown eyes, he wanted to—

"Brad, never look her in the eyes," Avery warned and tugged him up. "That's how she snookered my dad."

Len scoffed. "I would never corrupt our well-trained pup." At his wife's stern look, he muttered, "Narc."

Avery laughed, the sound free of familial burden, and Brad watched her, feeling that happiness blossom inside him into something more. Then her father broke the moment with some thoughtless comment about Avery looking foolish when she'd tangled with the Lab at the festival and leached the joy from her face.

He wanted to pound the guy—not a great reaction to have for his girlfriend's father—so he kept his gaze on his plate and finished his veggies.

When he glanced up, he saw June watching him with a sweet smile. She winked and dropped something to the floor.

Salty wasn't quiet about eating it.

And Avery wasn't subtle about letting her mother draw her father's attention while she reached for Brad's hand under the table and gripped it tight.

Chapter Twenty

AVERY HADN'T TALKED TO HER FATHER ONE-ON-ONE IN WEEKS, not since sharing dinner before he'd gone to New York. After being around him again, she sadly acknowledged why she hadn't made a better effort to see him.

For just a second there he'd treated her like someone he liked, teasing about her narcing him out. He'd talked *to* her, not at or about her. And that recognition had been amazing.

Yet in the same paragraph he'd belittled her in front of not only her mom but Erik and Brad as well.

Len looked from her to Brad and forced a smile. She could tell. "Say, Avery, could you spare me a minute?"

"Sure, Dad." Great. What would this turn into? More lectures? Opportunities for her to become something worthwhile? An arranged courtship with Erik? She'd been thinking about her relationship with her father for a long time. And none of her conclusions about dealing with him turned out well.

June nodded to the men at the table. "Brad and Erik can help me with dessert in the kitchen. How do you fellas feel about cheesecake?"

"Love it," Brad said.

"Yeah, me too."

June grinned. "That's too bad. I made apple pie."

Brad snickered. "Oh yeah. Your daughter gets that attitude from you."

June laughed, though Erik shot him a less-than-friendly look.

"Come on, Avery," her father said, heading to his study. "I won't keep you long."

She followed him, dread filling her as she walked the proverbial path of parental disappointment. But knowing nothing short of winning a Pulitzer would soothe her father, what choice did she have? Should she even bother trying anymore?

Ensconced in his study, complete with the oversized mahogany desk and bookcases, two monitors and a high-end computer, printer, fax, and landline—likely coded with a direct line to the director of the CIA, she thought with amusement—Len sat at his desk and steepled his fingers in front of him. On the walls behind and around them were pictures of her father in foreign countries, shaking hands with dignitaries, and accepting awards.

In the dining room Avery called an office, she had a poster of George Costanza, a *Seinfeld* character, posing in his boxers on a velvet settee. *The Timeless Art of Seduction.* She and Gerty regularly got the giggles when they looked at it.

Avery sat in front of his desk and waited.

"Honey, I'm really trying to understand you."

No, you're not.

"I spent a week with Erik, and what's he's doing is captivating. He's doing a series of exposes on corruption among our civil servants."

"Oh, so that's why you want him to talk to Brad? To see if he can dig up dirt on one of Seattle's heroes?"

Her father talked over her. "Erik said he'd be happy to talk to some people about getting you in at his paper. You'd have to start small, but you could easily work your way up. You're terrific with research. Even doing what you do now." Something he considered barely better than the scum one scraped off one's shoes.

"I don't want to work there."

"I know it's far, but the city has everything. Nightlife, action, theater—"

"Crime, homelessness, astronomical housing prices."

He snorted. "We don't have that here?"

"Here I have an apartment I can afford with my best friend. My

mother lives nearby." She said nothing about her father, not that
he'd notice anyway. "And I love my job." *I do. I really do.*

The revelation floored her.

She'd been trying to please her father for so long. And though
she kept trying to convince herself she liked what she did, it hadn't
taken. Until now. She was having fun. Emil liked so much what
she'd been doing he'd offered her not one but two raises—small
though they might be. And he wanted her as one of the faces of
Searching the Needle Weekly.

"You write stories about garden parties and Bigfoot sightings."
Her father scoffed.

"Yes, because garden parties interest people. The city is
known for its amazing blooms, something the people here have
a passion for. And it's not Bigfoot. It's Batsquatch, though the
Pacific Northwest tree octopus was seen just two months ago in
Bainbridge Island. I should know. I saw the tentacle tracks." She
did her best to keep from laughing out loud, especially because
she'd really annoyed her father.

He glared and let out a beaten-down sigh. "I'm just about ready
to give up on you, Avery."

"Why don't you, Dad?" Yep, it had finally come to a boil. She
was fucking done.

He blinked. "What?"

"I'm never going to be Erik. I don't want to do what you do. I'm
not Lennox King Junior. I'm me, Avery Dearborn, the new face of
Searching the Needle Weekly's Friday Feature. We help keep the city
in touch with its people. We do human-interest stories, fun pieces
on Pacific Northwest myths and urban legends. And we keep the
joy and love for our neighbors in the news.

"I want to make people laugh and not cringe when they look
for what's new online or in print. Life is about more than immigra-
tion reform and corruption in politics."

"That's right. Pretend it doesn't exist, like so many others, because that makes it all better." He scoffed. "Jesus, are you even my kid? Ignorance is not bliss. Ask anyone who's ever suffered oppression or discrimination."

That hurt. A lot.

"I'm not saying we don't have real problems, Dad. Or that I turn a blind eye to them. I don't. But why does life have to be all doom and gloom? Why can't I be an alternative to the ugliness of life?"

"It's not real."

"It's as real as ripping kids away from their families because an administration is trying to make a point, which I can't even begin to understand. It's as real as the many homeless in our cities, the mentally ill, the poor, the diseased. It's as real as the racism that never goes away, just gets covered up better by those in power. God, Dad, we have a lot of problems in our own city, let alone in our divided country. How about something that has everyone smiling? Or laughing? Or heck, clapping for? Stray animals need homes. People need jobs. Flowers need tending. Children helping and growing, raising awareness of the good in life.

"Why is talking about any of that less important than 'real news'? Why can't it go hand in hand with your kind of story, to show that the world isn't all crime and punishment? It's love and laughter too, Dad. Something I think you too easily forget."

She stood.

"You're just so smart, and I hate to see you not living up to your potential. Damn it, Avery, we paid a lot of money for you to earn that degree you're not putting to use."

Ah, there it was. The old college debt had resurfaced in the conversation. For a minute she'd been worried he might forget to mention it.

"Another underhanded compliment. Thanks so much." She sighed. "I wish, just once, you'd be happy for me and my choices. And for the record, we never had a formal contract outlining that you'd only pay for me to attend school if I worked in the career field of *your* choice. Which is funny, actually, because I *am* working in my chosen major, communications. So technically I should be getting your congratulations." She gave him a bright smile. "Oh, and my new Friday Feature comes with a pay raise, I'm happy to report." She raised a fist. "Yay, me."

Then she left before she gave in to the angry tears threatening to fall.

She should know better. Not once had he ever been happy for her doing what she wanted. She couldn't change him. But she could decide how much of her life he impacted from now on.

She saw her mother out back with the dog, taking care of Salty, and had another moment of apprehension. Were Brad and Erik playing nice? *I really don't need this tonight.*

She found them in the living room facing each other, like two gunslingers at dawn. Or rather, sunset. Keeping herself in the hallway out of sight, she listened in, trying to make out the conversation before she jumped in.

"You two are a couple then?" Erik was asking. "Not a fake pair?" He laughed. "She once tried to foist me off on her parents as proof she was getting out more, back in college. Before we were dating."

Shoot. She had done that.

She heard the back door open but kept her attention on the men in the living room.

"Nope. Avery and I are dating."

"Brad, no offense, but you don't seem her type."

"What is her type, Erik?" Brad had never used that fake polite voice with her, thank God. It sounded threatening, but Erik didn't seem to care.

"Someone like me, frankly. I'm not here to screw with you two. If she's happy with you, I'm happy for her. But I'll be honest. I miss her. I have feelings for Avery, and we have a past. If she's serious about you, I have no plans to get in her way."

Erik was such a jerk. Why couldn't he at least act like a dick and not some saintly guy looking out for an ex?

"Look, man. I get it. You two had writing in common. She loves her dad. You love her dad. Len's clearly crazy about you. But he's not that crazy about her, and that's why you guys will never work out."

Erik blinked. "What?"

What?

"Avery must have liked you a lot years ago when you went out. She's a picky woman, and she's not shallow. You seem like a nice guy."

Why does that sound so hard for you to say, Brad? She peeked around the corner, watching him, wondering if he was being honest or devious because she couldn't read him. And by Erik's frown, he couldn't either. Fortunately, both men were too intent on each other to look her way.

"Avery needs more than nice. She needs someone who will support her dreams, not try to make her into someone her father wants her to be. Did you know she's pretty damn good at her job? At making people smile? She's smart and funny, and she makes me laugh whenever I'm with her. That's a gift. Here she has friends. Family. People who love her."

Her heart quickened.

"You're in New York, right?"

Erik nodded.

"I just don't see her there. I mean, she could go, sure. But didn't she break up with you back then because you wanted to leave and she didn't?"

Erik tensed. "That's true. But we're different people now."

"I get that. But she's chosen to be with me, and you need to respect that." Brad sighed. "I'm not going to go all caveman and beat the shit out of you to prove I can." He looked Erik over, and Erik tensed even more. The poor guy. Brad would wipe the floor with him if he tried. "Avery is special, to me and everyone she knows. To you too, or you wouldn't be trying to get me to back off."

"I'm not—"

"Please. In your shoes, I'd do the same. She's one of a kind, and anyone would be lucky to have her. It's too bad her dad's such a dumbass he can't see how great she really is."

Avery's eyes watered. Brad really did get her. That big, badass fireman with the heart of tarnished gold. She wanted to march out there and tell Erik to get lost. But she held back, letting Brad and Erik have their moment.

Erik gave a short laugh. "Lennox King is nothing short of brilliant. Calling him a dumbass is like—"

"Trying to turn Avery into something she's not," Brad agreed. "And she's not yours, Erik. She's not mine either. She's a woman who can make up her own mind. So, give her your speech if you want. It's wasted on me. I know exactly what I want." He turned to leave the living room, and June hurried from behind Avery, having no doubt heard everything.

"There you two are. I'm sorry. Salty had to go out. But I'm done. Now let me wash up and we'll have pie."

Avery backed away and met them using another route to the kitchen, where everyone gathered. She and her father pretended nothing had happened between them. Brad and Erik did the same.

Avery wanted to laugh hysterically at the awkward silences punctuated by her too-chatty mother, everyone's stilted replies, and Salty's whines.

"You know, Mom. That was awesome. But we need to go," Avery said as soon as Brad finished his dessert.

"Amazing food, June." He smiled, and her mother looked giddy at the compliment.

"Don't swoon, Mom," Avery said drily. "He's not the Viral Viking."

Brad gave her a sidelong glance. "But I know the guy. You want to meet him?"

June nodded, and Avery huffed. "Don't create a monster, Brad. My mom wants to paint him."

"I really do. He's got amazing bones."

Brad gave Avery a wicked grin. "I can't wait to tell him you said that."

Having met the man, Avery didn't think he'd appreciate the compliment, though Rena might.

Avery nodded to her father. "Bye, Dad." She turned to Erik. "Erik, it was wonderful to see you. Thanks for coming to dinner. Have a great flight back." She grabbed Brad by the hand. "I'm so glad you got to meet Brad. He's special to me."

Erik took the not-so-subtle hint. "It was great to see you too, Avery. You have my number. Feel free to call whenever. If you just want to chat or feel like moving to New York…" he teased.

"Never. Seattle's my home." She gave her mom a hug. "Thanks for a terrific dinner. We need to go. Brad's on duty soon."

He didn't look at her, but she could sense his confusion.

Out in his car, he turned and said, "I'm off until Thursday, you know."

"I know." She let out a breath. "But if I had to spend one more minute near the great Lennox King, I might have killed the man. And we had too many witnesses for that."

He grinned, so beautiful, her boyfriend. Her lover. Damn it. Her heart.

"You know how they say to keep a secret a secret?"

"How?" she asked as he drove them back to his place.

"Be the only one who knows about it. Meaning you'd have had to kill everyone in the place. And I liked your mom. Erik and your dad, meh. Me? I'm tough to kill."

"Let's hope so."

"Seriously. I can withstand my brother's foul breath, Mack's dirty socks, and Reggie's manly sweat after a basketball game. Dude is rank."

She laughed. "I really do like your friends." She swallowed. "Better than Erik for sure."

He looked her way before focusing back on the road. "He wants you back."

"He can't have me. I'm taken."

She saw Brad's lips curl, and he reached for her hand to kiss the back of it before placing their joined hands on his leg. "Yeah?"

"Yeah. Klingon is it for me. I swear."

"Smartass."

She leaned over to kiss him. "Brad, I..." *Too soon to say it. Don't ruin the moment, dummy.*

"What?"

"I heard what you said to Erik. It meant the world to me."

He blew out a breath. "Oh. I didn't mean for you to hear it. I wasn't trying to out-dick him or anything."

"You...wait, what?"

"You know, prove my dick is bigger by threatening the guy. It's pretty obvious I could crush him without much effort."

Her manly boyfriend sounded so dang happy about that fact. She squeezed his hand. "We all know that."

"Right." He nodded. "But he needed to know talking to me was a waste of time. You're either with me or you're not. It's your choice, not mine."

"Not yours?"

"Hell, Avery. I'm with you right now. I like being with you."

I love you so much right now. Marry me. Have babies with me. Let our many dogs—no cats—hump your legs instead of mine. She took deep breaths to steady herself.

"You okay? Your glasses are steaming up."

"With annoyance. Sorry. Just remembering what my father had to tell me." She gave him a brief rundown, loving him even more when he sided with her.

"He doesn't know you very well, does he?"

"He doesn't want to know me, and he never will." She paused, and they both said, "His loss."

She smiled at him. "You are getting very lucky tonight."

Silence filled the car, and she looked at him with concern. "You okay?"

"No. I'm in pain. My dick is so hard right now I'm afraid I might come without you. With you is better, for sure."

"You sweet talker."

"I can't help it. You steamed up your glasses, and a few fantasies came to mind."

"Like what?" She asked him questions, like any good investigative journalist worth her salt would. When he told her, she swallowed hard. "Drive faster so we can put your hypotheses into proof."

Brad smiled. "Sure thing, Lois. Just promise you'll wear the glasses."

"Call me Lois again and I'll kick your ass."

"With the glasses on."

She sighed. "With the glasses on, yes. You big weirdo." But she couldn't help grinning as they pulled into his apartment parking lot.

"Hot damn. And as a firefighter, I don't use those words lightly."

―――――――――――

The next three of his four days off, Brad spent time with the guys and Avery. He and Avery had sex every night as his place. And Oscar and Gerty seemed eternally grateful that he gave them space, keeping Avery overnight.

He still worked out with the guys, still played games or included Avery in some, but not all, of his activities. He took their new togetherness with a sense of caution, as did she, asking before committing to spending time together. He didn't want to overwhelm her with too much of the guys—Tex especially. And she didn't want to intrude on his friendship.

They seemed to mesh really well.

Especially in the sack.

He groaned as she bobbed over him, having surprised him with a quick welcome-home blow job in the bedroom after he'd come in to change Wednesday night. With the guys waiting for him in the living room, having to keep quiet about killed him.

She rose after he almost died from a combination of ecstasy and heart failure and licked her lips. "Mmm. I was hungry." She winked and left the bedroom while he hurried to splash water on his face and pretend he hadn't just seen heaven for a few short minutes.

Man, he fucking loved her.

Bam. There it was again. That blasted L-word in conjunction with Avery. Their dinner at her parents' Sunday night had bonded them in an unexpected way. He'd seen what she'd been dealing with her whole life, and while he empathized, he didn't offer pity she didn't want. But he gave her compassion and a shoulder to cry on whenever she needed it—which she'd used the other night after watching *Up*, a freaking cartoon.

Who knew an animated clip of two old people falling in love could be so damn heartbreaking?

He refused to admit he'd been crying a little too.

She made him laugh. She made him mad. And that anger turned to passion way fast. She'd insulted his love of all things Marine Corps by saying the Navy must be superior, and in front of Reggie no less. "After all, the Marines are in the Department of the Nav-eee." Her singsong answer had gotten under his skin. Their relationship had been touch-and-go. The USMC was sacrosanct to Brad's way of thinking.

Then, after their dirty, angry sex, she'd admitted she'd been teasing. That the Marines rocked and everyone else was second best.

Still, he was holding her to that apology until she admitted, in front of everyone, what she'd told him.

He exited the bedroom and found the guys lounging while Avery was nowhere in sight. "Where'd she go?"

"She looked way too smug, hoss." Tex swung a bottle of cola around. "Said she stopped by to say hi then left. She'll swing by tomorrow if she can though. At the station."

Reggie gave an ugly smile. "Where Hernandez and the others will be waiting."

Brad narrowed his eyes at the three troublemakers. "And don't think I haven't noticed a lack of Ken making it with every swinging dick action figure in town. You guys have been waiting for her to come by, haven't you? Some big elaborate scene meant to freak her out."

"Now, Bradford." Tex sighed. "We love you, man. And we really like Avery. Why the hell would we do that?"

"I see you, Mack," Brad said without looking at his partner for tomorrow.

Mack shrugged. "I have no idea what you're talking about."

He and Reggie had air high-fived.

They spent the next hour bitching about B shift, the LT's hard-on for cleanliness lately, and the fact everyone kept wanting to get a dog they couldn't realistically care for without help.

Mack smiled. "But you could, Brad. I bet your girlfriend would watch him for you. Because she lurves your muscles so much."

Tex snickered, and Reggie tried to hide a smile.

"I'm done with all of you. Get out. I'll see you in the morning, bright and early."

"You know it." Reggie and Mack left.

Tex hung back. "Hey, man. Did Bree call you about the calendar? She won't tell me shit."

Brad felt for him. Bree was in no way talking to him again. She'd taken his picture for the calendar and disappeared from Tex's life. "She talked to Avery. Actually, Avery did an interview with her about Pets Fur Life. The calendar will be out next week, and she's already sold a mess of preordered copies and wants to print more."

"Oh, hey, that's great." Tex blew out a frustrated breath. "She ignores me, won't return my calls, and is driving me insane."

"Avery told me she put in a good word about you, about how responsible and helpful you are. But it didn't work, huh?"

"Nope."

"Tex, maybe you should move on."

"I was trying to. I might have if we hadn't had that calendar to do. Now I'm hooked on the witch all over again." He groaned. "Son, I am dyin' over here while you're getting your freak on."

"Not sure what you're talking about."

Tex snorted. "Please. You two were awful damn quiet. Then she leaves looking right smug, and you staggered back into the living room with that shit-eating grin."

Brad flushed. "Oh, shut up."

"I'm leaving. Just thought I'd share how jealous I am."

"That does make me feel better."

Tex shot him the finger.

Brad laughed and waved him goodbye.

And dreamed about Avery and a future he wanted but didn't know if he deserved.

Chapter Twenty-One

BRAD HAD HAD BETTER DAYS. AVERY HADN'T BEEN ABLE TO get free and visit. He and Mack had been balls-to-the-wall busy all day long, including one major accident near the station that had paramedics and ambulances swarming. Teenagers hopped up on drugs driving in a convoy to a party in Beacon Hill.

The paramedics took on the worst cases. Ambulances had been called, and while they waited, Brad and Mack worked on a teenager named Chris, the boy just turned sixteen and driving when he shouldn't have been, hopped up on something.

The boy seized before going unconscious, so they shoved his ass on the gurney and rushed him toward the nearest emergency room.

He'd done his best, but the boy had been unresponsive during the better part of the trip, waking at the end only to turn to Brad with tears in his eyes, weakly calling out for his mom.

"I'm so…sorry." Chris sobbed, his breathing uneven, his pulse weak and growing weaker.

"You'll be okay, Chris. You stay with me."

"Just tried it. The one time. My…birthday."

"I know. You'll get through this."

"Tell…M-Mom. Love her. Didn't mean to…" He passed out again. And this time nothing Brad did woke him up.

"*Shit*. Hurry, Mack," he yelled.

"On it."

Brad provided CPR nonstop, with nothing else to do but pray.

The ER doctor met them as they pulled up, but it was too late. He hadn't saved the boy. Just like Brad hadn't saved that man last year, the small family from a house fire two years ago, Dana…

Brad focused on breathing, on the here and now, staying in the moment so as not to spiral. This was the job. He knew it. Sometimes they lost people, but more times than not they helped those in need. He would concentrate on that.

They returned to the station, not talking, both he and Mack used to tough cases, but the ones with sad endings like this broke their hearts. They had just cleaned out and resupplied their vehicle when they had another call come in.

"It's gotta be a full moon," Mack muttered.

Brad shut off his feelings and forced a smile. "Tell me about it."

By the time their shift ended, everyone had been put through the wringer. He'd gone an hour over and missed Avery's Friday morning segment. He called her to apologize and had to leave a message on her cell.

He drove home, trying to shake off his despair. Fuck, but that kid had been just sixteen. A stupid experiment with drugs had ended a promising life. The boy had wanted his mother to know he loved her. What kind of life had he been living? Had they gotten along and he'd made a mistake? Or had he taken drugs to escape his life and then regretted it? Like Dana had tried to escape.

Dana… He felt so damn sad.

Brad would contact the police department later, find out who'd contacted the mother, and share the boy's last words, hoping it brought the mother peace.

Someone should know the truth, he thought, memories of Dana refusing to leave. Why had she not reached out to him? He could have helped. Or had he been so blinded to her life and what she needed, lost in his own selfish pleasures? He'd been out drinking with friends for the first time in a long time when she'd passed. And that hurt the most. He hadn't helped. He'd done nothing.

Just like with the boy, Chris.

He felt useless, worthless, and didn't want to talk to anyone.

After a shower, he slept for hours.

Revitalized and needing to reconnect, he decided to head to his mom's, in no mood to talk to Avery. He wasn't right, and he didn't want her to see him this way. He thought he might love her, the way he'd loved Dana. A true, deep, lasting love, and a little something more. And that scared the hell out of him, especially today.

On the way to Tacoma, Avery called. "Brad? I'm sorry I missed your call. Today was busy. I heard you guys were slammed."

"You did?" He hadn't planned on picking up, but some perverse part of him wanted her voice to hurt. He needed to know he would never have that kind of happiness with someone else because he couldn't do enough to save those who really mattered.

Except Avery's voice eased him, and that made it all worse.

"Yeah. I called the station and they told me you guys had been working all day yesterday and into this morning. You must be exhausted."

"I am." He didn't want to share what work had been like, so he said, "It was a tough shift."

She must have heard something because her voice softened. "Are you okay?"

"I'll get through it."

"Can I help? Want me to come over? Or do you want space? Tell me what I can do."

Just knowing she cared helped more than he'd thought it would. More than he deserved it to. "I'm going to check in with my mom. Maybe we can get together tomorrow?"

"Whatever you want. Just let me know." She sounded quiet.

"Yeah. Okay." He sighed. "Sometimes life sucks, you know?"

"I know."

"I'd better go."

"I… I'll text you later."

"Okay." He disconnected and drove to his mother's home. But when he got there, he found Oscar in the garage, staring at a bunch of open letters, two boxes scattered before him.

"Yo. Is Mom here? Rochelle?"

"Sorry, man. They're gone. I'm going through this to…" Oscar paused. "You okay? You don't look so good."

"Had a long shift is all. I'm tired."

"How about something to eat?" Oscar watched him, pocketed some papers, then put the rest back in boxes. "I was helping Mom clean up in here and one of the boxes fell. That shelf is for shit."

Brad saw the warped wood. "I'll fix it later."

"I can do it. Before I move out." Oscar smiled. "I'll tell you about it over lunch. But you have to make it."

Brad found he could laugh after all. "You never change."

"Neither do you." Oscar followed him back into the kitchen. "Something bad happened because you have that look."

"What look?" Brad dragged out fixings for sandwiches. "Make your own."

"Yeah, yeah."

He'd make sure to leave his mom some money for the food, always feeling guilty for eating so much. He had as a teenager and still ate like a monster.

As a teenager. Chris.

He blinked away stupid tears, balling up his grief for a life gone in the blink of an eye.

"You want my good news?" Oscar asked.

"Sure." He cleared his throat. "Well?"

"I'm moving out."

Brad hadn't expected that. "Seriously?"

Oscar flushed. "Don't sound so surprised."

"Where are you moving to?" He paused. "Not in with Avery and Gerty?"

"No. We just started dating. Moving in together that soon is the kiss of death."

Brad knew that. He also felt foolish for secretly wishing Avery would then need to move out…and in with him. That they might one day live together, be together, as something more than they were now. Which was what, exactly? A wannabe hero in love with the popular girl?

"You let our daughter die." Dana's mother's harsh words sounded clear as day. He could almost hear her father crying.

Oscar kept talking, and Brad homed in on his words. "...lame-ass living at home with Mom. I need my space, and it's time I was out of here anyway. Maybe Mom and Rochelle can finally come out and be together. You know, share one place?"

"So you're moving where?"

"I'm not sure yet. Maybe, ah, near Fremont. I know a guy."

"If something comes up in my place, you want me to let you know?"

Oscar snorted. "Too rich for my blood. I'd rather not live too close to you either. No offense."

"Whatever."

They made small talk, Oscar mostly about Klingon and Gerty and how the job was really taking off. Brad started to relax.

Then Oscar hit him with a verbal punch to the gut. "You know, I think Dana would like Avery a lot."

Brad choked on his drink. "What?"

Oscar flushed. "I've been thinking about it. It's close to the anniversary of Dana's passing, and you're not the only one who thinks about her. I liked her too."

"She was my best friend." Brad didn't like sounding like a shit, but he owned her grief.

"I know that. I used to be jealous of you guys."

"I didn't know that."

"Yeah." Oscar sighed. "She was so cute, and you guys went everywhere together. Even in middle school, when it's not cool to like girls, she was your best friend."

"I loved her." Loved. Love. Was there a difference? Did it matter when you failed the one who counted on you the most?

"And she loved you. More than you know."

Brad refused to cry again. "I should have saved her. I should have seen how bad it was, but her parents were always on her ass, you know? And she never hinted she'd do anything."

"I know, man." Oscar pulled Brad in for a hug he didn't want.

He pushed his brother away. "I'm good."

"No, you're not. You never are around this time of year. I was so happy when you and Avery clicked. She's good for you."

"She's too good for me." Brad had seen fellow Marines die, friends in combat gunned down doing their jobs. He'd seen the people he couldn't save pass so quickly. But Dana, his best friend, had hurt the most. Gone, but none of them were ever forgotten.

"Look, you need to read this." Oscar handed him an envelope.

"What's this?"

Oscar shook his head. "Just read it." He stood, took his plate to the sink, and left the kitchen.

Brad frowned, the handwriting hard to read. He looked closer and froze, recognizing his name in Dana's flowy script.

Dear Brad...

His mother and Rochelle walked in the door. "Hey, sweetie." Rochelle's broad grin faded. "What's wrong?"

He looked from her to his mother, confused. "Mom, what is this?" He held the envelope to her.

She read it and paled. "Oh, that. It's nothing." Before she could take it away, he dragged it back.

"Vivienne, what is it?" Rochelle seemed confused.

"It's a letter from Dana."

Rochelle gaped. "Dana? Dana Crawford, that Dana?"

He nodded.

Rochelle gripped Vivienne's hand. "Viv, where did that come from? Did you know about it?"

"I...yes. It arrived after the poor girl died. About gave me a heart attack." She wouldn't look at Brad, her attention on Rochelle.

Oscar walked back in, saw his mother, and blew out a breath. "Oh boy."

"Wait." Rochelle frowned. "Viv, how long have you had this?"

"Yeah, Mom. How long?" Brad stood, confused and angry. And growing angrier. "Did you know about this the whole time?"

"You were hurting. You needed to heal, and Dana makes you sad. I wanted you to recover, Brad. The way I never did with your father."

"Oh, please. Not this shit again."

"Brad," Rochelle said. "Not helping."

He ignored everyone and read the letter.

Dear Brad,

I know by now you're reading this because I'm gone. I don't know when I'll go, but right now the snow is out and it's cold. Everything's hibernating, waiting to wake up again. But I'm so tired. I just want to sleep. Forever. I think about it all the time now, and some days I think it'll be my last. But I'm a coward, and I go on living.

I missed you so much when you went away, and now you're back and you're not the same. You're sad, and it kills me because I can see your pain. But you're still always here for me, and I hate it. I hate that I'm a leech, like my mother. Because I refuse to take you down with me. You're the best of us, Brad, and I want so much more for you than bad memories and guilt.

But this letter is about blame. And I blame them. I can't take Mom and Dad anymore. I'm twenty-four years old and I feel like a child, unable to talk back or fight for my rights. I just can't keep living inside, away from everything and everyone, while Mom clings and Dad barks at me for not being perfect. I want to please them. I love them.

I hate them. So much.

Why can't they just love me for who I am? The way you do.

You're going to be mad at me for a long time. I know you. But Brad, it's not about you. It's about me, what I want, for once. I did bad things, and I liked it. I hurt myself, but it was my choice, and that opened a door for me, showed me that drugs aren't always bad. I flew into the sky and floated for hours, for days, and I was blessedly alone. It was like heaven, if there is such a place. But then the drugs wear off and fear returns, and I come home. And I hate myself a little more.

But I've made my peace, and it's my choice. A choice you'd try to talk me out of, but I don't want that. I want you to live your life. To go be big, brave Brad. Be happy. Do it for me. Find a girl you love with your whole heart. Not like we were, but with a deeper love. The kissing kind that lasts. (Ha. You were good at kissing.) I wish we could have had that, but we both know our love was different. It was pure, and the most important thing in my world.

In my next life, I'll look you up. And if there is an afterlife after all—I still say there isn't—I'll watch over you. I swear. I love you so much. Please don't be mad at me for too long. Know I'm at peace, and that this was my choice. Find your peace, Brad, and when you do, never let it go.

Love, Dana

PS. For fuck's sake, do NOT let my parents guilt you about this the way they've guilted me my whole life. If anyone should get the blame for me leaving, it's them.

Brad read the note again, disbelief making him blind to the tears running down his face. "You knew, all this time, and you never told me?"

Vivienne crossed her arms over her chest and looked at him,

finally. "How many times have you told me to put the past in the past? This is sad and ugly. Dana was beautiful. Remember her that way."

"She's fucking dead! How do you think I remember her? As my best friend who intentionally overdosed and died."

"Brad?" Rochelle stepped closer. "What did the note say?"

"Read it." He pushed it to her.

She read it while he paced, clenching his hair, so mad at his mother he could punch holes in the wall.

"I felt guilty for years, thinking I could have done something to help her. She planned to kill herself long before she did it."

"Oh, Viv. You should have given him this," Rochelle said sadly. She looked at his mother, her disappointment clear. "Why would you hide this?"

Viv snapped, "He had breakdowns when he came back. She pushed him over the line. We all saw it." She looked to Oscar, but he didn't react. So she looked back at Brad. "I never wanted you to feel guilty, Brad. I wanted you to get over the grief. The way I never could. You were always so strong that when you shattered, it killed something inside me."

"Oh sure. Let's let it be all about you again." He sneered. "What the fuck, Mom? Dana was my best friend. Since *the second grade* we'd been best friends. She meant everything to me. Don't you think knowing she was at peace with her decision, not scared or frightened or in pain, would have helped?"

"She'd still be dead." His mother paused. "I know what that's like, wishing for that. I was a lot like Dana growing up. Death sometimes seems like the answer. I understand her, and I pity her."

He'd spent so many days and nights envisioning a terrified Dana, unsure what to do or say, alone, without him for support, making the only decision left to her. While he still didn't agree with what she'd done, he was glad that for once in her life, she'd made her own choice. Even if it was the wrong one. "Her parents bullied her for years. Made her do what they said when they said it. She lived a nightmare. All their warnings about what might happen if their good girl stepped out of line came true."

Oscar shook his head. "Poor Dana."

"Yeah." Brad wanted to blame someone. But her parents? His mother? God? Nothing made sense, especially not the relief he felt for not having failed her.

"You see? Knowing it makes no difference. She's gone, Brad." His mother tried to reach out to him, but he pulled away.

"It makes all the difference." And the anger came, the realization that Dana had planned it. It hadn't been a mistake she couldn't take back; he couldn't talk her out of it. Not now. Dana had lied, just like his mother. "No. I've dealt with a lifetime of your so-called truth. You bury your head, hiding from what makes you uncomfortable."

"Brad," Rochelle cautioned.

He'd had enough. His mother wanted to meddle with his life? He'd meddle with hers. "Since Dad died, you've lived with that grief. And when that wasn't enough, you forced us to live with it. Hell, Oscar never even knew him."

"He was your father. You will respect him," Viv said in a burst of strength.

"Oh, I do. It's you I don't respect." He sneered. "You say you loved him, but how did you show him? By letting your seven-year-old raise your son until your friend came in to take over? Life has always revolved around *you* and what *you* need. You know who helped Oscar when he was little? Me. Who cleaned up our messes when you were locked in your room, crying about the old man? Me. And then Rochelle came into our lives, and I finally had a break.

"Because *she* helped us. Rochelle saved me when I nearly lost it. She held me when Dana died and I could barely function. Not you. You were too busy worrying about your damn self."

"Oh, Brad. No, honey." Rochelle tried to stop him, but he would no longer be silent.

"And after sixteen fucking years of loving you and putting up with your shit, she's still living in the shadows because you're too weak to stand up and admit you love her. I am so done with you, I just can't…" He grabbed the note from Rochelle and stormed out of the house.

He was so angry. Betrayal stung, and he felt helpless because he'd just yelled at a woman who could barely handle a stiff breeze without blowing over. And his dead friend had sincerely thrown him for a loop.

"And fuck you too, Dana." He got into his car and drove.

And found himself at Avery's apartment.

———

Gerty answered the door because Avery was in the middle of getting changed. The day had been beyond productive, and Avery actually looked forward to hosting the Friday Feature next week. Twenty minutes! She couldn't wait. No, she could. What if she made an utter fool of herself though?

According to Alan, she'd drum up more media gold.

The jerk.

She smiled.

"Avery, someone here for you. I'm leaving. Bye."

"Gerty?"

She pulled her sweatshirt down over her pajama pants, set to relax for the weekend since Brad needed some space. The poor guy. He'd obviously had a bad day, and as much as she wanted to race over and offer comfort, she worried she'd be too much in his face if she did. She'd never dealt with this before, helping a boyfriend through a bad day. Not a bad, these-edits-are-impossible day, but more like a someone-died-on-my-watch day, because she had a feeling it had been more like that.

She walked out into the living room and stopped when she saw a towering, smoldering Brad Battle. He looked so mad. Not sexy mad, scary angry.

"Brad?"

Then she saw the expression in his eyes, wounded, confused, so incredibly hurt.

She hurried to him and offered the best hug she knew how to give. "Oh, Brad. I'm here."

He hugged her back, then scared her when he started crying. Silent tears wet her shoulder, and she just kept hugging him, wishing she knew how to help.

She finally managed to get him to sit on the couch. "What's wrong?"

"Everything." He laid his head back and stared at the ceiling.

He said nothing else.

"You can tell me." *I won't judge you.*

"I... Can I just sit here with you?"

He sounded so damn sad. Her heart broke for him. "Sure." She had no idea what the hell had gone down today. Would it be wrong to call one of the guys? Would that be intrusive though?

She sat stroking his hair, and he closed his eyes.

She thought he'd fallen asleep when he started talking. "A boy died in my truck today. His birthday. He'd just turned sixteen, thought trying a new drug would be a good way to celebrate with his buddies, and died. We fished him out of a five-car wreck."

"Oh my God. I'm so sorry."

"Then I found out my mother hid a note from my best friend who died. Dana killed herself, something she'd been planning for months. I thought it was my fault, that I should have been there. But it turns out she did it because she was tired of living, tired of her fucking abusive family."

Avery froze.

"That's why I was so freaked out when you did that article five years ago. I'd just come back from hell on earth. Had buddies die, but I was holding on. We all served our country with pride, and I wouldn't demean them by not respecting them in life and in death."

She blinked back tears, listening.

"But I had Dana. My best friend forever." He wiped a stray tear. "Even when I came back kind of messed up, we connected. Were friends. But fuck that. She killed herself. Her parents blamed me for driving her to it. They said when I was gone she missed me, and if I would have been here it would have been different." He swore some more. "I wasn't anyone's hero. I didn't want you to praise me because I felt like shit. But I got over it. Mostly."

"That's good."

He turned to look at her, finally, his eyes watery, bloodshot. "You'd think, right? Except today I learned Dana meant to die. She was thinking about it for months and never told me. I should have seen it."

"Really?"

"Really. She was my best friend. I should have helped her. Should have done more for that kid yesterday too," he muttered.

Oh boy. Brad had a bad case of hero complex, and she felt for him. But she had no idea what to say, and the guilt was eating him.

She tried the one truth that might get through to him. "You can say all you want. Feel all you want. That's your right. But Brad, you have people who care about you. Who love you."

He stared at her, unblinking. There yet not there.

"I love you," she said softly, not sure he'd heard her.

He drew her close for a kiss, and she felt him tremble under her lips. Then he gently pushed her aside and stood.

"I'm sorry. I shouldn't have come."

"It's okay. Do you want to stay? Or take a nap? You can use my bed."

"No." He sighed. "I should go home. Get some rest. I... Sorry I unloaded on you like that. It's been a bad couple of days."

"It's okay." She wanted to hug him again, but he seemed distant. So she kept back. "Call me when you feel better, okay? And whenever you need me, I'll be there."

He watched her, the Brad she knew hidden behind a flat stare. He nodded, turned, and left.

And she could only watch him go, helpless, not sure if she'd helped him or hurt him more with the truth. That she loved him.

A sentiment he hadn't said back.

But hey, time would tell, wouldn't it?

Chapter Twenty-Two

IT WAS OFFICIAL. BRAD BATTLE TRULY WAS AN ASSHOLE. AVERY had offered support. Tried to be there for him in his time of need. When the great Brad Battle had been knocked down, she'd offered a shoulder to lift him up.

And then the fucker had ghosted her.

Two weeks and not a word. Just one text the day after he'd visited saying thank you and that he needed time.

He still went to work. His brother still dated Gerty. Oscar remained kind, funny, and frustrated because Brad had become distant with everyone. After sharing a more in-depth lowdown on what his mother had done by holding back the note, Oscar had also told them Vivienne wasn't talking to anyone either. Rochelle was taking a break, disgusted with her for the first time in their long relationship.

And the only thing Tex would tell Oscar was not to worry, that they were taking care of Brad.

"He's *my* brother, but his friends are taking care of him," Oscar complained to Gerty while Avery nodded with sympathy. "It's like Dana all over again. He's my big brother, but everyone else is entitled to help him but me."

Gerty scowled. "We should kill him."

Oscar sighed. "I can't. Not again. It felt weird last time."

Avery stared from one wacko to the other.

"On the computer," Gerty explained. "I had a buddy write him into the beta test I'm doing and let Oscar kill him. It turned awkward and...never mind."

Oscar was blushing.

Avery didn't want to know.

"I hate feeling helpless," Oscar growled. Klingon cocked his head, growled back, then pounced on Oscar offering sympathy licks.

Avery glanced at the dog, then at Gerty's gooey-in-love face. *Well, hell.* "You're keeping him, aren't you?"

"What? Oscar? Oh yeah. He's a keeper."

"The three-legged one."

Both Gerty and Oscar looked down at his crotch.

"Oh my God. I mean the dog!"

The pair snickered.

Gerty confessed, "The adoption went through last week. I'm so sorry! I meant to tell you, but then your archnemesis was back to being an asshole—sorry, Oscar."

"We're back to archnemesis and not Super Hunk FD?"

"No," Avery growled. She wanted to punch him in his big fat head. "His idiot friends have circled the wagon. No one will talk to me. I mean, if he's breaking up, he should at least do it to my face. We had sex, you know. That's getting pretty damn close."

"Uh-oh. She's cursing again." Gerty sighed. "I wish Alan were here. He's been so good with his diagnoses lately."

"He sucks too." Avery started pacing.

"It's the penis, right?" Oscar asked. "We all suck to you."

"Yes, it's the penis." She fumed.

Gerty kissed her boyfriend and whispered loudly enough to be heard by the entire complex, "Why don't you take Klingon with you for a long walk? I'll text you when it's safe to come back."

Avery rolled her eyes. "I can hear you."

"Okay," he whispered back as loudly. Then the jerk kissed Avery on the forehead. "I'm sorry, Avery. He's being a dick, and you don't deserve it. I know he really likes you. He'll come around."

Her eyes blurred. "Thanks." *For nothing. Who says I even want him anymore?*

"I'll be back later." He grabbed Klingon and some pet supplies and left.

Gerty put on water. "For hot chocolate." She pointed to the kitchen table. "Sit and talk to me."

"Why? You've heard all my bitching already. He had a bad day. A really bad day. Comes to me to vent. I listen. Learn his girlfriend killed herself. Oh. My. God. Talk about a bomb to lay on me. But he's grieving, so what do I do?"

"You listen." Gerty stood by the counter.

"I listen. I offer support. I tell him I fucking *love* him. I don't ask for it back. I'm being supportive. Then he kisses me once. Gets up like a ghost, floats away. A text the next day saying thanks. *Thanks?*" she yelled.

"What an ass," Gerty agreed. "He should have said thanks very much. Like, a lot of thanks."

"You're not helping," she snapped.

Gerty zipped her mouth closed.

"Two weeks and not a peep. I know he's having a hard time. But he could at least call." She blinked to stop herself from crying again. She hated crying! "He missed my first Friday Feature. And I killed!"

"You totally did." Gerty paused. "Sorry, pretend my lips are still zipped."

Avery sighed. "What did I do wrong?"

"Nothing. He's being a stupid man. He won't talk to his mom or Rochelle. Is icing out his own brother, which is making Oscar so mad. He and I have been talking about Brad a lot. Oscar told me he was tempted to drink, so he went to a few extra AA meetings."

"Good." Avery liked Oscar more and more. Such a great guy… who talked about his problems instead of wallowing in misery.

"Oscar is pissed. I don't know how much longer he'll wait to yell at Brad."

"I hope he does," she muttered.

"What about you?"

"Me?"

"How's it going with your parents? You said your mom is calling again. But your dad is still radio silent?"

"Yep. And I don't care anymore. I'm done trying to make him happy. Done trying to love a man who doesn't deserve me." She wiped her stupid cheeks. "I hate that I still love him. Why him?"

"Oh, you mean Brad."

"Yes, I mean Brad." Avery hiccupped. "My dad's an ass. Nothing I do will ever make him happy. But Brad. Is this payback for the interview five years ago?"

"Now that's just stupid. Sorry. He's being an ass, but even he's not that immature to make you fall in love with him then ghost you. I mean, it's ingenious and evil. Something *I* might do. He's not devious enough."

She sighed. No, her Boy Scout of a boyfriend wasn't. What he was she didn't yet know. But her notebook of insults had room for more. "I'm getting the book."

"Good. I came up with a few more names we can call him."

"It's almost full. You've been very creative." Avery got up and hugged her friend. "I love you, Gerty."

"I love you, too."

She yanked Gerty's hair.

"Ow, ow, ow. Let go."

"Adopting a dog without my say-so? I'm bringing the pain. It's in the contract."

"A roommate agreement on a sitcom is so much funnier than when you do it in real life," Gerty said, rubbing her sore scalp. "I have a few insults for you too."

"Don't make me tell Oscar about your sordid cybersex with our landlord."

Gerty's eyes widened. "You wouldn't."

"No, I would never do that. But I scared you, didn't I?"

"That was really wrong. Just evil." Gerty laughed. "No wonder we're best friends."

Two days later, on a bright and sunny Sunday afternoon, Oscar looked in the rearview mirror of his truck at Klingon in his crate, all buckled up in the back seat. "Yeah, we've had enough of his abuse."

Klingon panted, overjoyed to be in the car, one of his favorite places on earth.

"Time to take control of the situation."

Klingon barked.

"Good dog."

Oscar had mentioned he had some errands to run, so he and Gerty were spending the afternoon separately so they could work out some gaming "kinks" later when they went to bed together.

Avery normally put on music while she slept, keeping the noise loud enough so she could hear nothing but Gerty's muffled giggling if she heard anything. Feeling for her, Oscar was close to signing on the dotted line for his new place, a small efficiency near Gerty and Avery's pad. He had enough to afford it, living by himself. And they took pets! And, well, he'd offered to do the heater/AC repair work for free. That helped.

Avery had been a champ, never complaining when he stayed over, giving him and Gerty space, and never throwing in Oscar's face what a fucking bastard Brad was being.

Every time he thought of how his brother was treating Avery, he wanted to punch him in the face. Gerty had shared details Avery didn't know he knew. The big L-word out there, and Brad just let it hang.

He pulled into his brother's apartment complex and saw Reggie's car. "Too bad. We're going in."

Klingon wriggled.

Smiling at his new best friend, Oscar picked him up and walked him on nearby grass to do his business. Then he looked around and, seeing no one nearby, hurried into Brad's complex. He didn't bother knocking on the door and walked in the middle of an argument between Reggie and Brad.

"Sorry, Reggie. I need to talk to him."

Reggie paused, took a good look at Klingon, and smiled. "Hey, guy. I know you."

Klingon barked.

Oscar put the dog in Reggie's arms. "Can you watch him for me while I talk to Brad?"

Reggie looked at the brothers and sighed. "Sure. Text me when it's safe to come back."

Almost what he'd said to Gerty the other night with Avery.

Oscar nodded.

"You don't have to go," Brad told his friend, ignoring Oscar.

"Quit being such a pussy. Talk to your brother." Reggie walked away with the dog, quietly closing the door behind him.

Brad sighed and waited with his arms crossed. "Well? Say what you came to say, then get out."

Oscar walked up to his brother and shook his head. Then, before Brad could guess his intent, he hit him. Hard.

Brad clutched his face. "Ow. What the fuck!"

His cheekbone had to hurt because Oscar felt like he'd busted his hand. "Jesus, you have a rock-hard head. Hit me back and I'll geld you." He glared.

Brad went to put ice on his cheek. "Get out."

"No. I'm done. You treat me like crap all the time. It's over. I'm going to say my piece and you'll never have to hear from me again."

Brad gaped. "What are you talking about?" He looked Oscar over. "Are you drinking again?"

That was all Brad needed. His little brother off the wagon

on top of all the emotional trauma he'd been dealing with since Dana—fuck, since *Avery*—had told him she loved him.

"Fuck. You." Oscar clenched his fists, looking angrier than Brad had ever seen him. "I'm still sober, asshole. No thanks to you. First it was Dana. You and your bestie playing games and having a blast. I was a burden, nothing more." *Where the hell was Oscar getting this?* "But with her you'd laugh and hang out. I tried. God knows I tried, but you never let me in. You left for the Marine Corps. I had issues. I drank. That was on me, not you," Oscar said before Brad took the blame for that too. Why not? Everything seemed to be his fault lately. "You came back sad. I wanted to help. But no. Because your pain is precious, and you can't let it go."

"That's a cruel thing to say."

"But true. You're always the guy responsible, aren't you?"

"I'm what Mom made me. She was too busy moaning for Dad to come back from the grave. You needed someone to care for you."

"But you didn't really care. You never really wanted me around."

Brad frowned. "That's not true, and you know it." Where the hell was this coming from? Was everyone out of their mind lately?

"It felt true. Then and now. You come back from Iraq, you go to Dana. You ignore me. You find new friends in the fire department, and you're thick, man, tight." Oscar made a fist. "I try to join you, you look at me like I'm trash."

"That's not true at all. You were drinking back then, and—"

"*No.* No, I never came to you drunk. I wanted you to love me. And you shit all over me."

Brad started to panic when his brother, who never shed a tear, looked a little emotional. A lot emotional. "What is wrong with you?"

"Asshole. You won't let me in." Oscar rushed him, grabbed Brad by the collar of his shirt, and clung. And he was stronger than he looked. "I'm here for you. I want to help. Why do you keep shutting me out? What do Tex, Mack, and Reggie have that I don't?"

"Nothing, okay? Why are my problems about you?"

"Exactly." Oscar pushed him back. "Why is Mom's grief about you? Why is my drinking about you? Why is the fact Rochelle and Mom aren't out about you?"

"I don't—"

"Why is Dana's death about you? And Avery. Why is the best thing to happen to you in forever being ignored? By you."

"I... Look, none of this is your business."

"Fuck off. It wasn't your business when I was pissing myself drunk, but you had no problem dragging my ass to rehab. The way I see it, you're so used to feeling guilty about everything and having to save the fucking world that when you don't have to, you don't know what to do with yourself. Dana's dead. Not your fault. Marines killed by the enemy. Not your fault.

"Now, Avery upset because you left her? Not letting her in? *Totally* your fault, you asshole."

Brad clenched his jaw and winced when it pulled at his cheek. "Not your business."

"I'm dating Gerty, her best friend. I hear things."

Brad's nerves jumped. He couldn't eat. He couldn't sleep. He'd been exercising like mad lately to get a little peace, and he'd lost weight despite gaining muscle. "What things?"

"Why did you ghost her?"

Blame ate at him. "I didn't, I—"

"Stop lying, to me and yourself. Yeah, I'm an expert at it. So don't blow smoke up my ass. You had a kid die on you, then you found out Mom had lied and that stuff about Dana. You go to Avery to feel better. Then you never talk to her again."

"It's not like that."

"Bullshit. Did she make a move? Try to come on to you while you were upset or something?"

"No." She'd been kind. Sweet. Loving.

"Then what? Because my relationship isn't doing too well because of you."

Brad hadn't considered that. "I'm sorry, man."

"Don't be sorry. Just tell me the truth *for once in your goddamn life.*"

Furious at being lectured by yet another person who supposedly loved him, Brad answered, "*Fine.* She told me she loved me, and I bolted. Happy now?"

"But why?" Now Oscar just looked confused.

"Because… Because…" Brad slumped against the counter, his cheek throbbing. "Because I couldn't take it. Dana loves me and kills herself. Mom loves me and lies to me for fucking years. Then Avery loves me? Great. What's she going to do to me? Stab me? Steal me blind?"

Oscar sat in the kitchen. "Huh. Hadn't considered that angle."

"What?"

"I thought she said she loved you and pressured you to hear it back. Or she got all clingy or bitchy or something."

"No. She was nice."

"Pushy?"

"Kind." Brad sighed. "Sweet. I just needed space."

"But you couldn't tell her that. You blow her off for two weeks, don't even come to her big deal last Friday, and—"

"I came. I was there. Drove over with Tex and watched while we rode Aid 44. She was awesome." He paused. "I sent her flowers."

"No, you didn't."

Brad frowned. "Red roses with pink tulips. I did too."

"Huh."

"What does that mean?"

"I heard she got them from her coworker. Some guy named Alan?"

"That douche?" Brad snorted. "*I* got her the flowers."

"And she would know this how?"

Brad felt stupid. "They were red roses mixed with pink tulips. Tulips are her favorites, and the red because… Well, they look nice."

"So?"

Brad flushed. "Red roses mean you like someone. A lot. And she likes tulips."

"I like Gerty. Got her yellow roses to prove it."

"Dumbass. The roses are for love, okay?" Brad flushed. "They weren't cheap."

"And she has no idea you got them for her or even came to see her. Why bother?"

"Because it was important."

"Was it? Brad, what happened to you? My brave big brother who never let anything stop him from getting the job done. Complete the mission. Kiss the girl. What the hell are you doing?"

"I...don't know." Brad frowned. "I wasn't in a good place. I was kind of freaking out."

"Kind of?"

Brad glared. "When she told me she loved me, it got all messed up with the other fucked-up things I was dealing with."

"Is that why you won't talk to Mom or Rochelle? They're worried." He saw Brad's guilt "And they're not talking, by the way. Rochelle is really mad at Mom, and Mom's miserable."

"Good. She deserves it."

"Yeah? So do you."

Brad heard the anger. "Look, Oscar. I love you. I'm sorry if I acted like I don't. I just always felt so responsible to make sure you were okay. I guess being with Dana was not having to be a dad at age seven." He sighed. "I kind of grew up believing I had to help everyone. I helped you, Mom, Dana. My Marines." He thought about it. "But Avery is independent. She never leaned on me. Hell. I leaned on her more."

And he felt like shit for it.

"That's what love is, dumbass. Learning to accept help. To give and take. Man, you need therapy more than I do."

"Maybe." Brad felt terrible. "I don't know if Avery will forgive me."

"Would you?"

"If I really loved someone."

"Do you forgive Mom?"

"I will. Someday."

"How about Dana?"

"Yes. I was mad, but she had problems. Her parents…"

"Trust me. We were neighbors. I know." Oscar studied him. "What if you'd told Avery you loved her? You worked up the courage to lay your feelings on the line, and she left and never called you back."

Brad cringed. "I… I don't know. That would kill me."

"Congratulations. Now you know how she's been feeling since you crushed her. You've been a major ass. Are you still into her, or is it over? And if it's over, just have the decency to tell her to her face, okay? Because what you did is not only weak, it's cruel. And the Brad I know isn't like that."

Oscar was forcing him to see some hard truths. That it had taken his brother shamed him.

A slug to his arm hurt. "Stop hitting me."

"Then stop being a butthead."

"Butthead? That's all you got?"

Oscar smirked. "Oh, there's a whole book of insults dedicated to Avery's archnemesis."

Brad sighed. "I blew it."

"Totally. Now learn from your mistakes. Step one. Accept help and don't be a dick about it. You were a major asshole. I'm helping you to recover. It's okay to take my hand and take a step." He held out his hand.

"Don't be stupid."

"Take it, dickless."

Brad glared, but he reached out.

"Finally. One step at a time and we'll have you married before you turn sixty."

"Marriage?" Brad didn't know if he was ready for that. But he sure the hell was ready to get Avery back in his life. Letting himself dwell on how much he'd hurt her was worse than Dana's letter.

Find a girl you love with your whole heart. Well, he'd found her. He only hoped he hadn't destroyed the fragile emotion when he was finally ready to embrace it and all it entailed.

Oscar hit him again.

"Damn it. Cut it out."

"Work with me. I'm going to help you get your girl. And you will owe me for the rest of your life."

"Maybe I don't want her back." Even saying it felt wrong. "I do. I really do." Brad sank to the floor, his head between his knees. "Man, I fucked it all up. She'll never take me back."

"Forgiveness, Brad. It's a part of love. If I can forgive you for being a closed-off idiot, she just might forgive you for crushing her soul to nothing and living a literal hell on earth." He smiled. "Okay?"

"You are the absolute *worst* guidance counselor."

"Hey, I'm free. You get what you pay for." Oscar grabbed his phone from his pocket. "Can I text Reggie to come back, or do you need more time to pity yourself?"

Brad flipped him off.

"Great. Now let's help you unfuck your life." Oscar gave him a big grin. "Say it."

"What?"

"You know the magic words."

Brad groaned. "Seriously?"

"Say it."

"Oscar is great."

"Outstanding. Now say it again. With feeling."

Chapter Twenty-Three

FRIDAY NIGHT, AVERY STARED AT THE TELEVISION AND SIGHED. She'd been sighing a lot lately. Gerty had asked if she had developed asthma and, if not, to stop breathing so damn hard.

Which, okay, was kind of funny.

She dug through her rocky road, chosen specifically because she loved chocolate and because Brad hated nuts.

Her eyes watered. *Why? Why do the men in my life not want me?*

Stop. End scene. Too dramatic.

She could almost hear Gerty and Alan applauding her theatrics and stopped herself from going over the edge.

Erik had wanted her. So had several exes. And her father? His loss if he couldn't see how great she'd been doing. She was so done living her life to earn his approval. Emil loved her work. Pets Fur Life had gotten a huge boost between the calendar and her promotion.

And she still missed Brad like crazy.

Gah. Just like that, the man would pop into her thoughts. But Avery didn't need a man in her life. Even one that gave her massive orgasms. She'd bought a toy at one of those discreet shops downtown to help with her needs. She called it Better Brad. But it wasn't, not really, because she had to do all the work.

A lot like my relationship with Sergeant Jackass. Me giving. Him taking.

Except she remembered him seeing to her pleasure first. Including her with his friends. Standing up for her with Erik. Avery sighed.

Again.

She debated bringing out the dartboard for some practice and hung it on the back of the front door. Courtesy of Gerty, Brad's face had been tacked to it, and she was getting pretty decent about hitting him in the eyes. The board had made Oscar laugh and laugh. He'd even hit the bull's-eye twice.

The insult book had filled up. She had no more need of it to relieve stress. Avery had moved on to not wanting or needing a man ever again, watching violent movies on Netflix and doing such a great job at work Emil gushed about her progress.

She flicked through her watch list on TV, not finding a blasted thing she wanted to see.

The door jiggled, and the knob turned. Since only Gerty had the key, Avery turned back to the television. "What did you forget?" she asked.

"To say it back."

She froze, not having expected her archnemesis to walk in the door.

"Gerty lent me her key." Brad said nothing more.

And she sure had nothing to say to his sorry ass. She kept her gaze straight ahead, the back of her head on fire because she could feel his gaze burning a hole through it. She absolutely would not regret the fact he'd arrived to see her looking much less than her best. Her PJs offered comfort, and he could kiss her not-sorry ass.

"I'm here to grovel."

Hmm. That had promise. *No, still not interested.* Yet she waited.

He walked around the couch and stood between her and the TV. When she continued to say nothing, he turned it off. Brad looked handsome and strong yet drawn. He wore jeans and a nice sweater, appropriate since Seattle had forgotten they'd entered early May.

He held two vases full of pink tulips and a large gift bag.

"For you." He put the flowers down on the coffee table.

She looked at them then back at him, giving him the silence he'd wanted. Well, he could have as much space as he wanted too, and damn the hurt that balled in her gut.

"I'm sorry, Avery."

"Great. Get out." She tried to look beyond him at the blank TV screen, doing her best to press the remote, but it refused to turn on.

"It's all my fault." His words rushed together. "You were so great, so nice. I couldn't handle it. I—" He blinked at the dartboard. "Is that my face?"

"Yep." She dug into her rocky road and bit hard through a peanut.

"Ah, okay." He turned back to her, looking...nervous?

"I also have a book of insults, just for you. Leave me a few bucks on your way out and I'll email you a copy."

He groaned. "Avery, I'm so, *so* sorry." He held the gift bag to her. "Open it. Please."

"If I do, will you leave?"

He nodded.

Her heart twisted. But she wanted him gone, didn't she?

She opened the bag to find several gifts buried in the tissue paper. Expensive chocolates. A word-of-the-day calendar. A new *Seinfeld* poster to go with the one in the dining room, this one a portrait of Kramer. Gerty would flip.

Also inside, a small wrapped box. A bit large for a ring, but still, it looked like jewelry.

"Open it."

She did and saw a beautiful pair of ruby earrings she'd envied, having seen them while shopping with Gerty one day. They weren't cheap.

She pushed the box back toward him. "I can't—"

"No, please." He handed her the last wrapped box from the bag, this one the same size as the earrings. "Before you open this one, just let me have my say, okay?"

She wanted those earrings. She didn't want the one-sided attachment that came with them. But if he'd leave, she'd hear him out. Didn't mean she had to forgive him.

"Look, you know what happened to me the last time I was here. I was a mess and should never have come." He dragged the coffee table to sit on it, uncomfortably close to her now.

She edged back.

He sighed. "But I did come to you, because lost out there in my own head, driving around, I wanted comfort. To be with someone I care about. And I automatically drove here." He watched her, looking for a reaction she had no intention of giving. "You were lovely and kind. And then you told me you loved me." His voice cracked. "I, ah, I didn't handle it well."

She couldn't help the huff that escaped.

"It fucked me up," Brad admitted. "Because I didn't think I was ready for that. My mother has loved me forever, and she's never been there for me when I needed her, lost her in own pain. I spent my growing years being a dad to my younger brother. And I was only a kid when that started. It made me pretty responsible at a young age, and it's stuck with me. Through my family, the Marine Corps, and now as a firefighter."

She could see that.

"Oscar came to talk to me. Read me the riot act for not being a good brother. And I deserved it." He brushed a shaky hand through his hair, and she remained perfectly still, now wanting to hear the rest of it. Oscar hadn't mentioned talking to Brad.

"I guess I treated Oscar more like a responsibility than a brother. And I love him. I mean, he's my brother, and he thought I didn't want him around. I did, I just didn't know what I'd been doing to him. I love the guys I work with. They're brothers in the truest sense, but Oscar is my *family,* my little brother. And now he knows he matters the way he should."

Brad reached for her hand and held it tight. She hoped he couldn't feel her clammy nerves.

"Avery, I made a mistake, okay? A big one. Just like I lumped Oscar in with my messed-up feelings, I did the same to you. I had just learned that my mom and Dana betrayed me, the women in life who loved me. Then you told me, and all I could think is, what will *she* do to me? It's like an awful trend."

She had to add, "Yeah, kind of like why do all the men in my life want me to be something I'm not or leave me?"

He flushed. "I deserved that. But Avery, you're different. I know I haven't committed myself in my other relationships with women. Not like with you. You make me feel the way I did with Dana, like I could tell you anything and you'd support me no matter what. And yeah, that sounds like it's all about me again, but it's not. I'm trying to say I trust you. And I love you."

She didn't want to hear it, not when she'd finally decided to ditch him for good. "No."

"Yes," he said and tenderly rubbed her hand. "You scare the crap out of me. You're funny and smart and sexy as hell. I think you're amazing, and the fact your dad can't see that says something about his character, not yours."

That was just one of the nicest things to hear.

She felt herself softening and reached down, deep inside her, to hold onto her self-respect. She deserved so much more than a simple apology. "So, ghosting me until your brother talked some sense into you, that's how we'll work this relationship? Something awful happens and you'll disappear, and I should be okay with that because your friends are there to support you? Well, fuck me."

"No. I'm so sorry. I mean it. I should have called."

She didn't mean to show him, but she felt her eyes burning. "Two weeks ago was the start of my new show, and it meant everything to me. But you wouldn't know that because you weren't there."

"I was there."

"You—What?"

He nodded. "I stood in the back, where you wouldn't see me. Tex and I were on duty, but we swung by and luckily didn't get a call. I caught the whole thing." He cleared his throat. "I gave you flowers."

"You did not."

"The roses and tulips? Those were from me."

"But Alan said he got them."

"He's lying."

"He said…" She thought about it. Alan had actually said, *"Avery, you slayed out there! You're awesome. Oh, and I hope you like the flowers."* She'd been so touched she'd hugged him with thanks. "That liar."

"The flowers aren't important. You are."

She wanted badly to believe him, but she still hurt. "Pretty words, Brad, but actions speak louder, you know?"

He nodded. "I owed you. I still do, I know it. I, ah, I let the guys take pictures of me next to naked Ken and Amazon Barbie at the station. You're the Amazon trouncing me in all kinds of ways—some pretty damn perverted." He gave the ghost of a smile. "I'm now known as the loser who couldn't keep his girl. Wash jabs me every time they pose a new scene by putting a picture of my face over the Ken doll. They found dark glasses for the Amazon. You'd like her."

She liked hearing that, petty enough to appreciate being thought of as strong and not crying every night while her doll lookalike kicked Ken's ass. When he handed her his cell phone, she scrolled through a few funny-as-hell pictures of Brad looking pitiful behind Ken being whipped by Amazon Barbie.

"I donated money to Pets Fur Life in your name," he continued. "And I signed on for more dog adoptions, no cats. I'm hoping you might want to go with me next time."

He wanted a next time?

When she said nothing, just watched him, he swallowed loudly. "I also baked you a cake. It's at my place." He looked nervous. "It's awful. I can't lie. It's the fourth one I attempted, and I couldn't get the guys to eat the previous three. That's how bad they were."

"How hard is it to follow box directions?" she asked, doing her best not to smirk at his failures.

"I was making it from scratch." He sounded offended. "I was making you something with love. From the bottom of my heart. It doesn't count if it's not real."

Okay, that was a good one.

He glanced at the dartboard again before looking back at her. "Avery, I wrestled with how I felt about you for a long time, before that night at your place where I blew it. You mean so much to me, and it's like I've always known you. You get me, deep down. I see you. The real you. We're perfect for each other. But that means you have to forgive me." His hands fisted on his lap. "The way I've been working to forgive my mom. The way I forgive Dana for leaving me." He started to hand her a note from his back pocket then took it back. "I want you to read this, but not now."

He told her the gist of what Dana had written, and Avery felt awful for the poor girl.

"She told me to find my peace. And I have." He handed her the last gift, a small wrapped box. "I love you. I'm just sorry it took me so long to figure it out."

Avery had tried really hard to keep him at an emotional distance. But she was only human. She started crying. "Why did you just leave? Brad, you didn't say anything but thanks. Thanks?" She smacked him in the arm, pleased when he winced. "You broke my heart."

"God, Avery. I'm so sorry." He pulled her into his arms and let her cry it out. Stroking her back, whispering apologies, he sat with her in his lap until she stopped crying. "I love you, and I'm so afraid I ruined everything. I promise I'll never ghost you again. You know I have no problem telling you when you're wrong," he teased and wiped her cheeks.

She looked up at him, thinking she must be a mess while he looked like a Greek god. "I'm rarely wrong." She blinked to clear her tears, so in love with him it hurt. "You can't do that again. I can't be pushed aside like I don't matter. My dad does that, and I won't accept it. Not anymore."

"Good. You deserve better than that." He put the box in her hands. "Open it, please."

She froze. "It's not a ring, is it?"

His slow smile brightened her entire apartment. "Not yet."

She opened it and found a key. "A key?"

"To my place. And if I was a more romantic guy, I'd say to my heart." His eyes shone. "Avery, I love you. I want us to be together. To have you move in with me, I mean, eventually, after you have time to really forgive me for being such an ass."

"A douche."

"A jerk."

"A fuckhead to the billionth degree."

He smiled. "I should see this insult book, huh?"

"Warning, Gerty was pretty creative. But I was better."

He laughed and hugged her. "God, I missed you. So much. I know, it was all my fault. But I was so wrapped in guilt and misery. The guys called me names. They told me to talk to you. Tex was super pissed, said I was making the biggest mistake of my life if I didn't make it right. Reggie narced me out to Ed, my lieutenant." He shook his head. "But the bastard helped. Ed's a great guy. He's had a lot of practice with life issues, and he's helped me. His wife keeps him on his toes."

"I should meet this guy."

"You will," he promised. "My life is full of fires and rescues. My crew are my family." He cupped her cheek. "They already love you. But not as much as I do."

He kissed her, and she kissed him back. A short one because she needed a tissue to blow her nose with all the crying she'd done.

"My glasses are messy."

He put her on the couch and grabbed a box of tissues for her.

She knew she sounded like a foghorn when she blew her nose. Brad tried to hide a grin.

"You don't look so hot yourself, Bradford."

He sighed. "I couldn't eat or sleep too well. I was miserable and missing you."

"Good."

"I love how sadistic you are, have I ever told you that?"

"No. Tell me now."

"I just did."

"Tell me again."

Then he showed her how much he loved her, and they came together with a passion that blazed brighter every time.

———

Two weeks later on a lovely Sunday afternoon, Brad arrived with Avery to his mother's for a family barbecue. He knocked and followed Oscar to the back, where Rochelle was talking to Gerty, Klingon raced around chasing butterflies, and his mother stood, waiting.

"Go get 'em, tiger," Oscar muttered and went to play with the dog.

His mother looked nervous. The same as he felt, considering he hadn't talked to her since their spat a month ago.

Gerty and Rochelle paused, watching them.

"Hi, Mom." Brad held Avery's hand. "This is my girlfriend, Avery. Avery, my mom, Vivienne."

Avery smiled and took Vivienne's hand. "So nice to meet you."

"And you." Vivienne smiled. "I've heard so many good things about you from Gerty and Oscar."

Gerty waved like a maniac.

Brad wanted to laugh.

Rochelle joined Vivienne.

"And this is my fiancée, Rochelle." Vivienne looked at Brad with a blush on her cheeks. "I love her, and she loves me. We're getting married later this summer."

Rochelle laughed and hugged Vivienne. "We are. She asked. I said yes."

Everyone but Brad burst out with cheers and laughter, sharing hugs and congratulations.

Brad watched his mother. Avery and the others walked away to give them some space.

"Well? Are you okay with this?" she asked.

He smiled. "It's about time."

Her eyes filled. "I'm so sorry, Brad. For everything. I love you, honey. I wish I'd been a better mom. I never told you about what it was like growing up with my parents. I wish I'd been more like you. You have no idea how proud I am of the man you've become." She started sobbing.

"Oh, Mom. Don't cry." Brad hugged her. "I love you for who you are. Warts and everything," he teased, coming full circle.

Forgiveness had a magical power all its own.

———

An hour later, Brad sat with Klingon on the grass in the backyard, watching his family, which had grown with the arrival of his crew. Tex and Reggie flirted with his mom, while Mack remained glued to Rochelle and her homemade potato salad. Tex had brought a dog he was looking after, which did its best to blend in with the grass, sleeping under a table when not sniffing at Klingon or Tinker, his mom's dog. Gerty and Oscar kept challenging Avery to cornhole and losing, which she found funny as hell.

The insults flew back and forth.

He'd never had a better time.

"Yep, Klingon, life is good." The puppy lay sleeping by his side.

"I've been learning a lot lately. Avery's mom really likes me, though her dad is a loss. The guy still can't see how great his daughter is, though he did come to see her yesterday. Her articles are getting more popular now that her segment has gone viral. I think it was the slip and slide festival that put her over the top," he murmured. "Especially because she wiped out and came up in a very wet, very clingy top. Don't tell her I said that. But funny and sexy is really attractive."

And his woman had both. He smiled at her. She winked back before decimating Gerty on a beanbag toss.

He stroked Tinker's head, the dog lying next to Klingon. "Rochelle finally got Mom to go to counseling. She's dealing with her past. I'm hoping she'll get better. Rochelle thinks she will." He loved the fact he'd soon have an official stepmom.

"Oscar and I are working on a two-prong attack. We get Avery to move in with me so Oscar can move in with Gerty. It's genius. I'll probably have to put *Seinfeld* posters up in the apartment, but I don't mind. The Brad dartboard has to go though." He frowned at Tex grinning at Reggie. The idiot had told the guys at the station about it, and Nat had gotten her photographer husband to get a big blowup of Brad, which they'd taped to the heavy bag in the gym. Now everyone took a turn punching him in the face at work.

Which still made him laugh, though he didn't want it to be so funny. Avery seemed to take great pleasure in it, insisting he deserved it for what he'd put her through. He didn't disagree.

"And you'll be happy to know Pets Fur Life has a new leash— see what I did there?—on life. The calendar made a bucket of money. The shelter is going strong, for now. Though poor Tex is no closer to getting Bree to go out with him, but he's persistent. My bet is he'll wear her down with all that twang and country music."

Tex pushed his hat back and glanced over at Brad. He grinned and held up his middle finger when Vivienne gave him her back.

Brad returned the gesture. Klingon stirred, though Tinker lay snoring like a buzz saw. Brad pet the puppy, and the little guy climbed into his lap and went back to sleep. "Yep. Life is good. I've even been looking at rings. The keeping kind. But I'm going to wait until Christmas, after she's moved in, and I have time to convince her to say yes, before I let her pick one out."

The puppy snored, in harmony with Tinker.

Brad's friends laughed at one another. His family was all together, having fun.

Avery glanced over at and him and waved. "I love you, Bradford," she said loudly enough to be heard before nailing another hole in one, beating Gerty and Oscar once more. "Suck it, losers."

The guys milled around the game, demanding to be next.

His mother and Rochelle stood hand in hand, smiling at the gathering.

I've found my peace, Dana.

Klingon perked up and yipped, staring at nothing. But Brad froze, swearing he felt a kiss on his cheek, his best friend, so close, and suddenly he was flying, lost in the joy of love, family, and forgiveness.

Klingon raced over to Gerty.

After a moment, Brad joined him. And ended up losing to Avery twice in a row.

"My turn again." Tex nudged him out of the way.

"Five bucks says he loses," Reggie bet.

"You're on. The king of lawn games is a ringer." Mack rubbed his hands together.

"Bring it on, Station 44." Avery gave an evil laugh as she adjusted her glasses. "I love to make grown men cry."

Brad laughed, committing the day to memory. *Avery was his peace…and a raging inferno keeping him on my toes. He wouldn't have it any other way.*

Read on for a sneak peek at book 2
in the Turn Up the Heat series

BURNING DESIRE

Available August 2021 from Sourcebooks Casablanca

Eight months ago
Seattle, Washington

IT WAS ONE OF THOSE LULLS IN THE SURROUNDING NOISE THAT happen right before a most embarrassing discussion fills the silence. The firefighters in the station house had been talking and laughing, cooking in the kitchen, and coming in from the weight room to check out the kitchen's good smells. Then suddenly, everything seemed to stop, as if the world slowed down in time to hear Mack shoot off his big mouth.

"So, let me get this straight. On your big date last night, the chick *straight up tossed a glass of water in your face?*"

All eyes turned to the conversation happening a stone's throw away in the television area.

"Would you keep your voice down, damn it?" Tex McGovern glared at his buddy and prayed the others on B shift kept their big noses out of his business. He tossed the rest of them a scowl until they finally went back to their own boring lives.

Mack grinned then had the nerve to laugh. A lot.

Texan, firefighter, and former U.S. Marine, Tex sank deeper into the reclining chair, not seeing the game on TV as he relived his pitiful date. He reached for the comfort of his cowboy hat but tugged down the brim of a Seattle FD ballcap instead.

"Yeah, my life sucks." His twang sounded more pronounced, and he did his best to regroup, not wanting the others to know how much he hated what had gone down with a woman he'd grown to like way too much.

"Your life never sucks. You just move on to the next honey." Mack paused. "Why'd she throw water all over you? What did you do?"

Tex glared at his partner, a guy who should have had his back. "Why is this *my* fault?"

Mack raised a brow.

"I did nothin'. Not a thing. And it wasn't my date that splashed me, moron. It was the girl I broke up with two freaking months ago that drenched me. I finally got that date with Bree—"

"Bree of the sunny-blond hair, heavenly blue eyes, and body worshipped by men everywhere? That Bree?"

Tex frowned. Mack sure seemed to have memorized her picture from one shot on Tex's phone. "Yeah, she—"

"The woman you've been dying to go out with finally said yes? I thought she had better taste than that."

Tex flipped him off but lowered his voice when he saw two guys he'd rather not talk to right now glancing over at him. "Yeah, well, after the stunt my ex pulled, I doubt I'll ever see Bree again." He was miserable. "Mack, I'm tellin' ya, I broke it off with that woman two months ago. I had to block her from calling and texting me just last week. I didn't want to, but she wouldn't leave me alone."

Mack shook his head. "Tough being so tall, dark, and dynamic, eh?"

"It really is."

Mack rolled his eyes.

"Woman just wouldn't take no for an answer. Then she shows up outta nowhere at a place it took me weeks to get reservations at and loses it. She calls me a two-timer and a whore and throws my own glass of water on me! All while Bree is watching—"

"In shock and horror."

"—from right across our cozy little table."

Mack shook his head. "Man, that is just... Man."

Tex groaned. "I know. The ex takes off. Then Bree looks at me and tells me I should feel ashamed of myself. She left without letting me explain."

Mack coughed but didn't quite hide his laughter.

"It ain't funny!" Tex wished the rest of his crew could hear him. He knew *they'd* have given him the compassion and pity he deserved. "I mean, I've been trying to get Bree to go out with me forever. We texted and talked, but I had to beg her to meet in person. She has a thing against firefighters, for some reason. And now she probably thinks she was right when she was so wrong."

Mack opened his mouth to respond but closed it when two of the other guys on their eight-man shift beat him to it. Hell, the two approaching were idiots Tex rarely had patience for on a *good* day.

The ringleader, a guy they called Narc because he never kept anything to himself, smirked. "So, Tex, I hear you blew it with the chief's daughter." Next to him, Narc Junior, a guy who shadowed Narc's every move, laughed like the giant goon he was.

Tex blinked. "What?"

"You know, Brianna Gilchrist, hot as fuck, blue eyes, blond hair, big, ah, dimples?" Narc cleared his throat and looked around. Not seeing their lieutenant, he leaned in closer. "You had my respect for getting a date. God knows we've all wanted to. Couldn't close the deal, though, could you?" He held his phone to Tex, who watched a video of himself getting doused.

Tex leaned forward. "Motherfu—"

"What are you all doing over there? Slacking off?" their lieutenant boomed.

They all jumped. The LT had a mouth that didn't know the meaning of the word *whisper*.

Narc turned with a smile. "Not much, LT. Just bonding with the second-best unit in our squad."

"Suck it, Narc." Mack glared.

That earned a scowl, followed by a mean grin. "Say, LT." Narc and Narc Jr. approached the lieutenant and a few lingering guys who gathered to see what the fuss was about. "Check this out." Tex heard him play the video.

Mack shook his head and in a lower voice said, "Seriously, Tex? The *battalion chief's* daughter?"

Tex felt ill. "I didn't know who she was! Hell, I never even got her last name! I swear. We'd just met in person for the first time last night." First time and last time. Tex swore under his breath. As pathetic as it was, he wanted another shot at Bree Gilchrist. He'd had the hots for her since first seeing her picture on a dating app. She'd been sweet and funny online, their conversations never boring. But she'd been even better in person, as brief as their date had been. Just thinking about her made his heart race.

Too bad a petty ex had screwed him over. God, he should have blocked her as soon as he broke off with her.

His LT scowled at him.

Shit.

"McGovern, let's have a talk in my office."

Narc and Narc Jr. laughed at him. The others offered their condolences.

"It won't be so bad," Mack murmured. "Just tell him you're done with her."

Tex stood and sighed. "Not like I'd even started with her to begin with."

He hoped this would all blow over without any major repercussions from his chain of command. And that he'd manage to get over his small infatuation.

Even after the ass-chewing he got from the lieutenant to make better decisions, he still regretted that he'd never gotten a chance to show Bree how charming he could be. But her dad—the *battalion chief*? He shuddered, knowing his track record with women.

Better that it ended way before it had a chance to begin.

Five months ago
The Lava Lounge, Seattle

Hanging with the guys at a bar in Belltown, Tex enjoyed a cool pineapple margarita while his buddies Mack and Reggie razzed him for drinking something fruity. But come on, it was a tiki bar. How could Tex not have something with pineapple somewhere in the title? Brad sipped from a concoction mixed with rum and coconut milk and didn't say much.

The crew of four got plenty of second looks, some friendly and others not so friendly.

As firefighters, they had to stay in shape. But Tex and the guys liked to take it to another level. All prior military men, they knew the value of a good piece of gear on a mission. Hauling around equipment while wearing the fireproof suits and self-contained breathing apparatuses (SCBAs) that helped them breathe through smoke and ash had shown that having a fit body could mean the difference between life and death. For them as well as the public they served.

While they had bonded as brothers, both as firefighters and ex-military, they certainly had their differences. Tex and Brad had served in the Marines, Reggie in the Navy, and Mack in the Air Force. Tex did best with women, though Brad and Mack never seemed to be hurting. For two years Reggie had been in a long-term relationship with a woman. But recently things had grown rocky between them, so they'd gathered for a morale booster for the sarcastic bastard.

They were their own small family, supporting one another through everything, good and bad.

Which made it difficult to remember the good when the idiots continued to throw up to his face the fact that he'd dissed the battalion commander's precious daughter. Damn, but he'd thought that might have died down by now.

"Imagine," Brad said, a grin on his stupid face as he swirled his coconut mambo or whatever the hell he'd ordered. "In an alternate universe, Tex gets her to go out with him. She ends up bringing him home to meet the parents and he's all, oh, hey, Chief Gilchrist, how's it hangin'?"

Mack chuckled. "So pleased to meet you and the missus. Oh, and I'm sleeping with your daughter. She really is the hottest woman in town. And did I mention I brought my own raincoat to protect my hose? No worries on that score, chief."

Tex glared at Mack. "That was disgusting." To the others he said, "Can we let it go already? How about instead we talk about—" *Brad and all the women he's not dating? Reggie and his ballbuster of a gal?* Tex paused, hearing all that in his head, and knew they needed to change the conversation from women to something else. Reggie didn't look so happy.

Brad must have sensed the same thing, because he slapped Mack in the back of the head. "Idiot."

"What? Oh, come on. I'm kidding." Mack nodded at Tex. "He's been moping for months and needs to get over it."

Brad changed the subject. "You guys still okay with moving to the new station?"

Tex nodded. "Station 44 will be manned by the best and brightest our city has to offer. Of course they wanted us in the new place."

Mack agreed. "Well, that's true. I photograph well."

Tex saw Reggie's look of disgust and agreed. "I still don't know how your ugly face got on all the media stuff for Station 44."

Mack sipped from his beer. "What can I say? The public loves me."

"I mean, I'm much better lookin'." Tex flexed and tilted back his cowboy hat. He liked to think his bronze skin, a shade darker than Brad and Mack's but lighter than Reggie's medium-brown, glowed with sex appeal. His muscles clearly overpowered his buddies'... Well, if he ignored Reggie's huge neck, arms, and chest on account of all his obsessive weight lifting.

Behind him, a few women tittered.

Reggie finished off his beer. "You two make me want to drink."

"Right? God, I feel ill." Brad shook his head at Mack and Tex.

"Probably 'cause you're drinking all that sugar." Tex finished off his margarita and decided to slow down. "I'm with you though. This thing was good but way too strong."

"It's the tequila." Reggie nodded. "We should go work out and burn this off."

"Relax, fun-killer." Mack dodged the play swipe Reggie made. "It's Friday, and—"

"—trouble has once again found us." Brad sighed. "Bridal party, six o'clock."

They turned, and Tex saw what Brad meant. A group of six women wearing feathery boas and a mishmash of headbands showcasing tiaras and one set of demon horns had gotten into a verbal altercation with three large, aggressive men.

Tex could hear the suggestive comments across the bar from the three guys, and as if that weren't bad enough, the bouncer was dealing with two of their friends as well.

"Ah, hell." Tex decided to take one for the team. "I'll do it. Brad, you got into trouble last time."

"By all means." Brad waved him toward the mess.

"I'll go along to help if you need it, lightweight." Reggie smirked.

"This is why no one likes you." Tex walked through the crowd growing around the troublemaking jocks and bridal revelers. "What's up with all the noise?" he asked the woman closest to him.

The bride-to-be—who wore a *Bride-to-Be* sash that hugged her full rack—was a sexy redhead who looked livid. "These assholes keep trying to take us home. I'm just here with my girlfriends to celebrate my upcoming wedding. Giving blow jobs is *not* on tonight's agenda."

At the word *blow job*, the bar erupted into whistles and shouts of encouraging men, while several of the women in attendance shouted their support for the bridal party.

"I take it a blow job ain't a reference for a drink?"

The redhead scowled. "No, it is not."

Tex turned to the nearest asshole smelling like a brewery. "Look, man, it's obvious the ladies want you to leave them alone." He crossed his arms over his chest, saw the three inebriated fools eyeballing his biceps, and wondered if common sense would win out over lust and alcohol, always a poor mix.

The biggest drunk, a beady-eyed, bald guy who seemed the most vocal of the bunch, shook his head. He either worked out for a living or did some major steroids. He was *huge.* "Look, hayseed, nobody asked what you thought. Fuck off."

"Yeah, fuck off," one of his gym rat buddies seconded.

"You heard 'im," said the third.

A husky, feminine voice swore. "Oh, hell."

He turned to see a familiar blond demon. She wore tiny, red horns in her hair and sported a red feather boa.

Tex smiled widely. "Hey, Bree."

"This is not going to go well," Reggie muttered.

"I said get lost," Bald Guy said again. "Oh, I like red better than white." He goggled at Bree.

"No, *you* fuck off," the bride-to-be said, poking the big guy in his chest. Not exactly a smart move, because the man wrapped his arms around her and tried to get a kiss.

Before Tex could separate them, Reggie was there and shoved the inebriated man from the bride-to-be while steadying her. Tex quickly put himself between Bald Guy's buddies and the ladies before anyone could even think to grab Bree.

"Fellas, I really think you should reconsider," Tex advised in a polite voice, his arms loose, his fists clenched in warning. "Because I have no problem putting you down if you don't."

Fortunately, they seemed to have more sense than their friend. They took a good look at him, at Reggie, then at their friend swaying on his feet and swearing, and left.

"I could have taken him," Bree said, breathless, as she adjusted her horns.

"I'm sure you would have, darlin'."

"My name is Bree, Romeo, not darlin'. Or don't you remember?"

She was *talking to him*. He felt light-headed with joy. "I—"

A scuffle sounded behind him. When he turned to investigate, he saw Mack muscling Bald Guy to the floor, facedown, jerking the drunk's arm behind his back.

Reggie held his hands up in surrender. "It's all Mack. I'm just here looking out for the lovely lady getting married soon."

"Aw, aren't you cute." The bride-to-be had a hold on Reggie's thick forearm and watched him with adoration.

Tex grinned and said to Mack, "Go for it, MP." *Take the military out of the cop, but you can't take the cop out of civvy life.*

Mack sighed. "That's SF, for Security Force. I was Air Force, not a damn... Never mind." He turned to the crowd. "Can someone get the cops over here?"

"Already on it." The bartender gave a thumbs-up, his phone at his ear.

"I just wanted the demon, to be honest," Bald Guy was slurring from the floor. "But the bitchy bride would have been okay too."

She's my *demon.* Tex glared at the dick on the ground. "Want me to hold him till the cops come?"

Mack shook his head. "Hell no. We are not having any more trouble. We are here to drink and find women. Period." He smiled at the crowd gathered around them. "Anyone free for a beer?"

The bar erupted in cheers as many congratulated them for

stepping in. Then talk turned to them being firefighters at the new station.

Tex had been watching Bree, wondering if she'd try to make a break for it before letting him talk to her. As she started to edge away with her friends, he planted himself like a tree in front of her. "Hey, Bree. Can I talk to you for a sec?"

"If you don't want him, I'll keep him busy," a sexy woman with a sparkling, pink tiara offered.

Bree gave him a disdainful once-over. "Trust me, he's no good for you."

"Says you."

Tex winked at Bree. "Well, I say—"

Bree dragged him away before he could finish his sentence, into a quieter area apart from the fracas.

She planted her hands on her trim hips, and he couldn't help noticing her nails matched the horns poking through her honey-blond hair. "Okay, Tex. What do you want?"

He felt suddenly tongue-tied, unable to speak as he drank her in. Damn, but she was pretty, her hair loose and flowing down her back, jeans painted on, T-shirt clinging to her curvy top. The woman was just so tall and toned. Her light-blue eyes shot sparks as she watched him watching her, and he thought the devil horns appropriate.

"Sorry," he said, not meaning it. "But you are rockin' that outfit." She blushed. "Oh, stop. What do you want?"

"I want a chance. What happened last time wasn't my fault." "Oh?"

"Darlin'—Bree," he hurried to correct, "I'd broken up with Vanessa two months before we went to dinner. I swear." He crossed his heart, pleased to see her looking at his buff chest. But that didn't seem to impress her enough. She still looked annoyed. "She was stalking me online, so I blocked her. Then she followed me to dinner! That ain't right."

He swore her lips curled into a smile before they flattened. "Okay, so you're not a cheater. You're still a firefighter and serial dater."

"Hey, I never lied. I told you that before we went out." He frowned. "But you never mentioned who your dad was."

"Because I didn't want anyone using me to get up the ladder. You know, in the fire department?"

"Ha ha. Ladder. Funny." He did his best to keep his gaze on her face and not her heaving breasts. Because the girl was breathing pretty heavily, and only a dead man wouldn't notice. "Come on, Bree. I like you. I mean, we connected when we were messaging and talking on the phone, right? I like your looks, sure. You're gorgeous. But you made me laugh, and I thought you liked me."

"I did," she grudgingly conceded.

"Then why not go out for a real date?"

"I've been busy lately."

"With your photography. I know."

"Stalk much?" She raised a brow.

He flushed. "Nah. I just… I looked you up after I found out your name. Same as you did me. Trust me, dating you would not make me popular at the station. I just want to be with you, not your dad."

"Oh, so sex then we move on?" She looked him over. "Sure. When and where?"

"I… Wait." He scowled. "Nope. We aren't gonna just have sex." He felt his face heating and had no idea why, though she seemed fascinated by his discomfort. "Damn it. I just want a chance to get to know you. Is that wrong?"

"I guess not." She still didn't seem sure of him. "We can try again next week, if you want."

"I do." Did he.

Her slow smile mesmerized him. "Okay. I'll unblock you on my phone and message you the details."

"Perfect. See you then."

========

Four weeks ago

Bree gritted her teeth as she worked the Pets Fur Life calendar shoot, using members of the new Fire Station 44 to make money for the financially challenged charity. She could totally get behind helping strays find good homes. If it took biting back her scathing commentary about Tex McGovern being a no-good liar capable of grinding up a woman's emotions, then so be it.

He lingered near the others, shooting her side-glances but not saying much. Smart of him. She hated to admit it, but in a sea of man candy, Mr. December stood out as the sexiest lollipop of the bunch. She loved his looks and wasn't too superficial to say it. For the shoot, he wore faded jeans, a black T-shirt plastered to his chest, and that stupid cowboy hat that looked way too sexy on him. He might as well have held up a *Ride this Cowboy* sign. Sadly, she'd have to fight herself not to volunteer.

But Bree knew what many didn't—the rest of him didn't match up to the outward hero.

Several inches taller than her own five-eleven, his muscular frame was one anyone would envy. He had shaggy, black hair and light-gray eyes, a square jaw, and stubborn tilt to his head. His bronze skin tone only highlighted the brightness of his eyes. She couldn't define one thing she disliked about his looks.

Which she hated.

The blasted man had made her go back on her principles to give him a second chance. She'd let that alleged womanizer back into her life, only for him to show out as someone not worth her time yet again.

She might have believed his ex-girlfriend had set him up on their first date, but Tex standing Bree up on their second date? No warning or explanation of his absence until *two days later*? Who did that? No way she believed that lame excuse that he'd tried to call her and had phone problems.

"Bree?" A pretty woman with bright-blue eyes sidled up to her. "I just wanted to thank you for doing all this. I'm Avery, by the way. I'm doing the pet segment on *Searching the Needle Weekly*."

"Oh, right. I love your Friday morning show. You and Brad are hilarious together." The pair argued with each other and tried to set each other up on a popular streaming channel, as if playing an evil dating game. "And a little more than friends, hmm?" She hadn't missed the kiss Brad had plastered on Avery a few minutes ago. A hop step from beating his chest and proclaiming her his possession, Bree thought, though Avery wasn't complaining.

Avery blushed. "Ah, well, that's new."

"Hey, good for you. But don't stop giving him crap on the show. You ask me, it's good to see a hot fireman taken down a notch."

"You're telling me. Brad's responsible, nice, and handsome. He's a firefighter, a natural-born hero. I'm just a nosy reporter." Avery shrugged. "It's tough going up against Mr. Perfect."

"I'm behind you. Heck, I'd love to adopt one of your strays, that's if I can ever get my schedule under control." Bree had been photographing people and events nonstop for a year. She needed a break, though she couldn't complain the money hadn't been good. "Then again, once the animals appear on your show, they're adopted out pretty quickly. Or is that just made up to look good?"

"No, the animals really are adopted that fast." Avery nodded. "I'm so glad we're helping to find them good homes. I know Pets Fur Life appreciates it. I also know they're thrilled you gave up your time for this. I don't think they could afford to do the calendar without you."

"When Tex mentioned it, I had to help."

Avery studied her. "I didn't realize you knew Tex."

"What gave it away?"

"The way you clenched your jaw when you said his name."

"Ah, that." Bree didn't say any more, and Avery didn't ask.

"Well, I just wanted to come over and thank you for letting me stay through the shoot. It was amazing watching you work."

"It didn't hurt that all my subjects were either cute and furry or handsome, did it?" Bree nodded to the hair stylists busy flirting with several of the guys. She waved at the stylists, who smiled and waved back before turning to the shirtless firemen standing close by.

"Let me add my thanks, boss," her assistant said as she passed. "I love weddings and portraits, but this is why I went into photography. Half-naked men and puppies."

Bree rolled her eyes.

Avery grinned. "I have to agree. Well, I'm taking off. Just wanted to say hi now that you're winding down. Oh, and…"

"Yeah?"

Avery cleared her throat. "This is none of my business. I have no idea what happened between you and Tex before. But he's a great guy. He's genuine."

Bree sighed. "Another one drinking the Kool-Aid."

"I said my piece. And no, he didn't pay me to say that." Avery laughed. "So, now that I've annoyed you by mentioning Tex, how about agreeing to an interview? I don't just do the pet part at *Searching the Needle Weekly*. I run local stories about our community too, and I know our readers would love to know more about you."

"Seriously?"

"Yeah. And with the positive buzz we've been getting, the publicity can only help."

"Sign me up."

They agreed to a time the following week.

Avery left, and once everyone else had cleared out, Bree took one last look around before leaving as well.

The hour had grown dark, but in the parking lot, she spied Tex leaning against his truck, looking at his phone. Her car was the only other vehicle in the lot.

As agreed for doing the shoot, Tex kept his distance. He didn't flirt, and she treated him like a professional model. She'd said the bare minimum, all in regard to the photoshoot, and had been pleasant, if aloof.

In the growing dark, he didn't look at her, and she didn't say anything, just got in her car and left. But in her rearview, she saw him head out after she'd pulled away, turning at the stoplight when she went through.

Huh. What did that mean? And why did it make her heart race that he'd cared enough to see her safely into her car?

Acknowledgments

I'd like to thank Donovan for sharing his wealth of knowledge about Seattle's firefighting and medical practices and personnel. You are a wonderful help to the Seattle community, and especially to a writer unfamiliar with the life of a firefighter. Any mistakes in this novel are mine alone.

And for my agent, Nicole, I can't thank you enough for all that you do. Thank you.